RHOMBUS

RAY PASQUIN

Second Edition (2024) ISBN:
978-1-957351-50-6
Rhombus
Author: Ray Pasquin
Co-Editor: Margie McCurry
Second Edition Proofreader: Lyda Rose Haerle, Pipa Aldoro
Original Book Cover Design: Pamela Trush
Second Edition Cover Design: Michael Nicloy
Interior Design & Layout: Griffin Mill

PUBLISHED BY NICO 11 PUBLISHING & DESIGN
MUKWONAGO, WISCONSIN
MICHAEL NICLOY, PUBLISHER
www.nico11publishing.com

Be well read.

Quantity orders may be made by contacting the publisher via email: mike@nico11publishing.com or by phone: 217.779.9677

Also by Ray Pasquin:
Operation D

Contact Ray Pasquin's management:
g7agent@aol.com

Printed in the United States of America

*Dedicated to the memory of
Albert, Anne, and Bill Pasquin.*

I miss them all each and every day.

RHOMBUS

MOST SECRET:

London to Washington

Recently recovered from an undercover agent's laptop. Agent compiled info three days before he was skinned alive and tortured to death near Geneva.

–Thomas, MI6

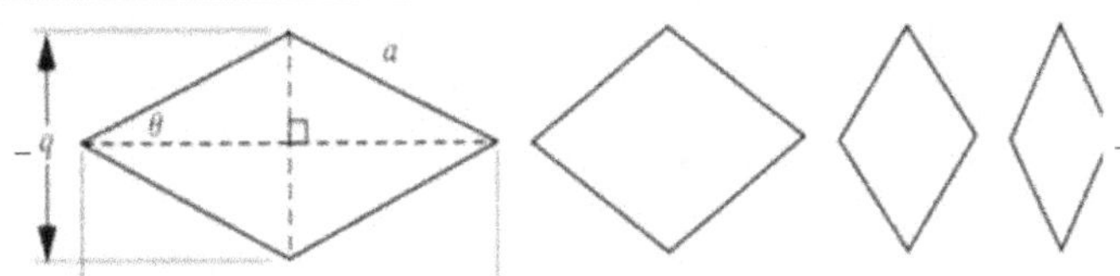

Rhombus - [Definition]

A quadrilateral with all four sides the same length; and both pairs of opposite sides parallel. - An equilateral parallelogram, 'one and the same' in all.

Assassin - [Definition]

As a general term: a person or persons who commit murder for a fee; especially killers who execute a politically important person. When capitalized: a member of a specialized group or sect often sent out on suicidal missions to murder prominent enemies; like the Shia at the time of the Crusades; or the present day al Qaeda suicide cells in Iran and Iraq.

Rhombus Assassin - [Definition]

One of four equally sadistic female killers; the four are parallel and identical in their methods and prowess; hence the name Rhombus. They are skilled executioners who have formed one of the world's most proficient extortion and assassination squads, receiving huge fees for their services.

Rhombus stalks and eliminates political and personal enemies; performing their horrific work clandestinely, with absolutely no link to the person or organization that has hired them.

<u>CIA Note:</u> Believed to now be somewhere in Switzerland or France!

Chapter 1

The End of Summer

Bang! Crash! Boom! The cannon-like sounds of explosives going off in the air startled Ambassador Elmer Dawson.

Though he knew they'd be coming, he'd briefly forgotten about them and he smiled at his momentary absentmindedness. These were the opening salvos of Venice's annual *Balducci* fireworks show, the extravaganza that takes place every September 4th outside the Grand Canal's plush Hotel Verona. The raucous celebration, a yearly tradition in Venice, was one with which the diplomat was quite familiar. Yet, this year, Ambassador Dawson had other things on his mind. Hence the red, white and green blasts now illuminating the sky above Piazza San Marco somehow didn't seem as inspiring as in years past.

It had been a noteworthy end of summer for Elmer Dawson, the distinguished United States ambassador to Italy. As in previous years, he'd officially completed his formal overseas duties on August 1st. The next morning, still following his usual practice, he dutifully hopped onboard the Trenitalia train from Rome to Milan to spend a few days consulting with some diplomatic colleagues at Milano's *Carlton Baglioni Hotel*. After that, however, things changed considerably; 360 degrees from the ambassador's customary year end routine. The following day, Dawson rented a sleek and uncharacteristically flashy Jaguar F Type sports car, and drove it from Milan to Venizia in order to meet up with the stunning young woman with whom he was having a glorious affair.

At a private party in Rome, sometime back in mid-July, Elmer had been introduced to this dazzling beauty. The two immediately hit it off, and surprisingly, *she* had made the first move on him.

Smiling at the memory of that first encounter, Elmer readily admitted to himself that this role reversal had tweaked his normally placid ego. The couple's initial meeting, at the home of some Korean diplomat whom the ambassador hardly knew, was followed by several picnic lunches and romantic, candlelit dinners. It quickly evolved into a marvelous affair, one that should have been implausible given the difference in their ages and personalities. He, an unadventurous, rather conservative married man in his sixties, and she, a striking jet-setting bachelorette in her late twenties.

What followed during the last half of July, and all of August, was a magical whirlwind of sensual romance and nonstop pleasure. The tryst with his beautiful new lover had delighted Elmer, though it was tempered by the fact that his wife and sons back home would have been appalled and saddened had they known of the affair.

Likewise, as a prominent U.S. government official, one who might soon be tossing his hat into the political ring, Elmer Dawson recognized that his behavior must always appear to be correct and proper. Accordingly, he and his young mistress, Terry, had been extremely careful never to be seen in compromising situations or settings. If anything, she had proven to be more discreet and worried than he about the affair becoming public. Thus far, thanks to this mutual practiced prudence, their secret romance had been totally veiled.

Elmer glanced at his watch: 9:35 p.m. Where was she? They had agreed to meet outside the hotel at 9:30, take in the sights along the Grand Canal for a while, and then have a late dinner at Locanda Rosa, the Verona Hotel's serene rooftop restaurant. As the ambassador anxiously looked at his wristwatch again, a low, sensual voice answered the question. "Hello, darling. Sorry I'm late."

Beaming at the dark-haired beauty who'd suddenly appeared, Elmer Dawson replied softly, "No problem, Terry. I haven't been waiting long." He pointed to the sky. "The fireworks are just beginning. I'd almost forgotten about them. Let's watch for a while, shall we?"

Terry smiled sweetly and took his arm in hers. Content just to be with one another, the two lovers enjoyed the pyrotechnic display for a half hour or so. They then strolled along the canal listening to the melodic sounds of Venice's singing gondoliers. As they did so, a large *traghetti*, the only public-style gondola still used by resident Venetians, slowly glided past. The happy families inside it were merrily singing along with their gondolier, as the crowded vessel made its way up the canal.

Smiling at the scene, and then at each other, the two lovebirds finally strolled back to the Verona and took the hotel's diminutive elevator to the al fresco restaurant up on the roof. They were soon sitting comfortably in a dark corner of the superb eatery enjoying the first of their delicious Bellini cocktails.

"This is heaven," Terry Harrigan, a stunning twenty-eight year old brunette, exclaimed with a smile. "The view is breathtaking and I've heard they have the finest Florentine beefsteak in all of Italy."

Elmer nodded. "That they do, Terry." He shrugged his shoulders sheepishly. "I'd originally wanted to take you to *Osteria da Fiore*, Campo San Polo's incredible restaurant. But some of my diplomatic colleagues eat there nearly every night, so we might have been spotted." He gestured toward the mostly unoccupied, well-spaced tables from their secluded booth. "I thought this place would be more private."

"It's lovely, Elmer." The couple then clinked their glasses festively, toasting the blissful two months they'd spent together in Italy.

Gazing into the eyes of his attractive companion, Ambassador Dawson sighed resignedly. Tonight he'd have to tell his new love that he'd soon be leaving for his compulsory three-month furlough in Washington, D.C. His official duties in Italy were over for another year, and in just four more days he'd be going home. Back to his wife and family. Taking another sip of his cocktail, Elmer *silently* wondered how Terry would take the news. As for his own feelings about it, one thing was abundantly clear. Somehow he'd have to find a way to keep this beautiful young woman close by. Terry's incredible sensuality and their growing relationship had become absolutely addictive, and Ambassador Dawson readily acknowledged that he couldn't live without her now. He was completely captivated by this divine nymph, the young woman who had stolen his heart so quickly. It was almost as if she'd gracefully made him fall for her. Made him a willing puppet to be erotically and wonderfully used and enjoyed. And Elmer had happily accepted it all, savoring every delicious moment.

Glancing over at Terry again, he recalled how he'd been instantly captivated by her splendor, her fashionable sophistication, and the air of mystery surrounding her. And yes, by her incredible sensual allure as well. Terry was part of him now, someone he could never let go. Some of this might still be vanity, the exciting realization that such a young, attractive woman could actually fall for him. Yet, most of it was love. The incredible realization that he had once again fallen in love with someone.

As Elmer pondered the situation, his thoughts turned to his wife, Mary. In his heart he already knew that there was no way he could willingly return to that mundane relationship again. The boring monotonous alliance in which he and his wife were currently locked. Their thirty-year union suddenly seemed stale and unexciting.

Elmer was painfully aware that he couldn't just walk out on his wife, for several reasons. There were his three sons, of course, and also his political aspirations to consider. The ambassador was contemplating a run at the Senate in a year or two. And a messy divorce involving a beautiful young mistress would certainly hinder that.

Even with those potential complications to contend with, Elmer Dawson knew that he could never completely abandon Terry at this juncture. And Elmer wouldn't consider a life without her now. Yet, what could he really do, even if he did somehow convince her to come to Washington with him? Perhaps rent her a small apartment in nearby Alexandria, or somewhere further south. Some place close enough to D.C. so that he could see her on weekends. Or on the occasional nights when his family was out of town. Maybe Terry would agree to something like that. At least until his mandatory presence back in Washington was over. His four-week furlough followed by the required two-month interval at his Washington office. After that, perhaps they could discreetly return to Italy and once more enjoy each other's company during the ambassador's next tour of duty in Rome.

Elmer wondered if Terry would even consider such an arrangement. After all, he'd be asking her to pull up roots, follow him halfway around the world to America, and then join him back in Italy again. It was a lot to ask. For that matter, what did he really know about Terry's goals or her personal life? Practically nothing at all. Everything about her, along with their surreptitious love affair, had been necessarily shrouded in concealment. She even used different names whenever they entered a hotel or restaurant.

Dawson shook his head and silently asked, "And what about Terry *herself?*" All she'd ever told him was that she had once lived in the Chicago area, came to Europe at a young age, and now occasionally worked in Milan as a 'freelance fashion consultant'. Whatever that meant. As the ambassador once more reflected on the situation, his thoughts were cut short by his attractive dining companion.

"There's something on your mind, isn't there, Elmer?" She gently touched the back of his hand.

"Oh, it's nothing, really."

His nervousness showed that he wasn't being truthful and she softly told him so. "Come now, darling. You can't fool me."

Elmer grinned. "I suppose I can't, Terry." He looked over at her, this time more reflectively. "I guess I'm just a bit melancholy knowing it's the end of summer." Pausing a moment, he knew it was time to come clean. "And I – well, you see, Terry, I'll be flying back to Washington in a few days, and I loathe the thought of leaving you. These last few months have been precious to me. And I..." He hesitated once more, a bit embarrassed, but then continued, "It seems I've fallen in love with you. Don't ask me how it happened. It just did. Now the problem is – I don't think I can live *without* you."

Elmer Dawson was surprised at how easily those very personal words seemed to flow once he'd made up his mind to say them. He smiled at her, hoping she too felt the same way, and was immediately encouraged by the warm expression on Terry's lovely face.

"I've fallen for you too, Elmer. The past eight weeks have been wonderful for me as well. But let's not talk of goodbyes until later. Let's have a great meal, drink some wine, and then enjoy a cognac back in your apartment suite. We can discuss the future a bit more comfortably there. Don't you think?"

Gently taking her hand under the table, Elmer smiled, enthusiastically. "Let's do just that, Terry." And for the next few hours they laughed and basked in the cheerful radiance of the open-air rooftop restaurant, savoring both the scrumptious *Tagliatelle al brasato* and each other's company.

~

It was well after midnight when the giddy couple arrived at Elmer's darkened suite on the hotel's ninth floor. As was Terry's rigid practice during her occasional overnight stays with him here, she made sure to enter the ambassador's suite only during *late* hours. Likewise, Terry always exited very early in the morning. Most evenings she merely visited Elmer here, returning to her own hotel, the nearby *Amanita,* and the suite Elmer had conveniently procured for her there.

As an extra continual precaution, Terry had checked into the smallish *Amanita,* and all of the other Italian hotels for that matter, via fictitious names. This one in Venice as 'Betty Cummings'. Additionally, on the rare occasions when she had to be introduced to someone – say a headwaiter or the concierge strolling by their table – it was always as some fabricated name. 'Miss Watkins' and 'Miss Thomas' being two of her favorites. Though steadfastly practicing all these precautions, the twosome had luckily never run into anyone the ambassador worked with or even knew. Thankfully, their clandestine love affair had been completely veiled, even on nights like this one.

Still laughing at a joke Elmer told in the restaurant, the duo entered the ambassador's hotel apartment via its long, narrow hallway. Ambling into the suite's spacious living room, they kissed each other tenderly and quickly made themselves at home.

Dawson's plush *Appartamento ammobiliato* was comprised of a sumptuous living room, a sizable master bedroom suite, a small kitchenette, complete with stove and fridge, and a roomy walk- in coat closet located right off the elongated entrance hallway. Turning on the living room lights, Elmer strolled over to the suite's iPod music system neatly concealed in a small bookcase. He chose some classical numbers, knowing that Terry enjoyed this particular collection of works by Vivaldi. As the first selection began playing, she turned and smiled at him. "Pour me a Remy, please, darling. And one for yourself."

She smiled again and then slowly made her way toward the bedroom, where she kept a few wardrobe items and a change of clothes for her sporadic overnight stays here. "I'd like to – what do they always say in those old movies – slip into something a bit more comfortable."

Terry winked at him seductively, knowing that the familiar cliché phrase, along with her deliberately tempting gait, would make Elmer pant with anticipation.

Spellbound, the Ambassador observed her every move, watching hungrily as she disappeared into the bedroom. He then nodded his head assertively, firmly deciding that this very night, this very moment, he'd ask her to come with him to Washington and then back to Italy. Come with him *everywhere* for the rest of his life!

Yet, how would Terry react to such a bold proposition? Would it be anger, shock, or sweet acquiescence? Elmer wasn't sure. He only knew he needed her and was certain she needed him too.

Lost in deep thought, with the lively Vivaldi music now filling the parlor, the ambassador neither saw nor heard a sound as three shapely female figures, each dressed in black, emerged from their hiding place in the apartment's oversized coat closet down the lengthy entrance hallway. They had arrived at the hotel a few hours earlier disguised as maids, entering Dawson's suite with an extra key they'd obtained from their fourth colleague. The three wraithlike silhouettes silently began inching toward the living room, where an unsuspecting Elmer Dawson sat with the back of his neck fully exposed to them.

Chapter 2

R

The three female stalkers crept closer to Ambassador Dawson, moving stealthily without a sound. While they did so, Terry Harrigan suddenly reappeared from the bedroom. Her abrupt arrival, along with the strange clothing she wore, startled Elmer. He had never seen her in such bizarre attire.

Clad entirely in tight black leather, including a pair of exotic high-heeled riding boots, the previously demure Terry had somehow been transformed into a menacing looking vamp via this harsh, sinister outfit. It appeared to be molded directly onto her shapely body. As she stepped out into the bright overhead lighting, Elmer Dawson could see that she was holding some sort of thin metal object in her right hand. Something he couldn't quite make out. Terry had a strange, distant expression on her face, and the dark, unusual eye shadow she sported made her look even more threatening. Her eerie facade actually sent a cold chill up Elmer's spine. She was breathing heavily, with a sly grin that appeared more ominous than friendly. Taken aback by her alarming aura, Elmer Dawson recoiled in uncertainty.

"Terry?" the perplexed ambassador finally managed to whisper. He was about to ask what was happening but never got the words out. In a lightning quick strike, one of the three stalkers – a tall, powerful redheaded woman – slipped a thin leather strap around Dawson's neck. With the skill of a practiced expert, she twisted the garrote tightly, so taut that the stunned diplomat couldn't breathe. She then roughly jerked him to his feet.

Before Elmer's hands could instinctively grab for the leather binding that had suddenly and effectively cut off his air supply, a second assailant, a shapely ash-blonde girl, swiftly pulled off his expensive sports coat. Grinning maliciously, she pushed the button on the pearl-handled switchblade she was holding, and methodically cut off Elmer's shirt, undershirt, trousers and boxers with several smooth motions of the knife. Giggling at the naked man, she brusquely stuffed a thick rag deep into his opened mouth. Shoving him back down into the chair, the blonde then took several pieces of thick rawhide from the front pocket of her black jeans and skillfully secured his flailing arms to his sides. She next tied his ankles together and then slowly backed away, admiring her handiwork. In a matter of seconds, before he could even comprehend what was happening to him, it was impossible for the gagging ambassador to budge. Naked, and seemingly choking to death, Elmer Dawson was now a complete and helpless captive.

Brushing away a few strands of her streaked blonde hair that had annoyingly fallen over her eyes, the knife-wielding woman again inspected the prisoner. Satisfied, she nodded to her red-haired associate. Only then did the muscular redhead release her constricting grip on the captive's neck, reluctantly loosening the leather binding that was still around his throat.

Dawson, who had slowly started to turn a purplish blue, gasped loudly, his flared nostrils desperately laboring for a precious breath of air. Even now, it was hard for him to breathe with the thick rag stuffed tightly down his throat. Clad only in black socks, Ambassador Dawson frantically tried to assess his shocking situation. Unable to move or make a sound, he watched in wide-eyed terror as the four women gathered in front of his chair.

Terry Harrigan, still showing that strange, portentous sneer, glared at the ambassador with a look of total contempt. She slapped him hard across the face several times. "You stupid old fool, how I have longed for this moment!"

With a wave toward the three other women, she informed, "Allow me to introduce my colleagues, Mr. Ambassador. Standing before you are Anita, our red-haired beauty, Suzanne, the attractive ash-blonde to my right, and Doreen, our other blonde colleague. The four of us make up the greatest team of assassins ever assembled; male *or* female. We faithfully follow the traditions of our celebrated sisterhood, those select female warriors who came before us." Terry beamed with obvious pride. "We are paid the most because we achieve the most. You should feel honored, my dear Elmer, to know you've been targeted by the best there is."

Moving in closer to the nude captive, Terry further explained, "Our assignment regarding you began back in June. My role was to meet and seduce you in order to make sure we'd be able to keep this evening's appointment with death." With a cold, hard glare, she looked Dawson directly in the eyes. "For tonight you will surely die, Elmer."

The expression of incredulity on the shaking man's face seemed to ask why, to which Terry replied, "The *why* of it is not important. Suffice to say, a prominent client has paid us a staggering sum. He wants you dead and that's all that really matters. That and the satisfaction we get from carrying out a perfectly planned execution." Terry grinned, smugly. "There is also the matter of those government files I've seen you carrying in your attaché case from time to time. The files marked 'confidential' that you lock away in your case each night. We'll need them very soon, for an important mission we've been planning. One that will be our grandest coup yet!"

With another nod toward her three lovely accomplices, Terry continued, "You see, Mr. Ambassador, our aspiration is to uphold or surpass the accomplishments of our predecessors. Those cherished sisters of death who walked similar paths. And, by doing so, achieved more notoriety than all of our competitors put together." Terry Harrigan stiffened her body and stridently exclaimed, "The successful completion of the enterprise I alluded to will end all debate on who's the best. Thanks in part to you, we will soon be hailed as the finest assassins the world has ever known!"

Terry chuckled, mockingly. "Pity you won't be around to see the international headlines, Elmer. But at least you'll die knowing that the little tryst you and I began here in Italy was the genesis for it all." She sneered at him derisively. "That's why my alluring charms were needed for the affair. although it was easy to trap a fawning old fool like you."

Two of Terry's partners laughed loudly at their leader's taunts. The third one, Doreen, the seemingly shy natural blonde, did not. She was obviously uneasy with this man's looming execution, just like she'd been with some of the other horrid killings.

Immediately sensing Doreen's reticence, Terry Harrigan frowned angrily, making a mental note of her cohort's annoying and potentially dangerous hesitance. Terry had always been suspicious of this woman, the enigmatic Doreen Lacy. As the fourth member of their group, Doreen had literally been forced upon them. Thrust onto the team merely to placate Doreen's influential mother, an original founder of their sorority of death. True, Doreen had her strong points, particularly when it came to ferreting out secrets about prospective new targets. Yet lately, she was maddeningly uncooperative and often apathetic. Especially when it came to vengeance slayings.

Terry frowned again, this time inwardly. Despite the fact that Doreen had been pushed on them by a founding queen, this squeamish and unpredictable girl would have to be eliminated. 'Taken out' for security reasons. Some convenient accident would have to be arranged down the road. Nodding to herself, Terry Harrigan turned her attention back toward the quivering Ambassador and addressed him.

"Let me make one final point eminently clear, Elmer. Concerning our time together these past few months. I abhorred *every* minute I spent with you. The only thing that kept me going was the delicious thought of your wife and children learning some of the lurid details." Terry grinned, cruelly. "When the police investigate your death, as they surely will, a few spicy tidbits are bound to come out. Except for my identity, of course. Thanks to my careful and continual insistence on no *real*

names and no open introductions whenever I was with you, I'll never be implicated vis-à-vis your demise. Fact is, no one in Europe, or in the States for that matter, even knows my or any of my team's actual surnames. We have no record at all." Terry bowed in mock appreciation. "So, thank you, old man, for your help in keeping it that way. Your assurance of secrecy during our affair was exactly what we needed."

Savoring the look of fear on the gagged man, she added, "At least you were right about one thing you said earlier tonight, Elmer - *dead* right. For you, it really is the *end* of summer. The end of *all* your summers!"

Once more, three of the four women laughed loudly at this last remark. Relishing the moment, they were truly enjoying the torment of this man before his rapidly approaching death. To them it was an erotic game, an exciting, sensual sport that they continually loved playing. The fact that they would soon slay an important government official also buoyed their senses.

The smirking Terry, still holding the thin metal item in her left hand, casually walked over to the kitchen area, making her way to the small gas stove. Only then did Elmer Dawson fully recognize the object she was carrying. When he did, his eyes grew wide in horror. For the malevolent Terry Harrigan, or whatever her real name might be, was holding a menacing-looking branding iron!

Still wide-eyed, the terrified ambassador watched as the woman he thought he'd fallen in love with held the branding iron over the stove's blue gas flame for several minutes. Satisfied that it was now smoldering, Terry walked back to the naked captive with a strange look of contemplation. One akin to a spider carefully studying a fly caught in its web before proceeding.

Holding the branding device near, so that the trembling Dawson and her three pretty sidekicks could feel the searing heat wafting from its amber glow, Terry nodded to Anita. The sultry redhead grinned and picked up the leather noose from the floor. With obvious perverted pleasure, Anita again slipped it over Elmer Dawson's head and around his neck. She then began to tighten the noose by repeatedlytwisting its ends.

Trying in vain to breathe, the ambassador's face started to turn blue for a second time. The merciless Anita, clearly an expert in the sadistic art of slowly strangling a victim, was careful not to kill this one too quickly. While the captive desperately fought for each precious breath, Terry Harrigan, along with her shapely collaborator, Suzanne, excitedly began searing their prisoner's body from head to toe. Using the scalding branding iron viciously, the two women took turns with it, laughing cruelly as they did so. Especially when they pressed the sizzling metal against the man's most sensitive parts.

Their reticent fourth colleague, the squeamish Doreen Lacy, stood well away from the vicious torture. Though she knew the importance of this man's execution, and the fact that it was a prelude to their most significant assignment yet, Doreen nevertheless closed her eyes and tried to *will* her mind away from the brutal scene. She would have much preferred that they simply shoot this man, wondering, as always, why her three associates insisted on this unnecessary agony for all their victims. Doreen winced and shivered as she heard the man's muffled screams. Though his pain must have been unimaginable, the rag stuffed deep down his mouth was working effectively, limiting even the loudest of the ambassador's suppressed shrieks.

Eventually, the sick, sweet smell of burning flesh was almost too much for Doreen to stomach, and several times she nearly vomited. Then, mercifully, it was all over. Elmer Dawson, United States Ambassador to Italy, was dead, slowly choked to death as his naked body was being tormented with a searing branding iron.

Disappointed that their perverted fun was over, Terry, along with her two drooling partners, untied Dawson and lifted his charred, naked body from the chair. Carefully placing his corpse on the floor near the sofa, they coldly observed the dead man's eyes, which were still frozen open in abject terror. Even now the shock and pain was evident on the ambassador's ashen face.

"Go to the bedroom and grab the black attaché case that's lying under his bed," Terry ordered. "That's undoubtedly where the info we'll need will be. And while you're in there, grab all of Dawson's jewelry. I still want to keep the Italian police guessing awhile about a possible robbery motive. Even though they'll soon rule that out once they analyze the murder."

Terry Harrigan then glanced down at her fingers and grinned slyly. Like her three attractive partners, she was wearing specially made latex *Acrin* fingerprint simulators on each hand. Just as she always did when visiting here. Thin finger coverings that hid one's actual prints and replicated others. Satisfied, she called out to her cohorts who were heading toward Dawson's bedroom, "Grab all my clothing that's in there too. Everything except for that new pink negligee you'll find hanging in the bathroom. I put it there a few nights ago. It's never been worn but it should add some spice to the tabloid stories." Chuckling loudly, her three associates promptly made their way into Elmer's room.

Ten minutes later, they returned with one of the Dawson's large suitcases, now filled with Terry's clothes and shoes, the ambassador's black attaché case and a few other government folders. Also packed inside were Dawson's wallet and jewelry, this to help bolster a potential homicide/theft motive.

Now wearing Elmer's long brown raincoat, retrieved from the hall closet, Terry glanced around the apartment one last time. She then placed the branding iron, now completely cooled via the small kitchen sink, into the suitcase as well. While doing so, she again eyed the lifeless, tortured body of Elmer Dawson sprawled on the floor. Nodding her head with pride, Terry exclaimed, "That's about it, girls. We've done it! Carried it out exactly as planned. There are no authentic fingerprints to trace, no names, and no real clues. Just the appearance of an apparent robbery, coupled with a sadistic homicide. Or perhaps a violent lover's spat. Whatever they suspect, it should keep the Venice *Polizia* guessing for months. As for my role in any of it, the only thing they could possibly have to go on is the negligee, and a few isolated rumors about some phantom brunette named Betty Cummings. A brown-haired woman who may or may not have been spotted with the Ambassador tonight."

Laughing triumphantly, the wily Miss Harrigan winked at her partners and then began to slowly remove her expensive brown wig, the excellent hairpiece she'd worn since that first day she met Ambassador Dawson. Struggling to pull off the firmly attached wig, she at last revealed her *real* hair - long, gleaming blonde dyed locks, almost golden in color.

The other women in the room smiled back with approval. For their sultry leader, Terry Harrigan, was *not* a brunette; nor was she 'Betty Cummings', some mysterious dark haired beauty. She was, in fact, a striking, longhaired blonde, one with no criminal record or fingerprints, no affirmation of her actual name, and someone who'd never even been to Italy prior to the last six months. Consequently, it would be virtually impossible for Interpol or Venice's *Polizia Giudiziaria* to find anything at all on her; particularly since they'd be looking for some shorthaired brunette with fingerprints that didn't match anyone's.

Terry placed the brown hairpiece into her large handbag, walked to the front door, and took a cursory look down the deserted outside corridor. Satisfied no one was about, she and her fellow assassins calmly exited Dawson's apartment suite. Although tonight's immediate goal had been accomplished, they were well aware that their *real* task was yet to come.

Carrying one large suitcase and two smaller pieces of hand baggage, the four women began the long trek down the fire emergency exit stairwell located at the end of the ninth floor's hallway. They walked briskly, climbing all the way down to the *Verona's* deserted basement parking garage.

Learning from a slightly inebriated bellman who Anita had met in a local bar four days ago, they knew in advance that the hotel's archaic security cameras, along with its one and only house monitor, hadn't worked properly in weeks. The women thus left the hotel sight unseen.

Beaming with confidence now, the pretty quartet of death strolled out into the humid darkness and boldly ambled down several of Venice's back alleyways. Eventually stopping near a small prearranged side canal at precisely 1:45 a.m., they soon spotted a sleek motor launch approaching the canal bank. It appeared almost magically, as if an apparition slithering through the mist. Nodding to the husky driver, who they knew well, the four women hopped onboard. Then, just as quietly as it had appeared, the boat swiftly vanished into the haze.

~

Several hours later, the golden Venetian sun gleamed down on the Piazza San Marco. A few minutes before noon, a pair of hotel chambermaids knocked softly on the double doors of Ambassador Dawson's suite. After getting no response to their polite but continuous knocking, they finally let themselves in with a passkey. Their screams came simultaneously as they spotted the stretched out corpse of Elmer Dawson lying grotesquely on the apartment's living room floor. The dead man's eyes were wide open, staring hauntingly into space, and there was dried blood caked on his naked body.

Still shrieking hysterically, one of the maids, the older of the two, somehow composed herself and frantically began phoning the front desk. While she dialed, the other trembling chambermaid glanced down at the Ambassador's tortured corpse and noticed that one single letter had been repeatedly burned all over his body. That one letter, viciously branded onto the man's flesh, was a large, rounded *R.*

Chapter 3

Departmental Secrets

Two weeks later and some four thousand miles from Venice, Italy, two men made their way toward a nondescript office building on Madison Avenue in New York City. One was a tall, distinguished grey-haired gentleman, accompanied by his shorter, stockier guest. The building they approached, a 13-story edifice officially known as the *Tyler Center* is similar to most of the high-rise structures in midtown Manhattan, with one unique exception. It's one of the few Manhattan high-risers owned and operated by the U.S. government.

The lower eight floors of the Tyler building accommodate several dull bureaucratic agencies; mundane population-recording offices along with a number of insignificant Census Bureau hubs. These lower floors hardly ever attract visitors or draw any interest.

It's the *top* five floors of the Tyler Center, however, that make this building anything but ordinary. For these higher floors contain the offices of G5, a classified intelligence department answering directly to the President of the United States.

Since the late 1970s, G5 was, and still is, one of America's most effective intelligence agencies. It is also one of its most secretive. The private nooks, conference rooms, secured files and diverse, hi-tech communication centers situated here are used by G5 to develop and authorize covert government operations. Missions that are carried out in all parts of the world by dedicated secret agents who willingly risk their lives in order to keep America safe. It was to one of these restricted top five floors that Colonel Peter McPhail, G5's Director, and his distinguished visitor from the CIA, Admiral James Collingwood, were now headed.

McPhail and his guest strolled to the very back of the building. Nodding to the two armed guards stationed there, McPhail and Collingwood flashed their government IDs. They then made their way through a narrow rear alleyway where two more sentries were patrolling. Briskly walking through this hidden passageway, one monitored by several closed circuit video cameras, they soon arrived at a shabby-looking freight elevator. Before entering it, they passed through a small airport-type security screening booth located directly in front of the lift. Successfully 'screened' now, the duo entered the elevator. Colonel McPhail slid his specially coded keycard into a thin slot on the elevator's right-hand panel, and the two men were soon being whisked up to the 13th floor.

To anyone seeing these rather ordinary-looking gentlemen, similarly dressed in conservative grey business suits, nothing would have called attention to the fact that each man guided one of his nation's most powerful intelligence bureaus; Peter McPhail's ultra-secretive G5, and Admiral James Collingwood's CIA, where the admiral was second in command at the Agency.

The two government honchos rode the elevator in silence, each man in deep thought about the other. Quickly exiting when they reached the building's top floor, they were greeted by yet another armed guard, this one in full protective armor. Showing their ID's, McPhail and Collingwood saluted the lone sentry and then walked a few more steps over to the main reception desk. Colonel McPhail smiled and addressed the smartly dressed secretary seated behind it.

"Afternoon, Miss Wilson."

Ginger Wilson looked up from her computer. "Good afternoon, Colonel."

McPhail pointed to his guest, a frequent visitor to G5. "You know Admiral Collingwood, of course."

"Of course, sir." Ginger nodded to the CIA visitor. "Nice to see you again, Admiral."

The CIA man nodded back at her.

"We'll be in my office a while," McPhail informed. "No interruptions please, unless it's an absolute emergency."

"Yes, Colonel. I put a fresh pitcher of ice water on your desk. Or would you or the Admiral rather have coffee?"

"Don't think so, thanks. They practically drowned us with espresso at *Wolfgang's* restaurant. But do me a favor, Ginger. Please call down to that special class now in session. Tell them I might need one of the attending agents in a bit."

"Will do, Colonel." And with that, the two men headed for McPhail's private office suite.

Ambling down a narrow passageway, they soon came to the opened door of Nancy Gallo's cubicle, Colonel McPhail's personal secretary. Her smallish office was located directly outside of McPhail's plush suite. The G5 chief greeted her warmly.

"Hi, Nancy. Told you I'd be back before two o'clock."

"Yes, sir, you did." She nodded to Admiral Collingwood. "Hello, Admiral, good to see you again. Did you and the Colonel enjoy your lunch?"

"Ate too much like always, Nancy."

Nancy Gallo chuckled as McPhail explained, "Jim and I will be in conference for a while. I told Ginger that I may need one of the agents soon. I'll buzz you when the time is right and perhaps you can go and retrieve him for us."

"Certainly, Colonel. I checked the attendance sheets. There are four agents in session today. The other two are absent."

McPhail frowned, knowing both of those men were on dangerous overseas missions. One of them, an agent presently on assignment in Saudi Arabia, hadn't reported in for over a week now. His contact messages were likewise overdue, and the colonel was extremely worried about him. Thinking about the missing operative, McPhail half listened as his secretary added, "Just let me know which man you'll want from downstairs, and when, and I'll get him right up to you."

"Sounds good, Nancy." Colonel McPhail and Admiral Collingwood both nodded to her and then made their way into McPhail's office.

Upon entering, they were met with a loud "hello" from Quack, McPhail's beloved pet parrot. Quack was a beautiful and extroverted Amazon Yellow Nape, a demonstrative bird that Peter McPhail cherished. Simultaneously grinning at the cage, the men threw off their suit jackets, loosened their ties and sat down in the leather armchairs in front of McPhail's large desk. It was Admiral Collingwood who got down to business first.

"Well now, Pete. I know you've been dying to ask me why I'm *really* here in New York." He chuckled. "Aside from enjoying the best sirloin in the city."

The two agency chiefs had deliberately not discussed 'business' during lunch. Each had a similar rule of trying never to do so when dining out, both for security and social reasons. There was time enough to worry about their respective bureaus after a good meal had been consumed, and over the years both men had learned not to mix business with pleasure. Yet, even though they hadn't discussed the brutal murder of Ambassador Elmer Dawson during their noonday feast, the Colonel was well aware that this was why the CIA exec had come. During McPhail's private conversation with the White House the day before, the president had given him a 'heads-up' on it. He looked Collingwood directly in the eyes and stated, "Well, I've got a pretty good idea why you're here, Jim. That messy affair with the ambassador might be a reason."

Collingwood nodded, sheepishly, not sure how to begin. McPhail, sensing his guest's uneasiness, quickly tried to put the visitor at ease.

"Don't worry, Admiral. I know a bit about your needs. The president briefly mentioned some of the details during our phone conversation. Told me you'd fill me in on the rest today. So please, fire away."

"Thanks, Pete." Admiral Collingwood leaned back in his chair and began, "This whole thing with the Ambassador is quite bizarre, Colonel. First off, it appears that Dawson was fooling around with a woman while in Italy. Happens a lot with these career diplomats stationed in Europe. Loneliness, boredom, who knows? According to a hotel bartender, whom we discreetly canvassed in Venice, Ambassador Dawson had occasionally been seen with a young brunette on his arm. Probably some Italian bimbo he met there, although nothing is really known about the woman. The barkeep said it was strictly low-key and very infrequent. He only saw Dawson with the girl a few time, mostly late at night. And he's not even sure if it was always the same lady or not. The ambassador usually kept to himself, and the few times he came in with anyone they always sat at a quiet table in the back. So this bartender, and everyone else at the hotel, wasn't really much help at all as to the woman's identity."

Admiral Collingwood watched McPhail pour himself a glass of ice water and then continued, "In any case, Pete, during their investigation right after the murder, Venice detectives found a woman's slinky nightgown in Dawson's suite. So obviously something was going on. As for the killing itself, Italian authorities aren't even sure if this gal was part of it or not. She might have left *before* the slaying and apparent robbery even took place. There was also some unsubstantiated gossip about a wild night of kinky sex gone horribly wrong. Could be true. Dawson was found naked, bound and gagged on the floor."

Collingwood looked over at McPhail and again shrugged his shoulders. He then added, "Interpol is now checking into another possibility: a deadly squabble between Dawson and a jilted boyfriend. Perhaps this was a revenge slaying carried out by some insanely jealous third party. You know, a scorned gigolo who punished and killed Ambassador Dawson in a rage of anger. They're still checking on the hotel's monthly visitor manifest, but as of yet no hints of any aggrieved third party have turned up."

The CIA man cleared his throat. "The one oddity here is that there's absolutely *nothing* at all on any woman or women who Elmer Dawson was seeing. No names, no friends, no nothing. It's a total blank. Even the few local names Interpol came up with aren't a match. There hasn't been a trace or any type of lead on this girl whatsoever. So, whoever Dawson was seeing seems to be a complete phantom. One who apparently has disappeared into thin air. That in itself is quite unusual."

"Any fingerprints?"

"There were plenty around but none that matched anyone of interest. Like I said, the woman's a phantom."

The Colonel frowned and declared, "People who have no friends, relatives or any record at all are quite rare, Admiral. I've found that they're usually professionals." McPhail smiled apologetically. "Sorry to have butted in, Jim. Please go on with your story."

"As I've stated, initially this killing didn't seem like anything more than a personal tryst, followed by some sort of violent fetish or quarrel gone awry. Certainly nothing we at the CIA would be interested in. These kinky love triangles are merely tabloid junk to us. Nobody's business but Dawson's. If the CIA had to follow up on every rumor of illicit affairs involving our government officials, we wouldn't have time for anything else. Heck, we had our own internal love scandal back with Petraeus."

Colonel McPhail grimaced at the memory as Collingwood acknowledged, "For that matter, even an overseas murder, even as violent and tragic as it was, isn't something we'd normally look into."

The CIA man gazed over at McPhail with a somber expression. "That is, until we learned that Ambassador Dawson's attaché case, which contained some confidential government papers, was also missing. Dawson's briefcase, along with all of his money and jewelry, were apparently taken right after the slaying. So it could have been theft, or even a potential blackmail motive."

"Blackmail?"

"Yes, Pete. Recently there's been a lucrative market for missing government papers and classified information. *Especially* anything American. Thieves and organized crime gangs have made a small fortune by first robbing, and then selling back, the documents they've stolen from us. Anything potentially embarrassing to the USA can bring in good money. These crooks and profiteers threaten to sell the information they've pilfered to tabloid publications, or to governments unfriendly toward us unless they're paid off. It can get real messy. Look what happened with those recent WikiLeaks when we refused to pony up." The Admiral shook his head. "Still, with the brutality of this Dawson murder, some smalltime blackmail motive just doesn't seem to fit."

"Was anything 'top secret' in Dawson's attaché case, Jim?"

"Not really, Colonel. But remember. Dawson was just an ambassador, *not* a senator or congressman. What he had privy to was probably just some diplomatic minutia. There were a couple of embarrassing letters criticizing Italy's ambassadors. And a few mild critiques of Italian foreign policy. But that's about it."

Collingwood thought on it a moment. "Yet there was one thing that could be of concern. And frankly, it still has me a bit troubled."

"What's that?"

"Dawson's papers included some private communiqués with the White House social staff regarding NATO's upcoming European 'black-tie' dinner. You know, that big VIP bash in Cannes, France, that the President is planning to attend next month. Right after the European summit. Apparently Ambassador Dawson had a few notes about it in his briefcase. Mainly info on who sits where and with whom. Fairly innocuous stuff that we can easily change. Although we obviously don't like anyone having advance knowledge of where and when the President, or *any* top American officials, are going to be at any specific time. But you know the Pres. He's adamant about being there. His biggest donors will be 'comped' there, and the president is firstly a politician. They'll undoubtedly change the seating arrangements now, and have the newest security machines about. Simply as a precaution."

Collingwood took another sip of his water. "By the way, Colonel, there'll be three or four other world leaders of NATO countries attending the gala as well. So naturally everyone is concerned from a security point of view." The admiral shrugged once more. "Then again, the international press has already been mentioning the event and the dignitaries who'll be gathering in Cannes next month. So it wasn't really a secret anyway. Plus, safety measures at the black-tie gala will undoubtedly be airtight. Now more than ever."

"Naturally," agreed McPhail.

"All in all, though, we're lucky there was nothing *really* classified in the ambassador's briefcase, Colonel. That being said, though, whenever government papers are lost or stolen overseas, CIA is obligated to get involved. So we quietly began looking into the Dawson murder itself. And, when we did, we didn't like some of the leads we found."

"What do you mean?"

"Well, there may be some rather alarming details in all this. Potentially troubling data regarding one possible gang of would-be killers. If any of those leads are true, it might make the ambassador's murder more than a simple crime of erotic passion. Or one jealous gigolo acting alone. We therefore need to get an inside operative over to Europe as soon as possible to see what gives."

"But not one of your own CIA operatives," McPhail affirmed in an almost directive manner. "One of *mine*."

James Collingwood twisted in his chair uneasily. "That's right, Pete. Normally, we'd do the job ourselves. Simply hand it over to one of our own agents. But the unique nature of one group of potential suspects calls for, ah..." Collingwood paused a moment, still a bit uncomfortable. "Shall we say, a *special* type of operative, Colonel?"

McPhail's stoic expression never changed as Collingwood admitted, "It seems we're going to need the services of a more *specifically* trained undercover agent for this particular assignment, Pete. Accordingly, my chief was informed by the White House that G5 might be able to help us out with that."

McPhail smiled. "Relax, Jim. The President filled me in yesterday on some of this. And it's definitely something we can give you a hand with. Just give me a few more specifics and I'll know better on how to help."

Admiral Collingwood rolled his eyes in gratitude as if a giant weight had just been lifted off him. "Thanks, Pete. My chief will be pleased. He would have skinned me alive if you guys weren't willing to help us.

Probably would have blamed me for poor negotiation tactics between agencies, or some such thing." Collingwood grinned. "Remember, Colonel. I'm only the number *two* guy at CIA."

"I understand, Jim. And please tell the CIA director that we're always happy to assist in any way we can. Just so long as the commander-in-chief *himself* gives us the official nod. That's the only way we're allowed to get involved." McPhail's eyes squinted slightly. "But what is it that you actually want from us? The President was rather vague on that part. Merely said it would involve one of our elite sectors."

"That's correct, Colonel. At least we *think* we may need the help of one of your, ah, specialized departments."

The CIA honcho got up from his chair and observed Colonel McPhail thoughtfully. He then inquired, "But let me ask you something first, if I may, Colonel. I certainly don't want to pry too deeply into your internal operations, of course. But we've heard some amazing snippets about your, ah . . . about a branch of yours that seems quite . . . well, quite unusual. I'm not sure if these stories are true or purely sensationalized, so I thought I better ask you about it first."

James Collingwood looked McPhail straight in the eyes. "I believe it's called your 'Super Stud' section?"

Colonel McPhail bristled, his expression showing both surprise and annoyance. It was obvious he was irritated by Collingwood's revelation. A covert sector he thought was not widely known, even to other intelligence agencies, apparently had people openly talking about it. Trying to remain composed, McPhail glared at his visitor and replied icily, "Yes, Admiral, we have such a department."

Sensing the colonel's displeasure, James Collingwood held up his hand. "I don't need to know all the inside details, Pete. Just a few generalities. It's essential in determining if what we have in mind could actually work."

McPhail forced a smile, somewhat mollified by Collingwood's last statement. "I understand, Jim. But what, exactly, do you want to know?"

"Well, do these, uh, super chaps of yours really have enhanced methods of captivating women? And are they actually *trained* to be irresistible to female targets in the field? I've only heard bits and pieces about it. A few tidbits concerning great-looking agents being able to mesmerize the fair sex via their looks, fancy etiquette, gourmet knowledge and faultless hygiene practices." Collingwood's face reddened, slightly. "And via their, uh, erudite sensual prowess as well. Believe me, it's relevant, Colonel, or I wouldn't be asking."

McPhail's expression remained stony. "What you've somehow managed to learn is fairly accurate, Admiral."

The CIA exec, trying desperately to reassure his host, promptly added, "Please don't worry, Pete. Only a few folks at my agency had even heard about this Super Stud section of yours. And they've been told to keep that knowledge strictly to *themselves.*"

Colonel McPhail smiled, his stern demeanor finally easing a bit. "Sorry to appear so paranoid about it, Jim. But anonymity and secrecy mean a lot to the security of that particular department. And for the safety of the agents themselves. Naturally I'm always concerned whenever *any* information comes out about them."

"I fully understand and agree, Colonel. I feel the same way about some my special operatives." Collingwood shifted in his chair. "Anyway, the last couple of days I've been trying my best to separate the Super Stud fact from fiction before asking for help." He grinned. "From the little I've learned, though, it's quite obvious that your Studs have infiltrated places and people we couldn't."

McPhail again grimaced. Apparently, CIA knew a lot more about the Super Studs than Admiral Collingwood was letting on. They obviously had their own methods of finding out classified information about a rival bureau. Making a mental note to have a stern talk with Kevin O'Rourke, G5's security chief, Colonel McPhail shrugged his shoulders and replied.

"Yes, Admiral, some of what you've heard about my Super Studs is correct. The Studs have proven to be an extremely effective force when the assignment calls for ferreting out secrets from females around the globe. In addition to being six of the best-looking men on the planet, they've also been thoroughly instructed on virtually every aspect of being irresistible to women. And I mean *everything.* From being skilled in perfect hygiene, to wine recognition, fine dining and correct wardrobe choices; to fostering alluring, passionate relationships with unsuspecting female targets."

James Collingwood silently wondered who the teacher was on *that* particular topic. He chuckled inwardly as his G5 host explained more.

"Our Super Stud agents have been fully coached on everything a woman would want in an ideal man. We've done meticulous study on it. Still do. These specially trained agents are well-honed stud machines, meticulously trained to be irresistible to the fair sex. Obviously, extraordinary looks was the first thing we looked for. It wasn't easy, checking out thousands of magazine ads, Hollywood hunks, inside referrals, and incredibly handsome faces. They were then trained to be schooled on every conceivable aspect. Including some seemingly trivial things, like using the most effective toothpastes, soaps and deodorants."

McPhail sat back in his chair, now warming to the task of informing this rival honcho about his favored Studs. "It took us nearly three years to find who we feel are the six handsomest men in the world. We used computer programs, hundreds of modeling websites, portrait files and various fashion magazine records to locate them. The candidates were initially judged strictly for looks by a panel of debutantes, savvy female jet-setters and knowledgeable modeling agents."

Now spellbound, Admiral Collingwood listened closely as G5's director gave more details. "Nothing at all is left to chance with our Super Stud operatives. Once a month they attend classes here. Courses that pertain to all the things I've mentioned - from hygiene to fashion. As a matter of fact, one of those classes is in session right now."

The Colonel took a long sip from his water glass and further explained, "Yet their most important training comes from noted psychologists who instruct our agents on how to slowly entice and captivate a woman. Then, using their looks and guile, to bring the targeted relationship along until the female we need inside information from can be 'turned'. Sounds a bit zany, I know. But it's succeeded beyond our wildest dreams."

"Amazing," Collingwood marveled.

"Yes it is, Jim – and it works. All of our Super Stud proficiency, training, and groundwork has helped these men conquer important female targets around the globe. The women surrounding powerful men and leaders who, in many cases, are America's most dangerous enemies. Like that Middle Eastern mistress, codenamed Elda, who was having an affair with Osama bin Laden's most trusted courier. One of our Studs got to the woman and mesmerized her. The inside info our man obtained during the fling eventually led the way for the SEALS to get bin Laden."

Recalling the mission, a trace of pride came across McPhail's weathered face. "You'd be surprised at how successful the Super Studs have been for us in recent years, Admiral. Simply by using their striking faces, their skilled approach with the opposite sex, and their craftiness." Colonel McPhail gave a thin smile. "I don't know if *all* the stories you've heard about the Studs are factual or not. But let's just say that if you need a good-looking agent to coax something out of any female in the world, I have six of them specially trained for just such an assignment."

James Collingwood nodded affirmatively. "Okay, Colonel, that settles that, then. But before I present CIA's formal request, let me hit you with a rather 'left field' question." Collingwood again shifted his body in the plush chair. "In your professional opinion, who would you say are the world's most effective assassination and extortion groups?"

Colonel McPhail was momentarily caught off guard by the query. He pondered it a few minutes and then reflectively gave his reply. "Well, offhand, there's that Fuji group from Japan. They've spelled major trouble for the authorities and for their unfortunate victims as well. Fuji is quick, deadly and effective. *Asian Death* is their appropriate nickname."

McPhail contemplated the question further. "There's also that Asesinato faction from the Philippines. Kidnapping, terror bombings and vengeance slayings have been their specialties for decades. As far as I know, no one's been able to control them."

"No one has," agreed Collingwood as the colonel continued.

"Needless to say, more recently we've had to contend with terrorist groups from the Middle East. The Taliban elite squads, ISIS and those volatile al Qaeda jihad factions." McPhail frowned at the thought of those gutless fanatics. "And of course, right here in America, certain divisions of organized crime frequently give us fits, along with their Mafia cousins in Europe. Those gangland families and sleazy 'hit men' of theirs have always been tough to oppose. Killing and extortion comes easy for them. Over the years they've managed to infiltrate several legitimate businesses."

"All excellent choices," Collingwood admitted. "But you've left out the *queens* of the pack, Colonel. Perhaps the most secretive and effective assassination squad of them all – *Rhombus*."

"Rhombus? You mean those four women who were active on the continent some years back Jim? I haven't heard anything about them in quite a while. Thought Interpol might have caught up with them."

"Unfortunately, no Pete. Although the original four Rhombus women are long gone. They've been replaced by a younger, prettier and much more sinister quartet of killers." Collingwood sighed. "Apparently, after four years of relative inactivity, they're at it again. We recently learned that it was Rhombus who killed that U.N. Administrator in Madrid last year. Skinned him alive first, and then threw his flayed body on a side street near the Plaza de Oriente. Brazenly dropped him right next to the United Nations offices there."

McPhail winced as Admiral Collingwood gave more details. "And just a short while ago, after being hired by a German crime syndicate, the new Rhombus foursome skillfully kidnapped a high-ranking Canadian diplomat's wife and child. Did so while the family was vacationing in Austria. Rhombus nabbed them even though the man's family was traveling with two armed security guards. It was a near-perfect abduction. The German syndicate got millions from Canada for the safe return of the abducted family, along with the release of one of their own members who'd been serving a life sentence. No telling how much the Rhombus gals made on the deal. The story was deliberately kept out of the papers for fear of copycat attempts by other extortionists."

Colonel McPhail nodded his head and informed, "I heard about that kidnapping, of course. But since it didn't concern my agency, I didn't pay much attention to it. Thought it was just another one of those European mob jobs. Didn't know it was Rhombus."

"It was *definitely* Rhombus, Pete. And though their fees are said to be extraordinarily high, these Rhombus women are not just in it for the money. Scuttlebutt has it that they get their jollies by pulling off flawless kidnappings and violent killings. They're said to be practicing sadists as well. Both personally and professionally. Sadists who have some odd social habits: whips, chains, that sort of thing. It's probably true, since most of their slayings show incredible brutality, spiced with merciless torture. They're quite a menacing crew."

Admiral Collingwood rubbed his forehead and poured himself some more water. "And here's the kicker, Colonel. We now have reason to believe that Rhombus might have been involved in Ambassador Dawson's murder."

"How'd you find *that* out?" asked McPhail. "From what I remember about them, the Rhombus group was always extremely secretive about their dirty work."

"They usually are, Colonel. In fact, that's the main reason the bad guys hire them; proficiency with complete confidentiality. But this time the few rumors that we ferreted out came from the client's side, *not* the killers'. Plus, there were some other possible Rhombus signs apropos the Dawson slaying. Though I emphasize the word *possible*."

"What are they, Jim?"

"Well, first off, there was a large single letter branded onto the ambassador's body."

"Branded?"

"Yes, Pete. Someone used a red-hot branding iron all over Elmer Dawson's body. Repeatedly burned the letter *R* onto him. We originally thought it was a Mafia touch. Still could be. In Cosa Nostra vengeance slayings, the mob's hit men sometimes carve, slice, or burn the letter *R* onto their victim's corpses. It's done to warn others that the killing was an act of gangland revenge. Hence the *R*. So, initially we at the CIA thought it could have been the *Mafia* who killed Ambassador Dawson."

McPhail again nodded.

"But then, just last week, some new leads popped up. Leads that could indicate the *R* on the ambassador's body was a sadistic trademark of Rhombus. So now we're back to square one, Colonel. And that's the rub. In addition to the tryst angle, it could also be the work of the Mafia *or* Rhombus." Collingwood sighed. "Plus, there's still the remote possibility that it was simply a jilted boyfriend acting on his own."

Colonel McPhail rubbed his chin in thought. "I can see you've got a real puzzle on your hands, Jim."

"We sure do."

"Any other leads?"

"Yes, Pete. Two of our European operatives managed to acquire some additional info late last week from our sources in Italy. It alleges that the Dawson killing was ordered by the Gitano mob family."

"*Carmine* Gitano? That dapper Mafia chieftain from Detroit?"

"That's the guy, Colonel. And as you're undoubtedly aware, Carmine Gitano has ties to Mafia families on *both* sides of the Atlantic. Two syndicates here in the States, operating out of Detroit and Chicago. And the other in Europe, headquartered in Sicily. The Sicilian faction is fronted by Gitano's uncle, Salvatore Gitano, although Carmine is still its leader. Regardless, it's one of the most powerful and dangerous of all the European mob syndicates."

McPhail quickly agreed. "I know. Over the years, G5 has had a few run-ins with the Gitano gang ourselves. Both domestically and internationally. They're a tough lot."

"That they are, Colonel. The worst of all the mobs. And there was good motive for Gitano's syndicate to be behind Dawson's murder. A few years ago, Ambassador Dawson sabotaged a bid by one of Gitano's deported lieutenants to come back into the States."

Admiral Collingwood took out some handwritten notes and glanced at them as he explained, "The case involved Donnie *'Little Man'* Sorentino, Carmine Gitano's favored second lieutenant. Apparently, Ambassador Dawson learned that Little Man was running a narcotics ring out of Florence. Dawson passed the info on to the U.S. Justice Department, who then quickly put the kibosh on Gitano's plans to bring Donnie back. They say Carmine Gitano never forgot it. So there was definitely incentive for a 'hit'."

McPhail scowled angrily, always repulsed by the mob's tactics.

"Of course," admitted Collingwood, "we're still not certain whether that was the reason behind Dawson's murder. Or even if the 'hit' was in fact contracted by the mob. But then, late last week, a few juicy European rumors pointing that way surfaced in Como."

"Rumors involving the Gitano crime syndicate?"

"Yes. Both them *and* Rhombus." Collingwood frowned and shrugged his shoulders. "Of course, these types of spicy tidbits are always prevalent whenever a U.S. official is killed in Europe. It's big news over there, and every two-bit hoodlum from London to Portugal seems to boast about either doing the deed himself or knowing all the inside details. Whether they actually do or not is another matter. Most of the time these gangland stories are nothing more than pure braggadocio."

"I understand, Admiral."

"Be that as it may, here's the deal, Colonel. One of our CIA moles was at a bar near Lake Como when some minor-league gangster strolled in. Apparently this thug was half drunk already, and he began bragging to a few of the late night regulars, enthralling them with his dramatic 'inside' tales regarding Elmer Dawson's assassination. Our informant kept buying this hood drinks, and pretty soon he *really* opened up. Claimed his Mafia boss, Carmine Gitano, had hired 'four gorgeous women' to carry out the hit. That snippet, along with this letter *R* thing, immediately swayed our suspicions back toward Rhombus. They're the only female assassination squad we know of. Plus, over the years, they've occasionally been hired by the Mafia families."

"Could be a fit," concurred McPhail.

"That's what Interpol thought too, Colonel. So, in view of that, we promptly ordered two of our best European operatives to see if they could discreetly re-contact this hoodlum; the bragging barroom loudmouth. They couldn't find him anywhere, but they did manage to come up with some admittedly vague information he'd privately told one of the wait staff."

Collingwood cleared his throat and informed, "Initially, we didn't think much of it. That is until this talkative Lake Como drunk, the hood who'd started the rumors in the first place, turned up dead the day before yesterday. His body was found floating in Lake Garda with six knives sticking out of it. Furthermore, his tongue had been cut out. That's a known Mafia ritual used whenever an insider talks too much. Evidently the mob didn't want any further info circulating about 'four beautiful killers'. So maybe the hearsay regarding a female assassination squad could be true. If not, why did they eliminate this drunken loudmouth so quickly and violently?"

Just then, Quack, McPhail's pet parrot, screeched out a loud expletive from its ornate cage behind the colonel's desk. The two men laughed as Admiral Collingwood finished up his story.

"We had our agents tactfully question the bartender again. At first, he was understandably hesitant to say anything. Probably didn't want to lose his *own* tongue. But a handful of Euros soon had him singing like a bird. We found out that the drunk who was knifed to death was definitely a soldier in Gitano's European mob. And our operatives were likewise told that in addition to a huge financial reward, the four women who allegedly took out Ambassador Dawson were given full use of Carmine Gitano's magnificent yacht – the Zephyr."

"His yacht?"

"That's right, Gitano's amazing vessel, which, whenever in Europe, is usually moored in Monte Carlo. It's the largest and most opulent private yacht in the world. Comes complete with a full complement of gourmet chefs, a bevy of butlers, stewards, and maids. There's also, three separate swimming pools, a state-of-the-art Las Vegas-type showroom, and gold-plated trimmings in all the baths and bedrooms. It's said to be unbelievable – 'the 8th wonder of the world' according to *Yachtsman Magazine*. The Zephyr is large enough to travel anywhere on the globe, and it can sleep a small army of pampered guests while doing so. If full use of this magnificent craft was part of a big payoff – say, full use of Gitano's breathtaking yacht for a month or two on the Riviera – that's quite a tempting prize. Just the right type of stimulating reward that could have swayed the materialistic Rhombus women to do the job."

"Definitely," agreed McPhail.

Admiral Collingwood sighed again. "As to whether all these rumors are true or not, we just don't know for sure. Although we did receive some relevant information from Interpol a few days ago. Details on both the passengers and whereabouts of Carmine Gitano's yacht. The report was quite interesting. Seems Gitano's luxurious cabin cruiser is indeed moored in Monte Carlo. And custom officials have confirmed that there are four attractive female passengers onboard. So, if our hunches are correct, and if these women actually *are* from Rhombus, they could indeed be the Dawson assassins."

"I see," said Colonel McPhail.

"Of course, all this could still be unfounded gossip, Pete. Merely boastful gangland rumors started by some Lake Como drunk. For all we know, the four females aboard the Zephyr might just be some young chippies whom Carmine and the boys are enjoying in Monaco."

Admiral Collingwood glanced up at McPhail, pleadingly. "In any case, we desperately need to find out if Ambassador Dawson's stolen briefcase and those missing NATO files have any *serious* implications."

"Have you or CIA formulated any plan of action yet, Jim?"

Collingwood grinned, sheepishly. "Yes, we have. And that's why I'm here, Colonel. You see, from the little my agency has learned about this current group of Rhombus women, the only thing they're said to enjoy more than killing and torture is flaunting and flirting with good- looking men. We thus feel that a handsome and suave operative might be able to somehow mix in with those four yacht girls in Monaco."

The CIA man glanced out Colonel McPhail's large office window and peered down at the mounting traffic on Madison Avenue. He mused silently a moment. Then, with genuine concern on his face, he ended his plea. "That's probably the *only* way it can be done, Pete. Some sort of social entrée with the four women on Gitano's vessel."

Admiral Collingwood finally took his eyes off the office window and looked back at McPhail. "I'm afraid our own CIA operatives wouldn't be much help in this, Colonel. First of all none of them are trained ladies men. And secondly, there's been some growing identity leaks about our undercover agents in Europe. It seems the bad guys know our agents better than we do. So I'm afraid we wouldn't get within 1200 yards of Gitano's yacht."

Collingwood shook his head dejectedly and affirmed, "And as per asking for help from the Monte Carlo maritime authorities. The well- bribed Monaco authorities are said to be in Carmine Gitano's hip pocket. Consequently they'd never let us do any covert snooping around Zephyr. And they'd undoubtedly warn Gitano if the CIA asked them for any help."

James Collingwood got up from his chair and frowned. "We can likewise forget about any Monaco governmental support. Seems *Don* Gitano is as well connected in Europe as he is here."

Collingwood again looked over at his G5 host. "We were therefore hoping that one of your Super Stud agents, mingling in with Monaco's 'in-crowd', and hopefully with those four yacht women as well, might be able to ferret out some verifiable information for us."

Listening patiently, Colonel McPhail now had a clearer picture of things. He took out a small notepad, scribbled a few facts down, and exclaimed, "Then I guess we're going to need an agent who's *irresistible,* Jim. One that can find out who those yacht ladies *really* are."

The Colonel reached for his intercom button, pressed it down and was instantly connected to his secretary.

"Miss Gallo."

"Yes, sir?"

"Would you mind running down to that Super Stud classroom for me now? And once you're there, please bring Agent Christopher Seven directly to me. ASAP, if you please."

Chapter 5

Back on the Horse

"Gentlemen, may I please have your attention!" the attractive Australian nurse firmly requested. Her small Super Stud classroom audience promptly quieted down. Satisfied with their quick compliance, she walked over to the large blackboard that covered most of the front wall of the windowless room. "This afternoon's Super Stud class is about ongoing personal hygiene and cleanliness." She wrote the words 'hygiene' and 'cleanliness' on the board in large letters with a piece of white chalk and then resumed, "Today we'll be reviewing hygiene habits that are essential. That is if you want to continue to be flawless in the eyes and senses of women around the world. Chiefly, those beautiful female targets in the field that it's your duty as Studs to captivate."

After double-underlining the word *cleanliness,* the Aussie turned around and smiled at the four incredibly handsome men seated in front of her. "Please concentrate now, gentlemen - concentrate. I have a feeling some of you are half asleep today." She waited a moment and then resumed her speech. "Here at G5 we leave nothing to chance. You're expected to be perfect when it comes to personal cleanliness. And fully knowledgeable in all of the other Super Stud areas of expertise that we stress. Gourmet dining proficiency, social savoir-faire, wardrobe perfection and most importantly, practiced relational skills with the opposite sex." She wrote the word 'relations' on the blackboard in similarly large letters.

The two newer Super Stud agents sitting in the front row, both in early stages of training, listened respectfully. The pair of veteran operatives in the back row did not seem quite as attentive. They'd heard it, or something comparable, many times before. The two veterans glanced at each other with knowing smiles just as their mentor resumed.

"Today we'll also be reviewing the Stud *preferred* list. Those tried and true products that have been tested and approved for your usage."

Again, the newer men in the front dutifully watched as the dark- haired beauty from Sydney began writing a list of several name brand items on the blackboard. She started with *Listerine* Artic Mint mouthwash and ended it with *Dial's* Mountain Fresh bar soap.

Super Stud Christopher Seven, sitting in the very back of the three rows of desk chairs, yawned quietly. He couldn't help it, having listened to similar lectures before. Both from this same female instructor and from other qualified teachers. In addition to being a bit jaded by it all,

Seven was dog-tired. Last night's poker game at the New Jersey home of Dave Kelb, the head of G5's travel department and Seven's closest buddy, had lasted almost all night. Consequently he was now paying dearly for this lack of sleep. Nonetheless, he sluggishly took out his note pad and textbook.

Seven was certainly aware that these classes, which focused on being the 'perfect male' in the eyes of women, were no longer a matter of frivolity. Being attractive, clean and desirable to females around the world was certainly serious business to him. And to the other three agents sitting in the room. True, all of these cosmetic suggestions and preferred grooming products had once seemed a bit comical and silly. But not anymore. All of these men had seen for themselves that being as sanitary and appealing as possible often helped with the success of their missions. Consequently, whatever they could learn today, or in future classes, might be critical in the field someday.

Yet, even knowing all this, Christopher Seven just couldn't get his mind in gear. He smiled inwardly at the memory of last night's card game and tried his best to concentrate. Hoping to keep from drifting off, he blinked his eyes and tried to focus as the pretty Aussie continued.

"Of course, you gentlemen all recognize the proper tooth-brushing techniques, which were reaffirmed by our guest oral hygienist last time. How we brush our tongues as well as our teeth. And how you must always brush your teeth after each meal no matter *where* you are. If necessary, by using your small travel tooth-care kits, which contain oral care brushing and breath strips, a miniature folding toothbrush and toothpaste tube, plus a tiny plastic mouthwash bottle. All of these pocket-sized products can be used in a pinch. You should likewise be aware that there are certain odorous foods a Stud must *never* consume. Garlic-based dishes, raw onions, certain cheeses and..."

A soft knock on the classroom's partially opened door interrupted her forthcoming sentence. A bit annoyed at being disturbed, the perky instructor nevertheless forced a smile and greeted Nancy Gallo, Colonel McPhail's executive secretary. "Yes, Miss Gallo?"

"Sorry to interrupt, Ms. Craig, but the colonel needs to see Agent Seven immediately. I'm afraid Chris is going to have to leave you for a while."

Vanessa Craig, still miffed at the intrusion, knew that all of nel McPhail's 'requests' were actually rock-solid orders. She thus answered compliantly, "Of course, Miss Gallo." The Aussie glanced toward Christopher Seven, the Super Stud agent she secretly liked best. And about whom she sometimes fantasized. "Okay, Chris. Seems you're wanted upstairs."

"Yes, I heard," replied Seven, inwardly delighted for his rescue from the mundane classroom work. "Sorry to be leaving you so soon,

Ms. Craig," he added with staged regret. "Hopefully, I'll see you at next month's class." Then, after a playful wink to his fellow Studs, he happily followed Nancy Gallo out the door and over to the elevator.

Once inside, Seven pushed the *Floor 13* button and exclaimed, "I know I shouldn't be saying this, Nance, but I'm glad you came and got me out of there. I hardly slept a wink last night, and discussing toothpaste and foot sprays on two hours of sleep is a bit trying."

Nancy frowned. "No sleep *again*? What was it this time? Some coed you were entertaining 'til all hours, or one of those silly card games of yours?"

Seven grinned sheepishly. "It was the latter. Now, tell me, Nance, what's up? Does the chief finally have something for me? Heaven knows I need to get back on the horse again. I've been hoping for another assignment. Haven't had a *real* mission in months, while the rest of the guys are flying all over the planet." Seven sighed. "I've hardly done a thing for the old man. Or done much good for the agency either. Except for that Denver fiasco with the Syrian gal. And that turned out to be a complete farce." He scowled. "Ever since then, not much of anything. What gives? Has the colonel lost confidence in me?"

Nancy Gallo, fiercely loyal to her boss, Colonel McPhail, wouldn't let on about anything, even if she'd known. Nonetheless, she felt a bit of empathy for this handsome hunk and answered him sympathetically. "Of course, the colonel will have to tell you himself if it's a job or not. But I happen to know that he values you very highly." She smiled, sweetly. "Now come on, Poker Pete, let's get to his office."

The elevator door hissed open on the 13th floor where the two of them exited, nodding to the armed guard. They then made their way over to McPhail's office suite where Nancy softly knocked on the colonel's closed door.

"Yes?" came the familiar, deep voice.

"It's me, Colonel. I have Agent Seven with me."

"Fine." There was a mechanical buzz from the electronic lock and the door quickly opened.

McPhail waited a moment as Nancy and Seven entered the room. He then motioned toward Nancy. "Thank you, Miss Gallo. That will be all."

"Yes, sir."

The colonel watched his secretary exit, relocked the door via a button under his desk, and greeted Seven. "Afternoon, Chris." McPhail pointed toward the chair to his left. "This is my good friend and colleague, Admiral James Collingwood."

Christopher Seven hadn't noticed McPhail's visitor. A bit embarrassed, he promptly greeted the unknown gentleman, walking over to shake his hand. "Beg your pardon, sir. I didn't see you sitting there, with those high back chairs in the way."

"That's quite all right, young man," Admiral Collingwood replied, as he smiled a hello. "Very pleased to meet you." Collingwood then stared at Seven for a full minute, shocked at how incredibly good-looking this Super Stud operative was. And though James Collingwood was as straight as an arrow, and had been married to the same woman for twenty-two years, he unabashedly thought to himself that this agent of McPhail's was the best-looking human being he'd even seen. His thoughts were cut short by Colonel McPhail.

"Chris, the admiral here is second in command over at CIA. Of course that info is confidential."

Seven nodded his head. "Of course, Colonel."

"It seems Jim's agency may need our help with something in the south of France."

Seven's heart began racing as McPhail continued, "As you're undoubtedly aware from the recent newspaper and TV accounts, a United States ambassador was brutally murdered in a Venice hotel room a few weeks back. In addition to the tragedy itself, there's now some concern that the ambassador's briefcase, containing classified NATO information, may have been purposely stolen."

McPhail looked over at Collingwood and then back at Seven as he advised, "As a general rule, we at G5 wouldn't be investigating an overseas murder, no matter how brutal. Or be looking into some alleged burglary in Europe. Normally we'd leave that to Jim's people. But the unique nature of one group of possible suspects presents a tricky twist for the CIA. One in which a handsome male operative may be needed."

Seven, always a bit uncomfortable when his looks were being discussed, briefly glanced away from the two older men. Colonel McPhail frowned at the display and quickly added, "The criminal organization that might be responsible for this whole thing, and I stress the word *might*, is a foursome of attractive female assassins. A quartet of beautiful killers for hire who call themselves Rhombus."

"Rhombus?"

"That's right, Seven. Ever hear of them?"

"No sir."

"Well, though they've been somewhat inactive for a while, their organization has actually been around for quite some time. Albeit with different casts of characters over the years. A 'sisterhood of death' is what they used to call themselves."

Seven began wondering about his role in this while McPhail went on, "Of course I've heard bits and pieces about these women from time to time. Yet nothing recently. In fact, I'd assumed Rhombus had most likely been disbanded. But Jim here tells me that's definitely not the case. They're still around and they've recently pulled off a few slick European jobs."

The colonel picked up his handwritten notes and checked them a few seconds before going on, "CIA's overseas informants have confirmed that the current version of Rhombus is made up of younger women now. More resourceful and apparently much more attractive. Regrettably, they're also more vicious and lethal." McPhail stared Seven straight in the eyes. "So, if you decide to accept it, don't go getting any ideas that this mission is merely going to be some playboy jaunt to the Riviera. From what Admiral Collingwood has told me, this present collection of Rhombus women is as nasty as they come."

Christopher Seven felt a sudden chill as his chief explained more. "Right now, CIA's sources report that there are four 'women of suspicion' vacationing on some gangster's yacht in Monaco. Could be Rhombus. Or it might just be four attractive young ladies having a good time in bad company. In any event, that's what you're being called upon to find out. Utilizing your... er... sophisticated charms and looks, the idea is for you to somehow gain access to this foursome in Monte Carlo. Perhaps via some social interaction. Then, if they're connected to any of this ambassador crime, to induce one or more of these women to tell you all they know." McPhail gestured at his guest. "I'll let the admiral take it from here."

The CIA man turned to face Seven and then explained, "Our hope is that you can infiltrate this female clique through some type of amiable encounter in Monaco. Get them interested in you, socially, and then go from there. Unfortunately, that seems to be the *only* way."

Collingwood glanced down at his Interpol report, reread a few lines of it and then affirmed, "Usually Rhombus is extremely guarded when it comes to strangers, priding themselves on their strict anonymity. They normally like to slip in and out of places like ghosts. The most recent mob scuttlebutt, however, says that the current Rhombus women are totally secretive in every aspect. Except *one*." Admiral Collingwood grinned slyly. "And that one aspect is where *you'll* come in."

Seven nodded as the CIA honcho went on.

"Recent Interpol research revealed that this new, younger version of Rhombus supposedly has one glaring weak spot. When not on a job, they're said to be notorious flirts. Openly collecting handsome men as trophies and playthings, much like other women would their designer dresses, fancy cars or jewelry. And though Interpol's mob informers didn't know *who* any of the Rhombus females actually are, and probably wouldn't tell if they did; most of them swore that these women like nothing better than collecting male hunks. Whether that's true or not, no one at Interpol really knows. "

Admiral Collingwood again glanced down at his notes. "To quote their latest report. 'The Rhombus girls are said to be habitual trophy hunters. It's like a narcotic 'fix' to them. Showing off attractive males in the heady haunts of the *beautiful people*. The playgrounds of the rich and famous, where champagne flows like water.' Quote, unquote."

Collingwood closed his small pocket notebook and quickly finished up. "We therefore believe that if a good looking operative, posing as a carefree playboy, happened to be vacationing in their vicinity; especially one trained to be, ah, irresistible, like you and your Stud group. Contact with these women might be possible."

Colonel McPhail glanced toward Admiral Collingwood and then looked over at his agent. "Well, Seven, how about it? Care to take it on?"

Chapter 6

"I'll try to do my best"

S even nodded affirmatively. "Yes, Colonel, I'd like to tackle it. But there's one aspect which isn't clear. Why would this Rhombus group get involved in an ambassador's murder? Or even be interested in those NATO papers? Unless they're politically motivated, what would they have to gain from it?"

"A hefty fee, for one thing," Admiral Collingwood interjected. "Rhombus is basically a proficient, yet purely mercenary, killing squad. So, if they in fact knocked off Ambassador Dawson, then someone else must have hired them. Just *who* that someone is, along with a few other specifics, is what we at CIA need to know."

"I understand," nodded Seven.

"You see," Collingwood continued, "Rhombus only hires out to the highest bidders. And their fees are usually astronomical. They get top dollar because they're true experts – discreet and effective. Rhombus's 'tradition of excellence' the colonel mentioned is no fairytale. These present women, no matter who's currently at the helm, take pride in pulling off dangerous, near-impossible feats. Doing so with brilliant precision. Interpol, who knows more about them than anyone else, states that there's definitely some sort of bizarre honor code uniting each succeeding Rhombus foursome. After all, they've been operating for over five decades now. And each *new* version of Rhombus tries to surpass the former crews who went before them."

"A lot of the terror groups are like that," Colonel McPhail informed. "Take the Taliban, for instance, or this fanatical ISIS crew. They give tribal awards and extra money to the families of anyone outdoing previous executions or suicide bombings. Sounds nutty, I know. But apparently it spurs on new volunteers."

Collingwood nodded his agreement. "That's much like what they say about each succeeding Rhombus version as well. Apparently there's some sort of sick 'one-upmanship' that drives them to outdo their predecessors. Whether it's murder with viciousness, extorting some entity for big bucks, or kidnapping in proficient style, Rhombus seldom fails. Problem is this current Rhombus team operates so infrequently, it makes them quite difficult to get a handle on."

"Sounds like a pretty special group," admitted Seven.

Colonel McPhail again took over the conversation. "Right now there are basically three potential leads in this case, Chris." McPhail counted them out with the first three fingers of his right hand. "*One,* there are four attractive females currently vacationing in Monte Carlo on a yacht owned by the head of a top crime syndicate. *Two*, the Gitano mob would have had good reason to kill Ambassador Dawson, after Dawson prevented an important Gitano lieutenant from going back to America. And *three*, an informant, who the Mafia quickly eliminated, had openly boasted that it was four *females* who *whacked* Ambassador Dawson. This mob loudmouth got his tongue cut out for just *talking* about it. So there could definitely be a link there."

"Yet all that pales if someone had hired Rhombus to specifically obtain classified NATO documents," Collingwood opined. "If that's the case, this whole thing could be a lot more worrisome. We therefore need to know the *who*, *where* and *why* of it."

"Was anything else from Dawson's hotel suite missing; *besides* his briefcase?" Seven asked.

Admiral Collingwood again nodded. "Yes, Chris. Some expensive jewelry and all the money in the Ambassador's wallet." Collingwood shrugged again. "Robbery still could be a motive, although the brutality of the murder argues against it. Those missing valuables might have simply been a ruse to throw us off the trail."

McPhail quickly filled in the final pieces. "The idea is to get one of our Super Studs, you, to be precise, over to Monte Carlo. Then, using the cover of a carefree stockbroker, one who's vacationing on the Riviera. You're to somehow work your way into the social circle of the four women now vacationing on this gangster's boat. Once that's accomplished, you'll use your looks and your, ah, *charms* to gather the information CIA needs." Colonel McPhail again looked Seven straight in the eyes, confident that his good-looking operative would accept the assignment. The two men had a steadfast, unspoken agreement. Namely that Christopher Seven almost always agreed to any mission Colonel McPhail thought was right for him. "I've chosen you, because I think it's something you can handle smoothly. So, are you still game, Chris?"

"Of course, Colonel. Just so long as I'll be properly briefed on what specific information CIA would like to know."

Admiral Collingwood smiled his appreciation and handed Seven a large manila envelope. "This is the full dossier on the situation as it stands now. Call me directly with any questions. My secured cell number is inside the folder."

Seven reached out and took the file as the CIA man finished up. "Like I've stated, Chris, our main concern centers on that missing NATO information."

"I understand, Admiral. And thanks for your confidence in us."

McPhail gestured toward Seven. "It's all settled then. You'll leave for Europe the day after tomorrow. I'll have Nancy phone Kelb and have him make all the travel arrangements."

Seven grinned inwardly, wondering if his late-night poker pal, G5's travel director, Dave Kelb, was as sleepy as he was.

"You can use the next two days to study the CIA dossier," the colonel further instructed. "And to ask any questions you might have."

McPhail then turned back toward Admiral Collingwood. "I'd like Hank Carson – he's our number two man – to go over the entire mission with you in more detail, Jim. Preferably sometime tomorrow."

"Certainly, Colonel."

McPhail looked at Seven somberly and again warned, "Like I've told you, son, don't go taking this mission too lightly. If the women you'll be trying to gain access to are in fact Rhombus, all reports indicate that they are extremely cruel and deadly adversaries."

"I'll be on my guard, Colonel."

McPhail rubbed his chin, contemplatively. "By the way, Seven. The Admiral and I have been kicking around the idea of sending another operative with you on this one. Somebody from their agency who knows the European crime families well and who can likewise help with all that exasperating French and Italian red tape. A guide like that might be of help to you over there. Behind the scenes, of course."

The Super Stud frowned, always hesitant about working with others when he was undercover. "*Another* operative, Colonel?"

"That's right."

"Well, whatever you and the admiral think, sir. But I usually work better on my own."

"We'll see," McPhail replied, evasively. "I'll talk it over with my opposite number at CIA. Jim's boss. He might feel better if one of his own people is with you. If so, we'll arrange some type of quick meeting between their man and you. Set up a greeting code as well."

Colonel McPhail folded his hands and placed them on his desk.

"Now then, Seven. Any final questions or comments?"

"Not at the moment, sir. Other than I'll try to do my best."

Admiral Collingwood smiled his appreciation. He got up from his chair and walked over to shake hands with Seven. "I'm sure you'll do fine, son." He then winked at the two G5 men. "And if *half* the things I've heard about your Super Stud section are true. You should have no problems entrancing those four beautiful ladies in Monaco!"

~

Two nights later, on a foggy Wednesday evening, Christopher Seven was alone in the master bedroom of his stately red-brick home in Rutherford, New Jersey. Finishing up his packing for tomorrow's trip to Europe, he placed the last of his things into two large suitcases. As always, by making use of a printed Super Stud packing list, Seven made sure he'd be carrying exactly what was needed. With no item forgotten or overlooked. Carefully referring to the packing list, he methodically checked off each entry right after that particular item went into his luggage; both cosmetic and wardrobe-related.

Thinking of the perky Australian instructor, he likewise made sure that he'd packed his 'preferred' Stud hygiene products. These included extra bars of *Dial's* 'Mountain Fresh' soap, several *Old Spice* 'High Endurance-Original Scent' deodorant sticks, and some large tubes of *Colgate's* 'Baking Soda & Peroxide' mint toothpaste. Satisfied his inventory was complete, he closed and locked the suitcases just as a melodic voice from the second floor called up to him.

"Hurry on down, Mister Chris. Your dinner will get cold."

"Be right there, Angie. Just finished my packing."

Quickly making his way downstairs, Christopher Seven again reflected on how lucky he was that Evangeline Case, his indispensable African-American chef and housekeeper, had stayed on all these years. The inimitable 'Angelina' had become a loving family member. A surrogate mother to Seven and his brother, Tim, ever since their early childhood. Both brothers cherished and treasured her.

'Angie', as she was affectionately called, had quickly agreed to live with the boys, along with their *legal* guardian, Aunt Mary. Right after Seven's parents had both been killed in that dreadful airplane crash some 18 years ago. For health reasons Aunt Mary had finally left for a warmer climate. But Angie had stayed on, soon becoming an integral part of the family. Initially hired by Seven's mother, this amazing 76-year-old woman had been with the Seven family for over thirty years now.

"Made you one of your favorite suppers, Mister Chris," Angie announced as Seven approached the kitchen table. "A full oven-roasted turkey, string beans, cornbread stuffing and mashed potatoes with gravy. Plus, my special homemade dinner rolls."

"Sounds great, Ang. No one in the world can cook like you." Fully believingly his statement, Seven gave her an enthusiastic grin and a peck on the cheek. "I'm off to Europe tomorrow, where they have some fine restaurants. But after a few meals from those stuffy Michelin starred chefs, I'll soon be missing *your* fare."

Angie laughed delightfully. "Shoot, Mister Chris. You could charm the wings off a bird. Anyway, I hope you enjoy dinner."

They sat down at the kitchen table and bowed their heads. Seven said a quick prayer of thanks and they then consumed the delicious meal, teasing each other affectionately about getting too fat. After a second piece of Angelina's delectable whip-cream-layered *lemon chiffon pie*, a dessert treat he could never pass up, the agent left the table well sated.

Exiting the kitchen area, Seven paused a moment and glanced around the huge brick home. Like always, he reflected that the house was far too big for his present needs. Yet the 35-year-old redbrick mansion on Carlton Terrace was something his father, a successful car dealer, had personally designed. It was a cherished inheritance, and keeping it in the family all these years had brought Christopher and Timothy Seven closer to their dad's memory. The two brothers jointly owned the majestic home, even though Tim was presently working and living out on the West Coast. The brothers had talked about selling the house from time to time, but the memories they treasured and honored were just too great. Sighing as he recalled some childhood memory, the Seven slowly walked up the stairs.

Back in his bedroom now, the G5 agent sat down at a small writing desk. He stared glumly at his plush king-size bed, knowing that sleep wouldn't come easy tonight. It would be a restless night for several reasons. First of all he'd be flying into the unknown the following morning. Thus the usual pangs of excitement, always prevalent before any new mission, would undoubtedly keep him from a sound sleep. This was the case with most undercover operatives before they embarked on a new assignment. It was simply part of the job – 'the shakes' they called it, and the Super Stud knew he'd just have to endure them.

Taking out the CIA's Rhombus file again, he reread the pertinent info, now for the fourth time. His exhaustive study of the dossier the last two days had shown that this present Rhombus organization boasted a long, sordid history of murder, torture and terror. Some of the case notes regarding past punishment slayings had made Seven's stomach turn. Brutal murders with sadistic touches such as slowly hanging their victims with piano wire, or cruelly skinning them alive before finally murdering them. Seven shuttered, wondering if this newest version of Rhombus was as ruthless as their predecessors. If so, would the four women he'd be trying to gain access to in Monaco actually *be* Rhombus? He shrugged resignedly and tried to dismiss any further evil thoughts.

Taking out his plane ticket, the G5 operative glanced at it cursorily. He then placed it back inside his carry-on, next to his passport. The schedule called for a 9:30 a.m. British Airways flight to London, spending one brief night in the British capital; happily at the luxurious Dorchester Hotel. He'd then fly on to Nice the following morning, and, once there, rent a car at the airport for the short but scenic *cornice* drive to Monaco.

Seven definitely preferred morning flights when traveling to the continent, knowing that the effects of jet lag were greatly diminished by flying during daylight hours. Accordingly, G5's erudite travel department, headed by his good buddy Dave Kelb, always tried to book him on early flights whenever the Super Stud was traveling to Europe. Sighing at the thought of missing Kelb's next *all-night* poker party, he placed the coded Rhombus file in a large courier envelope and sealed it.

Knowing that a messenger from headquarters would be coming to pick it up from Angie sometime tomorrow.

Making sure all was ready for his early morning departure, Seven took his second shower of the day and then set the alarm clock for 5:10 a.m. Sleeping, as always, only in his *Hanes* briefs, he hopped into bed. After reading a few chapters in Exodus from his well-worn Bible, he turned off the bedside lamp, said his evening prayer, and then frustratingly waited for sleep to come. While he tossed and turned, the same thoughts kept crossing his mind: *Were his female targets in Monaco actually members of this merciless Rhombus band? And, if so, were they responsible for Ambassador Dawson's vicious murder?* One thing was certain. If the four attractive women currently vacationing on a Monaco yacht were indeed Rhombus, danger was definitely in the forecast!

~

The airport limo arrived promptly at 6:00 a.m. The driver loaded Seven's two large suitcases, his hanging suit bag, the *Wilson* tennis racquets and his two smaller carry-ons into the spacious trunk of a silver Lincoln Town Car. The G5 operative hopped in the back seat, and they were soon making their way toward the George Washington Bridge. Thankfully, the early morning traffic was still fairly light, and they pulled up to the British Airways departure area a speedy fifty-five minutes later.

"Thanks for the ride," Seven said to the driver, an affable middle-aged man named Hirsh.

"You're welcome, Mr. Seven. Have a safe flight."

Seven tipped him and watched the limo pull away with a strange tinge of melancholy. He then made his way inside the terminal. With over an hour to spare, even with the always-annoying body search and X-ray screening, the yawning secret agent bought a newspaper and sat down by the boarding gate.

Twenty minutes later, after reading all of the news that was worth reading, he took out his smartphone from inside his sports jacket. When he did, he banged his fist on the chair arm in anger, realizing that he had completely forgetting to turn on his cellphone this morning! It was an unpardonable sin, one that his chief, Colonel McPhail, considered the gravest error an operational field agent could make. McPhail steadfastly insisted that his operatives keep their cellphones on at *all* times. Especially when embarking on a new mission. Headquarters would have a severe reprimand for Seven if they'd been trying to reach him. Maybe even summoning him back and off the case as punishment.

Frowning furiously at his inexcusable forgetfulness, the seething Super Stud promptly pressed the smartphone's green 'on' button, noting glumly that there were indeed several messages waiting for him. Since he'd retired so early for bed last night, absentmindedly turning his phone off then, Seven now hoped these stored messages were merely late-night *personal* calls.

As the still fuming operative was about to check his voicemails, he glanced over his left shoulder and saw a tough-looking stranger seemingly staring right at him. Seven stared back, and only then did the man look away. The Super Stud nonchalantly placed his phone back in his pocket and tried to ascertain if he was being spied on, or not.

After another ten minutes of casually observing this shadowy figure, a stern-faced man in his early thirties, Christopher Seven was certain the stranger was indeed watching him. A chilling feeling of dread rapidly ensued. Beginning to sweat profusely, Seven nervously asked himself: *Could this man be part of the Gitano crime syndicate sent to keep tabs on me? Yet how can that be? How could my mission have been compromised already? Was there a Mafia mole working at CIA?*

Calming himself, Seven hoped he was simply overreacting. Maybe the pent-up excitement of the mission, along with his dread of a long flight over the ocean, had his mind playing tricks on him. While he reflected on it, he heard the first announcement informing passengers that British Airways flight 178 to London was ready for boarding. Though outwardly appearing relaxed, Christopher Seven couldn't stop speculating: *Will this sinewy loner be on my flight? Or is he simply an innocent bystander waiting on the other airplane across the way? In a few moments, I'll know.*

Five minutes later, when his row was called, Seven slowly ambled toward the boarding door. Calmly walking toward the aircraft, the Super Stud casually glanced behind him.

To Seven's utter consternation, his initial trepidation was quickly confirmed. There was no doubt about it now. The mysterious figure was indeed boarding the London plane as well!

Chapter 7

The Doc

Seven walked to his seat guardedly, anxiously waiting for the stranger from the boarding area to enter the plane. Like most undercover operatives, he could usually tell when someone was tailing him. Though stunned that the mob had somehow found him out already, the Super Stud nonetheless remained composed. Trying to make sense of it, he quickly found his window seat in row 14.

Once there, he slung his carry-on and his tennis racquets into the overhead compartment. Slamming it shut, he then placed his laptop computer beneath the seat in front of him. As always, everything on his personal computer was in strict G5 code; just in case it was lost or stolen.

Finally taking his seat, Seven carefully observed the onrushing hoard of passengers making their way to the rear section of the aircraft. Searching for the stranger, while surveying this parade of cheery travelers, he heard the familiar ring of his secured smartphone. The Super Stud answered it promptly, "Seven, here."

"Chris? Thank goodness! This is Nancy." Out of breath, Colonel McPhail's private secretary, Nancy Gallo, sounded extremely flustered, yet relieved all the same. "Thank heavens, I finally got you. I've been trying your cellphone for nearly three hours!"

Seven again shook his head at his carelessness and replied tersely, "My bad. What's up, Nance?"

"Colonel McPhail called me early this morning and said to phone you on your way to the airport. Knowing your flight wasn't till nine-thirty, the colonel told me to call you anytime between six-thirty and nine a.m." The G5 operative glanced at his watch and noted it was 8:45.

"The colonel said I'd be sure to catch you by then", Nancy continued. "Either in the limo or at the boarding area. I've been trying all morning, but all I got was your voicemail greeting. I left four separate messages on your cellphone but you never called back. That's not like you, so I began to get worried. I was just about to phone security but decided to try you this one last time." She paused and let out a nervous breath, obviously still shook up from not reaching till now.

Seven again apologized. "Like I said, it was entirely *my* mistake, Nancy. I didn't even turn on my cell till just a few minutes ago. Guess I was still half asleep. I haven't even retrieved any of your messages yet." Seven shook his head contritely. "Sorry, Nance. I simply forgot. I was about to check my voicemails when - ah - well, something's come up."

Again looking up and down the aisle to try and spot the secretive stranger, Seven inwardly hoped he hadn't gotten her into any trouble with the G5 hierarchy. "Too bad I put you through all this, Nancy. It shouldn't have happened." He then sheepishly tried to appeal to her, even though knowing her allegiance to Colonel McPhail was unassailable. "Hopefully no harm was done, Nance. But I'd appreciate it if you didn't tell the old man about this."

Nancy's reply was purposely evasive. "Can't promise that, Chris. You know the colonel. He insists that all agent indiscretions, especially that one, be reported immediately." She softened a little. "Anyway, we'll see. Incidentally, are you on the airplane yet?"

"Yes. The rest of the cattle are boarding now." Seven cradled the phone to his ear, still keeping an eye out.

"Is anyone sitting next to you, Chris?"

"Nope, no one. The row is completely empty."

"Well, here's the deal and the reason I was calling you. There's been an eleventh-hour change. The Colonel and Admiral Collingwood decided they wanted you to have some backup in Europe. They've apparently been up all night kicking around the pros and cons of it, and the pros eventually won."

Seven frowned at the prospect of having to deal with a partner on this mission as Nancy went on, "The Colonel was against it at first. But Admiral Collingwood and his chief said they'd really like to send over one of their own agents to work with you. Someone they've used before in Italy and France. Evidently this man of theirs also knows the Riviera well. So he could come in handy over there. The brass told me to assure you that this CIA agent will be under *your* direction at all times."

Christopher Seven grunted affirmatively and listened to the rest.

"The CIA's operative was hurriedly briefed during the early morning hours. Then rushed to JFK airport in an unmarked car. Just in case anyone was '*watching*'. He was supposed to somehow make contact with you at the airport this morning. That's why I was desperately trying to reach you. To give you the recognition codes and these other details."

She paused a moment and then further explained, "They've planned it so that he'll be sitting right next to you on your flight to London. In fact, the two of you should be the only passengers in the entire row. Both sides of the aisle will be completely empty, as will most of the seats around you, thanks to British Airways help. I guess CIA discreetly used their contacts with the airline to arrange that part of it."

Nancy caught her breath, rechecked her handwritten notes and advised, "I have this CIA fellow's description here if you just let me read it to..."

"Don't bother, Nance. I bet he's a slim man, brown hair, about thirty-five years old. And he's wearing a tan sport coat and blue shirt."

"Why yes," the astonished secretary confirmed, glancing at her papers. "But how the heck did you know all that if you didn't meet. . ."

"Oh, just a hunch," Seven interrupted. "What's this guy's password greeting going to be?"

He again heard her rustling through the notes.

"He'll say, 'Hi there. Man, do I hate these big planes. You never get your bags on time unless you fly those red-eyes to California." Nancy paused a moment before instructing, "Your response should be, 'I know what you mean. I travel to San Francisco every month and I always fly overnight." She then made Seven repeat it twice.

After obediently complying, the Super Stud gave another quick glance down the aisle and finally saw the CIA operative approaching. "Here he comes now, Nance. Gotta run. I'll bring you something from Europe. Goodbye, beautiful.'"

"So long, Romeo. Take care."

Christopher Seven put his smartphone back in his jacket pocket and waited. Sure enough, the CIA man made his way up the aisle and found the seat next to Seven's. This time there was a friendly smile on his face and his soft-spoken greeting dutifully contained the recognition code. "Hi there. Man, do I hate these big planes. You never get your bags on time unless you fly those red-eyes to California."

"I know what you mean," a smirking Seven responded, not really a fan of these somewhat juvenile but necessary recognition greetings. "I travel to San Francisco every month and I always fly overnight."

The stranger likewise grinned and held out his hand to shake it with Seven's. Continuing to speak in a lowered voice, he declared, "Glad that nonsense is over. And glad to meet you. My name's Vin. Vin Fieri. Most of my friends call me 'the doc,' or Doc Vin." He chuckled, loudly. "That's cause I spent two years as a medic's assistant in the Army."

The Super Stud nodded. "Nice meeting you, too, Doc. I'm Christopher Seven."

"I know. I was briefed early this morning." Fieri then stared at Seven a bit warily, still trying to figure something out. "I kept trying to make eye contact with you in the boarding area, Chris. So we could meet there. They said you'd be fully informed about it." Fieri shrugged his shoulders. "Guess you didn't see me."

Seven's face reddened. "I saw you. But I thought you might have been one of the bad guys." Seven quickly explained. "There was a cellphone mix-up and I wasn't filled in until just a few moments ago. One of the office secretaries finally got through to me and explained the whole deal. Glad she did, or I might have looked like an idiot when you gave me the greeting code."

The Doc laughed. "That's typical. The company higher-ups usually mess things up for we peons in the field."

"Afraid it was my mistake this time," admitted Seven. "Anyway, I'm glad we'll be working together."

"Likewise, Chris. Tell you the truth, I've been hoping for some action. This past year has pretty much been all paperwork at my agency. I worked a bit on that CIA Libya project awhile back. But that's about it."

"I hear you," agreed Seven, taking an immediate liking to this candid, easygoing operative. "My outfit hasn't used me much lately either."

Christopher Seven watched as the CIA operative stood up and loaded his small carry-on into the overhead storage compartment. Seven then began sizing Fieri up with a trained eye. The 'Doc' appeared to be in his mid-thirties. He had brown, thinning hair combed back, and a decent-looking face. One that appeared to have a permanent smirk on it. Though rather slender, Fieri's solid, compact body looked hard and muscular. More importantly to Seven, the 'doc' seemed to be the type one could rely on if things got rough in Europe.

After wedging his carry-on next to Seven's things, Fieri sat back down and explained, "I know Italy, Monaco, and the entire Riviera area quite well from previous assignments. Although I haven't been back there in a long while. The past five years or so, my main stomping grounds have been Mexico and South America. And, occasionally, the Mid-East. So, no one in Europe has seen me around lately. And nobody knows I'm CIA either. Guess that was one of the reasons they agreed to send me along with you on this Monaco thing. That, and the fact that I speak fluent French and Italian."

Recognizing that his own foreign language skills were very superficial, Seven nodded his approval as Vin resumed, "Back when I was working Europe, I always stayed in the background. So, as far as we know, no organization on the continent has any current dossier or past 'cheat sheets' on me. My outfit was sure that no one, least of all Rhombus or the Gitano mob, would ever suspect I'm in U.S. intelligence. So hopefully I won't be a red flag around your neck if I'm seen hanging around with you." Doc Fieri rubbed his chin. "But we'll still have to come up with some innocuous way to get together in Monaco. In case anyone should start focusing in on us. They're always wary of newcomers on the Riviera." He looked over at Seven and asked, "Where you from, Chris?"

"New Jersey. Rutherford, to be exact. Bergen County."

"Know it well," the doc replied. "I lived in Ridgewood a few years, not too far from your town. What high school did you attend?"

"Newark Conservatory," Seven answered, not sure where all this was leading to. "It's a small private prep school in Livingston. You've probably never heard of it."

Fieri laughed, slapping his left thigh. "Like heck I haven't. Newark Conservatory was my high school's biggest football rival. I went to Montclair Prep."

Christopher Seven grinned his recognition as the doc asked, "Did you play any sports there, Chris?"

Still wondering what any of this had to do with their meeting up in Europe, Seven nonetheless answered, "Yes. Varsity tennis and fencing."

"Good. We can use this prep school thing as a way to greet each other. You know, rival high school chums who suddenly meet and greet in Monaco." Fieri leaned closer, still speaking in a soft tone. "You see, Chris, strangers like us, staying for more than a few days in Monaco, will always attract suspicion. Consequently, both the mobsters and the casino managers have paid informants everywhere. The casinos are on guard for card counters and other cheaters. While the mob is looking for rival hit men and undercover cops. Hence the best approach would be for us to stage an animated *'chance'* meeting between old school friends. Preferably at the main casino. A lot of bartenders, dealers, and croupiers there are on the mob's payrolls. So we might as well use that as a *plus.*"

"What do you mean?"

"Almost everyone who comes to Monte Carlo eventually winds up going to their world famous gambling hall. That's why the 'wise guys' often use casino *moles* as their 'inside' eyes and ears. Like I said, the European mobs are constantly on the lookout for rival gang members. And they're equally on alert for French Interpol agents who creep in through Nice. Regardless, the mobster bigwigs love their gambling. So if you want to make contact with mobsters, or their pretty gun 'molls', Monte Carlo's renowned casino is still the best place to observe them."

Seven nodded his head as Fieri added, "Yep, those European *baddies* are always spying on one another. You can count on it." Fieri chuckled "In fact, the big joke around the Riviera is that they're all paying the *same* people for basically the *same* information.

~

Christopher Seven laughed dutifully, as the Doc further explained, "Nevertheless, two strangers like us, spending an inordinate amount of time in Monaco, will undoubtedly catch the attention of some casino mole. So we might as well use *that* as a way of getting our cover story out in the open. Yet, no matter what, we'll have to tread water carefully, knowing these powerful Mafia *Godfathers* are relentlessly checking on newcomers." The doc, chuckled. "It wouldn't be pretty if we're 'found out'. Or worse, *found out* with 10 stilettos in our backs."

"What do you suggest, Vin?"

"First we'll make certain that one of these casino spies see us meet and greet publically. We'll put on a big show of our *unexpectedly* running into each other." Fieri played it out: 'Well, well. I'll be darned! If it isn't Christopher Seven, the guy who used to kick our butts in tennis back in high school. What a surprise running into you over here!'" Doc held out his hands. "You know, that sort of thing. Later on we'll let it slip out that we're both stockbrokers who've decided to work *together* on a few potentially valuable stock prospects. This way it will seem more natural if we hang with each other now and then."

"Sounds like a plan," Seven responded, already appreciative of an ally who knew the Riviera's ropes so well. McPhail and the CIA were right to have sent him. "By the way, Vin, I'm staying at the Hotel de Paris in Monaco. Where are you bunking?"

Fieri's reply came with a cynical sneer of envy. "The *Hotel de Paris?* That's the top digs in all of Monaco. No way would my firm put me up *there.* Too luxurious and expensive for them."

Seven laughed as the doc opined, "Unfortunately I'm at the *Oasis.* A small dump several blocks from your place. But maybe it's better that way. Could be a bit awkward explaining why two long-lost school chums just *happened* to be staying at the *exact* same hotel. That might be too *much* of a coincidence for the mob boys."

Just then the pilot revved up his engines, going through his final checks and getting ready for takeoff. Fieri looked down at his watch and began to reset it to London time.

"They told me you'll be flying from London to Nice tomorrow, Chris. That's fine. It'll give you a chance to grab a few days in Monaco on your own. You know, to get the lay of the land. I'll be staying on in England this weekend to review some Interpol files that MI6 managed to come up with on Ambassador Dawson."

The doc shrugged. "Probably not much there to help us, Chris. But it's worth a quick look-see anyway. After I'm done with that, I'll take the *Eurostar* train to Paris, and then go on to Monaco via the TGV."

Fieri thought a moment and then proposed, "Today's Thursday. Why don't we plan to catch up in Monaco some time Sunday evening? Or, if better for you, Monday morning?"

"Fine, Vin. Like you said, that'll give me a few days on my own to explore Monaco. I might even check out the Monte Carlo marina. See if I can spot our four girls or that gangster's mega yacht."

Somewhat apprehensive about Seven's last suggestion, Fieri's reply was accordingly hesitant. "I guess that'll be all right. But be plenty careful going it alone. Carmine Gitano and his mobster thugs have a darn good machine in Europe. Particularly in the Riviera region. They've bribed most of the authorities there, so they're not afraid to use the heavy artillery if needed. Just last month, over in Menton, Gitano's gang brutally machine-gunned three mafia stool pigeons and their families while the families were in church. Killed them all, including two pregnant women. Carmine Gitano didn't get so much as a parking ticket, even though Interpol was sure he arranged the 'hit'. So make sure you have a reliable cover story and stick to it at all costs.

"Well, like they told you in your early morning briefing. I'm simply a jet setting stockbroker who made a small fortune in last month's unexpected blue chip bonanza. For now, I just want to party with it."

Fieri nodded his head. "Sounds okay."

"Of course," continued Seven, "my *real* mission is to somehow infiltrate the social sphere of those four yacht women. That is if these four gals are even on Gitano's boat. Hopefully, *if* I manage to meet any of them, they'll show some interest in me." Seven paused awkwardly, not knowing what Fieri knew about the Super Studs. "That's something I've been, ah, trained for, Vin." Seven shrugged. "I guess the toughest part of all this will be finding a harmless way to meet up with them."

Vin Fieri smiled confidently. "We'll think of something, Chris." And with that, the announcement came informing passengers that they were ready for takeoff.

Seven, not a big fan of flying, gripped his armrest as the wide-bodied plane hurled down the runway and abruptly thrust itself into the sky. The 777 banked sharply to the right, and then headed east toward the blinking green dot on its sophisticated guidance system that was London's Heathrow Airport.

As Christopher Seven looked down at the tiny specks of cars and trucks seemingly moving in slow motion, he wondered what lay ahead of him on the other side of the 'pond'.

The following morning, after an uneventful flight from London to Nice, Christopher Seven was once again collecting his luggage at an airport carousel. This one in the south of France at *Aeroport Nice - Cote d' Azur.* His enjoyable, albeit short, one-night stay in London, had included an exquisite late-night dinner at *Le Gavroche* on Upper Brook Street, one of his favorite restaurants anywhere. Happy to finally be on the ground for a while, he flagged down a porter and made his way over to the Hertz rental counter.

"Bonjour, Monsieur," said the pretty Hertz agent, a shapely brunette. Flirting with her eyes, she gave Seven a sexy smile, wondering if this incredibly handsome hunk was a film star from America.

"Hi," Seven greeted. "I believe you have a reservation for me. Under the name Christopher Seven."

The brunette reluctantly began looking through her papers, obviously disappointed that he hadn't responded to her flirting. Oh well, at least she could tell her roommate, Collette, that the man of her dreams had been to the counter today. "Oui, Monsieur", she replied. "Here it is. Mr. Christopher Seven, from New Jersey."

The Hertz girl made a copy of his driver's license and passport, filled out the rental form, and then handed him the keys to a sporty Mercedes E350 convertible. Seven thanked her and made his way out to the Hertz shuttle van that took him directly to his vehicle.

Headquarters had grudgingly approved Seven's renting such a pricey set of wheels, buying into his argument that it would better fit his cover as a 'suddenly affluent' jetsetter. Impressed with the car, the Super Stud placed his luggage in the trunk and slid behind the wheel of the gleaming blue vehicle. He quickly put the convertible's roof down, and, after an admittedly juvenile racing squeal of the tires, was soon exiting the airport area; heading toward the N7 northeast thoroughfare. Or, as the natives call it, the *Moyenne Corniche.* The Middle Coast Road."

The ride up and through the middle corniche was absolutely breathtaking, and Seven found himself thrilled to be motoring in this picturesque area of France. He was likewise excited to be going to one of the most glamorous spots in the world - Monte Carlo!

Maneuvering along the winding road, the G5 operative took in the appealing sights. To his right was a splendid view of the sea, where the golden sun shined down on the stunning blue water. On the left was a charming mountainside vista, dotted with lovely French homes and villas. Seven hungrily envisioned the fine foods, breads, and pastries that were now being baked in their cozy brick-oven kitchens. He could almost smell the alluring aromas.

After this scenic forty-minute drive, the G5 agent pulled his Mercedes up to the front of the chic Hotel de Paris situated on the *Place du Casino,* directly across the street from the celebrated Monte Carlo gaming hall. He was immediately greeted by a formally attired parking valet. The smiling attendant bowed and promptly summoned a bellboy with the aid of a loud whistle.

As he entered the elegant lobby, Seven stopped a moment to admire the hotel's Louis XVI luxury, and to peruse its sophisticated shopping galleria. There were two well-known jewelry stores attached to the hotel, whose sparkling front windows displayed sixty-thousand dollar watches, and similarly high-priced diamond studded bracelets. There were also a number of designer dress shops where the prices were equally staggering. It had to be one of the most expensive shopping venues on the planet. As for the cavernous hotel lobby itself, the agent was impressed by the polished Italian travertine marble on the floor and walls, and the stylish gold leaf accoutrements everywhere. It gave the acclaimed hotel a regal feel, reminding him of Versailles. Basking in the lobby's refined elegance, Seven could clearly sense the ghostly presence of the rich and famous giants of history. Those notable names who'd once prowled and played in this very room.

The agent sighed softly, and then approached the front desk. Here he was swiftly and skillfully registered with chic European aplomb. A few minutes later, the Super Stud was standing inside his luxurious room, a balconied mini-suite facing the sea. Seven tipped the exiting bellman, unpacked his luggage and then set up his laptop computer on the suite's small telephone desk. After sending a short, coded message to headquarters, announcing his safe arrival, he followed that up with a shower in the palatial marble bathroom; using the plush Turkish towels hanging on the heated towel rack to dry himself. After putting on a stylish, collared polo shirt and white pants, he grabbed a small pair of binoculars from his carry-on bag.

Walking out onto the private balcony attached to his suite, the now reenergized operative zeroed in on the famous Monaco marina. It was situated a half-mile or so away. He had no trouble finding the Zephyr, Carmine Gitano's enormous yacht. It looked like a whale among minnows. Recalling Zephyr's profile and features from the CIA file photos, Seven noted that the mega yacht was moored off by itself on the far side of the marina. It looked powerful and impressive.

After making a mental note of its location, he put away the binoculars and made his way downstairs to the Café Jardin, the hotel's small, casual eatery, for lunch. The De Paris' two gourmet restaurants were closed till evening, but Seven was confident that the cuisine in the smallish Jardin would be similarly first rate.

To Christopher Seven, dining in or near France was one of life's greatest pleasures. Eschewing the Jardin's famous lunch buffet, he ordered off their regular menu instead, selecting a small house salad and the *Poulet du Monaco*. This latter entrée, a simple yet delicious roasted half-chicken, was accompanied by homemade matchstick *frites*. It was spectacular, and Seven again marveled at how the French were able to make any chicken dish moist and delectable. He wondered what his housekeeper chef, Angie, would think of it.

Enjoying his food and the white-gloved service immensely, the Super Stud refused to be distracted by the pair of gawking teenagers eyeing him from a neighboring table. Sitting with their parents, the leggy teens stared and giggled unabashedly at the handsome agent. Used to this type of female attention, a given byproduct of his amazing looks, Seven smiled back politely, called for his bill, and quickly left the table.

True to his ingrained Stud training, and once again thinking of the Australian instructor who emphasized brushing your teeth after every meal, Seven dutifully made his way to a smallish men's room just off the main lobby. Here, like always, he took out his pocket-sized tooth-care kit and used the petite travel toothpaste tube, along with its tiny bottle of Listerine mouthwash. Fully aware that most people would find this, and his other mandatory stud hygiene rituals, zany and compulsive, Seven again wondered what was wrong with having fresh breath and a clean body at all times. *What was so odd or silly about that?*

Shrugging his shoulders, he knew there was no sense rehashing this again. It was simply part of his job, the job of being as enticing and desirable as possible. As a government 'Super Stud', he was utilized for just *one* purpose. To be a well-honed, female-attracting machine - a male *'Stepford wife'*, so to speak. And while a great-looking face was part of it, Seven knew from experience that these obligatory hygiene routines helped make him even more pleasing to female targets. And since his job, and his duty, entailed being as attractive as possible to the opposite sex, he'd keep on practicing these hygienic customs. No matter *how* odd they might be viewed.

Exiting the bathroom, Seven strolled over to the valet parking desk and was soon driving the Mercedes convertible toward the Monte Carlo marina. Hoping to check out Mafioso Carmine Gitano's yacht close up, he likewise wanted to see if he might be able to spot any of his targets; the four attractive young ladies who just might be the most dangerous and sadistic females in the world!

Seven parked several blocks from the dock. Then, looking much like any other American tourist, via the New York Mets t-shirt he'd just put on, and the small digital camera hanging round his neck, he observantly strolled toward the marina. Walking down a set of narrow concrete steps toward the quayside, he was soon surrounded by a myriad of luxurious yachts.

"Wow!" Seven muttered under his breath upon arriving at the main wharf. "These boats are incredible!" He made his way closer, still amazed by all the opulent vessels. The distant view through the binoculars from his hotel room hadn't captured their true majesty. Or the exhilaration of actually standing amongst this flotilla of huge, exquisite pleasure crafts. Each yacht seemed more lavish than the next, with foreign flags flying from most of their masts. Most of the vessels came from England, Spain and Germany, though there were a few from Canada and the USA as well.

Suddenly, as Christopher Seven glanced down toward the far end of the marina, his senses quickened. There it was! All alone, in her *own* mooring, was the most magnificent craft of all. Carmine Gitano's incredible Zephyr! Regal and massive, the mobster's yacht looked to be void of any activity, with only two crewmembers standing near her gangway shooting the breeze.

Camera in hand, the Super Stud quickly made his way toward Gitano's vessel, following the bevy of gaping tourists who'd likewise spotted the gigantic Zephyr. The small posse of amateur photographers, Seven among them, eagerly filed over to Gitano's boat. The largest and most opulent of the yachts in the harbor, it was a popular target for the cameras. As the gawking group approached the mega yacht, one of the two uniformed crewmen, a husky, tough-looking sailor, held up his hand and spoke to them in a heavy Italian accent.

"Please'a folks, not'a too close. And no too many photo, please." He smiled politely, obviously used to the attention the huge yacht was getting. "I know you all wanna picture of our'a beautiful Zephyr. But for the security reasons, the owner, he donn'a want too many photo. So only one'a picture each, please. *Capisci?* – You understand?" Seven and the other tourists nodded to him. "Feel'a free to look'a few moments, though. We quite'a proud of her."

The muscular crewman beamed with pride, obviously pleased by the fanfare and attention that Zephyr always attracted. And though he performed his security duties ably, and non-offensively, his stern expression and husky shoulders firmly conveyed to the crowd that anyone *not* following his orders would be quickly shooed away.

After gaping at the Zephyr for ten minutes or so, the small flock of tourists finally moved on to take photos of the smaller crafts moored on the other side of the wharf. Seven did not. Standing his ground, he smiled at the brawny crewman and asked, "Don't suppose you could take a few more snapshots of me in front of your magnificent yacht? My friends back home would love to see them."

"Sorry, signore. Like I said. One'a picture, *only*. And I saw you already take'a yours already."

"I'd make it worth your while," Seven assured, quickly taking out a twenty-dollar bill from his wallet.

The crewman glared at him suspiciously, his voice beginning to rise. "Look'a, mister. I ain't gonna tell'a you again! *No* more'a pictures!"

Seven knew better than to press it any further. He was about to back off and leave when a low, feminine voice coming from the yacht's top railing called out, "What's the problem, Rio?"

Christopher Seven immediately looked up Zephyr's long gangway and saw one of the most striking women he'd ever laid eyes on staring down at him. When he did, his heart nearly skipped a beat. Not from this ash-blonde's looks, although she was extremely attractive. But by the startling fact that he might actually be gazing at a member of Rhombus itself!

Chapter 9

Suz

⁓

Seven and the crewman both glanced up at the young woman standing at the yacht's railing. The beefy deckhand waited a moment and then angrily began explaining, "Dis'a guy wants to take'a more picture, but I told'a him no more photos. You know what the boss says."

The ash-blonde beauty slowly sauntered down the gangplank. Smiling at Seven and the crewman, she addressed them both. "I don't see how a few photos taken by this gorgeous creature could hurt anything."

The blonde then turned toward Seven. "Hi there, handsome. I've been eyeing you from my cabin. Asked myself – where did *that* spectacular specimen come from?" She shook her head. "I must be getting careless to have missed a hunk like you. I thought I knew every attractive male under eighty here on the Riviera. Where have *you* been hiding?"

Seven grinned back. "Just got in from New York. I'm here on holiday, hoping to have some fun and break the bank at the casino." Pointing toward the Zephyr he added, "I adore yachts and ships of all kinds. And your boat is the most beautiful vessel in the whole marina."

"The boat's not mine," the girl corrected. "Belongs to a friend."

"Well," responded Seven, "whoever's yacht it is, it's magnificent! I simply wanted to get a few pictures of me standing near her for my envious friends back home. Didn't mean to cause any fuss with the owner. Or with this sailor here. Sorry."

The woman eyed him cautiously a moment but then seemed to relax. "Sure, I understand, mister. That's how most folks react to the Zephyr. Here, give me your camera. I'll take the pictures for you." Grabbing his Nikon, she positioned him closer to the yacht and calmly snapped a few photos of Seven standing in front of it. The girl then handed him back the camera.

"Thanks a lot. By the way, my name's Christopher Seven. I didn't catch yours."

"I didn't give it," she said, firmly. Her voice was definitely American. "But the name's Suzanne. Most of my friends call me Suz."

"Okay, Suz."

Her eyes again showed a trace of caution as she asked, "So you like yachts, eh?"

"That's right. Always have, ever since I was a kid. Like to own one someday, although I daresay it won't be as big or as luxurious as yours."

"I just told you. The tub's *not* mine. Anyway, let's talk about you. How long are you going to be in Monte Carlo?"

Seven answered evasively. "Oh, I don't know. I did really well on Wall Street the past few months. I'm a day trader, self-employed at the moment. Despite the current trends, I recently made a huge blue-chip killing. Felt I owed myself an extended vacation after that. So, here I am on the scenic Riviera. After that, who knows? May go on to Spain or Italy." He feigned pondering it a moment. "I'll probably stick around here awhile, though. Two or three weeks in Monaco might be fun. So long as this warm weather holds."

"You come alone, mister?"

"Yep. Just little old me."

Suzanne glared at him, guardedly. "That's a bit odd. A man with your looks and no rich wife or gorgeous mistress on his arm."

Seven chuckled. "I thought I'd find a few of those here. After all, Monte Carlo is supposed to be *the* place for jet-setting debutantes and wealthy divorcees on the prowl. At least that's what I've heard."

The girl frowned. "Don't believe everything you read about this town, friend. It's not some nonstop fantasyland, custom-made for bachelors." She then grinned widely, seemingly loosening up a little. "Oh, there's plenty of action and fun around here – as long as you know *where* to find it."

"Well, perhaps you can show me *where* to look," Seven pushed

"Perhaps."

She again eyeballed him. Was there a trace of skepticism in her eyes? "Just don't press me," she ordered. "I don't like being pressed." She gave him a haughty gaze. "Besides, *I'm* the one who usually does the pressing. Especially when I see something I like."

Seven smiled but didn't reply.

Inspecting him from head to toe for a full thirty seconds, Suz seemed satisfied. "You know what? Maybe I and my friends might enjoy having someone like you around. You know, to brighten up the neighborhood awhile. We gals kind of crave nonstop amusement. But I warn you. We're all insatiable trophy hunters. Party animals who like having male scalps on our belts. And you're about as good-looking a scalp as I've ever seen."

Seven decided he'd better display a bit of backbone and not appear overanxious. He purposely frowned his reply. "Well, I don't know about *that* part. I've never been a trophy before and I'm not sure I want to start now." He gave her a dour gaze. "And who are these other gals you're talking about, anyway?"

"Oh, just some friends I'm vacationing with." She giggled, wickedly. "We'd certainly make it worth your while, *if* you know what I mean. Maybe even get you a ride on this yacht, too. Or at least a private tour."

Suzanne glanced down at her diamond-studded wristwatch. "Oops, gotta go. I have a pedicure scheduled in *Zephyr's* spa and I can't keep my toes waiting." Giving him a parting wink, she cooed, "Well, so long, friend. Maybe we'll see you around."

"I hope so," replied Seven, a bit lamely.

"You do, huh?" She again stared at him rather curiously. It was still tough to ascertain if her expression was one of interest or suspicion. Suzanne shrugged her shoulders. "Then we'll just have to see what the future holds, won't we, handsome? But if we don't connect again, goodbye and good luck. Particularly with your *own* trophy hunting. Although you'll quickly find out that Monaco has a small and select circle when it comes to the *really* beautiful people. Anyway, ciao for now."

The assertive beauty then glanced back toward Rio, the Zephyr's apelike security guard. He was frowning disapprovingly, obviously annoyed with the juvenile banter going on between this brash American tourist and the girl. Suzanne tossed back her blonde-streaked hair and addressed Seven one last time. "Oh, and one more thing, handsome. If I were you, I'd take Rio's advice very seriously and not come snooping around here anymore. Especially with that camera. The yacht's owner is a very private person who doesn't take kindly to snoopers." She then turned and made her exit, leaving the warning at that.

Seven watched her shapely body amble back up Zephyr's gangplank and disappear into main salon. Nodding an awkward farewell to the still-annoyed Rio, the Super Stud made his way back to his car.

~

The rest of the day went by quickly and enjoyably for Seven. His first stop, after changing at the hotel, was the Monte Carlo Country Club, home to perhaps the most beautiful tennis setting in the world. Technically located in the community of Roquebrune-Cap-Martin in the Alpes-Maritimes, rather than in Monaco itself, the club's elegant red- clay courts are encircled by a bevy of multicolored flowers and lush landscaping. Offering an incredible panoramic vista of the azure sea below, the perfectly groomed tennis courts seem to hang in midair. It was almost as if they were magically suspended out over the water; as if they were part of the sea itself.

Looking down at the six courts, Christopher Seven was truly awed by the breathtaking view. He could see why the *Monte Carlo Open*, played here every spring, drew such enthusiastic raves from both the ATP players and the sold-out crowds.

Hoping he'd be able to keep his mind on the tennis match rather than the magnificent surroundings, the G5 agent eagerly made his way down to the courts via a steep brick stairway. Playing three excellent sets with the amiable French pro, Philippe, Seven surprisingly won two of them.

After showering in the tennis club's elegant wood-paneled locker room, he next drove to a martial arts academy located near the Avenue de Castellane. Both the academy and its black belt instructor had been recommended by a fellow agent, and the skilled *Sensei* turned out to be a topnotch trainer. He tossed Seven around unmercifully, working on the defensive counter moves that the G5 higher-ups liked best. These strictly self-protective 'counters' were the martial moves most stressed in Stud basic training. Colonel McPhail and the other agency honchos obviously wanted their Studs to be able to defend themselves, especially when undertaking dangerous missions abroad. Yet McPhail didn't want them to be *too* proficient or offense-minded. No black belt champions or karate chopping '*Robocops*'. Complex martial moves like that might give away their cover. And possibly compromise the confidentiality of their top-secret department as well.

That being said, all Super Studs were required to constantly keep up with their martial arts instruction, whether home or on the road. They were trained to be fit and tough. Able to at least defend themselves in a physical or fight situation. Accordingly, Seven dutifully booked another two-hour karate session for later in the week.

After finishing his martial workout, the G5 operative grudgingly visited the adjoining weight room for thirty-five minutes of lifting. This, along with an arduous session on their various strength-training machines. Now ready to collapse, Seven drove back to his hotel, took a soapy whirlpool bath, followed by a cooling shower, and then relaxed on his bed for a while. Deciding to retire early, he ordered and quickly devoured a delicious room-service filet mignon dinner, relishing the sublime béarnaise sauce and the potato au gratin that accompanied it. He then plopped back down on the bed and began reading the stirring book he'd brought along, RD Foster's Viet Nam classic, *One Day as a Lion.*

Yawning tiredly, Seven glanced over at his travel alarm clock, noting that it was now 8:50 p.m., Monaco time. Despite the relatively early hour, and the fact that his mind was still functioning in the even earlier New York time zone, he resisted the urge to visit the celebrated casino across the street. Instead, he used his secured cellphone to check in with G5 headquarters, and was soon speaking with one of the afternoon switchboard operators, a pleasant woman named Peggy. After giving her his agency recognition code, the Super Stud was politely told that both Colonel McPhail and his second in command, Hank Carson, were both out of the office. Leaving a simple coded message for the colonel, he informed his chief that he had seen Gitano's yacht. And that he'd also made contact with a good-looking blonde. One who was supposedly 'vacationing' onboard. As for whether she was Rhombus or not, Seven advised that he was obviously uncertain after this initial meeting. But that he would do his best to find out.

Ten minutes after the call ended, the weary operative crawled under the harsh, yet comfortable French sheets on the suite's king- size bed, said his nighttime prayer and was almost instantly asleep.

While Seven slept soundly, worn out from his active day and the remaining effects of jet lag, several events began rapidly taking place onboard Carmine Gitano's luxurious mega yacht. Events that would include intrigue, abductions and unmerciful torture!

Chapter 10

'Tradire La Cosa Nostra'

Sometime around 10:00 p.m., at the now nearly deserted Monaco yacht marina, several of Carmine Gitano's mobster crewmen suddenly appeared on the wharf's seldom-used rear boardwalk. Entering from a narrow side road, this jovial bunch appeared to be carrying two of their inebriated shipmates back to the Zephyr.

To anyone witnessing the action, it simply looked as if the two drunken sailors, both out cold, were being hauled back onboard Gitano's yacht by a group of their more sober mates. As the eight abstemious crewmen carried their seemingly intoxicated brethren, they laughed and sang loudly, as if returning from a fun-filled 'night on the town'. The reality, however, was a far different story. One with a very sinister motive indeed.

Since no one was actually around the Zephyr to witness this innocuous revelry, the charade that Gitano's men were now staging turned out to be an unnecessary one. Nonetheless, it was a prudent precaution. For Gitano's six henchmen had just abducted two rival Mafia chieftains. Skillfully surprising their stunned victims at a private meeting taking place in the backroom of a billiard parlor near St. Tropez. The two staged 'drunks', now being dragged onboard Zephyr were, in fact, two rival mob bosses whom they'd just kidnaped. It had been a faultless abduction.

A week earlier, Gitano's capable intelligence network had been furtively provided with information as to exactly where and when these two mob bosses would be gathering tonight. Armed with the inside details of this secret conference, the wily *Don* Gitano promptly made arrangements for his soldiers to snatch the rival capos. With stiletto blades and silencer-equipped revolvers in hand, Carmine's men had swiftly and quietly eliminated the four armed guards stationed in front of the pool hall. They then broke into the pool parlor's back room and callously grabbed their astonished quarry.

Quickly putting the two captives to sleep with a fast-acting, needle-injected sedative, they exchanged the business suits the two mob bosses were wearing for a pair of standard crewman's outfits. Then, tossing their sleeping hostages into a nondescript van, they speedily drove off toward the Monaco marina and the waiting Zephyr. The kidnapping had been slick and efficient. The type of drill Gitano's European syndicate was skilled in carrying out.

As the big yacht pulled out of the harbor and raced toward the open sea, the two captured gangland capos were still out cold. Tied tightly to two metal poles, their bare feet and ankles had been placed into a pair of large pails. This, to form what the mobs euphemistically call 'cement shoes'. Accordingly, each bucket was filled with quick-drying cement.

Carmine Gitano, with a gin and tonic in one hand and a long Cuban stogie in the other, waited patiently as his henchmen began reviving the two captives with several hard slaps to their cheeks. As Gitano heard the muttering of the bound duo, indicating they were finally coming out of their drugged stupor, he turned and addressed the muscular crewman behind him. "Nalco, go get the girls. They'll want to be in on the fun."

"Yes, Don Gitano."

"And tell them to hurry it up. I want to feed these two bums to the fishes by eleven o'clock. There's a championship fight on the satellite TV I wanna see tonight."

"Will'a do, boss." And with that, Nalco Incartti, the Gitano gang's main enforcer, ran down to the guest cabin area located on deck three.

Gitano watched closely as his goons continued to revive the prisoners. Ten minutes later, the ill-fated captives were fully awake, their eyes showing genuine fear as they came to.

"Well, well," Carmine chuckled. "Enjoy your nap, boys?" He grinned widely. "I guess you both know why you're here. One word: greed." Gitano walked closer to the captives. "Me and my uncle have repeatedly warned you to stay away from southern France. Away from *my* designated territory. But instead, just like a couple of disrespectful amateurs, you completely ignored our warnings. Ignored them *despite* the firm ruling of last January's Cosa Nostra council meeting in Sorrento. The council fully agreed with me."

Carmine Gitano shook his fist. "You two have been constantly trying to take over my Riviera enterprises for months now. Specifically my narcotics and call-girl action. Bad move, fellas. *Real* bad move."

With his hands tied behind his back and his feet encased in the quickly hardening cement, Antoine Minirri, the older of the two prisoners, sighed nervously. This French capo, a wiry, harsh-looking man, was the acting head of France's notorious *Unione Corse*. The secretive Corsican Mafia. Though knowing his position was extremely tenuous, the aging gangster tried his best to remain calm and steady. As a man of gangland authority, he was used to being respected, and, as such, felt his words and his stature might still save the day. He looked up at his captor and spoke in a low, controlled tone.

"Don Gitano, I admit that we've never been close friends over the years. But I have always respected you. I tried to reach out to you and your uncle many times. To see if we could resolve our differences and do business *together*. Maybe we still can."

Minirri looked Carmine Gitano directly in the eyes. "Along with the central syndicate of Don Carpi here, our three organizations could virtually rule *all* of Europe if we worked together. No one would dare stop us. That's what my meeting with Tony was about tonight."

Antoine Minirri paused a moment, hoping to see some positive reaction from his abductor. Sadly, Gitano's face was stone cold and unsympathetic. Though troubled by his captor's unresponsive expression, Minirri nevertheless forged on. "Don Gitano. If you kill us now there will be a great war between our syndicates. Many good men will die and millions of dollars might be lost. Untie us and let us calmly talk this out."

Carmine Gitano didn't answer. Instead he looked at the other bound man, Antonio 'Little Tony' Carpi, the infamous head of the San Remo *Bleau* syndicate, and addressed him. "And what about you, Tony? Do you likewise think we three can be partners?"

Antonio Carpi knew all too well that there was no sense trying to talk Gitano into sparing them. The fact that they were here as prisoners indicated it was already too late. It meant that the other European crime families in Italy and in France had given their blessing to the 'hit'. If not, Gitano wouldn't be risking an all-out war. It was a clever setup of betrayal by the other mobs, and Little Tony Carpi was fully aware of his grim situation. Nonetheless, he turned to Gitano and responded.

"You must already have the go-ahead to kill us from the other European families, Carmine. If not, we wouldn't be here like this. Still, what Don Minirri just said is true. If we three joined forces, we'd be unstoppable." He frowned knowingly. "But somehow I don't think that's what you want."

Gitano grinned. "You were always the perceptive one, Tony. And you are correct. You've indeed been sold out. Sold out by the other mob families as well as by your own people. It was unanimous. All the syndicate bosses, including your top lieutenants, wanted both of you eliminated. You broke far too many rules, and you've been way too selfish. Made life difficult for all the European mobs."

Shaking his head, Carmine Gitano further explained, "Starting tomorrow, two new capos will replace you as heads of your syndicates. They likewise gave their okay to *whack* you, agreeing it was my right to do so. Since you and *Don* Minirri invaded my territory, openly defying the repeated decrees of the Cosa Nostra council."

Gitano took a swig of his drink and explained, "I'll be meeting with your replacements sometime next month. By then, any hard feelings of those still loyal to you will have died down. Hopefully, even the initial anger of your hotheaded son, Frankie." Carmine shrugged his shoulders. "Who knows, Tony? I know Frankie's temper is legendary. But maybe, once he calms down, he'll see that tonight's 'hit' was simply business and not personal. Anyway, as for you two are concerned, it's too late. You're both gonna die tonight and your bodies will be tossed into the sea."

Taking a puff of his big cigar, Gitano added, "Out of respect for your positions as Mafia *Dons*, your deaths should be quick and painless. By rights, you should be shot in the head, as is the privilege of your *capo dei capi* rank. However, neither of you deserve that honor anymore."

Carmine Gitano feigned giving the decision some more thought. "To tell you the truth, I'm still not sure *how* you should be *wacked* tonight. Technically, you both violated that capo code when you defied the council and moved in on my domain; *tradire La Cosa Nostra*. By blatantly ignoring that Mafia mantra, and the Sorrento Committee's warnings, you two should be tortured to death without honor. Exactly like cheap, low-ranking hoodlums would be." He looked at them coldly, as if contemplating something. "I'm still considering the option of torture."

Gitano rubbed his chin, once more pretending to ponder the situation. He then smirked vindictively and informed, "Perhaps I'll leave it up to my four yacht guests. Let *them* decide your fate."

As if on cue, four beautiful women appeared. They were led over to the captives by Nalco, Carmine Gitano's main enforcer. Carmine gestured a polite hello to them and promptly introduced the women to his prisoners. "Gentlemen. These ladies are my lovely shipboard visitors. Anita, Suzanne, Terry, and Doreen They kind of enjoy watching victims die slowly. So I promised them that privilege tonight. Let's just say, as part of their well-earned reward for a recent job they did for me."

Gitano smiled at the girls and pointed toward the bound captives. "And these, my dear ladies, are the former heads of two of our rival companies. Pity they can't move forward to greet you. But, as you can see, they've both been fitted with new shoes."

The women laughed loudly, as did Carmine.

"Can we help throw them into the sea, Carm?" asked Anita, much like an excited child requesting a new toy.

"Of course, my dear. Right after Nalco shoots them in the head."

Shoots them?" Terry Harrigan protested, her voice showing staged disappointment. "What type of punishment is *that*, Carmine?"

"What do you mean?" Gitano asked with a wink, playing along with the sadistic game he and the women had arranged earlier. "What's worse than losing your life?"

"A lot of things," Terry replied. "At the very least they should be thrown into the sea with their cement anchors while they're still *alive.*" She motioned toward her three lovely associates. "That's what we'd like to see. Isn't it, girls?"

Two of her cohorts squealed with delight, clearly in full agreement. The fourth girl, Doreen, looked away, showing absolutely no enthusiasm.

Carmine Gitano patiently explained, "I don't know, ladies. According to Mafia tradition, these men are supposed to be given a respectful coup de grace; a quick and painless death." He again rubbed his chin in thought. "Of course, they've technically lost that privilege." He glanced over at Terry Harrigan and again winked. "Are you sure that's what you and your friends want, Terry?"

"Absolutely! You promised us we could choose the killing method and that's what we want. Along with a few *other* things." She giggled callously. "In fact, why don't you leave their execution to us? We'll make sure they eventually die, but in a manner we'd enjoy."

Gitano held out his hands and looked over at the two captives apologetically. "Sorry, fellas, I tried my best for you. But I owe these ladies big time." He barked out a harsh laugh and began walking down to his bedroom suite in order to watch the televised satellite boxing match

One of the prisoners, Antonio Carpi, suddenly yelled out to him, "Wait a minute, Carmine! This is *not* what Cosa Nostra procedure dictates! We are to be given the final respect that's due us as Mafia Dons. Have your man shoot us now and be done with it. That's our right. The heck with these stupid broads!"

Gitano stopped in his tracks and slowly turned around. Again displaying an expression of counterfeit sorrow, he promptly replied, "These women are my honored guests, Tony. And I would never disappoint such lovely visitors."

And with that, Carmine raised his right hand and waved a final good bye, declaring, "Proceed girls. These bums are all yours. Enjoy yourselves."

Terry Harrigan waited a moment. Still grinning, she approached the two bound men. "So we're stupid broads, huh?" She grabbed Carpi's hair and roughly pulled his head toward her. "Do you have *any* idea what it's like to slowly drown, my friend?" Terry asked. "Once we toss you into the sea in your cement shoes you'll slowly begin to sink. They'll be no escape from the pressure and the pain as your insides explode in agony."

Terry chuckled and finally let the gangster's hair go. She was obviously enjoying every delicious minute of tormenting these men, as were two of her attractive cronies.

The fourth gal, the reticent Doreen, merely stared down at her fingernails, again trying to will her mind away from what she privately deemed unnecessary and immature theatrics. Doreen longed to be somewhere else. Anywhere but here.

The opposite was true for Anita, Terry and Suzanne, who were gleefully observing the ashen, frightened faces of the two captives. Terry again addressed them. "Before we throw you punks into your watery grave, alive of course, we have a little surprise in store for you." She motioned toward her shapely red-haired mate. "Anita, go to my cabin and bring back my branding iron. Right after you've heated it up to a white-hot hue in the upper galley oven."

Grinning proudly, Terry Harrigan walked closer to the now-shaking captives and roared, "I'm going to show these two bums what Rhombus is all about!"

Chapter 11

Danger for Dessert

The following day, a bright and humid Monaco Sunday, Christopher Seven woke up early and well rested. After showering, shaving and completing his other morning grooming routines, he slipped on a yellow *Peter Millar* polo shirt and tan trousers. A few moments later, at exactly 8:30 a.m., a loud knock on the door announced that room service had arrived. Greeting Seven amiably, the cheerful French waiter walked out onto the suite's private balcony and placed the delicious-looking continental breakfast on the veranda's small glass table. Then, after receiving a generous tip, the server smiled a 'Merci' and took his leave.

Seven relocked the door and walked out onto the patio to eat breakfast. Lowering his head, he said his customary prayer of 'grace', and then eagerly began consuming the tasty food, particularly enjoying the fresh-baked, buttery croissant, which was still warm from the oven. Only in France, Belgium or Monaco could one find them this airy and delicious. Finished with his morning meal, the G5 operative again brushed his teeth and then powered up his secured laptop, which was sitting on the suite's small writing desk.

As expected, a coded e-mail had come in during the night from headquarters. The message contained some inside information taken from a report written by a fellow undercover operative. This non-Super Stud field-agent had briefly crossed swords with Mafia boss Carmine Gitano a few years back while on an assignment in Chicago.

Leaning back in the plush desk chair, Seven read the entire report carefully. Quotes from the account stated that *Don* Gitano had proved to be 'ruthless and cunning', and 'was a hard man to fool'. More alarming to Seven were some other details affirming that Gitano 'frequently resorted to vicious retribution on those who crossed him'. This strong-arm punishment was quickly and cruelly dished out by muscular mob henchmen whenever their boss was shown up, cheated, or lied to. Some of the reprisals included 'having acid thrown into a victim's face', along with 'painful butchering by way of long ice picks'. And yes, 'murder' could also be in the mix if the offense to Gitano was bad enough.

Continuing his reading, the Super Stud shivered, knowing he might be crossing swords with the malicious mob boss during this present assignment. As for Carmine Gitano himself, the memo stressed that the one thing *Don* Gitano respected, in either friends or foes, was 'self-assuredness'; someone who wouldn't be bullied or pushed around. In the Chicago agent's own words: "When dealing with Carmine Gitano, it is imperative to demonstrate that you can give as good as you get. In every encounter with him it's vital to show that you're just as clever, resourceful and tough as he is. Be assertive and never back down to him. Only then will Gitano take you seriously and allow your interaction or business with him to continue."

The G5 agent nodded his head. This last admonition might be extremely important re his current assignment. Thankful for the emailed pointers, tips which might come in handy down the road, Seven turned off and locked his laptop. He then grabbed his wallet and comb and exited the room, hanging the bilingual - *Service please/Service s'il vous plaît* - card on the front doorknob.

Ten minutes later he was driving the rented Mercedes toward the Avenue la Turbie for an interdenominational worship service at *The American Church of Monte Carlo.* Whether at home or on the road, Christopher Seven tried his best to attend church every Sunday and was thankful that this English-speaking house of worship was conveniently located near his hotel.

After the service, with its inspiring sermon from the book of Romans, the G5 operative walked back to his car, put the Mercedes top down and drove by the marina. Slowly cruising past the pier, Seven noted that the Zephyr was no longer docked there. He now wondered whether Gitano's mega yacht was simply out for the day or on a longer, extended voyage somewhere else. If that was the case, Seven hoped his four pretty targets wouldn't be sailing with it. If they were, what would be the effect on his mission? Would his assignment be postponed, relocated, or possibly even scrubbed *before* it got started?

Frowning at all three prospects, Seven's thoughts quickly turned to the perky ash-blonde beauty he'd met here the day before. The rather rough-and-ready girl called Suzanne, or 'Suz' to her friends. Had she stayed behind in Monaco or was she now sailing away on Gitano's yacht to parts unknown. Disappearing for good with those 'friends' of hers?

Seven knew there was no sense speculating. Perhaps Fieri could find out something about Zephyr's whereabouts via his CIA contacts. The Super Stud shrugged his shoulders. There was nothing he could really do about it anyway. Other than informing headquarters and then waiting until the Zephyr hopefully returned to Monaco. When and if Gitano's mega yacht did come back, Seven would again have to try and arrange another 'chance' meeting' with Suzanne. Hopefully one that wouldn't draw suspicion.

With all these thoughts firmly in mind, he slowly motored away from the pier and began the short drive back to his hotel in order to change for another round of tennis with Philippe. Grinning knowingly, he was certain that the lanky French tennis pro would be gunning for revenge after Seven's narrow victory yesterday.

While Christopher Seven toiled away on the red clay tennis courts of the Monte Carlo Country Club, Carmine Gitano's spectacular yacht was slowly making its way in from the open sea, cruising back to its mooring berth at the Monaco marina. As the luxurious vessel gently pitched and rolled on the suddenly choppy seas, the mob chieftain and his four attractive passengers were still buzzing about last night's sadistic fun: the torturing and drowning of Gitano's rival Mafia bosses.

Terry Harrigan and her Rhombus partners had finally dumped the screaming captives into the sea sometime around 2:00 a.m. The bound prisoners had first been tormented with Terry's scalding branding iron as she repeatedly burned the letter *R* onto their naked bodies. Periodically pausing to reheat her iron in the nearby galley kitchen.

After hours of this brutal torture, the women, with help from Gitano's main enforcer, Nalco, finally flung the bloodied Mafia *Dons* into the water. As their cement-shoe anchors began dragging the rival gangsters to the bottom of the sea, the Rhombus girls laughed with perverted glee. Giggling loudly when they heard the last garbled screams from the captives. Anita, Terry and Suzanne then applauded each other. It had been quite a spectacle!

Thinking about these stirring events again, the Rhombus foursome now sat around an elegantly set patio table on the yacht's expansive lido deck. Ready to dig into the head chef's appetizing lobster lunch, they eagerly relived last night's fun with their Mafioso host, Carmine Gitano.

"You should have seen Carpi's face when we finally picked him up and tossed him into the water, Carm," laughed Suzanne. "He looked like a shivering rabbit about to be consumed by a rattlesnake!"

"I can't believe those two sissies were actually mob bosses," Anita chimed in, as she broke off a piece of freshly baked bread and buttered it. "Both of them screamed and pleaded like little girls."

"I know," said Gitano. "Those bums kept me up half the night with their wailing. How long did you gals keep it going with that branding iron, anyway?"

"About four hours," Terry Harrigan calmly informed, while dipping a piece of lobster tail into some drawn butter. "We had to pause several times to reheat the iron." She glared over at Gitano. "You told us to give them the works, so we did. Rest assured that your underworld rivals were sufficiently punished."

"They deserved it," Gitano barked, sipping some wine from the elegant Waterford glass in front of him. "Minirri and Carpi violated every Mafia dictum there is." He then grinned perceptively. "But don't try to pretend that you and your partners tortured those two punks on *my* account, Terry. You gals loved every minute of it, like you always do." He winked at his attractive guests. "I know what turns you ladies on."

"Sure, we like the rough and wild stuff from time to time," Terry admitted, suddenly a bit miffed by Gitano's smugness. "Anyway, you promised we could have those two bums for our amusement. What we did to them was our business. Pass the rice pilaf, please."

With that, Carmine Gitano and the Rhombus women consumed the rest of their tasty meal, casually discussing the vicious torment and watery death of the captives as if they were conversing about some television reality show.

~

Two hours later, Christopher Seven had finally finished his tennis match with the club pro, Philippe, this time losing a tough, competitive match in three sets. He then drove back to the hotel and took a long hot shower in his mini suite. Feeling clean and refreshed, Seven threw a towel around his lean body, and plopped down on the plush bed. Grabbing his smartphone, which had now been adjusted to make and receive international calls, he tried twice to phone his CIA colleague, Vin Fieri, without success.

The Super Stud shrugged. In all probability, Fieri wasn't even in town yet, presumably coming in tomorrow. And though Vin had mentioned he might arrive in Monaco sometime late Sunday night, he also said that it was more likely he'd get here on Monday morning instead. Now assuming the 'doc' wouldn't arrive until tomorrow, Seven got up from the bed and contemplated his evening and his wardrobe.

Walking over to the closet, he decided that tonight he'd finally pay a visit to the celebrated Monte Carlo Casino across the street from the hotel. Do so for two reasons. First, and admittedly self-indulgent, he naturally looked forward to experiencing the opulence and romance of perhaps the most famous gaming house in the world. 'The Grand Dame of gambling halls'. Throughout its storied history, some of the Casino's legendary patrons had included King Farouk, Sarah Bernhardt, Aly Khan and the infamous Mata Hari.

The G5 operative grinned widely as he thought of Mata Hari. She, like him, was a spy whose role was to obtain information from the opposite sex, primarily relying on her looks and guile. Seven's own task was much the same, and he therefore sensed a kindred connection to the nineteenth century temptress.

Reflecting on that brought him to reason number *two* for visiting the renowned gaming hall. Seven had been told by the hotel's knowledgeable concierge that almost all of the Riviera's globetrotting 'in-crowd' would be there tonight. According to the concierge, Sunday evening was when the showy 'VIPs' and 'beautiful people' converged on the gaming club. The jet-setting countesses, prowling gigolos and mega-rich 'movers and shakers' wouldn't dream of missing a Sunday night at the famed Casino. Sunday after dark was when Monaco's notable visitors showed off the fruits of their labor. The night when they openly flaunted their expensive wardrobes, glittering jewelry, and their high-priced sports cars. Consequently, if Seven hoped to run into Suzanne again, the fashionable Casino would undoubtedly be the place she'd be tonight. That is if she hadn't already left town for some extended voyage onboard the Zephyr.

The agent again shrugged his shoulders. He could only strategize so much. In any event, if the smug Suzanne was still in town, Sunday night at the casino would be Seven's best chance of running into her. Perhaps she'd have those 'friends' with her as well. Now feeling confident, Seven opened the closet where his sport coats and suits were hanging and carefully considered his attire.

All Super Stud operatives had been issued a stylish and expensive wardrobe to utilize in the field. Perfect clothing to complement their amazing looks. Colonel McPhail's staff of well-informed researchers had rightly reasoned that the combination of the two - great looks with flawless fashion - would help make the Studs even more desirable to female targets. Accordingly, elegant wardrobe ensembles had been painstakingly designed by an eccentric but very capable Englishmen named Godfrey; G5's erudite fashion guru. And though the Studs could certainly change or deviate from Godfrey's wardrobe recommendations, they seldom did. Over the years the Englishman's stylish choices had helped them lure beautiful women throughout the world.

After perusing the garments now hanging in the suite's walk-in closet, Seven selected a fashionable beige sport coat from *Diante,* one of Europe's best clothiers. Glancing down at his printed Super Stud wardrobe card, Seven noted Godfrey's accompanying suggestion. The *Diante* fawn jacket, with a pair of expertly tailored black pants, a white French- cuffed dress shirt, and an eye-catching brown-and-gold striped silk tie *from Ruffini's Eleganza* collection. A pair of expensive black *Bruno Magli* loafers and black cotton dress socks finished off the assemblage.

Now impeccably outfitted with Godfrey's erudite ensemble, the Seven opened the small wall safe mounted inside the closet, using the personal code that he'd programmed in earlier. Here he retrieved some striking pearl cufflinks and his *Rolex Gold Diamond Masterpiece watch.*

This costly 18K-yellow gold timepiece, studded with large diamonds, was one of only two very expensive jewelry pieces that Christopher Seven owned. He had treated himself to this pricey wristwatch after a big slot win at the *Bellagio* during a vacation in Las Vegas. Doing so right after winning a $5.00 slot's sizeable jackpot. Seven smiled at the memory of immediately rushing to the jewelry store in Bellagio's chic shopping mall, *before* he'd be tempted to give his winnings back into another slot. He quickly purchased the watch with cash and never went back to the slots that trip. Still thinking about the Vegas memory, the Super Stud agent slipped on the Rolex, set it to the correct 7:55 p.m. local time, and exited his suite.

As he made his way down to the lobby, via the hotel's ornately mirrored elevator, Seven began anticipating the evening ahead; starting with tonight's dinner at Alain Ducasse's extraordinary restaurant, *Le Louis XV.* This landmark gourmet eatery, located on the hotel's ground floor, was one that Seven had been looking forward to ever since hearing he'd be traveling to Monte Carlo.

"Ah, here we are, monsieur," greeted the smiling Maître D from the entrance podium. "Monsieur Christopher Seven, eight o'clock, for one. We have a nice corner table for you. This way, s'il vous plait."

Seven followed the Maître D to the far end of the room, surveying the restaurant with a cultured eye. The hotel's lavish dining hall was literally a palace of gold: gold draperies, gold chairs, solid-gold light sconces on the walls and even a stunning gold carpet nicely accented by soft burgundy tones. Portraits of courtesans on the walls peered down from their gilded frames, likewise bestowing the elegant eatery with a refined ambiance. Small touches of luxury were everywhere. There were even petite footstools for the female patrons underneath their chairs. The well-spaced dining tables were set with fine crystal and cutlery, and each table had a lovely sculptured silver bird resting on it. It made Seven think of Quack, Colonel McPhail's pet parrot.

Despite a handful of empty tables, Seven knew that the restaurant was completely booked tonight, just as it was most every evening. He'd been fortunate enough to procure a table via a last-minute cancellation and a sizable tip to the hotel's concierge. As for the clientele, they appeared to be a mixture of well-to-do American, European and Asian guests. There were a few recognizable celebrities and several members of Monte Carlo's upper-crust society as well.

Most of the restaurant's female patrons, dutifully accompanied by their rich husbands - or more likely their goldbricking gigolos - were ostentatiously clad in gaudy diamonds and pearls. Yet, nearly all of them stopped eating when Christopher Seven entered the room, lowering their forks and eyeing his incredible looks contemplatively. Doing so much to the dismay of their escorts. As always, the Super Stud politely smiled back at them and then sat down at his magnificently set table.

After an excellent champagne cocktail aperitif, Seven began his dinner by choosing a selection from the 'garden section' of the menu: the vegetables and fruits en cocotte. His next course was a mouthwatering entrée from the menu's 'farm' section'; a charbroiled rack of Pyrenean lamb roasted in the open fireplace. The pink and juicy meat, one of the best racks of lamb Seven had ever eaten, was accompanied by delicious scalloped potatoes. And the half bottle of the superb red Bordeaux, which the sommelier had enthusiastically recommended, made the meal even more pleasurable.

After finishing his memorable dinner, Seven reluctantly passed on the vast selection of cheeses from the menu's 'pasture land' section. He did choose a desert, however. A flaky strawberry Napoleon, served with a large dollop of freshly whipped Chantilly cream. And though, like always in Europe, he couldn't get the French waiter to bring him coffee with his dessert, he waited patiently and had a satisfying cup afterward.

Now relaxing and enjoying his second *Cafe Americano* along with some delicious petit fours, Seven called for and paid the staggering bill with his American Express platinum card. He was about to savor one last sip of the freshly brewed coffee before taking his leave, when suddenly, all of his senses heightened.

Glancing toward the restaurant's front door area, the Super Stud witnessed a friendly commotion of laughter and loud voices, followed by the sight of Suzanne, the shapely ash-blonde he'd met at the pier yesterday. Immediately tense and alert, Christopher Seven felt his skin slowly begin to shiver, when he heard the Maître D stationed at the front podium deferentially call out, "Ah, good evening, Mr. Gitano. Nice to see you back so soon. Especially since you've again brought in the four prettiest women in all of Monte Carlo!"

Chapter 12

'Window Dressing'

Whirling around to hide his face and collect his thoughts a moment, Seven turned his back away from Gitano's arriving party. Fortunately, he could still observe them by way of the large mirrored panels on the dining room's far wall.

The Super Stud watched closely as the Maître' D walked Gitano and his guests over to a prime table for six in the center of the room. Seven easily recognized the infamous Mafia chieftain from the many TV and newspaper headlines about him. And from the CIA's file photos as well. Carmen Gitano - the so-called *'debonair Don'.*

The big man, said to be a generous tipper, was laughing and shaking hands with several of the wait staff who went out of their way to greet him. It was akin to a Roman emperor waiting for the fawning peasants to kiss his ring. The mob boss was accompanied by Suzanne and three other very attractive women. A muscle-bound hulk, obviously some sort of bodyguard, brought up the rear, dutifully scanning the room's other patrons. This apelike 'enforcer' looked completely out of place in the elegant restaurant. His wrinkled sport coat was way too tight for his massive chest and strapping arms. Fidgeting a bit, the burly guardian seemed very uncomfortable being in such heady surroundings.

As Gitano's group arrived at their table, Seven slowly turned back around. Shortly after he did so, Suzanne, the sassy streaked-blonde from the marina, glanced his way. A look of momentary uncertainty formed on her pretty face, followed quickly by one of animated recognition. Grinning widely, she immediately left her tablemates and strolled over toward Seven's table to greet him.

"Hi there, handsome. Break the casino yet?"

Seven smiled back. "Hello, Suz. No, not yet. But I'm planning to clean them out later tonight."

"That so? Well, maybe we'll see you there. We always play on Sunday evenings whenever we're in town." She motioned toward Gitano's table. "Come on over a minute and say hello to my friends. I told them about the gorgeous creature I bumped into yesterday. But I'm not sure they believed me."

Christopher Seven, though excited about this unexpected opportunity to be introduced to the other targets of his mission, was unsure on how he should play it. Especially with this Mafia boss and his gorilla bodyguard sitting at the same table. Nevertheless, he rose from his chair and accompanied her to Gitano's table.

When they arrived, Suzanne grinned smugly and announced, "Hey, gang. Let me introduce my good-looking friend to you. The one you thought didn't exist. And remember girls, I saw him *first.*"

Christopher Seven, a bit uncomfortable by the syrupy words, nevertheless nodded politely as Suz began the introductions. "The three lovely ladies you sitting here are Anita, Doreen and Terry. They're my - uh," she paused briefly, looking for the right words. "My *business* associates." Seven smiled a hello.

Pointing toward Carmine Gitano, Suzanne next informed, "The dapper gentleman sitting at the head of the table is Carmine, our host here in Monaco." She chuckled. "The host with the most." Then, turning toward the muscular security man, she informed, "And that big galoot sitting next to him is Nalco. Nalco is our resident nursemaid. Watches out for all of us." Suz sneered, "But don't let that monkey suit he's wearing fool you. He's tough as nails. And don't mess with him either. Or you might wind up in the hospital." Suz laughed loudly. "But most of the time he's a nice, quiet fellow, aren't you, Nalc?"

Nalco blushed. "If you'a say so, Miss Suzanne."

Suzanne giggled at Nalco's discomfiture and then addressed the other three women again. "Well, girls, here he is. The hunk I was telling you about yesterday. I bet you all thought I was making it up. Especially the 'great looks' part.

The three females sitting at the table eyed Seven from head to toe, as if sizing up a racehorse before the Derby. It was obvious they found Seven's looks compelling, and they made no bones about saying so. Much to the annoyance of the clearly jealous Mafia Don. The attractive blonde woman named Terry, sitting at the far end of the table, was the first to comment. "Well, you weren't lying about his looks, Suz. This guy's a keeper. What'd you say his name was?"

Suzanne shrugged apologetically. "I kind of forgot his name, Terry. I just remembered that gorgeous face."

"My name's Chris; Christopher Seven."

Terry sniggered at him. "Seven? And that's supposed to be a *real* name? What was wrong with eight, nine, or ten?" The other girls laughed, as did Seven, used to jokes about his last name.

Carmine Gitano, sitting at the head of the table, didn't show any amusement at all. The Mafia capo was used to being the singular center of attention. Especially when he was entertaining *these* particular women. Gitano immediately became resentful of the good-looking stranger whom his female dinner guests were now fussing over. The mobster's neck and face began turning an angry red, his animosity a direct consequence of the hidden crush he harbored on all four of his attractive dining companions. Their unabashed fascination with this guy, Seven, or whatever his name was, was rapidly sending the Mafia kingpin into a silent rage. He took an instant disgust to the handsome tourist, his hostility further fueled by the childish flirting of the four women. The Mafioso glared at Seven threateningly. Clenching his fists he coarsely enquired, "Suzanne said you were snooping around my boat the other day. Is that what you were doing, friend? Snooping?"

The G5 agent, surprised by both the gangster's tone and his menacing question, nonetheless answered it politely. "I wasn't snooping at all. It's just that I'm a huge fan of luxury yachts. I've always been fascinated by them. I get a real thrill out of seeing them up close." Seven smiled. "And yours was kind of hard to miss. It's one of the largest."

"It *is* the largest one, pal!" Gitano pompously shot back, still eyeing the Super Stud in a threatening manner. "Where you from, pretty boy?"

"New Jersey," Seven answered truthfully, likewise forming an instant abhorrence of this bullying gangster. Annoyed with Gitano's boorish manners, and remembering the memo from headquarters about 'always being assertive with Carmine Gitano', Seven brusquely asked, "And how about you, Carmine? Where are *you* from?"

Gitano barked out a derisive laugh. "Where am *I* from? A guy could get slapped asking a question like that, mister."

Christopher Seven refused to give ground. "Well, you asked me, so I'm simply asking back."

Not accustomed to anyone speaking to him this bluntly, especially some two-bit stranger, *Don* Gitano was momentarily caught off guard. The mob king remained silent for a few seconds, grudgingly admiring the visitor's bravado. Then, figuring this naïve tourist obviously didn't know who he was speaking to, the mobster merely shrugged his shoulders and informed, "Let's just say I'm from here and there."

Amused at the cagey *non*-reply, the G5 agent likewise said nothing. An awkward silence ensued, which Seven used to size up Gitano.

Carmine Gitano was a hefty, muscular man somewhere in his mid-forties. He was dressed in a very expensive brown suit, and vanity spewed from every inch of his persona. With flashy diamond rings on four of his perfectly manicured fingers, Carmine's huge gem-studded wristwatch made Seven's Rolex look like a toy. Gitano's wavy brown hair was combed straight back, and his curly locks looked as if they had just been professionally styled at some expensive hair salon. Gitano had a decent, tough-looking face, marred by a small scar running down the left side. The mobster tried to hide the scarring by way of a thick, artificial suntan, though his 'sunburn' had the telltale signs of a tanning salon, rather than any actual sun. It was another indication of the man's enormous vanity. Yet, beneath these enhancing aids, and store-bought indulgences, was the unmistakable force of a strong and ruthless thug.

Trying to ignore *Don* Gitano's angry stare, Seven continued sizing the Mafia capo up. Although on the short side, perhaps five foot eight at most, Gitano possessed a solid, husky build. He had a rock-hard, barreled chest and chunky, muscular arms and hands. Hands that looked strong and sure. Seven was certain that during the early years of Carmine Gitano's meteoric gangland rise, those same hands surely must have strangled, shot, or knifed many victims on their way to the top of the Mafia food chain. In short, *Don* Carmine appeared to be a very formidable character indeed, and Christopher Seven took an immediate aversion to this overbearing brute. And judging by Gitano's jealous scowl, and the uncomfortable tension now permeating the table, this hatred between the Super Stud and the Mafioso was clearly mutual.

Terry Harrigan quickly sensed the hostility between the two men, and for some reason tried to ease the bad blood that was rapidly developing between them. "Let's get back to you, Seven," Terry interjected. "How long are you going to be around here?"

The Super Stud agent decided to play it down. "Oh, I don't know, Terry. I'd originally planned to stay here a while. But now I'm thinking of moving on to Spain. Nothing much seems to be happening in Monaco. And from the little I've seen, the action's not as hot as I thought it'd be. So Madrid and then Mallorca might be a better option for me. I have a couple of fun-loving friends there, so I'll probably leave in a day or two."

"What's your hurry?" protested Suzanne. "Why not stick around?"

"Stop promoting things, Suz!" barked an angry Carmine Gitano. "The guy says he wants to go to Spain. So let him."

"Oh, don't be a party pooper, Carm," the leggy redhead named Anita protested. She looked Seven over again and exclaimed, "Listen mister, we girls are always looking for new 'window dressing' here on the Riviera. Nothing we like better than making those snooty European dames envious with good-looking catches on our arms. So why *not* stay? We'll show you all the hot spots. And trust me, we'd make sure you enjoy *every* minute of it."

"Absolutely," Suzanne chimed back in. "Who knows? Maybe Carmine might even agree to take you out on his yacht for a quick spin. *If* we gals ask him nicely enough."

"Yeah," echoed Anita. "You said you love yachts. Well, Zephyr is the top of the heap. Getting a jaunt on her would *really* be something you could tell your friends back home about.

"Hold the phone there, Anita," growled Gitano. "We don't even know this guy. It's a bit early to start planning a slumber party."

"Oh come on, Carm," implored Suzanne. "You know that when we see something *this* hot we just have to have it around a while." She grinned. "You have your toys, we have ours."

Though bristling at being treated as a piece of bartered meat, Christopher Seven nonetheless remained silent, knowing full well the *first* objective of his mission. He merely listened as Gitano glanced at the four women and unenthusiastically informed, "Well, I can't say I'm crazy about the idea. Having this brazen no-name around for any length of time. But you four chicks seem to have a way of getting what you want from me." Then, completely disregarding any opinion Seven might have about it, the mob boss grudgingly acquiesced. "I guess I could put up with him. For a *little* while, anyway."

The Super Stud agent decided he'd better show some self-respect and a bit of independence. "That's all right, Mr. Gitano. I appreciate the offer. But I wouldn't want to force my company on anybody who doesn't want it. And judging by your rather reluctant reply, it's obvious you're not too thrilled about it. I can certainly understand that. Me being a stranger and all. Naturally I'd love to be able to visit the Zephyr. And getting to actually *cruise* onboard her would be a dream come true. But I have my own plans, and they don't include Monaco anymore."

"Look, pal," Gitano roared. "When, and if, I say you're comin', you're *comin'!*"

Knowing the mobster had just been hooked by his *own* bullying ego, Seven was inwardly thrilled. Nevertheless, he decided to tweak Gitano a bit more by refusing to readily agree. *Despite* the Mafioso's edict.

"Like I said, Carmine, my tentative plans are to move on to Spain, so we'll just have to see." He smiled an adieu to the table. "Anyway, I've got to run now. Pleasure meeting you all. Hope you enjoy your meal here. I certainly did." Then, satisfied that he had indeed stood his ground with *Don* Carmine Gitano, the Super Stud gave a farewell nod to the table and calmly made his exit.

A seething Gitano waited until Seven left the restaurant before tersely carping, "I'd like to rip that guy's head off! Who does he think he is with his 'we'll have to see' garbage?" The mob boss reached for a piece of bread and buttered it angrily.

Just then, and for the first time all evening, the timid Doreen Lacy, the fourth female at the table, finally spoke out. Completely ignoring the irate ranting of her gangland host, she dreamily decreed, "Is that guy, Seven, the best-looking man you've ever seen, or what?" Doreen's faraway, childlike expression was akin to being in an idyllic trance. Much like a high school freshman longing for a handsome senior. "I can't wait to see him again! And I hope it's soon."

Doreen's infatuation with the great looking stranger was palpable, surprising and amusing the three other three women with her bold proclamation. The shy Doreen was usually reticent and indifferent when it came to men.

"My, my," teased Anita. "Our bashful little Doreen has *finally* found someone who gets her blood flowing." The other girls chuckled loudly as Anita continued, "That guy's looks are truly amazing, Dor. I'll grant you that. He'd definitely be a good trophy on our wall."

"I'll say," agreed Suzanne, likewise ignoring Carmine Gitano's angry scowl.

"I guess you weren't exaggerating about him, Suz," admitted Terry Harrigan. "He's some hunk. And Anita's right. He'd make a great crown on the Rhombus mantelpiece."

"If you ask me," scoffed Gitano, "he's nothing but a disrespectful punk. Just a cheap, insignificant gigolo. I'd like to get my hands on him and teach him some manners."

"So would I," grinned Terry. "Although it'd be a delicious shame to ruin that marvelous face of his with my branding iron." She sighed, pensively. "Yet I'm thinking about it!"

Everyone at the table, except for the diffident Doreen, laughed loudly, and then began perusing their fancy dinner menus.

Chapter 13

"Don't say I didn't warn you!"

After leaving the elegant hotel restaurant, Christopher Seven returned to his room and sent a short coded e-mail to headquarters. In it, he informed G5 that he'd just met his targets, as well as their Mafioso host. Then, after hiding his locked laptop away, even though most every code inside was changed monthly, he walked to the bathroom, brushed his teeth, and threw some cold water on his face.

Exiting the suite, and walking toward the elevator, Seven assessed the rapidly unfolding events. He was justifiably pleased with himself for achieving the first objective of his mission. Meeting the four yacht women socially, and paving the way for a possible future encounter.

As for his initial confrontation with Carmine Gitano, the Super Stud wasn't so sure about it. Had he overplayed things with his deliberately caustic demeanor toward Gitano? Or had he been *too* disagreeable to the Mafia kingpin? It was hard to tell. Seven had certainly stood up for himself with the gangster. The way the headquarters memorandum suggested he should. Yet, all that being said, he'd almost certainly rubbed the powerful Mafioso chief the wrong way, making an instant, full-blown enemy in the process.

Seven frowned, knowing that *Don* Carmine Gitano was definitely *not* the type of character you wanted for an adversary. Even so, if the memo from headquarters was correct in its assertion, perhaps Carmine Gitano had been impressed with Seven's independent manner. The G5 agent had refused to cower before Gitano, the way most people probably did when meeting him for the first time. Hopefully, Seven had gained some grudging respect from the gangster during this opening encounter.

Again thinking about the four women at the table, Seven knew he had piqued their interest. If only with his physical appeal. Yet, if this attractive quartet was indeed Rhombus, getting their attention was a vital first step. As for any future contact, the CIA dossier on the new Rhombus squad had stated that they *'collected'* good-looking playboys. Used them as objects to be 'played with', and then coldly discarded. "Trophies on the wall" was what one of the yacht gals had called it. Very well then. Seven would *let* them use him. At least up to a point. The agent grinned, exited the elevator and headed for the casino across the street

As for gambling tonight, Seven didn't think casino gambling was wrong or evil, and steadfastly felt it was simply entertainment; *not* a singular sin. Over the years, his conscience was fine with it, and he always enjoyed casinos. He'd once told his hometown minister that he compared 'diversionary casino visits' to playing 'bingo' at church socials. Or trying the lottery. Or even one's 'luck' on the stock market. Seven, a very religious person, recognized that his logic was thin. And over the years he and his kindhearted pastor had gone through several affable discussions and disagreements on it.

Even so, now standing near the entrance of the celebrated gaming hall, Seven was eager for the opportunity to finally step inside the impressive Belle Époque structure. He'd heard so many fascinating tales about it, like accounts regarding the late King Farouk. Known back then as 'the swine', Farouk devoured obscene quantities of food and drink inside the hall's refined French restaurant. One report claimed that Farouk had once consumed four roasted chickens and 85 oysters before losing a small fortune at the tables!

There was also a magazine article Seven had read, describing the night actor Richard Burton presented Elizabeth Taylor with the enormous *Kohinoor Diamond* right here on these very steps. Christopher Seven sighed, wondering if anything momentous would happen tonight. Smiling at the prospect, he showed his hotel ID card to the casino's uniformed doorman and walked inside.

Upon entering the famous gaming club, the frowning G5 operative was instantly disillusioned. Disappointed that many of the male visitors - sadly, mostly Americans - were dressed sloppily. Although they grudgingly wore sport coats, a rigid weekend rule here, under their frayed jackets were stained T-shirts or ripped polo tops. Most of them wore old sneakers as well. Seven frowned, dejectedly. So much for rubbing elbows with Cary Grant or Fred Astaire in tails. It seemed the casual crowd, the Disney World and Las Vegas fanatics, had seemingly taken over everywhere, dressing more for bowling than an elegant night out. Oh well. At least the magnificent crystal chandeliers and the gilded antique furniture still leant an air of old-world refinement.

Strolling over to the casino's main cashier window, Seven cashed several traveler's checks and then made his way over to a fifteen-dollar three-card poker table, perhaps his favorite table game. He sat down at the table's only empty chair, one that was situated between two beautiful coeds. They gave him a smile of welcome, which he promptly returned. Procuring six hundred dollars' worth of chips, the Super Stud settled in for an hour or so of nonstop action.

The object of the game is to get a '3-card hand' higher than the dealer's. Or better yet, to make some lucrative 'pair/plus' money with any pairs, flushes, or straights. In this game, a *flush* being three suited cards, and a *straight* being any three cards in a sequential row. The most renowned hand of all was the coveted '*straight flush*'; *sequential* cards of the *same* suit. That was where the big reward was.

After an hour of play, and adhering to his steadfast rule of only playing a hand when he was dealt an Ace, a king, or a pair; Seven found himself ahead almost two thousand dollars. This was mainly due to the inordinate amount of winning *'pair/plus'* hands, including two enviable 'straight flushes', each paying big money!

As Seven nonchalantly restacked his impressive pile of chips, the pit boss arrived with a new dealer, a large glass container of chips and two decks of unopened playing cards for the table. Not wanting to wait until this time-consuming ritual was completed, Seven thanked the dealer and slid a few chips his way. He then gave a friendly goodbye to his two lovely tablemates, one of whom had brazenly kept trying to invite him back to her Uncle's villa for cocktails.

Now what, the G5 agent asked himself. *Maybe some blackjack or perhaps an hour or so at the Texas Hold 'em table. Conceivably, by then, Suzanne and her three friends might wander in. It was only ten o'clock, and the night was still young.*

Seven glanced around the big room, detecting several pairs of probing eyes seemingly staring right at him. Remembering Doc Fieri's admonition that many of the casino staff were on mob payrolls, Seven was well aware that his activities might later be conveyed to Carmine Gitano. And perhaps to other mafia bosses as well. Nonetheless, he calmly moved about the casino with the ease of a happy-go-lucky American tourist, with a just-earned windfall.

Walking toward the Texas Hold 'em area, he noticed a large sign informing casino patrons that a *'Winner take all no-limit house tournament.* This to begin at 10:15 p.m. It required a two-thousand dollar 'buy-in' from each of the twelve contenders, with the 12 players competing at two tables of six. A $20,000 prize would be awarded to the winner, with the remaining cash going to the house.

Since Texas Hold 'em poker was a game Seven also enjoyed, and with the large stack of new chips he'd already won from the casino, he'd really only be risking 'house' money anyway. *Why not give it a go,* he mused. *Besides. It would be a good place to sit and wait for the yacht girls to arrive without drawing suspicion.* He excitedly paid the required two-grand 'buy-in', and was promptly escorted to Table Number 1, filling the sixth and final seat there. Now there was only one empty seat. The *last* chair at Table 2.

All of the other contestants, save one, were already at their respective tables and chairs by the time the *last-minute* Seven was seated. With his filling Table One, there was now only one unoccupied chair remaining. The final seat at Table 2, where the other seated contestants patiently waited for the sixed player to arrive. A large, cushioned chair had a "reserved" sign in front of it.

Nodding a 'hello' to the other participants sitting at his table, Table number 1, Seven wondered if his tablemates would be skilled or amateurish poker players. Suddenly the booming voice of Carmine Gitano could be heard approaching the last entry chair. The Super Stud shook his head. *So this was who the last seat was for!*

Gitano loudly greeted the dealers and pit bosses with a flurry of staged animation. Clearly in his element, he shook hands with several of them as he cheerfully made his way toward Table 2's final seat. But then, Gitano's broad smile turned sour, as he glanced over at Table 1, and observed Christopher Seven sitting there.

"Don't tell me *you're* playing here tonight, pretty boy?" growled the mob chieftain, as he slid into his chair. "Thought you'd be more of a tiddlywinks player." Gitano let out derisive laugh.

"I'm okay at tiddlywinks, but I'm better at hold-em poker," Seven replied, returning the gangster's laugh with a self-assured grin.

"Oh yeah," retorted the mob boss, suspiciously. "And where do you *supposedly* play?"

"Atlantic City, mostly." Then, merely to squeeze the big man, Seven fibbed, "I play in a lot of their larger cash tournaments."

"That so?" said Gitano with grudging respect. "Well then, you and I should be the only *real* players here. These French frogs don't know much about stud poker. Too interested in their fancy food and their hatred of Americans. That's why I love beating 'em here."

Gitano gestured toward the other players with unconcealed contempt. "Believe me, I ain't playing in this two-bit contest for the lousy twenty-grand prize. I pay more than that for my cigars. I play here most every year and I *always* win. Teaching these *Frenchies* a humiliating lesson every time I play.

Carmine Gitano again laughed loudly, despite the dirty looks he received from several of the French players sitting at both tables. "As for me," Carmine continued, "I usually play poker in Reno and Vegas. At their high-stakes tables. That's where the *real* action is. But I always play here in Monaco every time I come over. Never lost yet and never will. You could say I'm a poker legend around these parts. I *always* win 'cause poker is *my* game." He once more motioned toward the other players. "This should be easy pickings for me tonight."

The mobster glared at Seven disdainfully. "And as far as you go, you don't look like much of a player either. No matter *what* you claim."

Though Gitano outwardly showed confident bravado, deep down he was starting to worry about the cocky Seven. Perhaps this self-assured punk was telling the truth. Maybe he *did* play in high-stakes poker games, and, as such, he might be a genuine threat. Not wanting to ever lose here in Monaco, especially with the Rhombus women around, Carmine Gitano decided to try and scare Seven off. "Besides, if you *should* happen to get lucky and beat me here in front of all these people - well, that might have *severe* consequences. *If* you get my drift."

The Mafioso paused a moment to let his threat sink in. "So, why don't you withdraw and go have a cold drink? I'll pay you your entry fee back, and give you another two grand for your troubles." Gitano stared at Seven, waiting for Seven's submissive reply. It came quickly.

"No thanks, Carmine. I kind of like my chances."

Gitano's face and neck turned red with anger. "Okay, friend, it's your funeral. Don't say I didn't warn you." He left the rest unsaid.

Christopher Seven looked away a moment, determined not to show any trace of fear or respect for this pompous thug. He then turned back toward Gitano and calmly retorted, "Well, good luck, Carm. May the best man win."

"That's right, pal," the Mafia chieftain barked back. "And just remember, Mr. eight or Seven, or whatever number your name is. I *am* the best man, in every respect! They might as well hand me the prize money now!" Once more his disgusting laugh resonated noisily around the table.

Seven struggled to keep his emotions and anger in check, outwardly appearing to laugh off the arrogant bully's stinging words. Inwardly, Seven's blood was already starting to boil. Yet there was also optimistic anticipation as well. The delicious prospect of handing this egotistical tyrant his first loss here. Once more the G5 operative reflected on the theme of the headquarters memo: "The best way to gain Gitano's respect is to beat him at his own game." Seven now resolved to do just that. *So bring it on, tough guy. Bring it on!*

As the persona of the cool, calculating secret agent began taking over his psyche, Christopher Seven heard the ironic words of the pretty blonde croupier ring out loudly, "Mesdames et messieurs – the *big* game is about to unfold!"

Chapter 14

The Game is Texas Hold 'em

The Super Stud agent readied himself for what might one of the most important contest he'd ever undertake. The dealers at both tables began shuffling the cards, readying themselves for the big game. As they did so, a sizable audience made their way closer to the roped-off poker action. Most of them were there to get a firsthand look at the infamous Carmine Gitano. Or, as the media dubbed him, the '*Debonair Don*'.

Seven scrutinized the crowd, noting that the Rhombus girls were nowhere in sight. Perhaps they were gambling in another section of the casino. While he continued to survey the audience, the head croupier, a thin, attractive woman in her forties, with only a slight hint of a French accent, grabbed a handheld microphone. She smiled to the crowd and began calling out the tournament's details to the audience and players.

"Mesdames et messieurs, may I please have your attention. This is our no-limit, 'Winner take all' Texas Hold 'em tournament. All the participants will start with their buy-in, two-thousand dollars in chips. The action begins, and when any contestant loses *all* of his or her chips, that player is eliminated. The remaining three players from each table, six players in all, will then head to our *final table.* There they will battle until only two players are left standing. Those two finalists will then compete 'heads-up' - one against the other. The ultimate winner of that will be our champion and will take home twenty thousand dollars. *Bonne chance* to all!"

Christopher Seven took one last glance over his shoulder toward table number 2, where Carmine Gitano was sitting. The mob boss looked alert and ready, his nostrils flaring out like a racehorse at the starting gate. Everything seemed set now, and the G5 operative knew he'd best forget about Gitano for the moment and concentrate on his *own* playing. That is, if he hoped to meet up with the mobster at the final table.

Even though Seven's competitive nature drove him to win at nearly every challenge he faced, his goal tonight was not necessarily to win the tournament. Although a victory would certainly be sweet, and personally profitable. The objective now was to prove to this Mafia bully that Seven was not some meek playboy. To assert his independence to Gitano, and, if possible, be the player who knocks the arrogant gangster out of the tournament. After that, not much really mattered, although Seven certainly wouldn't mind the twenty-grand first prize. He grinned, sheepishly, wondering what his hometown pastor would think.

Still waiting on the dealers to finish up their shuffling, the G5 operative took in all of the sights, sounds and smells emblematic of most casinos around the world. The spirited yells and groans of the winners and losers, and the clinking of celebratory champagne glasses after a satisfying windfall. All of this was surrounded by the heady scent of expensive perfume, mixed in with the pungent odor of cigar and cigarette smoke. Unlike most American casinos with their preferred nonsmoking policy. The jingling bells, flashing lights and lively mechanical music coming from the numerous slot machines held a Pavlovian sway over their greedy customers. Yet somehow, all of these characteristic components seemed strangely appropriate; lending an air of glamour, adventure and even legitimacy to the patrons and setting.

Turning away from the provocative backdrop, Christopher Seven quickly got his mind back on the poker action. His table included a fairly benign group of affluent oldsters: four men, all French, and one woman, a sociable American in her late fifties. These opponents seemed to be an innocuous set of players, who in all likelihood weren't as practiced in stud poker as he and Carmine Gitano were. *The mob chieftain was probably right,* mused Seven. *My table should be easy pickings, unless I have a terrible run of cards.*

As the first dozen hands unfolded, the Super Stud found that his assessment of the group was, by and large, dead wrong. Although the two oldest men at the table, octogenarians in matching white dinner jackets, were indeed rather amateurish players, his other three opponents turned out to be excellent competitors. The heavyset, middle-aged woman on his right, an experienced poker player from San Francisco named Lucy Kenmore, was particularly skilled. Lucy, a pleasant, talkative lady, informed the men at the table that she frequently played at the Lake Tahoe high-stakes games. The other two players, younger men from Paris, likewise played a flawless, daring game. Both were excellent card players. Seven had his hands full and knew it. It was going to be difficult just to *make* it to the final table of six. Let alone meet up with Carmine Gitano in 'heads-up' action. Nevertheless, the more the game progressed, the more the G5 agent became totally relaxed, enjoying both the competition and the poker itself.

No-limit Texas Hold 'em was another of his favorite card games, mainly because it utilized skill and savvy rather than just pure luck. Each player is dealt two cards face down, called 'pocket cards'. After all of the tablemates receive their pocket cards, betting commences. This is called *pre-flop* betting. If two or more players stay in the pot, the dealer then begins to unfold five more cards. These shared cards are dealt face up as follows: the first three universal cards come out together and are called the *flop*. Further betting commences after the three flop cards are revealed. Again, if two or more contestants remain in the game, the fourth card, called the *turn*, is dealt. Betting and bluffing takes place once more, and if two or more players are still left to fight it out, the fifth and final card, called the *river*, is ultimately dealt.

The object of the game is to make the best *five-card* poker hand out of seven cards. Any combination from your own first two pocket cards and the five communal cards turned over by the dealer. Each player makes the best five-card hand he can from these seven cards, and must decide to 'check', 'bet', or 'fold', accordingly. Either by the strength of a genuinely strong hand or by bluffing your rivals into thinking you have something when you really don't.

The game's obvious dilemma is trying to figure out *what* five-card poker hands your rivals are actually holding; sniffing out bluffs from genuinely strong hands. With a myriad of possibilities, including the advantages of the 'button' and who's 'first to act', the action is nonstop. Antes and 'blinds' before each hand guarantee some sort of pot, and players can go *'all in'* at any time. That is, he or she can increase the bet by the entire amount of their remaining chips. Hence the term 'no limit'.

As predicted, the two older white-jacketed gents on Seven's left were soon out of the game, losing their chips when each of them went 'all in' at foolish times. Their loot was taken fairly evenly by the remaining four players, although Lucy Kenmore seemed to be the table's slight chip leader. Seven, technically running third, wasn't concerned. For though the cards can certainly run hot or cold, and doom even the best of competitors, the player with a proficient ability to *read* his opponents almost always prevails. A skilled Hold 'em competitor can usually spot an opponent's 'tells' as well. Those subtle inadvertent signs like a raised.

An hour later, it was down to Seven, Lucy and the two remaining Frenchmen at table one. Taking a moment to stand up and relax, the Super Stud stretched his arms. Observing him, Lucy Kenmore turned and said with a wry smile, "I don't know about you, but I don't care *who* wins this poker tournament. Just so long as it's not that beast, Carmine Gitano. I played against him here last year. He was extremely nasty and uncouth. And recently, I've read some sordid stories about him in the newspapers. Turns out, he's a notorious gangster! He's quite obnoxious to boot. Every time he wins a hand he pounds his chest and belittles his opponents. The man's an absolute brute."

Lucy gave Seven another smile and glanced down at his imposing stack of chips. "You seem to be a good poker player, young man. If you eventually knock me out, I can live with it." She whispered, mischievously, "As long as you take Gitano down as well."

Seven looked over at the woman's similarly impressive pile of chips and smiled back. "You're a long way from being knocked out, ma'am. Who knows? Maybe you'll take Gitano out yourself."

She grinned, widely. "That would be *real* sweet."

Ten minutes later, Seven won a sizable pot, this one from the youngest of the two remaining French players. It now appeared certain that Seven, the older Frenchman, and Lucy would be the three winners from table 1. Gitano, along with a thin, spectacled Spanish player and a short Japanese gentleman, had already won at table 2. As such, those three were assured of being in the final round. They now sat patiently, waiting to see who their opponents would be. A few moments later, Lucy Kenmore eliminated the younger French player, the lineup was set. It would be Lucy, Seven, and the Frenchman from table one, joining the three Table 2 winners at the final table.

"Would the remaining six players please be seated at table number 2," instructed the casino hostess. More spectators began lining up to watch the action as the woman's voice rang out again, "For the benefit of the audience, I will review the contestants and their stakes. These totals are approximate but very close to the actual counts."

She gestured toward the participants and began her summation. "From table 2 we have Messieurs Seiji Horito, Carlos Mina and Carmine Gitano. Seiji has a chip count of two thousand, eight hundred dollars and Carlos has three thousand, five hundred. Carmine is our current chip leader with five thousand, seven hundred. A hand for these fine players, s'il vous plait." There was a smattering of applause as Gitano stood up and bowed pompously, the only player to do so.

"What a jackass," murmured Lucy Kenmore into Seven's ear. The Super Stud laughed loudly as the casino announcer continued, "And, from table number 1, we have Madame Lucy Kenmore, and Messieurs Maurice Laval and Christopher Seven. Christopher has a stake of four thousand, eight hundred dollars; Maurice has three thousand, nine hundred; and Lucy has acquired three thousand, three hundred."

There was again applause as the smiling hostess added, "And, ladies, since Lucy is the only female in the tournament, we gals will just have to pull for her." Laughter and clapping commenced at this remark, particularly from the women in the crowd. The hostess then pointed toward Christopher Seven. "Lucy has also had the good fortune of sitting next to this amazing-looking gentleman. So even if she loses, she's a winner tonight!" More chuckling ensued along with a few wolf whistles, with a red-faced Seven laughing good-naturedly as well. Carmine Gitano, sitting on Seven's left, merely grunted with disgust, tired of again hearing about the good looks of this insolent young punk. The hostess quickly finished her spiel, "Okay, dealer. Shuffle up and deal!"

The dealer, a short Filipino, dutifully began shuffling the cards. Seven looked out at the spectators and noticed that three tough-looking hoods were now standing in the very front of the crowd. Gitano's Neanderthal security guard, Nalco, was right beside them. The four goons, who looked like extras from the *Godfather* movies, grinned a quick good luck to their boss, putting their thumbs up in support. They then turned their attention toward Seven, glaring directly at him with fierce, ominous stares. It was clear from their menacing expressions that they were trying to warn or intimidate him. Though momentarily taken aback, the Seven tried his best to ignore them.

With the first hand about to commence, Seven silently tried to evaluate the strategies and poker skills of his main rival. Being the natural bully that Gitano was, Seven guessed the arrogant mobster would never stop pushing. Pushing with either his play or his bets. Possibly that could be used against him. However, it could likewise present problems. In Hold 'em poker, an overly aggressive, and/or a reckless player can quickly spell trouble for everyone. Particularly if he's dealt decent cards. Seven would have to be wary of that.

The opening hand finally got underway, with the dealer deftly dealing each player his initial two pocket cards. The Super Stud knew that the first few hands between Gitano and himself would be important tests of tactics and wills. He therefore wanted to get off to a fast start if possible. Mindful of that, he watched attentively as the Japanese player, Seiji, opened with a bet of three-hundred dollars. Looking down at his two cards, Seven glanced at a ten and queen of diamonds. *Middle-of-the-road*, he pondered. *But suited and playable.*

Acting in sequence around the table, each player folded until it came to Carmine Gitano. He quickly raised the bet – six hundred to Seven, who was the last to act. Normally, Seven would have folded at this point, thinking the bet was far too high for what he held. Yet, knowing the mob chief's MO of wanting to dominate everything and everybody, Seven sensed that Gitano's strategy might be to win this initial hand no matter *what* cards he held. Not wanting the bullying Capo to get away with it, if in fact it was a bluff, Seven boldly threw some chips into the pot. "Call."

Seven's reward came immediately on the flop. Six of hearts, ten of spades, and the queen of clubs, giving him a strong two-pair hand. *Yet, how should he play it?* The G5 operative calmly waited, and soon heard Mr. Horito's "check," meaning no bet. This was followed by Gitano's annoyed "check," telling Seven that the mob chieftain likewise didn't want to risk a bet yet. And that his two rivals probably held mediocre hands with no help from the flop.

Sensing weakness from both his opponents, Seven didn't hesitate. "Five hundred more."

Horito folded immediately. Carmine Gitano glared at Seven for a moment and then loudly announced, "Call!"

The next card came, the turn card. It was a jack, a somewhat tricky card for Seven as it meant there were now 'straight' possibilities on the board with the ten, the queen and jack all showing. If Gitano held a king or a nine in his hands, he might be in the driver's seat. If so, Seven could be in immediate trouble. He waited for Gitano's play.

"A hundred bucks," the mobster finally droned, his words coming out dejectedly, without their usual bravado.

"Hmm," Seven mumbled, correctly sensing that such a small, token bet probably meant that his usually overaggressive gangland opponent didn't have much. If Gitano was holding something strong, his raise would have been quicker and much higher; trying to establish dominance right from the start. Then again, Gitano could be playing it craftily. A deceptive bluff was always a possibility. Thinking he probably should increase his bet, but deciding to be wary of an early booby trap, Christopher Seven merely raised another hundred dollars.

"Call," Gitano declared softly, now unable to disguise his frustration.

Seven studied the Mafioso's disgusted tone and expression, confident now that Gitano was bluffing and held nothing. The Super Stud smiled inwardly and waited for the river card.

The dealer flicked out the final communal card, the four of clubs. No possible help to either player. Seven knew he was the winner now and bet accordingly. "Nine hundred dollars." His intention at this juncture was not to slowly entice Gitano into betting more as proper strategy dictated. Seven's calculated aim was pure intimidation. Bully the bully while sending out an early message. Gitano threw his hand in, folding angrily. First round to Seven!

The action continued, non-stop. Two of the final-table players, Carlos Mina and Maurice, the nattily attired French gent, were soon eliminated. Now only four competitors remained.

Seven and Gitano each did well in the hands that followed. Though oddly enough they never really crossed swords again until an hour or so into the final-table action. It was then that a classic hand was dealt, one where Gitano was blessed with a suited queen and ace of hearts. Seven was dealt an ace and king of clubs, the powerful hand called *big slick*. Both players' pocket cards were strong, and Carmine Gitano's opening bet was suitably large; a stout twelve hundred dollars. Gitano's heavy bet caused all of the other players, save Seven, to drop out. The flop came: nine, queen, king - excellent cards for each remaining player.

Another round of betting ensued, and the pot promptly rose to twenty-four hundred dollars. It was on the *turn* card that Seven got burned. It was a second queen giving Gitano three of a kind. The mob king didn't even try to hide his joy at seeing the queen, nor his contempt for his opponent. "That's all, punk," he said with a haughty grin. "Raise! Three thousand."

Had Carmine not been so quick to step on Christopher Seven at this juncture, he might have suckered Seven into dangerously staying in longer. Indeed, the G5 operative had briefly toyed with the idea of going 'all in' with his powerful kings and the ace kicker. But *Don* Gitano had foolishly let his uncontrollable urge to crush and dominate get in the way of proper strategy. Sensing it, Christopher Seven quickly folded. Thanks to the gangster's bullying attitude Seven wasn't completely ruined. Yet, there was no denying it. The Super Stud's bankroll had taken a big hit. Equally agitating, Gitano had annoyingly retaken the chip lead as well.

Another half-hour passed. The G5 agent glanced down at his watch, noting it was nearly midnight. When he looked up, Suzanne and the other three yacht gals had suddenly appeared near the poker table. Wedging themselves in back of the rope, they were right behind Gitano's thugs in the front row. The attractive foursome, dressed to impress, had arrived with a horde of other casino patrons. Like them, the four women had just watched the cabaret show in an outer lounge. When Suzanne realized that Christopher Seven was playing at the same table as her gangland host, she seemed taken aback. Well aware that the volatile Gitano was savagely competitive and hated losing at *anything*. In fact, Carmine had told her to plan a black-tie poker 'victory' party on his yacht for tomorrow evening. She'd already invited several people.

Suzanne now wondered how the Mafia boss would react if he lost. Especially if he lost to *this* brash stranger. She, and two of her cohorts, Anita and Terry, didn't really care about Seven's eventual wellbeing. They just didn't want anything to spoil their *immediate* notion of 'showing him off' for a week or two.

Without telling Seven or Gitano yet, they'd already planned some tentative plans; to try and utilize Christopher Seven as 'window dressing'. Manipulate him with the lure of a brief jaunt on Carmine's fabulous yacht as bait. The three of them were planning to drag Seven to several of the Rivera hot spots. Smugly display him as one of their coveted 'trophy catches', while having some *private* fun with him as well. Afterwards, they'd coldly discard him like they did all of their 'trophy males'. Accordingly, the Rhombus women couldn't care less *what* Gitano or Nalco's men did to Seven later on. Just so long as they'd have him undamaged for a few glorious weeks.

In truth, only one of the Rhombus foursome, the reclusive Doreen Lacy, was actually worried for Seven's safety. She watched with genuine trepidation, biting her nails nervously. Doreen realized that if Carmine Gitano got angry enough, he was quite capable of having some of his thugs make sure that this great looking stranger wound up in a hospital for a long time. Or perhaps they'd order up something even *worse* for him. She'd seen firsthand what Gitano's men could do. Thinking on that possibility, and stirred by the strange, inexplicable infatuation she had for this man Seven, Doreen nervously continued watching. Hoping against hope that nothing ominous would take place afterward.

~

Twenty minutes later, there were just three poker combatants left in the tournament. One of them, the spirited Lucy Kenmore, though playing gamely against her two male opponents, had fallen to a *short-stacked* distant third. Gitano held the lead but it was now a narrow one, much to the gangster's annoyance. Sure enough, Lucy finally lost her remaining chips, defeated by a Gitano flush after she'd gone 'all in' with aces.

"Oh, that's too bad, Lucy," the hostess announced in a sympathetic tone. And then, "Mesdames et messieurs. How about a big hand for the little lady, Miss Lucy Kenmore! Nice job, Lucy."

The audience applauded warmly as Lucy stood up to leave. She extended her hand to shake with Gitano, who rudely pretended not to see it. Then, shaking hands with Seven, she commented loud enough for Carmine to hear, "I still think you'll beat this guy. Best of luck, Chris."

"Thanks, Lucy." Seven gave her a supportive smile just as the casino lady went into another speech.

"And so, ladies and gentlemen, we've come to 'heads-up' play – mano a mano. This will be for *all* the marbles, as the Americans say. Our two remaining players, Mr. Seven and Mr. Gitano, will now compete for the championship and the first-prize jackpot. Winner takes all!"

After waiting a moment she turned toward the spectators and announced, "Mr. Gitano is our chip leader with a little over thirteen thousand dollars, while Mr. Seven has nearly eleven thousand. It's still anybody's game. Good luck, gentlemen."

So this is it, the Super Stud reflected. *It's come down to Gitano and me. I guess it was meant to be!*

Chapter 16

The River of No Return

The opening few hands between the two poker finalists went fairly routinely. Whoever bet first usually took the pot. Seven knew that 'heads-up' play was different from all the other rounds. With just two players in the game, it was extremely important to stay aggressive.

A case in point was their sixth hand. Seven was dealt a suited ace and jack of hearts, a decent, solid beginning. Gitano's pocket cards were the 4 of spades and 9 of clubs, unsuited rubbish. However, Carmine Gitano shrewdly remained in the game, even raising a small amount. Wary, but liking his ace, Seven called.

The flop came: ace, king, jack, giving Seven a powerful two pair hand. Yet, Gitano raised $1,000. Surprised and concerned by the gangster's large bet, and fearing that his opponent likewise held an ace and possibly a king too, Seven merely called.

The turn card was another king. Carmine Gitano quickly responded with a hefty $3,000 bet. The G5 agent was flabbergasted and felt certain the mob boss held at least a matching king for three of a kind, beating Seven's two pair. Conceivably, Gitano had an ace as well, which would give him a monster full house. Although he didn't know it, Seven still had the much better hand.

The Super Stud paused a moment and then decided that he just couldn't chance matching such a large bet. Certainly not with a second king showing and Carmine's swift, assertive bet. His gangland opponent most likely held a better two pair, or quite possibly three of a kind. Maybe even a 'full boat'. After a moment of contemplation, Christopher Seven figured it was best to live and fight another day. He reluctantly threw in his cards, giving Gitano a sizable pile of chips.

Immediately after Seven's fold, the mobster, with theatrical flair, and also wishing to rub it in, displayed his hole cards to the crowd. He then started laughing, thrilled with his successful bluff. Though inwardly furious, the G5 operative showed no emotion. Although he did estimate that Gitano now had him by at least $4,500. Any more rounds like this one and it would soon be over.

Four more hands ensued, the players winning two each. With the odds now being in Gitano's favor because of his larger stack of chips, Seven knew he'd have to force the action if he wanted to win. He sighed softly and waited for the deal.

In every game of no-limit poker, there comes a time or a hand that can potentially be a huge momentum changer, a decisive and unexpected turning point. It can be a subtle play, a clever bluff, a 'bad beat', or perhaps a monster pot win. For Carmine Gitano and Christopher Seven, it happened fifteen minutes past midnight.

The Super Stud was down to approximately $8,100 in chips. Gitano's chip lead had ballooned to almost $16,000. With nearly a two-to-one chip advantage, the Mafia chieftain would soon be able to start playing power poker and squeeze the lifeblood out of his opponent. Seven recognized this as he looked down at his pocket cards, a miserable 4 and 9 of hearts. Carmine likewise glanced at his hand, which wasn't much better; a 10 of clubs and a 6 of spades. With a bluff in mind, Seven opened the betting, putting in a 'feel out' wager of two hundred dollars.

Gitano called. There would be a flop. The three communal cards came; the 4 of spades, the 6 of diamonds, and the 10 of diamonds. To his surprise, Carmine Gitano had drawn two pair. Seven had drawn one.

This time, the mobster played it smart and merely checked. The ploy worked. Seven, perceiving weakness, thought it a good time to bluff. He boldly raised Gitano's bid by $800, although he only held a feeble pair of 4's, pairing his pocket 4 with the lowest card of the flop. Gitano hesitated a moment, as if he held nothing, and then finally called. It was a good piece of acting and it totally fooled Seven. Both men leaned back in their chairs and waited for the next card.

Out it came, a jack of diamonds, no help for either player. Gitano, still being cute as he set his trap, hesitated a minute and then announced, "Check" in an annoyed tone. The unsuspecting Seven, again sensing vulnerability, immediately tried to steal the pot with another bluff. Buying into Gitano's hesitation ploy, the Super Stud raised a thousand. He was thus bitterly disappointed when Gitano, once again playacting, deliberated a moment and finally mouthed a rather tentative, "Call."

The pot was now well over $4,000, with Seven's reserves rapidly dwindling. Losing this hand would virtually cost him the contest. The sweating G5 agent continued to stay calm trying hard to hide his disgust at the unfolding events. He'd obviously picked the wrong time to bluff and was now about to pay for it. Like a condemned man walking to the gallows, Christopher Seven resignedly waited for the final 'river' card. The dealer flicked it over. It was another diamond, a queen. There were now four diamonds on the board. If Carmine Gitano held a diamond in his hand, he would now have an unbeatable flush. As it was, he undoubtedly had something far better than Seven's pathetic pair of fours. The mobster's betting would soon tell the story.

Fortunately for Seven it was Gitano who had to act first, and the Mafia chieftain now had his own problems. He, too, became very apprehensive when the fourth diamond came out, thinking the same thought as Seven: that his opponent was holding a fifth diamond and had just made his flush. The two pair that Gitano held, relatively small pairs at that, were nothing compared to a flush. In addition, Christopher Seven had bet heavily and quickly each time, most likely waiting for five diamonds all along. In all probability, Seven had indeed just made his flush with this last communal card, and now held an unbeatable hand.

Carmine reluctantly decided to 'check' and see what his opponent would do. "Check," the gangster again announced, this time showing genuine displeasure as he angrily stubbed out his cigar.

Up until now, the Mafioso had played his hand flawlessly. But checking irately with a massive pot on the table, was a very telling move. Especially from a forceful tyrant like *Don* Gitano. Knowing the mob king's propensity to quickly pounce on an opponent whenever he could, Gitano's annoyed "check" had broadcast weakness; obvious anger at this last river card. True, it could also have been a cleverly calculated move, one made to draw the remaining chips from Seven. But that type of systematic strategy just didn't fit *Don* Carmine Gitano. The whole night he had swiftly pressed on any monster hands. Immediately stepping on the other players whenever he'd drawn good cards.

A leopard doesn't change his spots, thought Seven. *If Gitano had made something big with that last card, he would have gleefully jumped on me.*

Reading a move such as this was the essence of no-limit poker. It was the difference between a good and an average player. Christopher Seven didn't hesitate, certain that had Gitano made a flush, or anything *really* good, there would have been undisguised triumph in his eyes. Along with a prompt desire to punish Seven in front of the crowd. Carmine Gitano was a decent poker player, but he was an egotistical dictator first and foremost.

There was no wavering in Seven's voice. "All in," he announced, knowing if the mobster called him now, the game, due to Seven's risky strategy, would be over.

Gitano slumped back in his chair. *So*, he surmised, *Seven has obviously just made his flush or he wouldn't be risking everything now.* The gangster thought on it again. *Or has he? Is this guy bluffing in order to get back at me for doing that to him? If I call now and he is bluffing, I've won.*

As the Mafia capo fingered his chips as if to call, the Super Stud's heart nearly skipped a beat. If Seven was called now, it was curtains!

The wily mobster again hesitated. Seven, now sweating profusely, tried to decipher why his pushy rival wasn't quickly acting one way or the other; either with a 'call' or a 'fold'. Uncharacteristically, the usually overaggressive Gitano was thinking things over. He knew he'd still have the chip lead if he folded to Seven now. Yet, if he matched Seven's 'all in' and then lost the pot, his annoying rival would suddenly become the chip leader, something that was psychologically devastating to the *Don*.

Carmine certainly didn't want to lose the chip lead now. Not with his four attractive yacht guests, his loyal bodyguards, and all of the other spectators watching.

No, Gitano finally decided. *It's too risky. Better to fold now than let the crowd see Seven take the pot and the chip lead with his flush. At least by folding now, I'll be able to steal some of his thunder with a good lay down.* Gitano looked directly over at his rival and announced loud enough for the crowd to hear, "I know you're probably bluffing, Seven, but it's no matter. I'll still have plenty of chips if I fold and I can easily beat a chump like you with those." With that, he folded his cards.

Christopher Seven, with a new lease on his poker life, calmly scooped up the large pile of chips. Although it was tempting to imitate Gitano's antics and show the crowd that he too could bluff, Christopher Seven made it a point of *never* showing his hole cards. To him, that was the ploy of an amateur; not a serious poker player. Instead, he responded by glancing over at the four yacht gals.

The game continued on. Surprisingly, most of the crowd had stayed around to watch, despite the late hour. Smelling blood, the engrossed spectators had sensed something personal going on between these two men, something that transcended a mere game of cards. Yet, who would come out on top: the notorious gangster or the handsome stranger?

The four yacht ladies also watched intently. Standing near Nalco, Gitano's strong-arm goon, they could hear the muscular hit-man hissing angrily every time Christopher Seven won a hand from the 'boss'. These women knew that it would be impossible to control Nalco's wrath if Seven managed to win the contest. Even so, they continued watching with a curious mixture of anxiousness and sadistic anticipation.

The next few rounds went back and forth, with the Super Stud finally pulling ahead in the chip count on one memorable hand, a wild round in which his two small pair beat Gitano's kings much to the gangster's displeasure. On it went, until the end came at exactly 1:00 a.m.

Both players began the final hand by getting tremendous pocket cards. Seven calmly looked down at two powerful queens. It was all he could do to hold back his satisfaction. But Gitano had been dealt an even *better* pair, no-limit poker's Holy Grail; a monster pair of aces!

While Seven again peeked at his queen of clubs and queen of hearts, Gitano likewise glanced down at his two marvelous bullets. Both combatants were now thinking the same thing: *How I do I reel my opponent in without scaring him off?*

With a huge smile on the inside but a blank expression on his face, the G5 agent opened the betting with $500. Doing so after Carmine's crafty 'check', hoping he wouldn't frighten the mobster into folding. After purposely pausing a moment, Gitano merely 'called', also playing his fabulous pocket cards in an uncharacteristically low-key fashion. The flop followed immediately. Two 4's and the queen of spades, helping Gitano get two pair but giving Christopher Seven a monster full house. *This might be it,* the G5 agent silently mused. *Just play it cool, Seven.*

"Six hundred," Gitano bid, in a low, composed voice. Glancing at his pocket queens for a third time, and then looking back at the 4's on the board, Seven called after his own contrived hesitancy.

The dealer waited a moment before turning over the fourth card. Unbelievably for Gitano, the turn card was an ace. Now, he too had a full house, one even *better* than Seven's full boat. Three aces over a pair of 4's! Yet, for once, the bullying mobster didn't pounce on his opponent. Instead, *Don* Carmine nonchalantly looked away a moment, playing with his snifter of cognac. "Check," he said, unemotionally. It was a superb act of restraint by the normally assertive capo and it totally duped Seven.

The unsuspecting Super Stud stared at the board, now concentrating on the ace that had just been dealt. Even if Gitano held an ace in the hole, giving him a strong two pair with the aces and the communal 4's on the board, it wouldn't be enough to beat Seven's full house. And if the bullying mob chief had anything better to start with, he would have already acted and squashed Christopher Seven like a bug.

Seven then reflected on his own cards, wrongly confident that he now had a nearly unbeatable hand: a loaded full house, queens over 4's. This was the game winning hand Seven had waited for all evening. *Yet how should I play it,* he again asked himself. *To best reel Gitano in? Should I simply make a small raise or should I go 'all in' and hope he follows?*

What Seven didn't suspect, however, was that, for him, the ace that had just come out on the board was the *worst* possible card that could have been turned over at this decisive moment. It had given his obnoxious opponent an even better full boat, aces over 4's. It was now the bullying gangster who had to force himself to stay cool and composed. This he did, admirably and uncharacteristically, like a spider watching a fly from afar.

"Another six hundred," the mob chief calmly announced, now hoping Seven wouldn't be scared off.

With only a trace of concern at Carmine's bold bid, the Super Stud studied the board again, wanting to be absolutely sure before going 'all in'. Staring at the ace and the two 4's, he once more played out the hand in his mind. If Gitano held a queen or an ace in the hole, it would give him a strong two pair with the 4's. Yet, two pair doesn't beat a full boat.

Seven wiped his brow and continued thinking on it. There were two other possibilities. Perhaps Gitano held another four. That would give him three of a kind, another good hand. But still not strong enough to win. Lastly, there was the chance that the mobster held both an ace *and* a 4. Gitano's three 4's over a pair of aces would then make a full house. But that particular full house wouldn't win either. Seven's full boat, with three queens on the top was still higher.

All of these thoughts now raced through the agent's analytical mind. The unsuspecting operative never dreamed that Carmine Gitano had initially been dealt the best pocket cards of them all, a huge pair of aces. If Gitano had been holding two aces, Seven was certain that the arrogant gangster would have bullied and pressed with them right from the start. Something the mob king hadn't done at all this hand. The now confident Seven once again reminded himself: *A leopard doesn't change his spots.*

"All in," Seven finally proclaimed, drawing a gasp from the spectators. They knew that the contest was over if Gitano likewise 'called'. Someone was going to win when the cards were turned over, and the crowed wanted to see who it'd be. And how they'd react

If Seven won the hand, Gitano would be out of chips and done for. And conversely, if Gitano won this hand, Christopher Seven would only have a few token chips left. Barely enough to ante. Similarly, the game would likewise be over, with Carmine the winner.

How would these two men reply to the outcome, whatever it was? Either way, the crowd wanted to see it play out.

"Call!" Gitano loudly exclaimed, drawing a gasp from the spectators.

What Christopher Seven had just heard initially thrilled him. But then, when he looked over and saw the strange, confident smirk on *Don* Gitano's angular face, Seven's euphoria quickly faded. An inexplicable feeling of dread suddenly came over him, something akin to a sixth sense. The Super Stud quickly dismissed the feeling, knowing he couldn't have imagined a better scenario. Here he was the slight chip leader, holding a monster full house. His abhorrent opponent had just called "all in" with an obviously lesser hand. This was what the G5 operative had wished for all night. He smiled confidently and sat back in his chair.

The casino hostess quickly made her way to the side of the table, again carrying her handheld microphone. "Mesdames et messieurs! Ladies and gentlemen. I think we all know that this is the moment of truth. I will now turn the cards over and call them out for the spectators."

The audience held its collective breath as the woman turned Seven's cards over first. When she called the pocket cards, "two queens", the audience roared, with Lucy Kenmore screaming out an excited "Yes!"

"Mr. Seven has a full house, queens over 4's," the hostess proclaimed. There was a big round of applause, with almost everyone in the crowd certain that Seven had just won the poker contest.

Christopher Seven looked over at Gitano, fully expecting anger and resignation. Yet, astonishingly, Gitano was grinning from ear to ear. The volatile gangster showed no signs of rage at all. Only a look of triumph.

Worried beads of sweat slowly trickled down Seven's side. Had he outsmarted himself? Been *too* confident? As if to answer his queries, Gitano's magnificent hole cards were slowly revealed by the croupier and the Super Stud quickly saw why his abhorrent opponent was grinning. The hostess had shockingly revealed Gitano's *better* hand! She too was stunned by the two pocket aces. Then, quickly composing herself, she dramatically announced, "With two pocket aces, Mr. Gitano *also* has a full house; a higher one, aces over fours. Mr. Gitano is now in the lead."

The beaming Mafia *Don* looked at the crowd and winked at his four lovely yacht guests. He then gave his bodyguards a jubilant 'thumbs up' and turned back to face Seven. "That's all, punk. You're finished."

Seven's heart fell to the floor, knowing that he'd completely misread his rival. The usually overassertive Gitano had held pocket aces the whole time. Yet never once had he bullied or pushed with them, totally contrary to his usual pattern. The wily leopard had indeed changed his spots!

For a full thirty seconds, Christopher Seven sat motionless. The shock of quickly going from victory to defeat had thoroughly numbed him. Gitano hooted loudly, laughing at Seven with all the contempt and hatred a man can show. The mob king bounced up and down in his chair like a giddy child. He again waved to the yacht girls, who were grinning back at him, their thumbs likewise held high.

The dejected Seven stared blankly at the far wall, not really perceiving anything going on around him. *So much for gaining this Mafioso's respect,* the stunned G5 operative mused.

The Super Stud was about to stand up and shake hands with his hated rival when he heard the casino hostess announce, "There is still the formality of the fifth card, folks," she said politely. "And, should he lose this hand, Mr. Seven will still have a few chips left."

Seven didn't care about that or anything else now. His few remaining chips would be meaningless. He'd barely be able to ante. Ironically, it was this final card, the river card that would officially confirm Gitano's insufferable victory. For Seven and his present mission it would be the 'river' all right. The river of *no* return'.

The disheartened agent shrugged his shoulders and sighed. The poker loss was of no importance now. His Super Stud mission was. And it was almost certainly over now. Or at least critically weakened. Carmine Gitano had crushed him like all of the others who got in the way. Seven simply wanted to slink out of the casino and never come back.

Now what? Seven silently wondered. *Try to somehow make up or suck up to this loathsome bully? Or just take it on the chin and try to work solely on the four women if I can? Yet, without Gitano's approval and interest, that would most likely prove impossible.*

While the drained operative gloomily thought on it, there was a great roar from the crowd! Seven was quickly startled to attention like a man breaking through the surface of icy waters. Not concentrating on the game, Seven hadn't even noticed the dealer turning up the last card, the *river* card. As his eyes fell on the card, his brain struggled to register the sight. It was a queen, a *fourth* glorious queen, giving Seven *four* of a kind and a miraculous victory! The Super Stud had incredibly pulled off a win on the very last card. The river had come through after all. An astonishing four of a kind that beat Gitano's formidable full house!

Quite a few in the audience, especially the French contingent, broke out in a loud cheer. Lucy Kenmore kissed the stranger she was standing beside. Several people came over to the table and slapped Seven on the back. The G5 agent nodded back and slowly collected himself, lifting his gaze toward his beaten opponent. It was now the mob boss who was in stunned denial, as the fate of the two men had astonishingly been reversed. Gitano suddenly found himself where Seven had just been. In the midst of a poker player's worst nightmare. Certain triumph had turned into a torturous 'bad beat' on the *'river'.*

Carmine Gitano sat frozen in his chair, his mouth wide open in disbelief. For a brief moment Christopher Seven actually empathized with his defeated rival. Yet Seven knew this last-minute victory over Gitano was significant for several reasons. Hopefully, it could help get the Super Stud on equal footing with the still stunned mob boss.

Christopher Seven held out his hand to shake, and, surprisingly, Gitano took it. But then, the mobster's face transformed abruptly, his lips curving into an evil, fearsome scowl. Slowly, Gitano whispered into Seven's ear over the applause of the crowd, "Don't count on spending any of the prize money, friend."

Then, with only swift revenge on his mind, Carmine Gitano, flanked by his strapping bodyguards, stormed away angrily, ignoring the outstretched hands and the calls of commiseration from the yacht girls.

Christopher Seven watched closely as the seething Mafia boss stormed out of the casino. The ominous warning Gitano had whispered in Seven's ear made the Super Stud rethink what, if anything, he'd accomplished via his poker gambit. True, as the headquarters memo suggested, Carmine Gitano seemed to be a kingpin who only respected those who battled him hard. Those who gave as good as they got. Yet, Gitano's threatening words still resonated in Seven's ear, and there had been no grudging respect in them. Only hatred and anger. No doubt about it. The Mafioso's fuming farewell had sounded like a genuinely dangerous threat.

Thinking on it again, Seven felt growing apprehension in the pit of his stomach. To be threatened by a powerful Mafia *Don* was nothing to take lightly. These gangland capos didn't make idle threats. And they certainly had the manpower to do something about it. Yet, was it *really* a definite warning? Or simply a case of an overly competitive bully letting off some steam after losing?

Before the G5 agent could dwell on it further, his thoughts were cut short by Suzanne, who had just edged up to the now deserted poker table with her three attractive girlfriends.

"Well, well," she caustically greeted, shaking her finger at Seven. "Now you've gone and done it. Carmine will be impossible to live with after this poker hoedown. No telling *what* he'll do."

"I'll say," echoed Anita. "If I were you, I'd keep my door locked and my windows closed when you go to bed tonight."

"Oh, maybe it's not as bad as all that," Seven replied, trying to reassure himself as well as the four women. "Mr. Gitano probably just doesn't like losing. Most competitive poker players are like that. Me included."

"That's what you think," Terry Harrigan exclaimed, pushing her way closer to Seven. "I don't know if you realize who you're dealing with here, handsome. But Carmine Gitano is not merely some timid Boy Scout enjoying a friendly game of gin rummy. He's one of the most powerful men in the world. And he's got several, ah, *associates*, who don't like seeing the chief shown up. They know their boss can't stand losing – *ever*. Whether it's in business, cards or with women."

The other three girls stared somberly as Terry continued, "And one more thing, friend. Carmine has a long arm and a lot of robust *acquaintances* when it comes to getting even with those who show him up, if you get my drift. Plus Carm's got a terrible temper."

"I'll say," Suzanne reiterated. "You're lucky he didn't take a swipe at you right here at the table."

Seven felt he'd better take this a lot more seriously and promptly decided to appeal to the women. "Gee, I never dreamed it was anything like that. Naturally, I've read about Mr. Gitano in the newspapers. But I thought most of his strong-arm stuff was just 'Hollywood exaggeration."

There were four simultaneous sighs at Seven's naivety as he lamely continued, "As for this poker contest, I was only trying to win a few bucks – that's all. I didn't think Carmine would mind. Matter of fact, I didn't even know he was playing here till *after* I signed up for the tournament. Besides, there were ten other players who could have beaten him."

"Yeah, but *you're* the one who did," warned Suzanne. "And that's all that matters to Carmine now."

Christopher Seven thought on it a moment and then, in a sudden flash of inspiration, decided that this Gitano thing might actually be used to the mission's advantage if played correctly. He rubbed his chin contemplatively and asked, "Do you suppose you girls could help smooth things out for me? Tell Carmine I didn't mean anything personal?" Seven looked at the women, pleadingly. "I wouldn't want him or his brawny friends to do anything rash. And believe it or not, I'd still like to tour that fabulous yacht of his. Especially if you four would be around."

Terry Harrigan, who, along with Anita and Suzanne, was likewise planning to use the bad blood between Gitano and Seven to their 'male trophy-hunting' advantage, stared at the Super Stud rather intently. There seemed to be a trace of uncertainty in her eyes.

The G5 operative watched Terry's expression closely as she answered, "Maybe we could help. But then again, *why* should we?"

Seven smiled. "Well, for one thing, I'd certainly like to spend some more time with you girls like you mentioned at the restaurant." He winked at them. "What was it you called it? - *Quality* time. The four of you seem to know where the action and fun is around Monte Carlo. I'm sure we'd have a good time finding it together." Hoping not to overplay his hand, he quickly added, "But I guess that's impossible after tonight. Seems I've really messed things up."

"Maybe, maybe not," Terry consoled. "Carmine's lost before, no matter what he told you. True, you're not one of his favorite people at the moment, but perhaps we can fix some of that. Truth be told, Carm owes us a favor or two. And what we girls want, we usually get. Even from Carmine Gitano."

She glanced at Anita, Doreen and Suzanne and then back at Seven before informing, "You're just lucky we decided earlier that you'd make a good plaque on our wall. You see, friend, we pride ourselves on collecting the best-looking male companions. Only the cream of the crop. And you obviously fit that bill. At least for the short run."

"Yeah," Anita further explained. "We enjoy making the women we run into green with envy. Especially those haughty Riviera jetsetters. That's why we only drive the most expensive cars, wear the best clothes and jewelry, and stay aboard the biggest yacht there is." She looked straight at him. "And why we only stockpile the best men to flaunt."

"Things might be fixed with Carmine," Terry added. "But if they are, you'll owe us *big* time."

Seven smiled meekly as Terry added, "In any case, you'd better lay low for a while and let us handle the peacemaking. If I know Carmine, he's probably already planning a little something for you. And it sure ain't a celebration party."

"I understand," said Seven. "Just let me know when the coast is clear."

Suddenly, Doreen, by far the quietest and shyest of the group, spoke up. Seven had never even heard her speak before. "Gee, Terry," Doreen timidly asked. "Do you think we should even *try* talking to Carmine?"

She glanced at Seven, worriedly. It was an odd expression of fear and affection and the G5 operative wondered if Doreen was somehow trying to give him a subtle warning. "Perhaps this fellow should just bolt," Doreen implored. "Get out of Monte Carlo as fast and as far as he can. Things might get dangerous for him. You know Carm and his people."

The other three girls glared at her angrily.

"Keep your mouth shut, Doreen!" hissed Suzanne. "Just let Terry handle things."

"Oh, I'm – I'm sorry," Doreen apologized. "I didn't mean to…"

"Don't mind Doreen, handsome," an obviously irritated Terry Harrigan cut in. "Sometimes Miss Doreen talks too much." Terry frowned at her bashful, blonde-haired colleague. "I've warned her before about it. Warned her that her careless trap may get her into *real* trouble one of these days."

Doreen blushed and hung her head shamefacedly as Seven silently pondered, *This beautiful, yet awkward woman, Doreen, seems to be much softer than her friends. She doesn't seem as polished or as callous as her three partners. If these yacht women are indeed Rhombus, somehow the serene Doreen didn't seem like she'd be involved in it.*

The alert Super Stud immediately began formulating plans to make Doreen his first conquest. Single her out for attack, much like a lion stalking the weakest antelope in the herd. With a friendly smile toward her, Seven softly assured, "It's okay, Doreen. And thanks for caring."

He gently put his hand on her shoulder and added, "Don't worry. I've been in trouble with angry gigolos and spouses before." He grinned widely. "Mainly jealous husbands who came home unexpectedly. Believe me, I've jumped out of quite a few windows."

The girls, delighted with Seven's faux confession, all began laughing, quickly quelling the awkward strain that had cropped up between them. "I *bet* you've jumped through plenty at that," chuckled Terry. Then, with a glance at her diamond-studded *Piaget* watch, she advised, "We'd better get back to the *Zephyr* pronto, girls. That is, if we're going to do this hunk any good. Carmine's probably back on his boat already, steaming, cussing and plotting."

Terry Harrigan motioned toward her three partners. "Maybe we can ease things for you, Seven. Start off by telling Carm that you weren't gunning for him personally. Just trying to win the prize money. I'll also remind him that we girls want to have you around a while; preferably in *one* piece. He'll understand that part of things. Carmine's well aware that we go in for attractive 'toys'." Terry shrugged her shoulders. "Anyway, we'll see. Hopefully, it'll work out. Like I said, Carm owes us."

"Yeah," echoed Anita. "Carmine may play it rough at times, but he can also be a gentleman when he wants to be. Especially with us." Anita raised her eyebrows. "Although *this* request might be tough for him to swallow. Anyhow, just leave things to Terry. She knows Carmine best."

Seven smiled his gratitude. "I will. And thanks for the help. I feel a lot better."

"Hold the phone there, friend," barked Terry. "I didn't say you've been pardoned yet. I simply said we'd *try*." She gestured toward the casino's front door. "Let's get moving, girls. If we're gonna try saving this guy's bacon we better begin right away." Terry looked back at Seven. "See you around, friend. If anything positive breaks, I'll call you." She grinned wryly. "If not, I'll bring roses to the funeral. By the way, where you staying?"

"The *Hotel de Paris*. Across from the casino."

"Okay, I'll phone you there. And remember, mister. If by some miracle we do get you on Mr. Gitano's good side, we *always* collect after a favor." With that, Terry and her three alluring colleagues sauntered out of the casino and into their waiting Rolls Royce limousine.

After watching them depart, Seven heard a man's voice call out to him. "Pardon, s'il vous plait, Monsieur Seven. Would you please come with me for your prize money?"

The Super Stud looked up to see the casino manager, a tall distinguished gentleman clad in a perfectly tailored tuxedo.

"Of course," Christopher Seven replied, suddenly recalling his pastor's adage about gambling, and hoping he hadn't been coveting this first-place prize money all along. "I'd almost forgot about it."

Seven followed the tuxedoed manager into a back office, where the casino exec explained the payment options. "I can write you a check for the entire twenty thousand now, which you'll be able to cash at the hotel's bank first thing tomorrow morning. Or, if you'd prefer, I can give you eight thousand dollars in cash right now, along with a promissory bank note for the remainder. I assure you we've never welched on a payment in over 120 years."

Seven grinned his acknowledgment as the casino honcho went on, "If you choose the *second* option, I can then wire the rest of your prize money to your personal bank in America." Dutifully attempting to drum up fresh business for his casino, the exec added, "That way, you'll still have a nice bankroll with which to play while here in Monaco. Plus a sizable balance waiting for you back home."

"That second option would be better for me," Seven advised. "I wouldn't want to carry around the entire twenty grand while I'm on holiday. Eight thousand is fine." He grinned. "I'll probably just give it back to you at the casino tables anyway."

The manger bowed slightly and took out a short form from his bottom desk draw. "Certainement, Monsieur." He passed Seven a sheet of instructions. "Please list your hometown bank details, or wherever you want your balence sent." Knowing that a contract from the famed Monte Carlo casino was rock solid, Seven sat down and began writing.

With business taken care of, the casino manager casually asked about Seven's future plans. Assuming that everything he said now would eventually wind up in the ears of the mob families, including Gitano's, the G5 operative answered evasively. "I'm still not sure, yet. In all likelihood, I'll probably be leaving Monaco soon. I'd like to visit some friends in Spain, although I haven't been able to contact them yet." He paused, pensively. "If that doesn't work out, perhaps I'll stay a few more weeks here in your beautiful principality."

"Trés bien, Monsieur."

Christopher Seven bowed, courteously. "Either way, I'm sure I'll be back to your fine gaming hall."

"Merveilleux, Monsieur. By the way, would you like an armed escort to your hotel? I have an excellent security team who pride themselves on protecting our large winners."

Seven laughed. "No thanks. Monte Carlo seems civilized enough. And I've only got a short walk back to my hotel." He chuckled again. "But if this was Atlantic City, I might take you up on it!"

With that, the casino exec bowed again and handed Seven a slip for $8,000 to bring to the main cashier window. Smiling politely, the casino manager observed attentively as his handsome customer left the office. Waiting a moment till Christopher Seven was out of sight, the casino man immediately picked up his telephone and made an important call.

~

After a celebratory glass of champagne in the chic casino bar, this to toast the thick wad of house money now in his wallet, Seven decided he wouldn't press his luck any further. Instead he decided to take a leisurely outdoor stroll and then head back to his room. Perhaps a bit of exercise might help bring on some sleepiness, as the agent was still wide awake, wired from all of the pent-up events.

Departing via the small rear exit doors in the back of the gaming hall, rather than the opulent main entrance in the front, Seven sauntered past the casino's lovely floodlit gardens and then headed down a small hill by way of several empty stairwells. The cooling night breeze from above was calm and fresh, and it was good to finally be out of the casino's smoky atmosphere. Happy to stretch his legs after the long session at the poker table, Seven headed toward his hotel to finally call it a night. But *what* a night!

Taking a deep breath of the clean air coming in from the sea, Seven casually surveyed his surroundings, noting he was somewhere between his own hotel and the *Fairmont, Monte Carlo*, the most Americanized of Monte Carlo's hotels. It was now well past 2:00 a.m. and not a soul was in sight on this beautiful, tranquil evening.

The Super Stud looked up at the twinkling stars, wondering what they held for him in the coming days. Shaking his head, he again replayed his improbable, last-second poker victory. It had been a near thing and he hoped something productive would come from it. Pausing a moment to admire the stunning full moon gleaming over the dark, cobalt water of the Mediterranean, the agent reluctantly turned and headed toward his hotel.

Ambling up a small knoll, he unhurriedly made his way toward the *Hotel de Paris,* passing through several back alleyways and deserted side streets. The last of these alleys, a long, narrow passageway with a singular lamppost, had a rounded sign at its entrance. On it were a painted arrow and a short message in both French and English stating that the *Hotel de Paris* was five blocks up ahead. With fatigue finally catching up with him, the now sleepy operative was glad that he was only a few minutes from his bed and some blessed sleep.

Seven was about halfway through the final underground alley, when suddenly, from out of the darkness, a heavily accented voice yelled out from behind him, breaking the peaceful stillness.

"Hey you'a, Seven. Freeze!"

The Super Stud spun around to face the voice, and when he did, a bright beam of light hit him in the eyes, temporarily blinding him. Then, materializing from out of the shadows, the apelike silhouette of Nalco, Carmine Gitano's strapping personal bodyguard, appeared. He was holding a large flashlight and was accompanied by his three brawny sidekicks. The same three thugs that Seven had seen watching the poker tournament. One of them, a fearsome-looking character with an ugly pockmarked face, was carrying a thick blackjack. The other two were armed with small bullwhips. All four men were grinning with malicious intent.

As they slowly began approaching him, Christopher Seven mumbled a silent prayer and prepared for the worst!

Chapter 17

'20-Cent' Beating

Seven shook his head. So much for Terry and the other girls 'saving his bacon', he glumly mused. This ambush had obviously been planned the moment Seven won the poker tournament. Shocked by the sudden appearance of Gitano's henchmen, the Super Stud tried not to panic. Hoping he could somehow reason with them, Seven answered back, "Hi there, Nalco. Where's Carmine and the girls?"

"Never mind 'a dat. We wanna have a little talk wit you." Nalco gestured toward the other men. "And we got a *present* for a you too. A little *gift* from the boss. So, what you say we take'a little ride." The gangster grinned, showing several missing teeth. "And when'a we get back, maybe your face ain't gonna be so pretty no more. Maybe you ain't gonna be alive no more either." The four goons erupted in laughter and continued approaching.

Christopher Seven watched them closely. Sweat trickled down his sides and he could actually feel his pulse quicken. *This is real trouble*, he warned himself. *And there's no sense trying to run away. This alleyway is too narrow and too dark for any escape attempts. Yelling for help won't work either. Gitano's probably paid off every cop in the neighborhood to stay away from this area tonight.* The anxious operative frantically tried to size up his slim options. *Perhaps I can talk my way out by using Terry and her friends as allies.*

The four thugs were now face-to-face with him and Seven felt the blunt end of a blackjack pressing into his stomach. He could smell alcohol on the breath of the goon that was holding it. "Let's get going, fella," the hood ordered in excellent English. "Follow me."

Then, unexpectedly, before anyone could make another move, a new voice was heard, this one coming from the entranceway of the underground alley. It surprised the mobsters as much as it did Seven. The Super Stud and his captors whirled around to see six armed casino security guards swiftly approaching them. Seven was never so happy to see anyone in his life!

"Are you alright, Monsieur Seven?" asked one of the uniformed guards, a powerfully built man with flaming red hair. "Our casino manager, Mr. Antoine, had second thoughts about you walking home alone with your winnings. He phoned us right after you left his office. Sorry we missed you leaving the casino. Didn't see you go out the back way, thinking you'd exit through the main doors in the front instead. Fortunately, one of my colleagues picked up your trail near this alleyway."

The casino guard eyed Nalco's crew warily, not certain as to what was going on here. Seven seemed fine. And as far as this casino man could tell, all was copasetic. "In any case, I think we should walk with you now", the guard insisted."

Seven, hoping to use the sudden turn of events to his advantage, decided to play things down and not implicate Nalco or his sidekicks. Not unless he had to. Perhaps he could somehow get into the good graces of Carmine Gitano by *not* incriminating this close-knit gangland tribe.

Though certain the well-trained casino men would see right through Seven's innocuous 'spin', the G5 operative nonetheless fibbed, "Thanks much, gentlemen. But everything's fine here. I know these four men. Their boss is a friend of mine. In fact, they've just asked me if I wanted to join them at the Fairmont Hotel for a celebratory drink. Regrettably, I had to pass. I'm kind of bushed after that long poker contest."

The Super Stud nodded toward the muscular casino squad. "Tell you what, though. Now that you fellows are here, and since my friends are going in the opposite direction, I wouldn't mind some company over to my hotel. Didn't realize it was so dark and spooky back here."

"Of course, Monsieur Seven," agreed the red-haired casino leader, well aware that Seven was holding back for some reason, but not wanting to press it.

Nalco and the other three hoods remained silent, awkwardly trying to hide their weapons under their coats. Seven walked past them without a word and quickly fell in with the uniformed casino team. Ten minutes later, he and his rescuers were standing in the lobby of the elegant *Hotel de Paris*. The G5 agent thanked and tipped them, despite their polite protests about the gratuity. He then made his way past the hotel's beefy nighttime security guards stationed at all the elevators, after first showing his room key. While he was being whisked up to his suite, the relieved operative whispered a silent prayer of thanks.

Entering his room quickly, after cautiously glancing up and down the deserted hallway, Seven double-bolted the door and plopped down on the bed, thoroughly drained from all the tension. The loud ringing of his room phone shattered the stillness, causing him to jump. Taking a deep breath, the Seven nervously picked it up.

"Hello?"

"Is this Christopher Seven?" asked the tense, female voice. "Yes."

"Thank heavens. This is Doreen."

Seven was truly surprised to hear from her. "Oh, hi, Doreen," was all he could manage to say.

"Listen," she stammered. "I have to be quick. I'm talking to you from a maritime Wi-Fi harbor phone ten minutes from the dockside."

Sounding extremely nervous, Doreen rushed her words together. "I shouldn't be telling you this, and maybe I shouldn't have done what I just did." After an awkward pause she added, "I did it because...well, I like you. I like you a lot. And I was worried for you." There was another short pause. "I've never reacted to a man like this before. Yet from the moment I saw you, I knew you might be different. I knew that...well, let's just say I thought you and I could be – well, really close. Something inside assured me of that."

Christopher Seven wondered what this was all about. Could it be some sort of trick or trap? Before he could speculate any further, Doreen nervously explained, "When we four gals got back to the yacht and tried to talk to Carmine about you, he refused to listen. No matter what we said, we just couldn't calm him. Terry finally settled him down a bit after a long, boisterous squabble. Carm grudgingly agreed that we could keep you around a while under *one* condition. Said he'd accept it only after he first taught you a lesson in manners. He told us he was going to send Nalco and the boys over to the casino to find you, and then have them give you a '20-cent' beating. That's a private term they use. Means it's only a fifth of what they *usually* do to people. No broken bones or permanent injuries, but it's still a painful thrashing."

Seven heard Doreen sigh into the phone. She then continued, "Anita, Suzanne and Terry went along with Carmine's decree, figuring you'd probably be up and around in a week or two. They also realized that this '20-cent' beating was the *least* amount of punishment you'd get from Carmine. Believe me, there's much worse scenarios."

Seven nodded. "I can imagine."

"I'm sure you can. Anyway, we four girls readily accepted Carmine's verdict. I had to pretend to go along with it too, even though I *didn't* agree. So, I waited till Nalco and his men left the Zephyr to hunt you down, and then swiftly got on with my plan."

Doreen stopped again, trying to steady her still-shaky nerves. Finally getting hold of herself, she nervously continued, "As soon as Nalco's posse left the yacht, I said I was going out for a moonlight stroll. I often do that, so there was no suspicion about it. I then quickly made my way to one of the nautical phones they have on the pier. The courtesy Wi-Fi phones for yachtsman and their staff to use. Next, I quickly and anonymously called the casino manager, Mr. Antoine. Told him I'd just overheard some men say they'd be going after you for your prize money very soon. Most likely confronting you a few blocks from the casino. Either there or someplace near your hotel."

Seven nodded silently as Doreen further explained, "Obviously caring about the reputation of his gaming establishment, Mr. Antoine was quite concerned and helpful. He told me not to worry and assured me that his security squad would get right on it."

"They did," said a grateful Seven, "thanks to you. But I –"

"No more talk," Doreen interrupted. "I've got to get back to the yacht before they start looking for me. Just wanted to make sure you were okay."

"I'm fine, Doreen, but –"

"Got to run," she breathlessly insisted. Then, unexpectedly, Doreen giggled girlishly. It reminded Seven of a high school freshman with a crush on a senior. "Perhaps you can show me your appreciation when we're alone," she cooed. "Bye for now."

Click—

The astonished Super Stud fell back on the bed. *Now what? Is this Doreen woman really on the level? Or is all this part of some intricate gangland plot? Oh well. At least I escaped Nalco for the time being.*

Fighting the urge to close his tired eyes and drift into restful sleep, Christopher Seven decided to send a coded e-mail to New York. Just as the Internet connection was being made, a loud banging on his suite's door brought an instant chill up Seven's spine. "*Uh oh?*" the Super Stud worriedly speculated. "*Maybe Nalco and his goons still want to give me their '20-cent' present!*"

Chapter 18

Il Strangolatore

The knocking on Seven's door became louder and more forceful. Once again in a potentially perilous situation, the Super Stud agent considered phoning hotel security and have them rush some strong-arm help up to his suite. Trying to calm himself, the G5 operative wiped his brow and thought on it again.

Calling the front desk might save him from a beating, but the ensuing uproar would undoubtedly result in an ugly public scene. In all probability, it would ignite a full-blown investigation by the Monte Carlo police; formally the difficult *Surete National*. Therefore a public investigation was something Seven wanted to avoid if possible. As for his G5 chief, Colonel McPhail always placed an agent's wellbeing and safety above all else. Yet that being said, involving the authorities would put a quick end to any chance Seven had of infiltrating the shady world of Carmine Gitano and his four pretty yacht companions. It might even compromise Seven's covert agency as well. Yet, what else could he do now? Take the thumping? Try to talk Nalco and his posse into sparing him? Maybe the latter was possible, though the odds seemed slim.

Seven hastily tried to reason things out, baffled as to how Nalco and his goons could have even gotten up here by the expensive suites. It was highly unlikely that the front desk would wave a bunch of uncouth hoods through to visit the hotel's 'high-end' section. The *de Paris's* strict privacy policy dictated that only specifically named visitors, those pre-registered as a patron's 'preferred guests', were allowed on the elevators. And the only name Seven had given his personal 'okay' to had been Vin Fieri's. As for Nalco's motley crew, surely the lobby security guards, stationed by the elevators, would know that four big galoots carrying bullwhips weren't 'preferred guests'.

As if to answer Seven's uncertainty, a familiar, friendly voice called out from the other side of the door. "Chris, open up! It's me, Vin. Vin Fieri, the doc." Fieri gave out a caustic chuckle. "Open up, unless you have some good-looking women in there. In that case, forget about me or get me one, too."

Laughing loudly, the relieved Super Stud unbolted and opened the door. The face of his CIA sidekick grinned back at him. "Thank goodness it's you, Vin."

"Yeah, it's me, all right. Sorry to break in on you in the middle of the night, but I've been frantically searching for you the past hour or so. I just came from the casino."

Fieri and Seven sat down in the suite's two comfortable easy chairs, where Vin quickly began explaining, "I arrived into town about midnight, totally bushed from all the traveling hassles. Went straight to my hotel, checked in and tried to get some much needed sleep." He frowned. "By the way, the place I'm staying at is a dump, just like I figured. Nothing at all like this palace."

Seven grinned as Fieri went on, "I figured you and I could catch up with each other tomorrow, so there was no need to call you or visit you this late. But then, sometime around 2:00 a.m., I was awakened by an urgent cellphone call from my European chief. He informed me that one of our Monte Carlo moles, a freelance bartender who periodically works the main casino, had just phoned his CIA contact. While serving several drinks to some two-bit gangster, the half-drunk hood suddenly opened up. Seems some good- looking American tourist had just won a heated poker contest from *Don* Carmine Gitano, and now a bunch of Gitano's goons were going after this American guy. *Bingo!* It wasn't hard to put two and two together. Figuring my new pal, Christopher Seven, might be in a mess of trouble, I threw some clothes on and hurried to the casino. Couldn't locate you there, so I rushed over here, praying I'd find you."

"I'm OK, Vin. But just barely. In fact, when you banged on the door I thought it was Gitano's boys coming to give me some painful payback."

Fieri shook his head and chuckled. "I thought I told you to lay low till I got here." He grinned sardonically. "Guess you've been doing a lot more than sightseeing these past three days, buddy boy. What gives?"

Seven promptly gave Vin a full rundown, leaving nothing out. He ended with the final details on the poker tournament, Gitano's warning, and the subsequent confrontation with Nalco and his thugs.

Doc Fieri gave out a low whistle as Seven finished up his report. "And that's why I was so worried when I heard the knock on my door just now. Thought it might be them. I was seriously contemplating calling security but I didn't want to compromise the mission with some extensive police investigation. I'll tell you one thing, though. This Nalco guy seems like one weird hombre."

"He is," agreed Fieri. "As a matter of fact, I came upon Nalco's Interpol file just yesterday in London. His full name is Nicola Incartti, although for some reason everyone calls him 'Nalc' or 'Nalco'. He's a born killer and a bizarre one at that. Both Interpol and the Italian authorities have tried connecting him to several murders and beatings. But thus far nothing's stuck. I guess Carmine Gitano's hack lawyers see to that."

Seven nodded.

"In any case, Scotland Yard swears Nalco's done plenty of dirty work for the mob. Murder, extortion, drugs, pimping, you name it. But always in Europe. The FBI nor the CIA have nothing on him in the States."

The doc shifted his body on the chair. He then began filling Seven in on Nalco's sordid history, using some of the info he discovered in London.

"Our friend Nalco came into crime at an early age. He lost both his parents to a car accident near Genoa when he was nine years old. Spent the next six years or so in various orphanages and reform schools, constantly involved in petty crime. Stealing hubcaps, breaking windows and beating up the neighborhood kids. Apparently he was a real weirdo with a violent mean streak as well. None of his relatives wanted to take the boy in. Seems young Nicola had two strikes against him. One, a unique physical ailment. And two, a mind that was said to be a bit 'off kilter'. Consequently, Incartti was raised in state facilities until he turned sixteen."

Fieri cleared his throat, leaned back in the chair, and tried to recall more of the details. "The Mafia showed an early interest in Nalco. Mainly because of that strange physical oddity I mentioned. You see, Chris, Nalco Incartti was born with an abnormal left arm> one that has little feeling in it and less than a normal man's strength. As a result, the boy's *other* arm, his strapping *right* one, gradually developed almost Herculean power. That often happens when one of our senses or one of our dual body parts is dead or dormant. The other one can become three or four times as strong. Blind people quickly acquire an overdeveloped sense of smell, or super-sensitive hearing. People with one bad leg can have another limb that's a great deal stronger than normal, and so on. I saw it every once in a while when working with a medic in the military. There's a fancy Latin name for it but we just called it 'compensation'."

"I've heard about it," said Seven.

"Well, with this guy, Nalco, his right arm and right hand became incredibly strong. I mean science fiction strong, Chris. The boy quickly realized it, so along with the amazing power he had from natural compensation, he took up heavy weight lifting and those controversial Asian strength meds. These, along with grueling Chinese holistic workouts nearly every day. Nalco had tons of sports steroid injections as well. All this to give his right arm even *more* strength."

Vin shook his head and added, "The combination of these things soon made him a superhuman freak. Italian doctors said they never saw anything like it."

The Super Stud sat spellbound as Fieri went on, "Young Nalc and his unique prowess quickly gained notoriety, and he became sort of a local legend. Arm wrestling in neighborhood gin mills, crushing things like billiard balls with his right hand, and betting against unsuspecting suckers on all sorts of seemingly impossible feats of strength. With his amazing right limb, Nalco just couldn't be beat. He won sizable bar bets in nearly every saloon throughout southern Italy."

Seven shook his head as the doc added, "Carmine Gitano's uncle, Salvatore Gitano, a Mafia underboss here in Europe, eventually heard about young Incartti. He decided to check the kid out for himself during one of Nalco's arm wrestling bouts. Some barroom matchup pitting young Nalco against a seasoned traveling circus strong-man. Like most of them, Nalco won it easily and Uncle Sal took an instant liking to the kid. Made some 'mad money' as well betting on Nalco against much older and bigger opponents. A close relationship developed between the teen and the gangster and Nalco Incartti was soon taken into the Gitano crime syndicate out of Naples. He eventually became a 'made man', and he's been with them over sixteen years now. In fact, whenever Carmine Gitano comes over here from America, Nalco is immediately dispatched to be Carmine's bodyguard, chauffeur and companion."

"From what I've seen of this Nalco, he sure is an odd sort", Seven. declared. "Grunts a lot and never smiles."

Fieri nodded his head in agreement. "He's a weird one, all right, Chris. The mob took him in as someone they felt they could groom for dishing out some unique Cosa Nostra *rivalsa.* That's Mafia lingo for reprisal or revenge. Punishment for doing anything the wise guys deem a serious transgression. Like when someone shows disrespect to a mafia chieftain." The doc frowned at Seven. "Exactly like you did, old buddy."

Christopher Seven wiped his brow, knowing he'd been lucky.

"Nalco and the Mafia were a perfect match," continued Fieri. "Young Nalc showed an immediate penchant for the rough stuff. Bashed and murdered his victims gleefully. Did so without any remorse whatsoever. He absolutely loved killing or maiming various mob targets."

The Doc paused a moment and then informed, "Now, here's the nutty part I mentioned about him. It comes directly from a reliable underground medical source we have in Milan."

Vin looked up at the ceiling, trying to evoke the dossier facts. "They say Nalco Incartti has developed such a lust for killing that it's become an addiction. If he isn't given the chance to murder or cripple every two months or so, he goes into uncontrollable rage. Ferocious tantrums and screams of frenzy, brought on by extended periods of what they've loosely termed *'violence apathy'.* Even the mob has trouble controlling him when he's like that."

"You can't be serious, Vin."

"I am. Deadly serious. Apparently, if Nalco hasn't killed or maimed anyone in sixty days or so, he goes absolutely bonkers. Especially, if he can't *strangle* someone with that crushing right hand of his. Consequently, the mob boys make it a point to try and find him a quarry every two months. That is, if they can. Male or female, young or old, it doesn't matter. Just so long as Nalco can exert his strangulation prowess on some poor victim."

"Lovely," frowned Seven. "I wonder what brings on his cravings."

"I don't know the technical name for those either, Chris; these bizarre yearnings of Nalco's. I once read about something similar in an army psychological journal. It theorized that in abnormally violent men, sadistic desires can be triggered by a unique form of satyriasis; recurring sexual urges that can only be fulfilled by brutal acts of violence or cruelty. Yet, whatever causes it, after two months of idleness, with no obsessive slaughter to gratify him, Nalco Incartti goes crazy. According to one source, if there's no killing or rough stuff to be done, the mob is forced to lock Nalco in some rented room, which he literally trashes beyond recognition. After a night or two of that, he supposedly calms down. The Mafia honchos then simply overpay the innkeepers for any damages, and give them firm orders to keep their mouths shut - or else."

Seven again shook his head as Doc concluded, "Gitano's gangland keepers know all about Nalco's problem and try hard to quell his violent yearnings when and *if* they can. Although Nalco Incartti's bouts of suppressed violence probably come in handy in the savage world of organized crime. Just think of the possibilities. A proficient hit man, who, as a rule, uses only his right arm to kill. So, there's no weapon to be traced. And a willing executioner who never says *no* to a job."

"It does sound like a perfect match, Vin."

"I'll say. The ideal assassin. A goon who loves his work, and one who's armed with a silent yet lethal modus operandi; strangulation. You see, Chris, strangling victims with his devastating right hand is Incartti's specialty. That's why, in mob circles, he's called *'Il Strangolatore'*. Once Nalco grabs you around the neck with that powerful right arm of his, it's all over. You're a dead duck. No one or no force can pry his big paw away. Rumor has it that right after one killing, Uncle Sal had to use a crow bar to get Nalco's hand off some murdered hood's neck. Big Nalc just wouldn't let go."

"What a brute!" Seven exclaimed. "And what a weapon Nalco's right arm must be."

"I'll say. The mob boys claim that Nalco's huge right paw is so strong it can actually crush billiard and bowling balls to smithereens. And he knows how to prolong the victim's agony too. A real sadist. Nalco can slowly but surely choke the life out of his victims. The mobsters know and respect him but they give Nalco a wide berth. Even his *own* people."

Fieri got up from the chair and again looked Seven straight in the eyes. "So you were very fortunate tonight, buddy boy, if that's what Nalco Incartti had in mind for you." Vin frowned. "Could be Nalco's sixty-day 'inactivity' was up. Anyway, it's a darn good thing this Doreen chick got you off the hook."

"I know," Seven replied, instinctively rubbing his neck. The Super Stud then grinned slyly. "Yet there is *one* benefit apropos what's happened tonight."

"What's that, Chris?"

"Well, for one thing, I can't wait to thank the lovely Doreen - *personally.*

Chapter 19

Trick or Treat?

Seven glanced at his watch. It was now going on 3:30 in the morning. He desperately wanted to get some sleep and sensed that his CIA colleague did too. Yet there were still things to discuss and several critical decisions to make. He walked over to the suite's small mini-fridge, grabbed two cans of *Sprite,* and handed one to Fieri.

"Now what, Vin? I need to make contact with those four yacht women again if G5's plan is going to work. Even though it might be suicidal to continue with an angry Gitano on the warpath. And now there's this freak, Nalco, to worry about. Like you said, it could be his sixty days of idleness have ended and he's out to strangle someone - namely *me*."

Fieri thought on it a moment. "I'd say the only thing to do about these four women is to wait it, Chris. I know that's tough, but you calling them, or making some other pushy move, could set off alarm bells over at Gitano's yacht. Besides, if they're as interested in you as they seem to be, they'll undoubtedly find a way to make contact. From what you've told me, they presumably want you healthy and unhurt to 'flaunt'. They'll also know when the coast is clear vis-*à*-vis Gitano and Nalco."

As if on cue, the room telephone rang. Seven reached over and answered it on the first ring, thinking it might be Doreen again. The woman's voice on the other end wasn't hers. This voice was cold and businesslike. "That *you,* Seven?"

"Yes."

"It's me, Terry." She seemed surprised to hear him answer, and puzzled that he sounded so normal. "Are you feeling okay, handsome?"

"I'm fine."

A bit perplexed, she nonetheless went on, "Sorry to call you in the middle of the night, but I said I'd get in touch with you as soon as I had something definite to tell you." Terry paused a moment. "I just wasn't sure if you'd be feeling too chipper tonight." She awkwardly explained herself. "I mean, after all that pent-up tension from the poker game."

"Like I said, I'm perfectly fine, Terry."

"That's good", she said, with no enthusiasm or feeling behind it. Still baffled as to why Seven wasn't being treated in some local infirmary, or nursing serious bruises in bed, Terry's indifferent tone suggested she couldn't care less that he'd somehow managed to dodge the Nalco posse. She shrugged her shapely shoulders and advised, "Listen, I think we finally got Carmine to settle down. And to hopefully forget about that crazy poker tournament." She chuckled. "Not a moment too soon, from what I heard. Rumor had it that Carmine was thinking of having some *friends* of his come visit you tonight. Apparently they didn't connect."

Seven remained closed-mouth about the Nalco incident, so Terry simply went on. "Anyway, a few minutes ago, Carmine promised to call off the dogs and a fragile truce has been declared. Thanks mainly to my insisting on it. In fact, as a token of Mr. Gitano's peace overture, you're going to get that chance you wanted to take a quick jaunt on the *Zephyr.* Though I'm sure it's more a favor to us girls rather than any gift for you."

"That's fantastic, Terry!" exclaimed Seven, hoping his staged excitement wasn't overplayed.

She seemed fine with it, however, and promptly began giving him the specifics. "Here's the deal. Tomorrow evening we sail on the Zephyr for an eight-day cruise to the Italian Riviera – Ischia, Capri, Naples and the like. Each port has some trendy nightspots that we always hit once we're docked for the evening. Chic, upscale places where the region's rich and famous go to party. We girls told Carm that we'd like to have you along. You know, window dressing like Suz explained."

Seven winked to Fieri and gave him the 'OK' sign as Terry kept explaining, "It'll be a fun-filled cruise along the Riviera and Amalfi coasts, carousing at all the hotspots. Those snobby European bluebloods we usually run into on the Italian run, especially those stuck-up Capri dames, always think they've got the best-looking sugar candy. Wait 'til they get a load of *you*!" Seven frowned into the phone as Terry informed, "We spend most of the voyage partying, skinny-dipping and visiting the best clubs. And we always finish the trip off in outrageous style, drinking ourselves silly at a winery Carmine owns near Moronti Beach. Should be an interesting clambake, if you're game."

"Sounds like fun," Seven replied. "But are you sure Mr. Gitano doesn't mind me tagging along?"

"I'm sure. I just talked with him a few minutes ago. He said we four gals can have whoever we want on this trip as long as we don't crowd him. So be ready with your suitcase and get yourself over to the marina chart house at four o'clock tomorrow afternoon."

She paused a moment, and then, as if remembering something, quickly added, "Oh, and listen. You better pack a dinner jacket or a tux if you have one. On some of the evenings aboard *Zephyr,* Carmine insists that his yacht passengers dress up formal-like. He wants all his male guests wearing those monkey suits. Sort of a fetish with him. Says it makes things more *civilized.* Anyway, Mr. Gitano's security manager will meet you by the chart house's passenger entrance at Pier 1. He'll check you in and see to it that you and your bags get aboard the yacht."

Christopher Seven wrote the details down as Terry finished up, "Now listen *carefully*, Seven. Me and the girls somehow got you on this yacht trip and it's we who stuck our necks out. So mind your manners and make sure you stay out of Carmine's way." She chuckled, caustically. "As I'm sure you know by now, Carmine Gitano has a very short fuse."

She waited a moment to let her words sink in. "As for the cruise and the partying – well, I'm sure we women will find a way for you to sing for your supper. In any case, at least you'll get that trip onboard *Zephyr* you claim you've been dreaming about."

"Thanks, Terry."

"You're welcome. See you tomorrow."

Seven hung up the phone and grinned at Fieri. "Well, I guess that's torn it, Vin. I was just invited by the yacht women for a week's trip on the *Zephyr,* hosted by my new pal, *Don* Carmine Gitano. I'm either in for the time of my life on the world's most luxurious private vessel; or I'm being set up for a swift and tidy gangland revenge." The Super Stud smiled. "Think I should go?"

Seven's CIA accomplice had a look of genuine concern on his face. "Well, Chris, it's entirely your call. But if I were you, I'd take the first plane back to New York and forget all about it."

~

The following morning was hazy and hot. Both Fieri and Seven slept in late, not stirring till 10:00 a.m. They'd agreed to meet back at Seven's suite after lunch in order to mull over some final strategy for the Super Stud's potentially perilous yacht trip.

After requesting a late check-out time from the hotel's front desk, Seven used what was left of his morning for a return visit to *the* Gosho Karate Academy on the *avenue de Castellane*, practicing his martial arts skills for two solid hours. Reflecting on last night's frightening encounter with Nalco and his hoods, the G5 operative was anxious to keep up with all his martial moves.

He then grabbed a quick lunch and swim at the *Monte Carlo Beach Club,* raced back to his hotel, and lifted some weights in their small gym, showering in his suite afterward. Once his bags were packed for the cruise, Seven phoned the concierge to arrange for one of the bellboys to take his rental car back to *Hertz.* He likewise made a tentative future reservation for his return to Monaco eight days later. Reflecting on a possible ambush once he was onboard *Don* Gitano's yacht, Christopher Seven hoped this next hotel stay would indeed be necessary.

Glancing around his room to make sure everything was indeed packed, the Super Stud agent took out his secured cellphone and made an international phone call to headquarters. For some reason, Colonel McPhail seemed uncharacteristically apprehensive about Seven's upcoming yacht voyage and said so. "Listen, Chris, you'll be all alone with this Mafia boss and his female cohorts once you're onboard that

119

boat. So, be extremely cautious and don't take any unnecessary chances. I smell real danger in this. Just remember, if those four women are indeed the newest version of Rhombus, they'll stop at nothing should they ever get an inkling that you're on to them."

"Yes, Colonel, I'll be careful."

"See to it that you are, Seven. And try to stay in touch with Fieri when and if you can. He's your only contact over there, and hopefully he can relay anything to us should it be pertinent." McPhail sighed. "Well, goodbye and good luck, son. Take care."

"Will do, sir."

Fifteen minutes later, Doc Fieri arrived at Seven's room. "Afternoon, Chris. What do you say we go down to the lobby and have a drink there instead of working up here? The bar is empty, so we can talk freely. I don't know about you, but I find it's easier to make plans with some booze in my gut." Seven grinned as Fieri added, "Who knows? We might even run into Nalco and Carmine for a genteel round of bridge."

"Those hoods probably can't even read, let alone play a heady game like bridge," laughed Seven. "But if you want a drink, I'm buying."

"You're on, friend."

With that, the two men made their way toward the elevator and down to *Le Bar Americain.*

A few minutes later they walked into the hotel's opulent cocktail lounge. It was cool, dark and completely deserted. Sliding into an isolated booth located in the rear section of the stylish barroom, Seven called out to a passing waiter, "Two Bellinis, please."

"Oui, Monsieur."

The agents then waited 'til the server was out of earshot. "Are you all packed, Chris?"

"Yes, just finished."

"Any more phone calls from your girlfriends?"

"Nope. And no messages either. Guess the next time I'll see them will be aboard the *Zephyr.*"

"I guess so. What are your plans for the voyage?"

Seven deliberated a moment. "Well, I thought I'd try working on this girl, Doreen, first. She seems the friendliest and also the most vulnerable, unless it's all been a shrewd act. I'll have to be careful though. The other three women may not like me singling out just one of them. They seem like a jealous, self-centered lot, so I guess I'll have to play up to *all* of them. Individually, and behind closed doors, of course."

Fieri chuckled. "Sounds interesting. And how about the Godfather, *Don* Gitano?"

Seven frowned. "He won't be quite as easy to contend with. Especially after our poker clash in the casino. I'll try to stay clear of him if I can, although that might be impossible for the entire eight days. But, when I do see Gitano, I plan to adopt a 'live and let live' attitude. Show him I'm willing to bury the hatchet without being too spineless about it. He's said to respect those who don't cower in front of him. At least that's what a headquarters memo indicated."

The doc nodded.

"In any case, my main objective during this yacht trip will be to do some subtle spying wherever and whenever I can. And to try to captivate and 'turn' one or more of my four female targets. If I can do that, we might be able to get some inside info on this Rhombus organization. Perhaps learn more about Ambassador Dawson's murder and those missing diplomatic papers too."

"Let's hope so, Chris. Yet it won't be easy."

Seven shrugged his shoulders. "I know it's a long shot, Vin, my getting one of those females to talk openly about things. But when women are in the initial stages of a desired relationship, I've found they're a bit more chatty and careless. My headquarters preaches that concept too. So, who knows? Maybe that'll be the case with one of my attractive yacht companions."

"I'll drink to that," said Fieri, as he took a swig of his Bellini.

"By the way, Vin, what have you heard about Gitano's yacht?"

The doc's face showed noticeable admiration. "She's absolutely incredible, Chris. Knowing you'd be cruising onboard her today, I reread the CIA's classified files on *Zephyr* this morning. Some of the ship's details are astonishing."

Fieri took another pull from his drink and read from his written notes, "Carmine Gitano purchased the Zephyr four years ago. Bought her from some Dubai sheik who'd originally built the yacht as a gift for his son. The vessel, then unnamed, was well over 500 feet long, and she had as many decks and amenities as a small cruise ship. It was, and still is, the world's largest private yacht, beating out both *Azzam* and *Eclipse*. Gitano offered 300 million for her. At first this Sheik wouldn't sell, having paid more than that for it to be built and still wanting the boat for his boy. But then, so the scuttlebutt says, *Don* Carmine made him the usual Mafia offer, one that *couldn't* be refused."

Seven smirked, knowingly, as the doc went on, "Whatever the case, after buying the yacht, Gitano immediately made several alterations. The passenger areas are now a fairyland of gold, marble, and unabashed luxury. But it's some of the *other* things on the vessel that makes it so unique. The Zephyr has a helicopter pad, a sophisticated intruder detection system, and even a German-built missile defense system. Both the bridge and Gitano's palatial master bedroom suite are fitted with bulletproof glass. And the yacht is equipped with an anti-paparazzi shield in the form of laser beams that sweep over the boat whenever they detect a CCD or photo signal. These beams, when activated, can instantly obliterate any unwanted filming, videos or photographs around or onboard the vessel." Fieri chuckled. "Obviously, Carmine and his gangland pals need their privacy and don't want any mug shots of their comings and goings floating around. Photos taken by various law enforcement departments around the globe, or those annoying European paparazzi exposures. Or even nosy tourists like you snapping too many pictures with their phone cameras."

The Super Stud chuckled.

"All in all, Chris, Gitano's Zephyr is quite a tub!"

"She sure sounds it. Can't wait to board her." Seven glanced down at his watch. "Well, guess I better be going, Vin. I'll try to call you via our secured cellphones whenever it's practicable. Though we'll have to assume that with all of these sophisticated electronic gizmos Zephyr has, they'll somehow have a way to listen in on all my cell conversations."

The doc nodded. "You can bet on it."

"So," advised Seven, "all our phone chats will have to be in the universal inner-agency lingo. The *nicety code*, as you feds call it."

"Know it well," Fieri replied. "It's standard for all CIA operatives." Vin laughed as he recalled using this primitive conversation disguise during several former assignments, playing it out for Seven. "Hello there, Cousin Chris. This is your cousin Homer, or your roommate, Harry, or your brother Herb, calling from my bird-watching trip in Ohio." The doc chuckled again. "Or some such touristy gibberish. Hopefully I'll be able to decipher what the heck you're really trying to tell me."

"I'm sure you will, Doc. In the meantime, see if you can get more info on those four yacht women. Maybe Interpol has something - passports, visas, anything at all. I'll try to charm some names out of them once I'm onboard." Seven signed. "Although whatever names I do get will probably be bogus. Yet, you never know. If they don't suspect me as any type of threat, they just might blurt out something truthful."

Seven again looked at his watch. "Gotta go." He sighed, softly. "Wish you were coming with me, Vin. Two is always safer than one."

"Me, too, Chris. I don't like the thought of your being all alone out there." The doc held out his hand and shook Seven's. "Good luck. And don't worry. Even though we'll have to talk in the *nicety* code, I'll be a quick phone call away at all times." He smirked, wryly. "Unless you're underwater after finding a horse head in your bed."

"Thanks, pal," laughed Seven. "Hopefully, I'll see you in eight days or so. If not, tell my brother I died gamely."

The grinning Super Stud threw some money down on the table for the drinks, nodded a final farewell to Fieri, and headed up to his suite to retrieve his bags. For better or worse, he was off!

Chapter 20

Toys Dripping in Blood

Seven's taxi ride arrived at the Monte Carlo pier at exactly 4:00 p.m. He paid and tipped his driver, who helped him bring his suitcases and hanging garment bag into the small, immaculate, chart house located at the front of the pier. The modern customs building was a beehive of activity, the nerve center for all of the private yachts and passenger vessels that were arriving or leaving Monaco. Seven made his way over to one of the three check-in windows and politely addressed the spectacled man standing behind it.

"Hi. I'm Christopher Seven, a passenger on Mr. Gitano's yacht. They said someone would be here to help me through customs and security."

Upon hearing the name 'Gitano', the counter man snapped to attention. "Yes sir, I saw your name on Zephyr's manifest. Mr. Gitano's vessel is moored in basin 30. His aide, Mr. Cassia, should be here momentarily. In the meantime, may I please view your passport and one other form of picture ID?"

"Of course." Seven handed his papers over and waited. While the customs agent was perusing it, making a few notes with a thin pen, the G5 operative heard a friendly greeting coming from behind him.

"Mr. Seven?"

"Yes?"

"Hi, I'm Frank Cassia, Mr. Gitano's social secretary." Cassia, a rather tough-looking, balding man, held out his hand to shake. "Very nice to meet you. Terry and the girls said you'd be arriving around four. Thanks for being on time. As soon as Joseph here is through with the customs and passport formalities, we'll get you right over to the Zephyr."

Seven replied with staged enthusiasm. "Thank you, Mr. Cassia. I just can't tell you how much this means to me! I've been fascinated with private yachts ever since I was a boy, and Zephyr is the cream of the crop. To think – I'll actually be *cruising* on her!"

Frank Cassia stared at him. Was there a hint of cynicism in his eyes? The Super Stud couldn't tell for sure.

After a brief pause, Gitano's employee simply said, "Yes, I understand. The Zephyr is the most celebrated private vessel in the world." Cassia then glanced over at the counterman. "Is everything in order with Mr. Seven's papers, Joe?"

"Yes, sir, everything's fine. He's all yours."

Seven waved a goodbye to the customs man and turned around to see his luggage being loaded on the back of a large golf cart. Gitano's secretary then walked over to the cart and motioned for Seven to join him. They both hopped in the cart's back seat, directly behind the overweight driver; a bearded Frenchman badly in need of a bath. The driver waited a moment, then pushed the electric self-starter, and slowly drove out through the front entrance via its opened double doors. They were soon riding on a narrow boardwalk, making the long trek out to Zephyr's mooring.

Seven turned to his companion and asked, "Will you be coming along on this cruise, Mr. Cassia?"

"Wish I was. Unfortunately I'm swamped here in Monaco. Tons of paperwork and some other pressing things I've got to attend to."

"Oh, that's too bad."

"Yes," agreed Cassia. "I would have liked to have spent some time with Terry and the girls. Always a lot of fun when they're along."

"Oh," Seven replied, trying to sound politely attentive. "Do they sail on Zephyr frequently?"

Again Cassia glared directly at him, and this time there was no doubt about the suspicion in his eyes. He brusquely replied, "No, not really." With that, they rode the rest of the way in silence.

As the golf cart pulled up to Gitano's extraordinary yacht, Christopher Seven felt his pulse race. Zephyr looked magnificent just as she had that first day; massive and beautiful. The yacht was a true work of art, a maritime masterpiece gleaming in spotless white paint, shining brass trimmings, and decks and railings made of polished teakwood. Six bustling seamen, smartly dressed in identical blue nautical outfits, were putting the finishing touches on her before she headed out to sea. They somehow added just the right touch to the seafaring setting.

Seven glanced up at the gangway steps leading into the belly of the luxurious craft. Two officers, clad in formal white naval uniforms, were standing near the top of it. There was no sign of Gitano or the women.

"We've arrived, Mr. Seven," Frank Cassia exclaimed, as the cart came to a gradual stop. "You can walk right up the gangway and onto the boat. One of the staff will show you to your cabin, right after the captain gives you a quick tour and his mandatory lifeboat drill."

"The Captain?"

"Yes, Mr. Seven. The safety drill is required by international law for all new incoming passengers. Most of the time the Captain handles it." Cassia pointed up the gangway. "That's him, at the top of the steps - Captain Sergio Bacca."

Seven nodded.

Well that's about it, Mr. Seven. We'll have your luggage loaded through the hold. It'll be in your stateroom in an hour or so." Cassia shrugged his shoulders. Sorry for any delay, but the provisions always come first. "

Yes, Seven mused to himself. *"Enough time for my luggage to be neatly rummaged through before they deliver it.*

Cassia smiled, cordially. "Enjoy your voyage, sir."

"Thanks. I'm sure I will." And with that, the G5 agent hopped off the golf cart and made his way up the gangway steps, truly excited to board Carmine Gitano's fabulous vessel.

Reaching the top of the steep metal stairway, Seven was greeted by the two officers standing near the railing. The shorter of the two, a well-tanned, stocky man with a grayish beard, extended his hand. "Welcome aboard, Mr. Seven. I'm Captain Bacca." He saluted smartly. "Mr. Gitano's compliments. He's in conference at the moment but asked me to see that you're comfortably settled in." The captain pointed toward the other officer. "This is my navigator, Salvatore Gracci."

Seven nodded to them both and asserted, "Thanks for the official welcome, gentlemen. Happy to be aboard. I've read a lot about the Zephyr. They say she's the most technically advanced yacht ever."

Captain Bacca bowed proudly. "That she is, Mr. Seven. Zephyr is currently the largest private vessel in the world. Eclipse held that distinction until Mr. Gitano purchased this one. I can't elaborate too much, for security reasons, but the ship weighs over 12,000 tons. And she's nearly 550 feet in length. We have the latest and best navigational, communication and technical tools, and she's fully stabilized. Among her many features, Zephyr has two separate water desalination plants, so we can thus sail anywhere in the world in safety and comfort." He beamed with pride. "Come. Let me show you around."

"If you'll excuse me, gentlemen," said the navigator, Gracci, "I have some charts I'd like to review before departure." He nodded a goodbye.

Seven nodded back and followed Captain Bacca through the promenade door, into the air-conditioned comfort of the main salon. Once they were inside, the captain began his official tour. "This is our central salon, Mr. Seven. The main passenger hub of the yacht."

The G5 operative looked around in awed astonishment. The roomy salon was much like the lobby of a small luxury hotel, complete with plush sitting areas, a reception desk manned by two middle-aged women, and a separate concierge desk. There was even a tiny banking center, flanked by two ATMs. Expensive oil paintings hung on the lavishly wallpapered walls, with fresh floral arrangements everywhere. An elaborate overhead speaker system was playing soft, soothing music.

"Here, passengers can obtain anything they desire," Captain Bacca informed. "The reception desk is manned 24/7. It's at your beck and call should you need anything while onboard. From a toothbrush to a full wardrobe. Our concierge desk is likewise open 'round the clock, in case you need to make future travel plans or any arrangements on shore. Golf, rental cars, restaurant reservations - just ask here." Bacca pointed to a small writing desk, which had two decorative house phones on it. "And naturally, you can call anywhere in the world at any time. Either from right here or from the comfort of your stateroom via our satellite phone system. State-of-the-art computers, located in the library on Deck 6, can likewise be used for any e-mails or other functions."

"Just like home," grinned Seven, genuinely impressed.

The captain smiled in agreement. "Let me show you some of our other areas, Mr. Seven, before your mandatory lifeboat drill."

What followed was a twenty-minute tour of pure opulence. The Zephyr had everything. There were three separate dining rooms, including the extravagantly chandeliered main dining hall. The outdoor lido area housed two beautiful swimming pools, and several whirlpool hot tubs. And the sunbathing areas had loads of lounge chairs."

Seven glanced to his right and saw a nifty rattan-themed bar and buffet hub near the largest swimming pool. The yacht also had a state-of-the-art spa and gymnasium, the latter equipped with a regulation-sized boxing ring. There was a small running track on one of the upper outside decks and an enclosed, high-definition golf simulator where passengers could challenge the toughest courses in the world. There was even a mahogany-paneled cigar room for nighttime cognac and brandy. It was located opposite an arcade filled with pinball machines and games.

To Seven's astonishment, the captain next walked him into an old- fashioned English billiard room. The Super Stud wondered how anyone could play pool on a rolling sea. Sensing his surprise, Captain Bacca promptly explained, "Each of the two pool tables in here cost over a hundred and fifty thousand dollars. The tables have a specially built gyroscopic leveling mechanism that counters the ship's movement. Consequently, the pool tables are virtually impervious to any rolling or pitching due to rough waters. Our guests can therefore enjoy a game of billiards in *any* weather." Seven smiled in amazement as the tour continued.

Bacca showed him several attractive bars and cocktail lounges situated throughout the yacht, each with a different motif. In addition to these cozy lounges, there was a small disco, a sports bar filled with several widescreen TVs, and a sizable show lounge, where the captain said Mr. Gitano frequently flew in top-name entertainers to perform.

Next, they walked into Zephyr's casino. Seven smiled to himself, knowing this was where the gangster could entertain his yacht guests and probably fleece them as well. Nonetheless, the casino, like all of Zephyr's other rooms, was impressive and stylish.

Near the end of the tour, they rode the small passenger elevator to the very top of the vessel, Deck 10, where Captain Bacca informed,

"I'm now taking you to an area that's normally closed to passengers, Mr. Seven. Guests aren't allowed up here for safety reasons. That's one of our most stringent rules." He quickly explained, "The heavy equipment stored on this deck can occasionally break loose in rough seas and potentially cause severe injury. Therefore, no one's *ever* allowed up here but the crew."

A bit confused, Seven nevertheless nodded as the captain added, "Once per voyage, however, I'm obligated by maritime law to bring all new passengers up here, as this is the deck where our lifeboat muster stations are located. Accordingly, this is where you'd come to in case of an actual emergency. If you ever hear the emergency signal, three short blasts on the ship's horn, followed by three longer ones, grab the life preserver stored in your cabin and make your way up here to Deck 10."

Bacca's voice became much sterner. "But you're *only* to come here in the event of an actual emergency. Other than that, Deck 10 is strictly off-limits to *all* passengers." The Captain's voice again grew forceful. "Guests are *never* allowed up here unless accompanied by a crewmember or officer. Like I said, bulky pieces of equipment we store here can swing wildly in the wind, or even break lose. And we've had a few mishaps."

"I understand, Captain," replied Seven, silently wondering if these *mishaps* were Mafia-ordered.

Captain Bacca forced a smile and his tone became affable again. "In any case, since this is also where our lifeboats are housed, naval law dictates that I must show all embarking guests the area they'd come to in an actual emergency. Our crew, who are trained proficiently in safety and fire procedures, would then direct you to a lifeboat."

Seven knew this Deck 10 'off limits' edict might very well be a self- serving command from Carmine Gitano himself. Maybe there were things up here that the gangster didn't want outsiders to see. Contemplating on how he could covertly sneak up here for another look, the Super Stud said nothing. Bacca's deep voice interrupted his thoughts.

"Well, that's our tour, Mr. Seven. Hope you enjoyed it."

"Very much so."

"Fine, then. And may I be the first to wish you a wonderful cruise. Our weather looks pretty good, so it should be a smooth voyage."

As they turned to leave and make their way back toward the elevators, the G5 operative noticed a massive object further up the deck. It was covered by a heavy tarpaulin. Pointing at it, Seven asked the obvious question, "What's that huge, tarped object over there, Captain?"

Bacca, at first a bit hesitant to answer, was quickly swayed by his noticeable pride. With a pleased grin on his weathered face, he proudly responded, "That's Mr. Gitano's latest toy, and she's a real beauty." The captain winked sheepishly. "I'm not really supposed to do this, but I hear you're a real yacht enthusiast. So I don't think the boss would mind."

He led Seven over to a circular area, threw back part of the covering canvas, and proudly revealed a brand new Ecureuil AS 350 helicopter. It was tightly secured in the yacht's heliport landing area by several thick bindings. The copter's sleek black body glistened majestically in the sunlight, looking space-aged and powerful.

Captain Bacca beamed. "How do you like her, Mr. Seven? The Zephyr is the only yacht in the world that houses one this sophisticated."

"Magnificent, Captain! Like everything else onboard."

The G5 agent then looked further up the deck, up toward another huge cylinder-shaped object. It was even *larger* than the helicopter. Whatever this thing was, it was situated near the very front of the deck, likewise hidden under a heavy canvas. This time, Captain Bacca, noticing Seven observing it, purposely ignored the object. Hastily shooing him away, the captain went silent for a moment. Frowning slightly, he firmly pointed toward a narrow stairwell and hurriedly ushered Seven down some metal steps to the deck below.

Here, one floor down on Deck 9, an assortment of expensive watercrafts were displayed. There was a large banana boat, several Jet Skis, six kayaks, and a bunch of brand-new wave runners. High-priced toys for Carmine's gangland cohorts and guests to enjoy.

With that, Captain Bacca's tour finally came to an end. It had been an amazing showing. In short, the Zephyr was very much a miniature cruise ship, a pleasure boat complete with lavish trimmings and every conceivable plaything a rich man could buy. Yet, Christopher Seven silently reminded himself that all of these toys, including the Zephyr herself, were fruits of crime, extortion and murder. Every single luxury and toy onboard Carmine Gitano's magnificent vessel was undoubtedly dripping with the blood of innocents.

"So, what do you think of our Zephyr, Mr. Seven?"

"She's incredible, Captain. I wish I could take a few photos for the folks back home, but I noticed several signs that said, 'absolutely *no* photos or videos of *any* kind'. Seven shrugged his shoulders. "I guess Mr. Gitano must have his reasons."

"I'm sure he does. Remember, Mr. Seven, Carmine Gitano entertains many prominent businessmen, politicians and international VIPs who cherish their privacy. I hope you understand?"

"Of course."

Just then, a smartly uniformed room steward appeared. "This is Aldo," the captain introduced. "He'll be your stateroom steward for the voyage. He'll escort you down to your cabin now." The captain held out his hand to shake. "I look forward to seeing you around the ship."

"Thanks, Captain. Both for the tour and lifeboat instruction."

The captain bowed gracefully as Seven followed the smiling Aldo to the elevator and down to Deck 5, the main passenger deck.

"You're in Stateroom 5, Mr. Seven. Like the Captain said, I'll be your steward this trip, so please call me if there's anything you need."

"Will do, Aldo."

They walked down a long corridor with numbered doors on either side. Seven guessed that Zephyr housed 30 or so passenger cabins, as there looked to be at least 20 staterooms on either side of the lengthy hallway. That would mean the yacht, when full, could take at least 60 passengers in her spacious cabins. Plus a sizable crew with their own quarters down on Deck 1. The G5 agent wondered how many other guests would be going along on this particular Capri voyage. And how many would be mobsters. He decided to ask Aldo about the passengers.

"Are there a lot of folks traveling with us this trip, Aldo?"

"Oh no, sir, we're nearly empty. I guess we'll only have around 16 passengers in all." They walked over to Stateroom 5, where Aldo slid the magnetic key card into the door's electronic slot. It opened immediately. "Here you are sir - home sweet home." He handed Seven the card key, pushed open the door and they walked inside.

The cabin was roomy and attractive. There was a single queen-size bed, a small sitting area and an unexpectedly sizeable bathroom. A flat- screen HDTV was mounted on the wall in front of the bed. The stateroom was tastefully decorated, with blonde woods and brass trimmings. It was complimented nicely by the blue carpeting and draperies.

Seven looked out the large floor-to-ceiling picture window and accompanying glass patio door. He was pleasantly surprised to see a small private balcony attached to his room. *Typical of Zephyr's luxury,* he reflected. *Her staterooms even have their own private verandas.*

"I've unpacked and put your things away, Mr. Seven. Your empty suitcase, carry-on and suit bag are now stored under the bed."

"Fine, Aldo," Seven replied, thankful he'd left his laptop computer and all of the coded files and CIA documents back with Vin Fieri. The affable room steward spoke again.

"There's fresh ice in the bucket, a fully stocked mini-fridge, and a 'welcome aboard' bottle of *Taittinger* champagne, courtesy of Mr. Gitano. We depart promptly at 6:30, and you've been invited to dine at Mr. Gitano's table tonight. 8:30 in the main dining salon."

Aldo bowed smartly, getting ready to take his leave. He took one last look around the cabin to make sure he'd explained everything. "Oh, yes, almost forgot. Let me tell you a bit about the room telephone. Just dial 9 should you need me for anything at all. If I'm off duty, you can leave a voice message or call the front desk.

Seven nodded.

"Well, sir, I hope you enjoy your voyage."

Christopher Seven held out a twenty-dollar bill but the steward politely refused it. "Oh, no sir, Mr. Seven. Thanks much, but Mr. Gitano wants us to work for the satisfaction of his guests, *not* their money. See you around, sir." And with that, Aldo took his leave, closing the door gently behind him.

Seven shrugged his shoulders and sat down on the bed. The mattress was firm and plush, undoubtedly an expensive European pillow top. *Now what?* he asked himself. *And what's all this about a dinner invitation from the Mafia boss? Is it truly a peace offering, or merely the 'last supper' before the slaughter?* Seven glanced at his watch; 5:35. In three more hours, he'd find out.

As the Super Stud continued to ponder it, he heard a knock on his cabin door. He got up from the bed and opened it, surprised to see Terry's beautiful face staring back at him. She walked straight in, closed the door behind her, and grinned seductively.

"Hello, handsome."

"Hello, Terry."

Then, without warning or explanation, she strolled over to Seven, threw her arms around him and gave him the longest, most passionate French kiss he'd ever received. Panting heavily, she grinned and said, "I just wanted to welcome you onboard *properly*. I'm down the hall in Cabin 18 if you need anything."

And with that, she slowly sauntered back to the door and exited the stateroom.

Chapter 21

Last Name Taboo

Two hours later, as Christopher Seven relaxed on the comfortable bed in his stateroom, the cabin telephone on his night table began ringing. He reached over and answered it.

"Mr. Seven?" asked the shrill, feminine voice.

"Yes?"

"This is Donna at the front desk. Welcome aboard."

"Thanks, Donna."

"You're very welcome. I wanted to let you know that Mr. Gitano has invited you to dine at his table this evening at 8:30 p.m."

"Yes, my steward mentioned it."

"I hope you're planning to join us, then?" "Absolutely. Please tell Mr. Gitano I'll be there."

"Lovely. Incidentally, tonight's dress code is *semiformal.* Sport coat and tie would be fine. I should also mention that we have different dress codes for each evening. It's usually dependent on whether we're at sea or in port." She mentioned each. *"Semiformal* dress means jacket and tie; and *casual* is no jacket or tie required. Although smart, country club attire is still expected."

"Sounds fine", said Seven as Donna concluded. "And on *formal* nights, Mr. Gitano insists on black tie with a tux or dinner jacket. You can find the appropriate dress guidelines displayed at the reception desk. Or in the shipboard info sheet that's slipped under your door each night."

She paused a moment, and then advised, "By the way, we may be departing Monte Carlo a bit late this evening. One of the passengers is still not aboard yet and we're waiting for him to arrive."

Again there was a brief silence, during which Seven heard another person breathing into the phone. Someone was obviously listening in. The G5 operative simply ignored it as Donna finished up her spiel about dinner. "If you would, sir, please meet me at the Polynesian Terrace at 7:45. That's the small cocktail lounge on Deck 6, one floor above you. I'll introduce you to Mr. Gitano's other dining guests and we can enjoy a cocktail before we all go in for dinner."

"Sounds great, Donna. I'll see you then." The Super Stud smiled at the room phone after hanging it up. So, it was dinner with the big man. *Don* Carmine was apparently playing his magnanimous host role to the hilt. *Oh well,* Seven mused, *might as well go along with it. And try to amiably cope with the mob boss as well. There's no sense making waves or being adversarial if I want to move around the ship freely.*

The Super Stud shrugged his shoulders, walked into the bathroom and took a *Bonine* motion-sickness tablet out of his drug case. He broke it in two and popped one of the halves into his mouth, swallowing it down with some Evian bottled water from the mini-fridge. This was the regimen he always used to avoid motion sickness whenever cruising. Half a *Bonine* pill an hour or so before departure, and then a quarter pill every morning while on a sea voyage.

Smiling at the memory of a past family cruise, he stripped off his clothing and stepped into the spacious bathtub, where he turned on the shower full blast. Soaping up liberally with his preferred *Dial* 'Mountain Fresh' soap and then shampooing his hair, the G5 operative was happy to find the yacht's water pressure streaming down from the *Grohe* multi-jet showerhead surprisingly strong. After drying himself with one of the bathroom's thick Turkish towels, he next used the small hair dryer mounted on the bathroom wall and followed that up with his usual grooming regimen.

As he finished, he heard some metallic static coming over the cabin's ceiling speakers. It was followed by the distinctive voice of Captain Bacca.

"Good evening, ladies and gentlemen. This is your captain speaking. I'd like to update you on our departure and route. I've just been informed that our final passenger has missed his flight connections and unfortunately won't be able to join us until sometime tomorrow afternoon. Accordingly, we will not be waiting here for him any longer tonight. We'll instead head out to sea a bit earlier than planned. Regarding our course, after hugging the Monaco coast awhile, Zephyr will turn west toward neighboring Nice. She'll then anchor for the night right off the French Riviera coastline. This way you can wake up to the beautiful waters of Saint-Jean-Cap-Ferrat and enjoy some swimming off the bow. Or, if you'd prefer, visit the area's charming nearby villages and beaches. Our delayed passenger will be arriving at Nice Airport tomorrow afternoon, which is quite near our anchorage area. Once our passenger arrives onboard, we'll then set sail for Italy around 6:00 p.m. tomorrow evening. The weather looks perfect, so I hope you have an enjoyable night. Sorry about this small change in our schedule, but it will not impede our agenda for the Italian portion of the cruise."

Christopher Seven sat down on the bed, wondering who this missing passenger might be. Obviously he had to be important for Gitano's yacht to wait for him near the Nice Airport. Maybe the Super Stud could find out more specifics during dinner.

Ten minutes later, he felt a slight, sudden vibration as Zephyr's powerful engines began to churn. At first there was no perceptible sensation of movement. But then, very gradually, Seven could definitely feel the mega yacht backing away from her mooring. The Zephyr stopped for a moment and then slowly edged forward, majestically making her way out into the Mediterranean Sea. After clearing the no-wake zone, the captain cranked up the power and they were off.

Thankfully, the ride was smooth as they motored beyond Monaco and out into the open waters. Zephyr then hugged the coastline, passing Cap d'Ail during her short journey toward Nice. Captain Bacca was taking it slow and easy and that suited Seven fine. Although he'd been on quite a few family cruises as a child and young teen, he wanted no part of towering waves and rough water, something, that as an adolescent, he never seemed to mind. The Zephyr might be the largest private yacht in the world, but she was, after all, still a yacht; and *not* a mammoth cruise ship. As such, there would be definite movement, and probably *'mal de mer'* for her passengers if the seas got bumpy. Hoping this good weather would hold, the G5 operative was confident that his Bonine would do the trick if it didn't.

Walking over to the stateroom's spacious closet, Seven promptly began contemplating his wardrobe for the evening. As he did so, he again thought of Godfrey, fashion guru to the Super Studs.

Seven grinned, recalling the many times he and the other studs had spent playfully arguing with Godfrey over 'fashion versus comfort'. "Before I came here to New York to work with you uncultured chaps," Godfrey would crow, "I was originally from London. I spent many years toiling in Seville Row, where I've dressed some of the most prominent and stylish men in the world. Including royalty! *They* never carped about comfort like you super chaps."

Seven and his fellow Studs would feign disbelief, causing Godfrey to pout incessantly. And though it was great fun to tease the eccentric Brit, the agents knew that Godfrey was usually 'right on' when it came to making the Studs' clothing look as striking as their incredible faces.

After choosing a tapered, cream-colored cashmere sports coat, Seven checked Godfrey's printed wardrobe card and saw that the Englishman recommended a beige dress shirt, black Italian dress pants and an elegant gold-and-black silk tie to go with it. Also suggested were black cotton dress socks and black *Magli* loafers.

With his hair perfectly styled and his clothes impeccably tailored, Christopher Seven knew he'd certainly turn heads tonight. For what seemed like the millionth time, Seven once again reflected on the blessing and curse of his good looks. He shrugged. What could he do, other than use them for the benefit of his country?

As he made his way to the elevator, up to Deck 6's Polynesian lounge, the Super Stud now hoped those looks would help him uncover some clues regarding Ambassador Dawson's brutal murder.

~

Entering the intimate cocktail lounge, themed in rattan, bamboo and an overabundance of orchids, Seven immediately spotted a group of passengers, including his four targets, seated at a large, oblong table. With drinks in hand, they were chatting amicably over the soft, mellow sounds of the Hawaiian guitar in the background. The four yacht women looked remarkably beautiful in low-cut dresses and expensive jewelry. Seven nodded to them just as a tall, thin lady at the table stood up to greet him.

"Ah, there you are, Christopher. I'm Donna from reception. Thanks so much for joining us. Allow me to make the introductions. I believe you already know Terry, Anita, Doreen, and Suzanne. Some of our other dining companions are also here."

She smiled and motioned toward two couples sitting near the end of the cocktail table. Seated there were a pair of middle-aged women wearing far too much makeup, along with their burly male companions who looked like 'extras' from the mob movie *'Good-fellas'.* They were all drinking Beefeater martinis.

"This is Frank and Doris from Chicago", said Donna. And sitting next to them are Giovanni and Marie, originally from Cleveland, now residing in Naples, Italy."

The men grunted an unenthusiastic 'hello', while their ladies simply gawked unabashedly. One of the women, the short redhead, Marie, stared at Seven and loudly exclaimed, "Where the heck have *you* been all my life, beautiful? I suppose Carmine's been keeping you behind closed doors." She glanced at the four girls sitting to her left. "Or is it Terry and her friends who've kept you caged?" Marie patted the empty seat next to her. "Come, sit by me."

"Hey, watch it there, Marie," cautioned her hefty companion, Giovanni. "Slow down, before you and this guy wind up overboard with the sharks!"

Everyone laughed, albeit a bit nervously, as the receptionist tried to lighten this rather awkward beginning. "Oh, don't mind Giovanni, Christopher. He's always kidding around about Marie like that. But I can assure you that he and his loving wife are inseparable."

"Yeah," chimed Marie, with a derisive frown. "Until he sees anyone in a skirt who's twenty years younger." Again there was edgy laughter.

Receptionist Donna merely smiled and then awkwardly explained, "As you've undoubtedly noticed, Christopher, with the exception for Mr. Gitano, we never use last names aboard the Zephyr. It's a firm rule of the house. So I hope you don't mind my calling you Christopher or Chris?"

"Chris is fine," replied Seven, knowing this last-name taboo was undoubtedly done to protect every two-bit hoodlum traveling onboard.

"Where you from, pal?" asked the Chicago hulk named Frank.

"New Jersey," Seven answered, with purposeful vagueness.

"Jersey, huh? I think I owned a brewery there once."

At that juncture they were joined by another couple approaching the table. "Oh, here's Edgar and Stella," Donna beamed, "Carmine's west coast accountants." Seven nodded politely toward the newcomers as they took their seats.

"Excellent, we're all here now," Donna informed. She gave her guests a staged smile and then snapped her fingers for the waiter. "Let's get Chris, Stella and Ed something to drink."

Seven ordered a glass of champagne while the new couple ordered white wine spritzers. The drinks came quickly, served elegantly by a smiling Filipino waiter. The G5 agent looked over at his four attractive targets, raised his champagne glass toward them, and proclaimed, "I guess it's time I toasted you ladies. This voyage is going to be incredible, as is this beautiful yacht. Thanks for getting me onboard."

The sultry redhead, Anita, was the first to reply. "You're welcome, handsome." She grinned savagely. "Just make sure to save your *thanks* for later." Anita then called back the waiter and ordered another round for Suzanne, Terry and herself, for some reason leaving out Doreen. Seven, listening carefully, made another mental note to keep working on her.

The Super Stud tried to casually engage the reserved Doreen, who was now sitting farthest away from him. Regrettably, this proved impossible with all the babbling and small talk going on around them. A chaotic half-hour of this insipid chatter ensued. Then, mercifully, their hostess, Donna, stood up and announced, "Well, folks, it's now going on 8:30. Shall we join Mr. Gitano in the dining room?"

The group of twelve rose simultaneously, exited the cocktail lounge and followed Donna toward an ornate circular stairway that led up to the main dining room on Deck 7. They were soon standing at the entrance of Zephyr's formal dining salon, *Rose Hall.* Seven was truly amazed at the restaurant's spacious dimensions, not at all like he'd expected on a private yacht. It was a good-sized room with at least twenty tables. Most of these were set for four, but there were a few tables for two and some bigger sized tables for groups as well. The largest of these, an elaborately set rectangle with fourteen elegant chairs surrounding it, was located in the exact center of the dining room. Sitting at it now were Carmine Gitano and Captain Bacca. The two men seemed to be watching intensely as a tuxedoed Maître d' led Donna's flock toward their table.

After they arrived, Donna gaily announced, "Well, Mr. Gitano, here are your dinner guests for this evening." She motioned toward the table and informed those arriving, "Ladies and gentlemen, please take your seats. You'll find a place card in front of each chair showing your designated seat." Donna then took her own assigned chair, one which was situated between the captain and Gitano.

Seven, amused at the formality, quickly found his specified seat. To his annoyance, he was not seated next to any of his four targets, wedged instead between the Chicago couple and the twosome from Naples. At least Terry and Anita were seated across from him so there might be a chance to engage them. Unfortunately, Doreen, Seven's main quarry, was again furthest away from him. Way down the opposite end of the table.

The Super Stud sat down and glanced over at Carmine Gitano. It would be interesting to see how the big man was going to play it with him. Would the Mafia *Don* be a gracious host? Or would he simply ignore Seven? The G5 operative didn't have to wait long for his answer. Gitano looked over at Seven and boomed, "Well, well, if it ain't my poker-playing friend. Thanks for joining us on this little yacht jaunt to Italy. Thought you might back out after our *disagreement* in the casino. And some other events thereafter. But you came aboard all the same. That shows guts." He grinned, stood up, and reached out his hand to shake.

A grateful and surprised Seven took it and replied, "It's me who should be thanking *you*, Mr. Gitano. Despite that silly poker contest, you've graciously allowed me to experience your amazing Zephyr firsthand. That was a truly magnanimous gesture."

The mobster seemed momentarily confused, probably because of the four-syllable word Seven had just used. He then barked out a harsh laugh and said, "Well, you should really be thanking the four gals sitting here rather than me for this boat ride." Gitano grinned. "They seem to have a way of always getting what they want from me."

Carmine Gitano then winked mischievously to the other guests sitting around his table. "But I wouldn't go feeling *too* comfortable yet, if I were you, pal. My compadre, Nalco, is *also* onboard this trip. And I'm sure he'll be thrilled to learn that you're traveling with us."

Everyone laughed except Seven, who instinctively rubbed his neck just as the Maître d' began handing out the large, gold-leafed menus.

Chapter 22

"The World's Greatest Mob Hit!"

armine Gitano rose up from his chair, raised his champagne glass, and toasted his dinner guests, doing so with surprising aplomb. Shortly after he finished, Zephyr's engines slowed down and then stopped completely. Seven guessed they were now somewhere off the coast of Saint-Jean-Cap-Ferrat. As four hovering waiters approached the dining table, the Super Stud felt and heard Zephyr's massive anchor being lowered. The yacht had arrived at its overnight anchorage.

The servers waited respectfully for Mr. Gitano to sit back down, and after he did, the lavish meal began. Three solid hours of superb cuisine, genial but guarded conversation, and several bottles of expensive wines.

After perusing the extensive menu, Christopher Seven ordered the *filet de boeuf en croute*; pink and juicy beef tenderloin encased in a buttery puff pastry. This excellent prime beef entrée, complimented perfectly by a glorious *Château Haut-Brion* wine the sommelier proficiently served, was truly first class. It rivaled Seven's favorite *'en croute'* dish, a puff pastry encrusted rack of lamb that he ordered regularly back home at *Claude's* restaurant in New Jersey.

Throughout the meal, Carmine Gitano proved to be a gregarious host, joking and laughing with his table guests, including Seven. Yet the G5 agent still sensed that, at times, he was being subtly tested by the Mafia chieftain. He thus tried to give as good as he got, whenever Gitano's biting humor was aimed at him.

As for his other tablemates, Carmine's uncouth 'associates', the Super Stud learned very little from them, other than the fact that they were all somehow connected to Gitano's so-called 'business interests'. They were undoubtedly mob connected as well. That was quite evident as they carelessly gave themselves away by coarse talk about this guy, or that man's *'territory'*, much to the annoyance of their Mafioso host. Disappointingly, there was little opportunity for Seven to openly engage his four female targets. He thus decided to try after dinner.

After the final cups of coffee and expresso had been consumed, Gitano again stood up and politely dismissed his guests. "Well, ladies and gents, I hope you enjoyed the chow."

There were several murmurs of satisfaction as the gangster went on, "The night is still young. 11:30 is merely the starting time for many of my boat's activities. The disco is open, as is the casino and all the bars are open as well. There's also a midnight singer in the main showroom. Some broad I hired from Vegas." Glancing over at Terry, Anita, Suzanne and Doreen, the mob chieftain apologized, "Sorry I can't be with you four ladies tonight. But I got a late meeting with some of my staff in the conference room. Maybe tomorrow night." He then gave a stern glare in the direction of Christopher Seven and then back at the four women. "Just make sure you girls behave yourself."

Satisfied he'd made his point, *Don* Gitano returned his attention to the rest of the table. "As for tomorrow, folks. Like the captain said, we'll be anchored near Cap-Ferrat all day, so you'll have plenty of time to check out the neighborhood." He grinned, widely. "They tell me there's a topless beach near the dock, so maybe I'll see some of you men there. Anyway, enjoy your night." He grunted a final adieu and made his exit.

The three married couples at the table all decided to go listen to the singer in the lounge. When one of the female passengers, the heavyset lady, Marie, asked Seven if he'd like to join them, the fiery Terry quickly and firmly chimed in, "Sorry, missy. Handsome is occupied this evening. He'll be with *us*."

Knowing Terry and Carmine's temper, the three couples then quickly said their goodbyes and left the table.

The Super Stud glanced around the now-nearly empty restaurant. Only a couple of tables were still occupied, mostly Zephyr's officers and staff. He then turned toward the four women sitting across from him. "Well ladies, if I'm *occupied*, what are we going to do this evening?"

"Oh, we'll think of something," the sultry Suzanne replied.

"Yeah," echoed her redheaded cohort, Anita. "But first, why don't we go have an after-dinner drink somewhere?"

"How about the English Pub?" suggested Terry. "That's the small, London-themed cocktail lounge down on Deck 4."

"Fine," agreed Seven. He winked at them, knowing everything was free onboard except the casino. "But I'm buying", said Seven. "I *insist*."

The girls all laughed, with the notable exception of Doreen who remained quiet and pensive. In fact, she'd pretty much been mute the entire night. Doreen looked down at her fingernails and said, moodily, "You people go ahead. I've got a slight headache. I think I'll go back to my room and read."

Seven was disappointed. Doreen was the target he'd most wanted to work on, as she seemed to be the weakest link of this pretty quartet. Showing no outward regret, he merely sympathized, "Gee, that's too bad, Doreen. Hope you feel better soon."

"Thanks." She then left for her cabin, walking out the dining room's main doors with a glum frown on her face.

Anita shook her head, irritably. "Glad *she's* gone. Doreen's been a downer all night. In fact, she's been that way the past couple of days."

Anita shrugged her shoulders, grinned, and then exclaimed, "Well, handsome, I guess you only have *three* of us to make happy now."

"Seems so," Seven replied, as they all stood up and made their way out of the dining hall.

Terry and Anita stopped in the ladies' room across from the restaurant's entrance. Seven likewise entered the small, immaculate men's room next door to it. Here, as required, he took out his Super Stud travel tooth care kit, quickly brushed his teeth and gargled with the pocket-sized *Listerine* Artic Mint. He then washed his hands and walked out to see Suzanne standing alone, waiting for her two companions.

Seven was about to say something to her when she suddenly grabbed him around the neck and kissed him fervently on the lips. A bit stunned, the agent said nothing. But he made a mental note to start putting his foot down if these women continued to use him as some type of erotic 'errand boy'. He certainly didn't want to appear to be a willing puppet to his four targets, meekly waiting for their next command. The Super Stud knew from experience that if he showed some backbone and mystery, rather than placid compliance, he'd ultimately become more desirable to them.

Thinking on this, he simply gave Suzanne a stern, annoyed look. Slowly moving away from her, Seven turned and saw Terry and Anita standing directly behind him. He wondered if they'd observed the kiss, and, if so, whether they were angry or jealous by it. It was hard to tell from the neutral look on both of their faces. The G5 agent remained silent as Terry brusquely ordered, "Follow me." The four of them then made their way to the elevator, which whisked them down to Deck 4.

The cozy British Pub had quite a few customers, including some of the attractive off-duty spa girls and Donna from reception. She was sitting at a small table with two of the ship's officers. It was a pleasant room decorated in an England motif, complete with a beautiful mahogany bar, an official English dartboard, and a full-sized, though nonworking, red London phone booth. Most of the clientele were drinking dark ale from the bar, enjoying the guitarist who played soft jazz in the background.

Terry motioned Seven and the girls to the back of the cocktail lounge, where they grabbed a table away from the other patrons. A waiter dressed in festive 'Old English' attire walked over and took their order. Apple martinis for the women and another glass of champagne for Seven.

While they waited for the drinks to arrive, Christopher Seven glanced at his three attractive companions, sizing them up with a professional eye.

Anita, the acerbic redhead, looked to be the toughest of the bunch, both physically and via her rough, caustic demeanor. She had striking green eyes and thick red hair, which she was wearing pinned up in a bun. She was by far the tallest of the girls, standing at least 5'9". Her excellent body was much more solid and heftier than her friends, and there wasn't an ounce of fat on her. Seven guessed Anita was quite athletic as well, probably someone who worked out daily in a gym.

Suzanne, the attractive 'dirty blonde', was the thinnest and most guarded of the women. Her shapely body was more delicate and feminine than Anita's, and she seemed to be more circumspect than the rest of her clique. Seven would have to be extremely careful in what he said to her, for she had a sharp brain that appeared to be permanently on 'high alert'. 'Suz', as she preferred to be called, had lovely blue eyes, a flawless complexion, and long flowing hair. Mostly blonde, with wisps of darker locks veined through it. She reminded Seven of a prettier version of *Veronica Lake*, the sexy movie goddess he'd seen in several old *Alan Ladd* movies from the 1940s.

Terry, the abrasive leader of the pack, was by far the hardest to figure. She was an absolute knockout, with shiny blonde hair that was obviously colored, for it seemed almost golden at times. She wore it alluringly parted to the side. The Super Stud knew instinctively that this woman was the most dangerous and calculating of the entire group, their unquestioned 'leader'. Though Terry could be friendly and helpful at times, she was also the type who would happily sell you out in order to get what she wanted. Seven was certain that this capricious female was an unabashed 'user'. And quite callous as well. A woman who would kiss you passionately on the lips while getting ready to stick a stiletto into your back. She was extremely perceptive and cunning, and the Seven knew he'd have to keep a wary, placating eye on her at all times. The enigmatic Terry was someone he definitely didn't want as an enemy.

"Here you are, folks," said the amiable waiter as he put down the four drinks. "Please enjoy."

Seven raised his glass. "Well, ladies, what should we drink to?"

Almost as if to prove the G5 agent's summations correct, Terry exclaimed with a sneer, "How about to your health? From what I hear, it almost wasn't worth much the other night." She looked him directly in the eyes. "Tell me, friend – is this nonsense about your 'loving yachts' really true? Or do you have *other* reasons for wanting to get together with Carmine and us?"

Christopher Seven was floored by the question. It took all of his professional training to remain composed. He calmly took a sip of champagne, and smiled through his answer. "Well, Terry, believe it or not, I am indeed a yacht 'groupie'. If we were back at my home in Jersey now, I'd gladly show you all the books, photos, and magazine articles I've collected on the subject. Yet, if truth be told, yes, I definitely *did* have another objective."

The three women eyed him carefully.

"You see, girls, when I meet four beautiful women on the prowl, I'd have to be extremely dumb *not* to try and follow up on it." He gave them a sheepish grin and added, "So I freely admit that when I first saw Suzanne, and then the rest of you ladies at the restaurant, my fascination with yachts took on even *more* interest!"

Terry, at first a bit skeptical, grudgingly smiled. Convinced for the moment by Seven's candid confession, she laughed, "Fair enough. I just wanted you to know that I didn't buy this 'little sailor boy loves his boats' thing a hundred percent." She and her two cohorts then settled back with their drinks. Continuing to enjoy the music, they took turns dancing with Seven, as the other women in the room watched with envy.

~

While the Super Stud agent was trying his best to captivate and gently probe his lovely targets, Carmine Gitano was below decks attending to his 'business meeting'. Way down on Deck 1, he sat at the head of a long mahogany table located in the yacht's sizeable conference room. Sitting with him around the table were the powerful Mafia chieftains of three other European 'families', each accompanied by his personal bodyguard. The apelike Nalco, Gitano's trusty protector, along with another Gitano soldier named Mario, were likewise at the table.

Officially calling the meeting to order, *Don* Gitano was all business now. Cold and vicious, he certainly wasn't the jovial host he'd forced himself to be at dinner. There were many things on Gitano's mind. Including his continued desire to extract some form of revenge upon Christopher Seven; the good- looking punk who'd embarrassed him in the casino. For the moment, this 'pretty boy' could wait. Although Gitano would be sure to address Seven at the end the meeting. Right now, there were more pressing matters to review.

"Okay," snapped Carmine, "let's get started. As you fellas know, we have less than four weeks to commence with our momentous plan. When it finally comes off, it will be the biggest and most historic gangland 'hit' ever carried out by organized crime. Bigger than Capone's St. Valentine's Day massacre, bigger than the Sparks rubout of Castellano and Bilotti, and bigger than the mob's hit on Marilyn Monroe after the Kennedy thing. It will be even bigger than Johnny Pro's hit on Hoffa. And it's gonna net me one *billion* smackeroos, which I've generously promised to share with you boys for your help."

The other capos looked at each other and grunted noncommittally as Gitano went on, "This enormous payday will be the highest fee *ever* earned for a gangland rubout. For that, we have our generous friends from Iran and North Korea to thank. By the way, those two countries have agreed to split the fees 50-50."

Carmine Gitano puffed his barreled chest out, proudly. "It's gonna be something they talk about for centuries!" He snarled a short laugh. "Guess you guys never thought we'd be school book material."

The other mobsters smiled back at him as Gitano continued.

"Obviously, the Mafia will only be *rumored* to be in on it. At least for the short run. Just like the Marilyn Monroe thing, we won't get any initial credit. Not until some savvy TV or newspaper reporter eventually stumbles on the truth. Hopefully not for another fifty years or more. But that's a *good* thing, since no one can spend a billion bucks in some federal prison." There were more grunts as Gitano added, "True, there'll be risks, but that's what we're getting paid the big dough for."

The big man stood up, stretched his arms. He then sat back down in his chair and began, "Now then. As for your individual roles. Let's review them one more time. Joey and his Corsican contacts have bribed or threatened the four catering hall people we'll need if any classified banquet questions come up. Or to let us know of any last minute seating changes from that Ambassador guy's notes. These catering hall managers are now firmly in our pocket. Gitano grinned. "Although they don't know what we're *really* up to."

Gitano then pointed to the stocky gangster sitting to his left. "And Willie Boy here has hooked the Rhombus 'escort guys' on some of those fancy drugs he's been selling in America. Those four embassy dudes will now do *anything* Willie tells them to, in order to keep their fix of narcotics coming. He's got 'em completely hooked."

"Anything we want, they'll do, Carm ," affirmed Willie, a gruff looking gangster with strong mob ties in Detroit, and also in Italy with the Carpi gang.

There were affirmative nods around the table as Carmine further informed, "And as for our friend Sino, here", Gitano pointed to his left, "He's the one who supplied me with the Korean doctor, one of the most important cogs in the whole plan. By the way, Sine, that Korean turned out to be a perfect choice."

Sino Fressi bowed his head slightly, a bit embarrassed by the praise as *Don* Gitano added, "Yes, gentlemen, so far, it seems that you're all completing your tasks satisfactorily. Although I'll need definite confirmation of that from my own people, as will the Koreans and Iranians. Verification, *before* any money is paid to you.

"Whataya mean?!" yelled Joey Taba, head of Sicily's notorious South Hill mob. "You promised we'd each be getting a four-million-dollar retainer. Something to hold us till the big money comes in. That's the only reason we agreed to sail on this Zephyr tub of yours. To get our retainer dough *here* and *now*! What gives?"

"Relax, Joey," Gitano countered. "Like I said, I got to confirm things with the North Koreans and Iran." He held out his hands. "Look at it from *their* point of view. You don't just give out twelve million smackers without confirmation. Once all the initial procedures have been successfully completed, you guys will be paid. But *not* before."

There was an awkward silence around the table. Sensing looming trouble, Gitano assured, "Don't worry, fellas, you'll get your initial million. Maybe not this week, but it'll be soon. Right after my clients confirm everything."

"Look," barked Taba. "We want our dough *this* week! Onboard this boat, just like you promised us."

Carmine Gitano's face began turning an angry red. Trying to control himself he again assured, "If the clients give their okay this week, fine. I'll hand you the money drafts myself, right here on Zephyr. But only *after* I get Iran's and North Korea's blessing."

The other two mob bosses grimaced angrily. Expecting something like this, they turned toward Joey Taba whom they had earlier picked as their spokesman.

"No deal, Carmine," Taba declared. "First off, we each want our million in seven days or less, or everything's off." Taba pounded his fist on the table. "And one more thing. You said last month that you and we would be divvying up the one billion total, with you getting three quarters of a billion right off the top. And with us three guys splitting the rest *after* all the expenses are taken from *our* end."

"Well?" said Gitano, still trying to hold his temper.

"No good," barked Taba. "We've been talking, and that's way too greedy. We now say – *you* pay the expenses, not us. With *another* hundred million going to us to divvy-up. After all, we're splitting our take three ways. And the feds can trace *our* roles in this just as easy as *yours.*"

Carmine Gitano slumped back in his chair, stunned by this last-minute squeeze. Inwardly seething, he glanced over at his own second lieutenant, Mario Gaya. Both of them had anticipated some resistance, but nothing like this eleventh-hour curveball. And nothing *this* sizeable. Thankfully, Carmine and Mario had made 'contingency plans', secretly negotiating separate deals with the underbosses of the families these three capos at the table headed. *Permanent* plans.

Unlike the anxious Gitano, Mario looked at the other mobster chefs with poised assurance. For the three 'Dons' now sitting at the table, along with their beefy bodyguards, would be 'hit' – *whacked* Mafia style right here aboard Zephyr! It had all been planned and approved by the European underbosses of these three chieftains.

Carmine Gitano glared at the three traitors sitting around the table, feigning affronted outrage. Playacting flawlessly, just like his wily poker persona, Gitano seemed to be angrily pondering the situation. After a moment of silence, and what appeared to be shocked reflection, he contrived to reluctantly concede.

"Okay, Taba, you win. You guys know there's obviously not enough time for me to argue or change things now. Too big a risk at this point.

But I don't like being held up like this. Suffice to say, I'll never *ever* work with any of you bums again!"

Joey Taba shrugged his broad shoulders. "Come on, Carm. Don't take it so personal. It's just business."

Gitano faked calming down. "Maybe, Joey. But I still say it stinks. What you guys are doing to me now is rotten!"

Now it was *Don* Gitano's turn to shrug his shoulders. "Oh well. I guess you people don't operate the way I do. In any case, you'll get the deal you want. And I'll have those retainer deposits for you as well. You'll get 'em before we arrive back at Monaco. Even if I have to lay it out myself from my own Swiss accounts. But if any of you guys try to hold me up *again* on this, I'll personally beat the snot out of you!"

The three rival Godfathers grinned, used to Carmine's theatrical rants. Happy to change the subject, Sino Fressi asked, "What about the Rhombus dames, Carm? Are they having any second thoughts?"

"You leave them to me," Gitano insisted. "But I can assure you that they won't back out on us."

Carmine Gitano, with a subdued expression on his bony face, slowly explained, "I know you guys find their part in this hard to believe. At first, so did I. But it's absolutely true. The Rhombus women don't want a dime for this caper. They only want the glory. To be assured that our worldwide press contacts, and our various media outlets, spread the word that Rhombus made the actual *hit* itself."

Carmine sighed. "Their motives are a bit complicated, so I won't go into it right now. But I've personally promised them that what they've insisted on will be faithfully carried out. And I meant it. The world will indeed know it was Rhombus."

Don Gitano stared at the ceiling a moment, his expression solemn and resolute. "That's all the four girls want and they're going to receive it. For I, Carmine Gitano, now swear, in front of all of you, that I will keep my sacred *Cosa Nostra* pledge to them." Gitano held up his right hand. "My life on it. It *will* be done."

"*Lo giuro su mia madre,*" Gitano's underling, Mario, softly whispered.

Carmine Gitano then crossed his heart with genuine emotion.

The other mobsters waited respectfully a few moments, and then Willie Boy Sassa, the third Mafia chieftain, asked, "What about this yacht voyage you wanted us to come on, Carm? I still don't get it. What if we're spotted? I heard you got a few civilian passengers onboard this trip. Maybe one of them might recognize us. The cops and Interpol could become real suspicious if word ever got out that four of Europe's biggest mob figures were meeting on the same boat. Especially once the big event takes place. That's why I was strongly against your insistence that we come on this yacht trip."

Gitano, hiding his *real* reason for bringing these three Mafioso rivals onboard Zephyr, turned toward Sassa and assured, "Had to be done. Where *else* could we go over things in complete seclusion? Away from our mob families and any possible stoolpigeons among them." Gitano smiled, confidently. "But don't worry, Willie. For one thing, the yacht's practically empty this cruise. Secondly, you guys will be out of sight the entire voyage, living and eating as 'new workers' down in the crewmen's area. Passengers aren't allowed down there. And as for my crew, believe me, they've been firmly ordered not to talk with; or bother any of the new guys. And not to ask any questions about them either. Trust me, they know to keep their mouths shut - or *else*."

Carmine shrugged his shoulders apologetically. "Sorry it won't be a luxury cruise for you and your bodyguards this time around fellas. Being stuck downstairs for the voyage. But it's only for a week or so, and I'll make sure there's plenty of topnotch liquor and chow for you guys. In any case, it was imperative that you came along in order to go over final arrangements and compensation." Carmine frowned. "Especially now, since you want your retainers up front."

The gangsters nodded as Gitano further explained, "And as for any informants or plants among the few passengers we have onboard this trip, don't fret. There are no civilians aboard of any consequence. Mostly just my gangland cronies, plus a few of those corporate honchos we deal with on the legit stuff. But they all know the score about keeping their traps shut. All they want is free food and booze."

Gitano frowned with annoyance. "Oh yeah, I almost forgot. There *is* one other passenger with us. Some worthless punk the Rhombus women insisted on bringing aboard last-minute. You guys know how the Rhombus girls are always grabbing good-looking gigolos and dragging 'em along. It's a real pain in the butt but I couldn't refuse them. Not this time, with everything they're doing for us. Anyway, this lowlife is nothing to worry about. Some freeloader from New Jersey. But don't fret. I'll make sure to have him carefully watched anyway."

Gitano grinned and ran a finger across his neck. "Besides, he may not even make the entire voyage. Nalco and I have a little score to settle with him, so there could be an *accident*."

The other mob chiefs laughed knowingly as Carmine finished up. "So just relax fellas and dream about all that loot we'll be getting. And be proud of taking part in history's greatest mob hit."

The Mafia *Don* leaned back in his chair and spoke slowly and very deliberately, wanting to make his next words sound even more dramatic. "Cause it ain't every day that some uncouth 'wise guys' like us can rub out the president of France, the prime ministers of England and Italy, and the President of the United States...all on the *same* night!

The following morning Christopher Seven was awakened by bright sunshine creeping through his stateroom's partially drawn draperies. He sleepily glanced at his alarm clock beside the bed, noting that he'd forgotten to set it after tiptoeing into his room well after 3:00 a.m. The clock now read 9:20 a.m.

Thinking about last night's partying with Terry, Anita and Suz, the agent grinned. He was justly proud of himself, knowing he'd made some real progress with these three women. Though admittedly he was a bit disappointed they wouldn't be around today. During last night's merriment in the English pub, Anita had casually mentioned that she, Suzanne and Terry would be engaged most of the day. Some 'personal appointment' in Antibes set up by the concierge. Anita had also revealed that their fourth colleague, the diffident Doreen, wouldn't be going with them. Doreen would be remaining onboard Zephyr.

Left to his own devices, the Super Stud decided he'd try calling Doreen's cabin right after breakfast. See if she wanted to have a late lunch with him. Either on the yacht or somewhere on shore. If so, it might be a rare opportunity to get Doreen alone without her three sidekicks mulling around. Thinking on it again, Seven walked into the bathroom for his morning shave, tooth brushing regimen and shower.

Twenty minutes later, dressed in white Levi's and a red-and-white nautical shirt, he perused the yacht's daily activity and information sheet. It had been silently slipped under his door sometime during the night. The G5 agent noticed that a buffet breakfast was continually served between 7:00 a.m. and 11:00 a.m. up by the Deck 8 pool. Deciding to breakfast there, he exited his cabin and headed for the elevator, leaving the *Please Service my Room* sign hanging on the door for his steward.

While riding the small lift, Seven silently vowed to start using the stairs instead of the elevators from now on. Do so as a means of getting some extra exercise to help work off the calories from all the tasty food onboard. He recalled a family cruise he'd taken several years ago with his parents and brother. Back then, one of the dining room waiters had told them that the only way to stay fit and fat free on a cruise, with all the rich cuisine consumed, was to "always take the stairs instead of the elevators." Smiling at the remembrance, Seven promised himself he'd start walking whenever and wherever he could, to go along with his daily workouts in Zephyr's excellent gym.

Upon reaching Deck 8, he saw a number of elegant patio tables set up under a blue canopy by the main pool. These lengthy tables, stationed along the far wall, were filled with every conceivable breakfast item.

Seven walked over to have a look. There were freshly made bagels, homemade pastries and breads, a huge selection of fruits and cheeses, steaming platters of bacon, sausages and home fries, and a 'freshly made French toast and waffle section.' There was even an omelet station for 'made to order' egg dishes. The agent shrugged and grabbed a tray.

Making his way through the tempting, calorie-laden glut of food, he chose the healthy route instead, taking plenty of fresh fruit, a plain multigrain bagel, and a small box of *Wheaties.* He also placed a cup of coffee and a large glass of his preferred 'fresh-squeezed' orange juice, one of his all-time favorite beverages, on his tray. The OJ had just been squeezed by a thin attendant standing behind the buffet table manning a *Zumex* juicer. Seven was about to carry his tray over to an empty table, when a passing waiter grabbed it from behind.

"I'll take that, sir," said the waiter. "Please follow me. Miss Doreen is sitting alone on the other side of the vessel and she'd like you to join her." Seven nodded and followed the server over to Doreen's table.

Arriving at Doreen's table, she smiled up at them. "Thanks for fetching him for me, Anzi. And please see to it that no one else comes to our table."

"Very good, madam." Anzi neatly unloaded Seven's food items, set them down on the table, and took his leave.

After waiting a moment, Doreen cordially greeted, "Beautiful day, isn't it, Chris?"

"It sure is. And what a breathtaking view of the shoreline. The water's so still and blue. One could almost reach out and touch the land."

"I love it when we anchor," Doreen responded, her face showing a delightful smile. "We're technically still at sea, yet the boat is completely motionless, anchored a mile or so out from land. A lot of nights we stop like this and have dinner under the stars. It's marvelous."

"Sounds it," Seven replied. "By the way, how are you feeling today? I missed you last night."

"You *did*?" Her surprised, pleased expression was endearing to him.

"I sure did, Doreen. I wanted to personally thank you for that Monaco business with Nalco. So since you weren't with us last night, I was wondering if you'd like to have lunch with me today. We could take the tender to shore, rent a car, and perhaps drive over to Eze. I've heard it's one of the most charming villages in all of Europe."

"Oh, it is," she gushed. "I used to visit there quite often when I was a kid. Haven't been there in a few years, so it'd be great to see Eze again." She blushed a bit. "Especially with you."

"Then it's a date," said Seven, unexpectedly charmed by this attractive, reserved young woman. It was a welcome change after being with her three acerbic girlfriends last night. Doreen's quiet simplicity was refreshing to him. "I'll come by your cabin in an hour or so," Seven informed. "Say around 11:45. I'd like to get a workout in the gym first, and perhaps a quick swim in the pool."

"That's fine. I'll be ready. I'm in Cabin 12. But how should I dress?"

"Casual but stylish is fine. I have a restaurant in mind that was recommended by a buddy of mine. He told me the place is fairly informal. But I'll bring a sports jacket just in case."

Still smiling, Doreen got up to leave. "Sorry to have to make you eat breakfast by yourself, Chris. But I scheduled a massage in the ship's spa for 9:45 and I'm already five minutes late."

"No problem, Doreen. See you later."

"You bet. And thanks so much for the lunch invitation. I was hoping we could somehow get together today." And with that she cheerfully strolled toward the elevator.

Seven watched her walk away and then finished the remainder of his breakfast in silence. Leaning back in his chair, he gazed out at the magnificent panorama of the sea and the French coastline. The turquoise water below him was dead calm and remarkably beautiful. It glistened dazzlingly in the bright Mediterranean sunshine. There was a soft, cooling breeze, making the setting even more idyllic. The G5 agent sighed, grudgingly admitting that he could now see why the rich and famous loved their yachts. And all the wonderful moments and vistas like this one that came with them. He sighed again, took a last drink of the delicious orange juice and got up from the table.

Finally alone, Seven silently deliberated if the time was right to do a bit of snooping. After all, that was why he'd come. Not to enjoy some lazy seagoing interlude in the sun. He ducked into a nearby men's room, dutifully brushed his teeth, and tried to clear his mind. *Now, where should I begin?* he calmly asked himself. The obvious choice was the yacht's top, restricted deck; Deck 10. During Seven's initial tour of the ship, Captain Bacca had seemed extremely wary of exposing too much up there. *Okay, then, I'll just have to explore that area for myself. Now then, how can I do so without drawing suspicion? And what about the yacht's sophisticated surveillance equipment?*

As he pondered these questions, Seven recalled his early spy training. Back then, his instructors had pointed out that the best and safest way to visit an area to spy on was through the 'front door', if at all possible. Actually *ask* someone to show it to you after coming up with a believable reason for doing so. That way, if you were detected, a somewhat reasonable explanation was easier to defend than being caught in the act of sneaking around on your own. "I asked someone if it was Okay" was always better than some lame, far out excuse.

Making his way over to the wrought iron staircase, he walked up the short flight of stairs to Deck 9, which was basically an outside sunning deck that housed some of Zephyr's water toys. Fortunately, no one was about except for a lone worker washing the deck with a thick black power hose. The worker's metal nametag said 'Emilio Rossi.' Seven smiled at him and greeted, "Excuse me, Emilio."

The crewman immediately turned off the hose and bowed politely. "*Si, signore*, can I help'a you?" Thankfully, his English was quite passable.

Seven feigned embarrassment and informed, "Sorry to bother you, but the other day, during the lifeboat drill with Captain Bacca, I think I might have left my sunglasses up on Deck 10. They're rather expensive *Porsche* glasses, so I'd really like to find them. I saw by the sign across the upper steps that Deck 10 is an area for crew only. I was thus wondering if you could escort me up there to have a quick search for them."

The crewman gave him a nervous, hesitant look, but Seven kept pressing him with sociable small talk. "By the way, Emilio, I'm half-Italian myself and very proud of it. What part of Italy are you from?"

Emilio beamed, delighted that one of Mr. Gitano's passengers was actually having a friendly conversation with him. Most of them treated him like dirt. "I'm'a from Tuscany, signore. Cerbaia, a small'a town outside of Florence."

Christopher Seven grinned widely. "One of Italy's most beautiful areas, Emilio. Bravo! As for me, my father's family was from Perugia. You know, where they make that great candy."

"Ah, Umbria. *Bellissimo,* signore!"

"Do you have family in Tuscany, Emilio?"

"Si." The crewman smiled, took out his wallet and proudly showed Seven a photo of his wife and his two young daughters.

"They're lovely, Emilio." The Super Stud took four twenty-dollar bills from his own wallet and nimbly placed them into Emilio's front shirt pocket. "For helping me look for my glasses," he pushed. "Please buy your girls some chocolate when you get home." Seven grinned. "But make sure it's from Perugia."

Emilio glanced around, apprehensively, but then bowed his head in gratitude. Shrugging his shoulders, he explained, "Usually we not supposed to go up'a there. Especially with passengers. But I think if we quick about it, it should'a be okay." He walked over to the metal stairway leading up to Deck 10 and cautiously removed the hanging sign tied across it; one that read: "Restricted – Crew only – Absolutely <u>no</u> admittance! Nervously looking around, he motioned Seven to follow.

Upon arriving at Zephyr's highest deck with crewman Rossi, Christopher Seven promptly walked away from him toward the other end of the deck. Seven then began making a show of searching for his missing glasses. The edgy deckhand likewise began looking, doing so at the opposite end of the deck. He yelled over, pleadingly, "Please'a be *quick*, signore."

Seven nodded and hurriedly made his way toward the canvas-covered helicopter. He searched around it a moment and then headed further up toward the ship's bow. Continuing the charade of rummaging for something lost, this for the benefit of any hidden security cameras, the G5 operative pretended to search in the corners and on the ground; casually strolling toward the very front of Deck 10. He soon came upon the other huge object hidden under a thick tarpaulin, the massive, cylinder-shaped item. After first making sure Rossi wasn't facing him, Seven grabbed the canvas cover and had a fast peek under it. He immediately recognized what he saw. Surprised but satisfied, the Super Stud pulled the tarp back down and once more pretended to continue to search for his specs.

A few minutes later, he walked back toward Emilio, who was still searching the opposite end of the deck. With a neat sleight of hand move, Seven pulled out his sunglasses from his pants pocket, held them high and happily exclaimed, "I just found 'em, Emilio." He pointed toward the front of Deck 10. "They were over there, near the railing, hidden by one of the lifeboats."

Rossi spun around to face him and gave out a relieved sigh. "*Bene*, signore. Now *please*. Let's leave'a here, pronto." And with that, the two men walked back down the stairwell and returned to Deck.

~

An hour later, after a short workout in the gym, followed by a dip in the pool and a shower in his cabin, Christopher Seven changed his clothes for his luncheon date with Doreen. Still trying to silently replay his weak 'missing sunglasses' explanation for trespassing on Deck 10, in case he'd been caught on any surveillance cameras. Seven knew it might not wash so easily. He thus decided to openly inform security about it later on, figuring the best defense was a good offense. Hopefully they'd let it go at that. If not, if Seven was even remotely suspected of spying, the vindictive Carmine Gitano probably wouldn't listen to any sophomoric explanations. A severe chastisement or something far worse could definitely be in the offing.

Shuddering at the thought, the Super Stud was nonetheless satisfied that the risk had been worth it. For underneath this second spacious tarpaulin, some forty feet from the helicopter, was something the undercover operative had never expected to see on anyone's private vessel. Seven's spying foray had revealed a small submarine, an eight man *Alvis* submersible manufactured in Groton, Connecticut. The agent was vaguely familiar with it, having seen one during a private tour at the Woods Hole Oceanographic Institution in Massachusetts.

Still astonished at finding it onboard Zephyr, Christopher Seven wondered what use a Mafia chieftain would have for a submarine on his yacht. He was also puzzled as to how a gangster like Gitano could even get hold of one. As far as Seven knew, these sophisticated mini-subs were only manufactured and sold to accredited scientific research organizations; or specialized U.S. Naval branches. Not gun-toting mobsters. Carmine must have bribed someone really well. Seven frowned. *Better get this info off to G5 headquarters ASAP.*

As the Super Stud made his way up the hallway up toward Doreen's cabin, his analytical mind raced rapidly, desperately trying to ascertain what the wily *Don* Gitano was up to. Little did Seven know, however, that two husky crewmen had quietly observed his bribe to Emilio, as well as Seven's Deck 10 spying venture. Doing so from their video monitoring station on the ship's bridge. They were now hurriedly making their way down to Carmine Gitano's master suite.

S even met up with Doreen just as she was coming out of her cabin. He smiled, took her arm in his, and they then walked down to Deck 2 where the 'tender embarkation station' was located. Since *Zephyr's* underbelly *was* too deep to go in any closer to shore, the yacht's motorized lifeboats were being utilized to whisk passengers between from the ship and the dock. A small sign, hanging by the open gangway door, said they'd be running the lifeboats, 'aka tenders', continuously until 6PM this evening.

After a short and smooth tender ride, Seven and Doreen were soon standing on a miniscule pier near the *Plage Ste-Helene.* Waiting for them there, as arranged by Zephyr's proficient concierge, was an *Avis* rented BMW Z4 convertible. After checking in with the Avis rep, Seven helped Doreen into the dark-blue roadster, and then hopped into the driver's seat. Their first planned destination was a mountaintop estate that Doreen had asked him to drive to, casually mentioning it while they were riding the tender in to shore.

Glancing over at his lovely companion, the Super Stud anoted that Doreen was the best looking of the four yacht women. Close to a 'perfect 10', much like a younger Bo Derek whom she slightly resembled. Her natural blonde hair fell softly over her shoulders, and her piercing blue eyes complimented her gorgeous face perfectly. She was dressed in tight-fitting white Capris and a clinging yellow blouse, smartly accented by some expensive gold jewelry. With her hair gently blowing in the soft side breeze, and wearing a pair of large, rounded designer sunglasses, she looked seductive, and also a bit mysterious.

Seven put down the car's retractable roof and was about to drive away when Doreen gleefully exclaimed, "What a great day for a convertible. It'll make our drive up to Eze even more enjoyable."

"It sure will, Doreen. And since our lunch reservation isn't 'til two, we'll have plenty of time to enjoy the ride. But tell me more about this old estate you wanted us to visit first. Sounds kind of adventurous."

"Actually, it was the home I grew up in as a young kid, right here in the south of France. It's located quite close to Eze, so I figured it'd be easy to visit today. The villa, named *Le Bleu,* was my father's old residence. It was his family's property for many generations. Sadly, Daddy lost it several years ago when he couldn't pay the two mortgages he'd taken out on the place. The bank eventually foreclosed, and losing the estate literally broke my father's heart. He died six months later."

She sighed, looked away a moment, and then continued, "No one ever purchased the property after that, and the bank people have pretty much given up on the place. It's fallen into severe disrepair, but I still like to visit there whenever I can. Brings back memories of the few enjoyable times in my life."

Seven said nothing, a bit surprised by Doreen's gloomy candor. She remained downcast for several minutes, then finally regained her smile again. Seemingly coming out of her pathos she informed, "It'll likewise be fun to see Eze Village again. I haven't been there in quite a while. We used to visit Eze a lot when I was a youngster."

"I'm looking forward to it, Doreen."

Seven then started the powerful 335 HP power turbo engine, and they were soon motoring up the middle cornice. With the car's top down, and the wind blowing gently on their faces, the drive was wonderful. Albeit a bit daunting with its sharp twists and turns. As the road got steeper and more rural, Seven had to be wary of oncoming cars, frequently pulling over to let the wild French drivers speed by on the narrow roadway. While doing so, the Super Stud thought of Monaco's Princess Grace, the lovely actress and princess who died in an auto crash right here on this cornice motorway. The G5 agent fondly recalled her dynamic role in Hitchcock's Riviera classic, *To Catch a Thief*.

Looking down from the mountain, the delightful vista below was enhanced by the azure water of the Mediterranean Sea. The G5 operative thought it one of the most scenic landscapes he'd ever driven. He hoped his pretty driving companion was also enjoying it. Yet, as they got nearer their first destination, the *Le Bleu* estate, Doreen once again grew sullen, showing little interest in the spectacular scenery. She became downcast and moody again, and Seven wondered if this sullenness would continue. And, if so, whether she'd be difficult to engage. Nevertheless, he was still confident he attracted her, and coldly continued planning ways to use her in order to ferret out information.

Twenty silent minutes later, the BMW convertible finally reached a large white dwelling situated on a secluded hilltop. As they neared the dilapidated front gate, the girl's depressed demeanor abruptly changed for a second time. She smiled widely, thrilled to see the old manor. "There it is! Le Bleu. Daddy's estate."

Seven pulled the car over a pothole-riddled driveway and parked on the right side of it. "Come on, Chris, let me show you around."

For the next half hour or so, Doreen gave him an informative tour. She cheerfully showed him the regal old house, the ancient underground wine cellar and the wooden barn behind the main dwelling filled with primitive tools and a pack of sleeping bats. The house and barn were in appalling shape, with broken windows and missing siding everywhere.

Seven doubted the place could ever be put back together, and understood why the bank no longer wanted it.

Moments later, the two of them were standing in front of a large man-made lake. It was the only part of the property that was still appealing, thanks mainly to its crystal-clear, blue water; the property's namesake.

"My dad and I spent a lot of time by this lake," Doreen explained, tears welling up in her eyes. "During my early childhood years, he used to tell me about the legendary flower mermaid of the Riviera."

"The flower mermaid?"

"Yes, Chris." She smiled, endearingly. "Daddy promised me that I'd always be protected by her. He told me that if I ever fell into this lake, or, for that matter, got into trouble *anywhere* in the world – the flower mermaid would make sure I returned safely to this very shoreline." Her face beamed. "And see? Here I am again, safe and sound."

Seven was charmed by her childlike fervor. He listened with interest as Doreen pointed toward the cluster of lovely rose bushes that lined the right side of the water's edge. "That's where the mermaid lives", Doreen declared. "In those flowers over there. Daddy explained that when she's not busy rescuing people, and bringing them safely back here, the legend says she becomes a rose and dwells in this garden. And, if you want her to, the mermaid can turn you into a rose petal too. So you can live with her here forever, just like in the storybooks - 'happily ever after'." Doreen sighed with a distant, forlorn expression "I sure wish *I* could live here. Happily ever after with the mermaid."

Confused by the distressed look on her face, Seven said nothing. Though he was genuinely touched by Doreen's sadness, and this wishful childhood fairytale, he was also aware that she just might be the fourth member of one of the most notorious and sadistic criminal bands in history. It was a strange dichotomy. One that seemed completely surreal in this tranquil, idyllic setting. Here he was, in all likelihood mingling with a dangerous enemy agent. Yet he was surrounded by blooming roses in a delightful lakeside locale. Listening to innocent childhood tales of some magical flower mermaid. The agent shook his head at the incongruity.

Soon, several small birds flew in and began chirping loudly, as if they too wanted to be part of the conversation. Doreen smiled at them. "Daddy and I both loved birds," she said, still with that poignant, reflective look in her eyes. "We used to bring them food and feed them here by hand."

"Your father sounds like he was a loving and wonderful man, Doreen."

"He was. Dad was my hero in so many ways." She looked out over the lake. "He and my mother split up for good on the day of my twelfth birthday." She frowned, disdainfully. "Some present, huh?"

Seven nodded sympathetically.

"From then on", Doreen reflected, "I was bounced around from one parent to the other. That is, when I wasn't away at my horrid boarding school in Geneva." Doreen grimaced at the memory. "When school ended for the summer, I spent most of my vacation time with mother in Paris. Even though Dad was the one I really wanted to be with. Especially here, during the few happy weekends I actually got to spend with him. My father had a quiet elegance about him and he was never demanding of me. Mother was the complete opposite; strict, harsh and domineering. She made me do things *her* way, whether they were right, wrong, or even deceitful."

Seven's senses immediately picked up at Doreen's last remark. He observed her growing anger closely as she finished the story.

"Mother more or less forced me into her way of life and wouldn't take no for an answer. It was always her way *or else.* And she wasn't one who spared the rod either. I can remember several painful beatings."

Again Doreen's resentment seemed to increase as she revisited more of her past. Her eyes had a detached, distant look to them. It was as if Seven wasn't even there. As if she was talking to herself. "Father was completely different. Always kind, and letting me be myself. He encouraged me to pursue whatever I wanted in life. Yet always good and normal things." Doreen stared straight ahead a moment. "The exact opposite of Mom, really. Daddy was gentle and laid-back, while Mother was a constant pusher. A domineering 'stage mother' who forced me into her career and lifestyle."

Seemingly coming out of her trance, Doreen finally looked over at Seven. "Oh well, one can't choose their parents, can they? I guess I was lucky to have *one* parent who was decent."

Seven mentally filed her admission of being 'forced into a certain lifestyle'. *Did that mean Doreen's role with Rhombus?* Seven wondered. *It just could be.* In any event, one thing was clear. The beautiful young woman sitting across from him was much more open and careless with her words than were her cohorts. Anita and Terry's's annoyance and fears about 'Doreen talking too much', were well founded. A weakness Seven had likewise discerned.

Certain now that Doreen was the one to work on, the weakest calf in the herd for the stalking agent to prey upon, Christopher Seven merely nodded his head.

Seven looked away a moment, carefully contemplating his next moves. First, he'd have to somehow 'lure out' more details about Doreen and her mother. Do so despite the maddening Gitano rule about 'no last names'. If he could somehow entice *real* names out of this girl, hopefully Doc Fieri could check them out through Interpol and the CIA.

Ten minutes later, they left Le Bleu estate for the short ride over to Eze. As Seven's rented BMW pulled into the charming village, Doreen became an animated companion again. Impressed by the town's enchanting motif, Seven understood the reason for her enthusiasm. He, too, was captivated by Eze's picturesque, *Camelot* aura.

Constructed on a rocky hillside, Eze Village had once been a fortified feudal outpost erected during the middle ages. Back then it was an armed citadel built to fend off raids from the Corsairs. Nowadays, the community is a popular tourist destination, with fortress-like structures, medieval fortifications, and unique rock formations; a labyrinth of quaint cobblestone streets, gas-lit taverns and quaint art galleries.

After parking the car in a narrow alleyway, Seven and his companion briefly explored the scenic village. Stopping first in a few of the old-world shops, they soon made their way into one of Eze's two celebrated art galleries – *Gallerie Sevek* and *Gallerie Doussot*. The G5 operative made Doreen smile as he wryly commented on some of the ostentatious artwork and their exorbitant prices.

At exactly 2:00 p.m. they walked into *Chateau de la Chevre* D'Or, the town's most renowned hotel and eatery. The famous restaurant proved to be a gourmet fairyland. A castle-shaped oasis of dramatic floor-to-ceiling windows overlooking the sea. Both Seven and Doreen were enthralled by the glorious setting and refined elegance.

After they were seated, the Super Stud ordered a Ker Royal for each of them and told the waiter to hold off with the menus awhile. Wanting to begin his subtle probing, Seven took Doreen's hand under the table and squeezed it gently. "I want to thank you again for pulling my chestnuts out of the fire the other night, Doreen. It could have gotten real messy with that guy Nalco in Monte Carlo."

"I know. I've seen what Nalco can do when he's angry and I didn't want that happening to you." She hesitated a moment before nervously confessing, "You see, Chris, from the first time I laid eyes on you, I wanted to get closer to you."

A bit embarrassed by the admission, her face reddened slightly. "Don't ask me how or why, but somehow I knew that if we gave it a try, we'd enjoy a special relationship." She sighed. "At least for the *short* run."

Doreen glanced down at the floor a moment. She then laughed uncharacteristically and declared, "I can't believe I just said that. Yet, you make me feel so blissful and serene. It's been a long time since *any* man had such an effect on me. That's probably why I decided to help you and warn the casino about Nalco's squad. Besides, I didn't want those apes to destroy your beautiful face." She reddened again. "It's the most divine face I've ever seen."

Seven gave her an affectionate smile of thanks.

"Believe me, Chris, I've *never* been impulsive or pushy when it comes to relationships. It's just that I know ours could be wonderful."

Christopher Seven, expertly trained to spot any semblance of a trap or deception, was sure Doreen's feelings were genuine. At least most of them. The Studs, via G5's vigorous psychological training, could almost always detect telltale signs that a woman was truly falling for him. And he knew that this one had – *head over heels!*

Even so, he coldly dismissed her feelings for him, focusing only on how he could exploit them. Now certain that Doreen was the obvious weak link of his targeted foursome, he still wasn't sure where to start with his probing. He couldn't just come out and ask her, *'Are you and your three friends part of Rhombus, and did you kill that U.S. ambassador?'* Obviously, if she, her three cronies, or Mafia boss Carmine Gitano even remotely suspected that Christopher Seven was a federal agent, Seven would quickly find himself on the first plane out. Or worse, his body lying in some dark alley with several knives stuck in his back. Instead Seven simply began with a few innocuous questions.

"Tell me, Doreen, how long have you known Mr. Gitano?"

"A while, I guess. He's ..." she paused a moment ." ... he's a 'business associate' for me and the other women onboard."

"A business associate? Seven probed, looking over at her. "What line of work are you ladies in?"

"Nothing important."

Undeterred by her unexpected stonewalling, Seven handled the rebuff with professional aplomb. He merely nodded and calmly perused the lunch menu.

Nothing of consequence was discussed for a while and they ordered and ate the delicious charbroiled 'Côte de boeuf pour deux' in polite silence. It was clear to Seven that this girl was on edge, as Doreen again became withdrawn and nervous near the end of the meal.

The G5 agent wondered if she was always this stressed or whether her tension was because of him. Glancing over at the demure, idealistic beauty sitting across the table, the Super Stud again asked himself, *Could this seemingly fragile girl really be part of one of the most ill-famed killing cores in the world? It still seems so illogical.* He shrugged his shoulders and ordered coffee for two to accompany the delicious petits- fours the waiter had just put down in front of them.

After a second cup, Seven called for and paid the check and then made his customary tooth-brushing stop in the empty men's room. A few minutes later, he and his lovely target were motoring back down the middle cornice toward the pier.

Arriving at the dock, they were immediately met by the freckled young man from Avis. He took the car keys, had Seven sign and initial a few forms, and then hopped in the BMW and drove it away.

Doreen and Seven glanced around the now deserted dockside. The tender to take them back to the Zephyr was nowhere in sight. Sensing their uncertainty, a tall crewman came over to explain.

"Sorry for the delay, folks. There's engine trouble with the main passenger tender and the other one is currently being utilized by the kitchen crew for supplies. We're getting a third tender down, but it will be at least thirty minutes before that one's ready to go. In the meantime, we have lemonade and snacks near the security guard over there. That is, if you'd care to wait here at the marina. If not, there's a small town not too far up the road with a bunch of shops and souvenir stands. And don't fret if you miss the next tender. All three tenders should soon be back up, running continuously right 'til 6:00 p.m. So you've got plenty of time to look around if you want." He held out his palms in contrition. "Anyway, sorry for the holdup." He then walked away.

Seven turned toward Doreen. "Want to take a stroll?"

"Sure. I'd like that."

Hand in hand, they wandered away from the small pier, passing a few roadside souvenir huts as they walked. Fifteen minutes later, they came to a deserted field filled with colorful flowers. Doreen motioned toward it and they hopped over a rotted wooden fence and strolled in. The wind was blowing gently and the scent of the flora and pine trees was pleasant and inviting. Unhurriedly making their way through the meadow, they eventually came to a small brook surrounded on both sides by clusters of mint leaves.

"Isn't this wonderful, Chris?"

"I guess. But I wouldn't want to get chased by some farmer's bull."

Doreen chuckled and sat down on the grass. She patted the spot next to her, the intention quite clear. Seven took his cue. Sliding down beside her, he knew he'd have to try and resist most of her advances as best he could. The scientifically tested Super Stud approach with any new target was to initially withhold as much of the physical stuff as one could.

The Super Stud agent tried to recall his department's textbook mantra. *Tease and tempt* in the early stages of a new relationship. But *never* give in completely. Slowly tantalize your female target in the beginning until she'll do most anything to win you over. This, assured G5's learned psychologists, will make your targeted quarry try *everything* she can to bond with you. Including revealing private or inside details in hopes of bringing you closer to her.

It might all be true, and it's worked perfectly before, Seven silently admitted. *But most of that strategy and scientific data was purely book talk; impersonal classroom statistics perfected by elderly professors.*

Christopher Seven shook his head, aware that here, in this tranquil meadow, is real life. A beautiful woman was sitting beside him, panting excitedly and whipping at his senses. Seven knew she'd be hard to resist.

Sure enough, as soon as their eyes met, Doreen leaned over and softly kissed him on the lips, her breathing warm and heavy. This kiss was different from those of the other yacht women. There was tenderness and feeling in it. Not simply raw physicality or 'one-upmanship' like the blatant advances of Terry and Suzanne had been. Seven threw his arms around her, instantly returning Doreen's kiss, as their tongues quickly came together in fervent starts and stops.

Moaning passionately, she pushed him down and lay across his lean body. Her kisses became more frequent and ardent while she massaged his chest after rapidly unbuttoning his shirt. As she rubbed her body against his, Christopher Seven desperately tried to control himself. He knew he'd have to implore all of his self-control if he was going to comply with the tested 'Stud' psychological procedures.

Suddenly, as Seven was frantically trying to win the battle within himself, Doreen stopped cold. She pushed him away and sat up. Disappointed and unsatisfied, Seven wondered what was happening. Was this another one of her mood swings? He watched her closely.

Doreen was smirking bizarrely with a dazed expression. One that had a look of madness to it. Her strange gaze instantly brought Seven out of the moment, his passion and desire quickly subsiding. He heard her say in an odd, detached voice, "Tell me, Chris, do you believe in love at first sight?"

"Well, I guess it depends on how you mean it, Doreen."

"Well, Suz said you kissed her the other evening after claiming you *loved* her." Doreen gave him another bizarre grin. "And Terry told me the same thing. That you likewise confessed your love to her in your stateroom."

"What?" Seven angrily exclaimed. "I never..."

Doreen put her finger across his lips to silence him. "It's okay," she assured. "I know all about it. I was just wondering if you feel I'm *different* than they are or if you think I'm part of the group."

Seven was dumbfounded, not knowing how or what to say. Obviously these four women compared notes at night, so what he said here and now would undoubtedly get back to the others. Yet he couldn't let these contrived tales of his being 'in love' with the other women slide. Not without telling Doreen as much. She was the one he wanted to work on, *not* them.

The G5 operative slowly sat up and gently took her hand. "First of all, Doreen, it was my impression that *they* came on to *me.* If truth be told, I was sort of surprised by it. I'm not saying your friends don't appeal to me, but yes – to me, you're quite different than they are."

Instead of being happy with his answer, as Seven assumed she'd be, Doreen frowned, angrily. "You don't understand," she pouted. "I *want* you to be in love with *all* of us. All four of us together, as one. That way, we'll all be *entwined*, just like Terry preaches. You see, we four women have a very inclusive bond. We desire to be 'one' in *everything* we do. Linked forever in life, with men, in feelings", she paused. "And even in *death!*"

Completely stunned, Christopher Seven silently asked himself, *what's going on here? These four females are all crazy!* He quickly decided to stall and try to sort things out. Get himself back to the planet Earth. "Well, Doreen, all this is a bit different for me. I'll have to think on it."

"Yes, you do that, Chris."

And with that, she calmly brushed some grass off her blouse and got up from the ground as if nothing at all had just occurred.

Twenty minutes later, Seven and Doreen boarded the tender for the short ride back to Zephyr. As the Super Stud looked out at the setting sun from his front row seat in the small watercraft, he was still anxiously trying to decipher – *What in the world is happening here?*

Chapter 25

The Long Scream

Zephyr raised anchor at exactly 6:30 p.m. and eased out of the picturesque *Ste-Helene* harbor some ten minutes later. Heading out to the open water, Captain Bacca turned the mega-yacht eastward toward the Italian coastline. Fortunately for all onboard, the seas were still calm.

After a lengthy shower in his cabin, Christopher Seven walked over to the closet and once again contemplated his wardrobe. The dress code for tonight was 'formal', which meant black tie and a tuxedo; or a ceremonial white dinner coat. Seven reached in the closet and took out his white dinner jacket, a specially tailored 'Super 100' formal coat from *Corbin*. He also grabbed a French-cuffed *Gitman* formalwear shirt and tailored black pants. A black bowtie, and matching cummerbund with black-patent leather shoes from *Frederico Leone*, completed the outfit.

While he attached the pearl studs and matching jeweled cufflinks to his shirt, the Super Stud wondered why a mobster as uncouth as Carmine Gitano would demand that all of his yacht guests dress up so formally. And why *tonight?* Perhaps it had something to do with the onboard arrival of the tardy VIP passenger. Some Korean doctor whom Doreen mentioned had finally arrived at Nice Airport to join the Zephyr.

All that Seven could get out of her about this Korean was that, in addition to being a close associate of Gitano's, he was a gifted surgeon who'd be coming onboard for the remainder of the voyage. Whatever the case, the G5 operative was glad he'd been advised to bring along formal duds for the voyage. Or, as Terry had crudely put it, 'make sure you bring a monkey suit for the black-tie nights onboard'."

Just as Seven finished putting on his Rolex watch to complete the elegant garb, there was a loud knock on the door. He walked over and opened it, surprised to see Anita standing in the doorway. The Super Stud hoped this wasn't going to be another impromptu 'kissing spree' these yacht women seemed to relish.

Scrutinizing him from head to toe, Anita smiled admiringly. "Hello handsome. Wow! Don't you look fine all decked out."

"Thanks, Anita." He eyed the striking black dress she was wearing. "You look great too. What's up?"

"Well, Carmine's hosting a gala chef's dinner in his suite tonight, and he's asked me to grab you and bring you along." She frowned with annoyance. "Seems our 'stick-in-the-mud' friend, Doreen, has begged out again." Her lips turned down, disapprovingly. "Figures. She's been a real wet blanket lately. But the rest of us girls will be there and we'll all need dates. Carmine likes couples at his black-tie dinners, if at all possible."

So, Suzanne is acting as Carmine's escort tonight, and Terry will be accompanying Zephyr's special guest, Dr. Hiun Kim." Anita quickly put her hand to her mouth. "Whoops! I forgot about that silly *last-name* rule." She shrugged, apologetically. "Don't tell Carm I accidentally blurted out the doctor's last name or he'll clobber me. Let's just call our new guest 'the doc.'"

Seven grinned, thinking of Vin Fieri, while making a mental note of 'Kim', the Korean's last name.

"Anyway," Anita added, "Since I'll need a beau for the evening, Carm and I decided I should come capture you. So, how about it? Will you be my date tonight?"

"I'd be honored."

She looked at him alluringly and grinned. "Thanks. I'll try to make it worth your while." Glancing at her watch, she advised, "I've got a few things to do now, but why don't you come by my room in an hour or so? I'm in Cabin 14. Let's say, sometime around 8:00 p.m. We can have a drink upstairs in the Crow's Nest bar and then mosey down to Carmine's suite after that. Dinner will be served at nine o'clock."

"Sounds great, Anita."

"Good. I'll see you later, then." And with that, she sauntered out the door and made her way down the hallway.

Seven grinned. These four yacht women were becoming quite a handful. *Oh well,* he reflected, *that's what I've come for. To interact with them and try to find out as much inside info as I can. Like this Korean doctor's last name that Anita accidentally blurted out. It'll be interesting to see what this guy's all about.*

The Super Stud glanced in the mirror one last time, turned out the cabin lights and exited his stateroom. He decided to stop in at the yacht's library and kill an hour or so. Perhaps use one of Zephyr's public computers to send a coded e-mail or two before picking up Anita.

Entering the elegant but empty mahogany-paneled library on Deck 6, the G5 operative continued to speculate on why Carmine Gitano wanted him at this private dinner gathering. *Something a bit odd there,* Seven mused. *And why had Doreen begged out again? She hadn't said anything during the day about not seeing him tonight.*

Shrugging his shoulders, Seven sat down at one of the computer stations and began sending out two thickly coded e-mails, fully aware that Gitano's electronic lackeys would probably be viewing them as well. The first message he sent was to G5 headquarters via one of their purposely nebulous public e-mail addresses; this one: *NYGstockquotes@ yahoo.com.* The other message, sent in the prearranged code that he and Vin had worked out, would be going to Fieri at his similarly innocuous e-mail address - *VFenterprises.com*. In both of these heavily veiled e-mailings, Seven asked for any known info on the Alvis mini-submarine and anything on a Dr. Hiun Kim of Korea.

Fifteen minutes later, a deeply coded reply came back from G5's New York headquarters. The only thing they had come up with, via some quick help from Interpol, was that Dr. Hiun Kim, of Ursan, North Korea, was a plastic surgeon of 'dubious character'. And that Kim had mysteriously left a thriving practice about a year ago. As for the *Alvis* sub, nothing much was added to what Seven already knew about it.

Doc Fieri's return email, likewise cloaked in heavy code, arrived ten minutes later. Again, nothing noteworthy on the sub. Other than it was definitely 'state of the art', and that it could safely transport up to 10 people at surprisingly deep depths. It was said to be much stronger than the *Titan* submersible, which ended in tragedy and loss of five lives, while trying to privately view the *Titanic.*

As for this plastic surgeon, Dr. Hiun Kim, the CIA reported that South Korean authorities had permanently suspended Kim's medical license three years ago. Shortly after he'd performed several 'questionable' and potentially dangerous 'operations'. Kim then went over to North Korea, where he now works and lives. Nothing further was known about him.

Finished with the computer work, Seven erased all the coded e-mails and their replies and then walked down to Cabin 14 to pick up his sultry, redheaded dinner date for their pre-meal cocktail.

~

"Maybe we can do something *really* wild and crazy to liven up this little boat ride!" Anita exclaimed raucously, loud enough to make a passing cocktail waiter's eyes bulge. "Like go skinny-dipping in the ship's main pool later on tonight."

Seven took a pull of his Bellini and quipped, "I'm not sure Carmine would approve. He's deemed tonight's dress code formal, and technically 'birthday suits' aren't black-tie attire."

Anita laughed with delight. "I guess you're right about that, handsome. But I want to have fun tonight. This tub of Carm's is getting a bit staid if you ask me. I'm getting tired of all the fancy food and elegant clothes. I want some excitement!" She took a swig of her third gin and tonic and asked, "You game?"

Seven grinned. "Why not? Besides, as your official 'date' this evening, it's my duty to follow your lead."

He looked over at Anita and smiled, furtively, watching for any telltale signs of her getting 'sloshed'. Quickly ordering another drink for her and one for himself, the agent hoped that more liquor might really open her up.

They were sitting at a snug table in the diminutive Crow's Nest saloon, a small cocktail lounge situated in the very front of the ship on

Deck 9. One floor below the 'restricted' top deck. The view out the floor-to-ceiling picture windows was breathtaking, and Seven could clearly see the twinkling lights of the Italian coastline off in the distance. He and Anita were the only two patrons in the place. The other six tables, as well as the four stools at the bar, were all empty.

After serving Anita her fourth drink, the bartender and attending waiter retreated back to their service stations behind the petite bar. They then quietly resumed their argument about *Manchester United* football, trying to give the young couple some privacy.

Seven appreciated their discretion, pleased that the two barmen were now out of earshot. He promptly began some gentle probing. "Tell me Anita, who's this hotshot Korean doctor we're having dinner with? It'd be nice to know who's dining with us."

Though she was definitely getting 'tight', Anita's slurred reply was nonetheless restrained. "Oh, don't go asking me questions, snoopy. Let's just say he makes women even prettier - more powerful and mysterious too." She growled playfully and began to giggle.

The G5 operative was about to ask her another question, when suddenly a long, terrified scream coming from several decks below was heard. It was barely audible at this height, but even so, the high-pitched wail had a desperate, horror-struck tenor. Seven immediately glanced over at his date. "Did you hear that, Anita?"

"Yeah. Sounds like someone slipped on a banana peel."

A few minutes later they heard the concerned voice of Captain Bacca coming from the room's overhead speakers.

"Attention, ladies and gentlemen! This is your captain speaking. We've just had an unfortunate accident. A man has fallen overboard, a crewman who was polishing one of the teak railings. Regrettably, he lost his balance during a sudden roll of the yacht and fell into the sea. I'm not sure if he was hit by our propellers or not. So I'm now preparing to stop Zephyr, lower two of our Zodiac life rafts located down on Deck 3 and attempt a search-and-rescue operation. We'll begin the procedure shortly and I'll do my best to keep you all informed."

Captain Bacca paused a moment, although the overhead speaker system was still on. Seven could hear several officers on the bridge excitedly conferring in Italian. A minute later the captain again addressed the ship.

"I'm sorry to say that the situation is very serious. I've just been told that the wind and sea have kicked up considerably, and there's a strong undertow, making swimming out there extremely difficult. There could also be sharks and other large predators in this area. Nonetheless, we'll do our best to find the crewman as swiftly as we can. Hopefully before it's too late. Thank you for your attention." And with that, the metallic voice signed off.

Christopher Seven immediately began speculating on whether this was truly an accident or, more likely, if Gitano's gangland hand was behind it. The Super Stud desperately wanted to get down to the outside decks and have a firsthand look at this supposed emergency rescue attempt. As far as Seven could tell, there had been no movement of the ship at all. The sea seemed dead calm. He looked over at Anita. "Let's go down and see how they're making out."

Anita frowned, angrily. "Let's *not...*" she slurred. "That crewman will probably be okay. Whether he is or he isn't, though, I want another drink. Let's just sit here and enjoy each other's company."

Seven was already up from his chair. "You can stay if you like, but I want to see if the crew can save that sailor before it's too late. Besides, maybe they could use some help. I'll be back as soon as I find something out." Anita again frowned as her 'designated-date' raced to the elevator.

By the time Seven got outside on Deck 3, Zephyr had finally come to a complete stop. Even so, the white object, whatever it was, was now a good distance behind them. Two of Zephyr's large emergency life rafts, manned by several crewmen, had just been lowered into the sea. They were now preparing to make their way out into the open water by way of the small outboard motors attached to the back of each raft. Surprisingly, there seemed to be no sense of urgency to this so-called lifesaving maneuver. No looks of concern on the sailors in the rescue dinghies.

A tough-looking Corsican seemed to be the rescue operation's team leader. Yelling a few orders in Italian from the yacht's back railing, he lethargically began shining a large flashlight out at the dark ocean behind them. A few minutes later, both rafts finally started motoring toward the bobbing white object, now a long distance behind Zephyr. The object appeared to be a man's body, though it was hard to tell from this distance. Whatever it was, it looked small and lifeless, aimlessly dipping up and down in the soft swell of sea. While Seven watched from the railing, a few passengers whom he didn't recognize began congregating by him. They were seemingly enjoying the seagoing spectacle, as if it were some TV reality show.

Several more crewmen and officers, Captain Bacca among them, had also arrived on the scene, their placid expressions showing little concern. The captain was impassively listening to his two-way radio as the rescue squads reported their progress. Seven could clearly hear the words 'morte' and 'senza vita' through the static of Bacca's radio, and the G5 agent knew intuitively that it didn't look good for the missing man.

Five minutes later, the first life raft finally reached the bobbing target, hauling the stiff object, now clearly the shape of a man, into it. Both rafts then speedily headed back to the yacht.

The moment the Zodiac rafts returned, several crewmen began hauling up the lifeless sailor facedown via a primitive roped scaffold.

Seven tried to get a better view of the body, but, when doing so, he was roughly pushed away by the muscle-bound Corsican who angrily yelled at him, "No passengers near here, mister! Crew only. Scram!" The G5 operative reluctantly backed away as ordered.

Despite the harsh warning, Seven continued observing as Zephyr's self-appointed rescue squad whisked the body down a narrow stairwell toward Deck 1, the yacht's lowest deck. Suddenly, the thick blue towel that had been covering the dead man's face and head unexpectedly came off, infuriating the Corsican and the men carrying the dead body.

Watching intently as the towel slid off the corpse, Seven's heart nearly skipped a beat. For even though Gitano's thugs desperately tried to hide the victim's face and head from view, two things were now frighteningly evident. First, the deceased man's neck hung hideously to one side, a telltale sign that this crewman almost certainly had a severely broken neck. The alleged rolling sea hadn't done that, nor had sharks or barracuda, for there was absolutely no sign of blood or torn flesh. *No,* mused Seven, *clearly this man had been brutally strangled just before being pushed overboard.* Without doubt, it was the unmistakable handiwork of Nalco, *'Il Strangolatore'*, Carmine Gitano's chief executioner.

More troubling than that, however, was the fact that Christopher Seven recognized the unfortunate victim. The dead man now being taken below decks was Seaman Emilio Rossi, the amiable father of two from Florence who had kindly allowed Seven to visit Zephyr's restricted area earlier that morning!

Chapter 26

"Careless people get into trouble!"

Guilt-ridden and stunned, Christopher Seven knew it was he who had gotten the unfortunate Rossi murdered. It was something the G5 operative would have to live with for the rest of his life. Gnashing his teeth in revulsion and shame, he slowly made his way back up to the Crow's Nest cocktail lounge, enraged and sickened by what he'd just witnessed.

Anita was waiting patiently in the dimly lit cocktail lounge. She was now sitting at the bar, chatting amicably with the waiter and bartender. She looked up at him. "What was all the fuss down below about, handsome?"

Seven didn't even bother to hide his anger and disgust. "That seaman who they claim *fell* overboard. He didn't make it. He's dead."

Anita glanced down at her fingernails and replied mundanely, "Oh, that's too bad." Her tone and expression made it obvious that she couldn't care less. The Super Stud now wondered if she and her three cohorts had somehow been in on it.

"Of course," Anita added, "accidents do happen. Especially onboard a moving ship. After all, we are at sea, at the mercy of the weather. Tough luck, whoever he was."

"A crewman named Emilio Rossi," Seven brusquely replied, not caring if she was suspicious as to how he knew who the dead man was. "Did you know him?"

"I've bumped into him from time to time," admitted Anita. "Seemed like a nice enough chap. Oh well, I'm sure good old Carmine will pay the funeral expenses and send a check to the man's family. He always does. Anyway, what do you say we forget all about it and enjoy the evening? Besides, it's time for our highfaluting dinner party." Inwardly revolted by Anita's blatant lack of concern for the murdered man, Seven reluctantly got back into his role and followed her to the elevator.

Carmine Gitano's other guests had already arrived at his spacious first-floor master suite when Anita and Seven finally strolled in. Everyone was enjoying hot canapés and iced champagne, served deftly by a formally uniformed waiter. Some Sinatra standards were playing through the cabin's expensive iPod system, and in the center of the room, a beaming Carmine was jovially holding court with two couples. Spotting Seven and Anita, he loudly greeted them. "Well, well, look who the cat's brought in. It's my favorite redhead, Anita, and her date, Mister Poker Guy. Welcome. Have a drink and grab yourselves some chow."

Though he couldn't put his finger on it, there was something about Gitano's smirking expression that Christopher Seven didn't like. Accordingly, the Super Stud's keen instincts told him to be on 'high alert' tonight. Inwardly worried, Seven still managed a smile and took a glass of champagne from the cocktail waiter. Carmine then made the introductions for Seven's benefit.

"You know my friends Suz and Terry, of course. And the couple to my right is friends of mine from Chicago. Mario and Tina." Again using no last names, Gitano tilted his champagne glass toward Mario, his trusted lieutenant. "Mario is my...how should I put this...my *implementation* expert. He's also the most loyal of *all* my people."

Mario smiled widely as the mafia boss continued, "And Tina, sitting next to him, is Mario's, ah...his personal *comforter.*" Carmine and Mario roared with laughter.

As Seven nodded toward the gruff looking couple. Mario's well-stacked moll, Tina, eyed the Super Stud from head to toe and gushed, "Hi there, mister. Too bad I ain't fifteen years younger."

"Cool it, Tee," growled her 'date', Mario, "Before I wallop you one." Mario then turned toward Seven. "You gotta be wary of Tina, mister. She'll charm the shirt and pants off you - *literally!*" The G5 agent dutifulyl chuckled

Carmine Gitano then introduced the other man, a refined-looking Korean gent, impeccably dressed in a stylish black tux. "And this is our guest of honor tonight. The honorable Dr. Hiun. Huin is his first name, of course. You people know my rule about last names."

Seven winked at Anita and then held out his hand to shake. "Pleasure to meet you, Doctor." The Korean said nothing, merely giving Seven a quick bow.

"OK," barked Gitano, rubbing his hands together. "Now that intro business is out of the way, let's eat." He clapped loudly and two waiters magically appeared, coming out from the small galley opposite the suite's master bedroom. One of the waiters, a tall man named Lino, pompously began giving a short recitation.

"Ladies and gentlemen. Our executive chef, Alberto, has prepared a wonderful tour de force for your dining pleasure. You'll be starting with Chef Albert's famous minestrone soup, followed by an appetizer portion of his homemade *lasagna Verdi al Forno.* After that will come your main course. An elegantly baked *plume de veal steak scaloppini parmigiana,* the chef's superb version of that famous dish. Desert will be a light and fluffy *Zabaglione,* warmed tableside. And now, if you would ladies and gentlemen, please take your seats."

The mouth-watering feast then began, complimented nicely by the sommelier's wine choice; a rich *'97 Siro Pacenti Brunello di Montalcino.* Christopher Seven had to admit it. Gitano's' staff had presented a masterpiece of Italian feasting at its best. The homemade lasagna sheets, encased in an exquisite Bolognese sauce, were aided by just the right amount of *béchamel.* And the main course was perhaps the best tasting 'veal parm' that Seven had ever eaten. So tender he could cut it with a fork. As he consumed the delicious food, Seven again wondered how this boorish Mafia tough guy managed to surround himself with the most civilized luxuries. *Oh well,* Seven mused. *Money can indeed buy anything.*

Dinner continued pleasantly enough, although to Seven's frustration he couldn't really connect with the reserved Korean doctor. Or learn anything about him from the other guests.

Near the meal's conclusion, Seven excused himself for his tooth brushing routine in the suite's fancy powder room. He then returned to the table just in time to hear Gitano's troubling announcement.

"First of all, ladies and gents, I want to apologize for that little mishap we had this evening. With the guy who fell overboard. Rossi, I think his name was." Glaring directly at Christopher Seven, Gitano tersely added, "Then again, the crewman who died, this Rossi guy, carelessly broke one of our most important safety rules. Rules made to protect him and everyone else on the ship. Rossi was careless. And careless people get into trouble around here."

Seven suddenly felt the accusing eyes of all the other dinner guests focusing on him. Trying to remain composed, he decided he'd better say something about this morning's sunglass episode. His reckless spying venture that had gotten poor Emilio murdered.

"That was certainly tragic news about your crewman," the Super Stud began, calmly playing with the spoon by his empty coffee cup. "Ironically, I'd just met the fellow earlier this morning. He seemed like such a kind and helpful man. You see, I had misplaced my sunglasses somewhere onboard, and I thought I might have left them on the yacht's top deck. You know, back when Captain Bacca gave me my lifeboat tour. Anyway, your crewman, Emilio, was kind enough to let me have a quick for them look up on Deck 10." Seven held up his right hand. "Properly accompanying me at all times, of course. Mr. Rossi firmly explained that he was obligated to tag along with me because Zephyr's top deck is strictly off limits. He firmly stated that passengers must have a crewman with them at *all* times while they're up on Deck 10. And that no one can go up there unless it's for drills or emergency reasons "

The condemning eyes of his fellow dinner guests continued to bore into him but Seven kept going, "As a matter of fact, I was meaning to mention it to you tonight. Didn't want you or the captain thinking your crewman did anything wrong or against the rules. Or that I was on a restricted deck *without* being properly accompanied. In any event, I'm truly sorry about your man."

The Mafia Don stared at Seven for a full thirty seconds, displaying a nasty sneer that showed he wasn't impressed by the confession.

"So *that's* your story, pretty boy?" Gitano probed.

"Yes. That's exactly what happened."

The mobster's face turned red with anger. He slowly made a fist with his left hand and barked, "Well, pal, despite your little sunglass fairytale, you *did* do something wrong. *Very* wrong. You were in a restricted zone even though warning signs are clearly posted. And I heard from the grapevine that money changed hands as well."

Seven nodded. "I tipped Mr. Rossi, if that's what you mean."

"Tipped him?!? *Bribed* him is more like it. I hear it was almost a hundred bucks you gave Rossi! That's a lot of dough to tip someone for a lousy pair of shades."

Seven felt his palms begin to sweat as the Mafia chieftain pretended to reflect on the situation. Gitano winked over at Mario sitting to his left. "Well, Mare, what do you say about all this?"

"I don't know, CG. Pretty boy here deliberately broke the rules. I think that calls for something a bit harsher than a verbal reprimand." Gitano callously nodded his head in agreement. It was obvious to Seven that the two mobsters had rehearsed all this ahead of time. "So, what do you suggest we do then, Mare?"

Mario glanced at Seven. "Well, you said this guy thinks he's a gambler. You know, with his poker prowess. So I'm sure he wouldn't mind taking a chance at the *Scegliere* game."

"Oh no," stated a smirking Carmine Gitano, "he wouldn't mind at all. In fact, I'm certain he'd *love* to play."

Christopher Seven wondered what all this was leading to, especially the nonsense about a 'game'. At least he now knew the reason he'd been invited to Carmine's private dinner party. He was here to be publicly 'called out' in front of the yacht gals and these other creeps. Gitano had obviously been fully informed about Seven's spying foray on the top deck. Presumably beating all of the details out of the unfortunate Rossi before he was slowly strangled by Nalco. And now the Mafia boss wanted to make Seven sweat in front of Gitano's mobster cronies. Especially the yacht women who'd shown such interest in the handsome stranger.

Apparently, Carmine Gitano was still intent on getting his revenge on Seven - one way or another. Well, the Super Stud wouldn't go along with it meekly. He was determined to remain strong, no matter what was in store for him.

Smirking back at his host, the G5 agent asked disdainfully, "What's this *game* garbage all about, Gitano?"

The mob boss leaned back in his chair and began explaining, "Actually, it's a medieval contest. One they've played in Italy for centuries. Only in this game the loser gets a very painful beating." He gave Seven a sarcastic grin. "But that shouldn't worry a sporting guy like you, should it, pal? After all, you're the chap who *never* loses at games. Unfortunately for you, though, you're also a guy who likes to snoop where he doesn't belong. Like under other people's tarpaulins."

Carmine snapped his fingers. Within seconds the apelike Nalco and two other thugs appeared from the galley. Seven didn't like the crazed smirk on Nalco's greasy face.

The Mafioso pointed to his burly henchman. "You remember Nalco, don't you, Seven?

The Super Stud said nothing.

Gitano stood up and barked out some orders to Nalco and Mario. "Take this bum to the gym and question him thoroughly. If you don't like what you hear from him…well, let's just say there might be another *accident* tonight."

The two hitmen nodded to their boss who added, "After you guys grill him, we're gonna make him play the *scegliere* game. As punishment for snooping around my ship. My dinner guests and I will be along later to enjoy the beating this punk is gonna get from Nalco."

"Okay, boss," Mario replied. He motioned to Seven. "Let's go, fella." Seven shrugged amicably, as if not having a care in the world.

"Sure, Mario, I'm coming. But aren't we going to have some brandy and cigars first?"

Much to Carmine's annoyance, Terry and the other girls laughed loudly, admiring Seven's spunk and surprising courage. The reserved Dr. Hiun also seemed to admire the bravado. The Korean smiled, clapped his hands together, and bowed his head in respect.

"Get moving, punk!" Mario growled.

Seven got up from the table and smiled toward Anita, Suzanne and Terry. "Don't suppose you gals would care to vouch for me?"

Terry was the first to respond. "Sorry, friend, but you shouldn't have been nosey." She yawned, indifferently.

"Oh well", Suz declared. "Guess we girls will have to find *another* hunk to show off. Since you'll undoubtedly be hospitalized and out of commission for a few months. Besides, nobody likes a would-be hunk with a scarred, swollen face." Suz shrugged her shoulders. "No biggie, though. Good-looking gigolos are a dime a dozen in Italy. Although finding one with *your* looks might prove difficult."

Anita, Seven's 'date' for the night, quickly turned on him as well. "It's simple, handsome. You did something wrong, so you have to pay the piper. But look at it this way. At least Carmine's allowing you to play the *scegliere* game. That gives you a one-in-three chance to escape a good thumping." She shrugged her shoulders. "You might just get lucky."

The sultry redhead then eyed Gitano with a stern expression. "But listen, Carm. Just make sure the game is on the up and up this time. Just like you promised us this afternoon. No tricks. Remember. Handsome here is technically *our* guest."

"Yeah," echoed Suzanne. "After all, you fully agreed that we could have him to display during our jaunt to the Italian Riviera. And we're still kind of hoping to show him off. In one piece, *if* the game is fair. And *if* he beats the odds."

Suzanne gave Carmine a beseeching expression. One that even the stone-faced gangster found hard to resist. "Besides," she added, "this guy might have simply made a mistake in judgment. Could be he really *was* looking for his sunglasses."

Gitano reflected on it a moment and then held up his right hand. "Okay, ladies, I give you my word. I'll see to it that Mario has a nice friendly chat with your play-pal up in the gym. No rough stuff, just talk. Unless he loses."

The three women nodded in sequence as Carmine added, "I also promise you that the *scegliere* game will be on the square. If Seven wins, he'll get no beating. But if he loses, your good-looking friend gets a full pasting from Nalco. Absolutely no mercy." The Mafioso looked over at the three women. "Agreed?"

"Fair enough," nodded Terry.

"Yeah," mumbled Anita. "So long as the game is on the up and up. Like I've said. At least that gives him a one-in-three chance."

For the first time all night, the Korean doctor, Huin, spoke up. His voice was soft yet assured. "I agree with the women, friend Carmine. I too want the game to be just." He looked over at Seven. "I admire this man's bravado. He seems like a warrior. And in Korea, even condemned *Sul Sa* warriors are given a slim but honorable chance at survival. Let it be so with this fellow. Your word on it, please."

Carmine solemnly held up his right hand. "You got it, Doc. My word on it, just like I promised the gals. If he chooses correctly, he'll be allowed to walk away unscathed."

But then, hiding his face from his dinner guests, Carmine Gitano turned around towards his two husky soldiers. Sporting a vindictive grin, he winked at Nalco and Mario who were standing directly behind him. The wink's hidden meaning was obvious and both mobsters immediately got the message - pledge or no pledge, they would make *sure* that Seven lost.

Don Gitano again winkled at his henchmen and then turned back around. "Okay boys," he loudly proclaimed, "It's all settled then. A nice, friendly chat with Seven, followed by an *honest* game of *scegliere.*

The mob chieftain took a long swig of his expresso and calmly ordered Mario, "Now then. Take this bum over to the gym. It's time we finally see what he's made of."

Christopher Seven was led to a waiting elevator and ushered up to the Zephyr's gymnasium on Deck 8. Entering the surprisingly spacious gym with his guards, Mario, Nalco and two other goons, Seven was pushed onto a metal stool located alongside the regulation-sized boxing ring. Nalco stood over him, breathing heavily, and ready to pounce if Seven tried any wrong moves. Mario, Gitano's main enforcer, grabbed a bottle of *Evian* water from the ringside ice bucket, took a long swig, and then took off his tux jacket to promptly begin the interrogation.

"Okay, fella. Mr. Gitano and his guests will be along momentarily. He's got some business to discuss with Dr. Huin first. But like the boss said, I'm in charge of his *information* department. And that's what I want from you now, mister. Information and plenty of it."

"Fine," replied Seven. "Ask away. Although you'll probably find my answers rather dull and boring. Like I've been telling everyone around here, I'm just an ordinary Joe from New Jersey. And I certainly didn't push your crewman Emilio into the sea, if that's what you think."

"Don't be a smart aleck or I'll break your jaw," barked Mario. "I need to know what you're *really* doing on this boat. You see, pally, Carmine never bought your nonsense about being a yacht enthusiast. As a matter of fact, he thinks you're working for a rival gang. So do I. Either Carpi's crew or Big Eddie Manero's."

Inwardly relieved these hoods were barking up the wrong tree, Christopher Seven laughed loudly, "Me, a *gangster*?" He laughed again. "Are you kidding, Mario? I'm simply a tourist who was lucky enough to meet some attractive women. Just hoping to have a good time with them. Wouldn't *you*?"

Mario shrugged his broad shoulders and declared, "Maybe. Maybe not. But you've got a lot to answer for, friend. Like entering the *exact* same poker tournament as the boss right after you just happened to meet him in the *exact* same restaurant a few hours earlier. Coincidence? I doubt it." The mobster frowned. "There's also the matter of your bribing one of our people to get a look upstairs." He pointed upwards. "You see, friend, all of these little *coincidences* just might add up to one big setup."

The wily enforcer gestured toward his three beefy confederates. "We happen to know that there are certain people and certain 'families' who want to know more about Mr. Gitano. Specifically, inside details concerning his daily routines, his travel schedule, and some confidential particulars about this vessel. Those same people may want to 'surprise' Mr. Gitano the wrong way. And at the wrong time. Capisce?"

Mario glared at Seven accusingly. "Could be you're working for one of these 'families' on the sly."

Seven was surprised and thankful that these hoods apparently thought of him as a possible rival mob informant rather than a government agent. And although apprehension that he was a rival gang member was probably just as dicey, the Super Stud was nevertheless glad about their faulty assumptions. He wondered how he should play it now.

Resolving that the best tactic was to stick to his present cover story at all costs, he decided to keep insisting that he was merely a yacht buff. One who simply jumped at the chance to get onboard the luxurious Zephyr. Especially when four alluring females invited him.

As Christopher Seven hastily tried to think of ways to fine-tune his alibi, the G5 agent glanced over at Nalco's huge right hand; wondering if he could resist any upcoming torture dished out by this uncouth ape should they try to force him to talk. Seven's reply was thus extremely guarded.

"Listen, Mario. I don't know who or what these *families* you're talking about are. But do I look like a gangster? You guys are forgetting one important fact. I was *asked* on this jaunt by Terry and the three other girls. *Not* the other way around. So, unless those four ladies are likewise part of some imagined conspiracy, your suspicions are laughable."

Mario rubbed his chin in thought. What Seven just said made sense. Yet there was still that troubling bribe to the crewman. And Seven's calculated peek under the submarine canvas. Somehow Mario's instincts, aided by years of beating confessions out of cringing prisoners, was telling him that this good-looking passenger was hiding something. Gitano's slimy enforcer just couldn't put his finger on *what* that something was. Mario's musing was interrupted by Seven.

"Tell me, Mario, what's this Scegliere game all about?"

The mobster gave him a cruel smile. "You really want to know, pretty boy?"

"Yes."

"OK, then." The Mafioso sat down on the empty stool in front of Seven's. "The game of Scegliere is a simple one. We put three grapes, all the exact same size and shape, into a tall wine goblet - one green and two purples. Then we blindfold you. All you have to do is pick the green one out of the chalice and you're safe. You win. If you pick one of the purples, however, you get a vicious thrashing from big Nalc over there."

"Sounds plain enough," Seven replied. "And like Anita said, it gives me a one-in-three chance. But why is Gitano insisting I play this senseless game?"

Mario pointed his finger at Seven's chest. "First off, even you would have to admit you've got a good beating coming to you. Payback for that casino poker stunt after Carmine ordered you to drop out. And, more concerning, punishment for snooping around Zephyr's top deck after you bribed a crewman. The problem was *how* to damage you without upsetting the four girls. For some reason they wanted you around unhurt. Who knows *why* with those screwy broads?"

The mobster shook his head and continued, "You were lucky you didn't get it back in Monte Carlo the other night. Nalco should have taken care of things right then and there." Mario grinned. "But you won't be lucky for long, buddy boy. 'Cause tonight you're finally gonna get what's coming to you."

Christopher Seven knew he was in for it and wondered if he could somehow talk these thugs into changing their minds. He decided to give it a try. "From what I've seen, Mario, Mr. Gitano appears to be a very private person. You know, with his 'no last names' decree. And with all of Zephyrs' high-tech security measures. Don't you think *two* suspicious deaths on the same day, and during the same voyage, might be rather hard to explain to the Italian authorities?"

"Who said anything about your being *dead?* After you play the game and lose, you'll get a nasty licking from my friend Nalco here. And though it'll be ruthless and plenty painful, thanks to Nalco's expertise, there'll be no killing blows. Just enough blood and pummeling to ruin that pretty face of yours, and put you out of commission a few months. This way, there'll be no more talk from the girls about *'showing* you off'. And no need to keep you aboard this yacht, either."

Mario glanced toward Nalco, who was already panting with sadistic anticipation. "After the big guy beats the tar out of you here, we'll throw you in the yacht's infirmary for the night. Then, first thing tomorrow morning, after the boat arrives at Capri, we'll drop you off at a local medical center we know. The staff there is on our payroll so they don't ask questions. They'll stick a few bandages on you and quietly make arrangements to get you to a Naples hospital. And that will be that."

The gangster again shrugged his shoulders while adding, "If any details of your thumping leak out, we'll simply tell the cops it was a spat between two guys over one of the yacht women. Nalco's been in trouble with the law before. So a few greased palms should get him out of any police difficulties. He'll doubtless get the usual fine and warning."

The Super Stud frowned. "You guys think of everything. But what if I manage to *win* this silly game of yours? I distinctly heard Gitano promise the girls, and that Korean doctor, that the contest would be a fair one." Seven frowned. "Although, somehow I doubt that."

Mario chuckled. "All Carmine promised was that if you picked the right grape you'd be cleared. And he'll happily honor that pledge." The mobster laughed again, this time louder and with more malice. He then motioned to one of his lackeys. "Jilly. Bring out the grapes while I tell this sucker more about the game."

Jilly, a stocky thug with a permanent frown, dutifully walked over to the small refrigerated storage area in the back of the gym. The main fridge inside it held various fruit and cheese snacks for Zephyr's exercise buffs, after they work out. Jilly quickly returned with two small clusters of grapes; one bunch was purple and the other green. Both sets of grapes were exactly the same size and shape, the only difference being their color. Mario quickly explained.

"These are some of the sample grapes we're bringing along to Carmine's winemakers for his *Procida* winery. There's a lot more of them downstairs in the storage hold." He handed the grapes back to Jilly. "The game of *Scegliere* likewise uses grapes, just as it's done for centuries. Like I told you, three grapes are put into a large wine goblet; one green and two purples. If the blindfolded player picks the green one he's safe. But if he should choose one of the *purples,* he suffers the consequences."

Seven listened closely, trying to get the essence of the contest as the gangster went on, "During the Renaissance period, Italian noblemen liked to use the Scegliere game when one of their workers, or some local peasant, committed a petty crime. It was a good source of amusement for the wealthy guests and visitors who frequented the feasts and parties at various estates. Observing a potential victim nervously playing the game, and then watching as the loser got flogged, or beat to a pulp, was great fun for them." Mario smiled. "Just like it'll be for Carmine and his guests tonight. Especially for the three girls. They always enjoy the rough stuff."

"I bet they do," frowned Seven. "So I'll just have to pick the green grape and disappoint them."

"We'll see," said Mario with a devious expression, one that the G5 operative didn't care for. "By the way, Seven, there's one other directive I forgot to mention. The 'accusare' rule."

"What the heck is *that?*" Seven asked.

"You see, should a Scegliere contestant lose his nerve at any time *before* picking his grape - say he tries to get out of playing the game by claiming that the contest has been rigged or is corrupt - then that player automatically forfeits and gets his punishment *immediately*. So there's no whining and no accusations about a potentially 'fixed' game. Forfeiture due to 'accusare' has been a main edict of Scegliere for centuries. That way, there's absolutely no finger pointing. Or bellyaching about fairness allowed. If you publicly accuse the game of being fixed, or even *hint* that I, Carmine, or the game's other administrators are being dishonest, you'll lose before you start."

Seven frowned, glumly. "Don't worry, Mario, I'll take my chances. I won't foolishly accuse you or your boss and fail without even *trying*. Like you, Nalco, and Carmine are probably *hoping* I do. But why do I have the distinct feeling that you and Carm have managed to rig things?"

Mario grinned. "Careful, friend. You almost lost the game then and there via the *accusare* rule. Good thing for you the game hasn't officially started yet."

The mobster snickered knowingly. "Yet, I'm surprised at you, pal. Thinking we'd unfairly *fix* things? Don't Carmine and I look honest?"

"Yeah. About as honest as Al Capone and Frank Nitti."

The Chicago enforcer howled with laughter. "Come on now, pally. You heard Mr. Gitano assure his guests that if you picked the right grape you'd be fine."

The Super Stud answered, derisively. "Yeah, I heard him. And I take great comfort in Carmine's assurances. I couldn't think of a more trustworthy guy. Other than Bernie Madoff."

Mario jumped up from his stool and slapped Seven hard across the face. "Still the wise guy, aren't you, punk? Well, maybe what I tell you next might end your cockiness."

The seething gangster sat back down and explained, "Normally, a Scegliere player like you has a one-in-three chance of escaping his punishment. To win tonight's game, you'd simply have to reach into the goblet, pick the winning green grape, and *not* either of the purples."

"Well?" pressed Seven.

The gangster grinned. "Well, that's gonna be rather difficult for you tonight mister. Cause Jilly here is gonna make sure that the wine goblet has only three *purple* grapes inside it. No green grape at all, just three loosing *purples*. So no matter *which* grape you pick from the cup – you're gonna lose, chum!"

Seven watched dejectedly as Jilly grabbed three purple grapes and walked over to the goblet to do his dirty work, gently placing the trio of condemning purple grapes into the chalice. Mario nodded and declared, "I don't mind telling you all this now, punk. Because if you try to protest, or accuse us of *any* improprieties *whatsoever,* you'll automatically lose the game through the 'accusare rule'. In fact, Carmine is counting on that since Doc Huin and the girls know the accusare regulation too." The Chicago enforcer laughed heartily, as Christopher Seven quietly tried to summon his courage.

~

Ten minutes later, Carmine Gitano and his dinner guests strolled into the gym, carrying half-filled brandy glasses. Two new thugs and their female 'molls', heavyset bimbos whom Seven hadn't seen before, had joined the party; one which included Terry, Anita, Suz, Tina and Dr. Hiun. Giggling excitedly, they reminded Seven of the ancient Romans coming to see an exhibition of blood and torture at the Coliseum.

Observing the small horde as they filed in, the G5 operative was surprised to see the expressions of sadistic expectancy in their eyes, particularly on the women in the group. They were literally panting, clearly longing for a spectacle of pain and gore. *They're just like the heartless house guests of those medieval noblemen,* Seven mused. *Enjoying this upcoming Scegliere game and the ruthless punishment to follow.*

As for Anita, Suzanne and Terry, their plans to 'display Seven as window dressing' were completely forgotten now. At this point, all these women wanted was some sadistic fun. To see a screaming victim bloodied and beaten. They had apparently written Seven off. Or had they?

The Super Stud shook his head. Though not surprised by their new personas, he was taken aback by their blatant vindictiveness. A further indication they could indeed be Rhombus.

"Okay, Mario," boomed Carmine Gitano. "Did you have your little chat with poker man here?"

"Yes, Chief."

"And?"

"His answers weren't satisfactory. Scegliere is definitely in order."

"Did you explain the rules to him?"

"Yes, Carm, all of them."

"Including the *accusare* rule about no accusations or protesting?"

"Yes sir, the rule was fully explained."

Gitano nodded. "Good. Then let's proceed with the contest. And tell Nalco to be ready with plenty of his rough stuff. I promised the girls that if this man loses, they'd be witnessing some heavy-duty punishment here tonight. I want Nalc to put on a *real* sensational show for my guests. Drag it out, and make this bloodied punk scream and suffer."

Seven again glanced over at Suzanne, Terry, and Anita. They each sported a strange, almost savage look. One that the G5 agent had never seen on them before. It was as if these three women had turned into different people; heartless and menacing. They sat transfixed, waiting for the impending bloodshed and torture. Much like a treat to a child.

Even Tina, Mario's older moll, seemed to have sadistic longing in her eyes as she eagerly exclaimed, "I've seen Nalco work on a few other saps who lost at this game. It was really something. Gosh, how those losers howled! And right before a Scegliere beating begins, they usually strip the victim naked. It should be a great show. So let's grab us a ringside seat, ladies!"

The guests, including the reserved Dr. Huin, sat down on folding chairs that had just been brought in by two uniformed crewmen. Holding snifters of expensive brandy, Gitano's visitors eagerly waited for the medieval spectacle to commence. So did the Mafioso Don, who would finally get his revenge on the brash Mr. Christopher Seven. Watch Nalco pummel him down to size in front of the three women whom Gitano secretly desired for himself.

Seven was brusquely led to the center of the boxing ring for all to see. Some large bed sheets were then spread over the ring's canvas floor, ostensibly to keep most of the victim's blood from being splattered on it during the punishment. Mario walked over with a dark blindfold and placed it around Seven's face and eyes.

Now completely blind, the sweating agent wondered what he could do or say to avoid his fate. Sadly, he could think of nothing. If he tried to alert the assembled audience of Gitano's treachery, fixing the game with the three condemning purple grapes now inside the chalice, Seven knew these mobsters wouldn't wait any longer. They'd simply claim that he'd lost the game on the *accusare* rule and have Nalco start right in on him. Seven's only hope now was to see if his martial arts could help fend off the worse of Nalco's blows once he lost the game.

"All right mister pretty boy," Mario ordered, loud enough for the spectators to hear. "Reach in and pick your poison. And no fondling or trying to size up the grapes. They're all exactly the same size, shape and feel anyway. Just grab one like a man and hand it over to me. I'll then show it to the crowd. If it's the green grape you can go. If it's purple - well Nalco will take over from there."

The hushed audience watched closely, all wishing this handsome victim would lose so that the *real* show could begin.

Christopher Seven slowly reached into the goblet and grabbed the convicting grape, momentarily hiding it in his clenched fist. As he did so, Mario moved in closer to retrieve it and show the result to the wide- eyed crowd. Then, unexpectedly, Seven popped the grape into his mouth and promptly swallowed it.

"Yes!" the Super Stud yelled, triumphantly. "I just picked the green one! Any wine enthusiast can taste the difference. The grape I swallowed was tart and crisp, definitely a green and *not* a sweet purple." Seven quickly removed his blindfold and announced to the audience, "I'm sure if Mario pours out the two remaining grapes from the goblet, and shows them to you folks, they'll obviously be purple. They have to be since I just picked and swallowed the *green* one. And in accordance with Mr. Gitano's solemn pledge to all of you, I've won the game."

Momentarily stunned, and looking for some direction, Gitano's enforcer glanced over at his fuming boss. The Mafia chieftain reluctantly nodded. Shrugging his shoulders, Mario obediently turned over the goblet. When he did so, two purple grapes fell into his open hand. "They're purple all right," the gangster unenthusiastically informed.

Seven stared over at Carmine Gitano and exclaimed, "Guess it's just my lucky day, Carm. And thanks for keeping your word. The contest was indeed on the 'up and up', just like you promised us. If not, I couldn't have won. You're a man of supreme integrity, Mr. Gitano." The G5 agent then waved to the disappointed crowd and stepped down and out of the boxing ring.

Strolling over to the three astonished yacht girls, Seven addressed them amicably. "Sorry to spoil the party, ladies, but like Anita said earlier, I had a one-in-three chance. Luckily I made it. And now, if none of you have any objections, I'm going for some champagne to celebrate my victory." The three women nodded their heads in hesitant approval.

Dr. Hiun, who was seated near them, bowed, clapped his hands in admiration, and grinned widely. Acknowledging the praise, Christopher Seven courteously bowed back. He then turned and glared directly at Gitano. "Thanks for an interesting evening, Carm. If you think of any other little games we can play, let me know."

And with that, the Super Stud calmly exited the gymnasium.

Chapter 28

The Key to the Kingdom

Seven quickly made his way down to his cabin, still shaken from the near-miss beating that seemed unavoidable only a short while ago. He felt justifiably proud of himself. Aware that Carmine Gitano was a man who respected cunning and independence from friends or rivals, the G5 agent was again hoping he'd scored some points with the big man. And also impressed Anita, Terry, and Suz. Nodding with self-satisfaction, he picked up the cabin telephone and dialed Doreen's room. She answered on the first ring, her voice low and sullen, as if expecting bad news.

"Hello?"

"Hi Doreen, it's me, Chris."

Doreen was both shocked and thrilled to hear from him. "Chris! But how did you ..."

"It's okay," he calmly informed her. "Let's just say I've had an interesting evening playing some crazy game Carmine cooked up. Lucky for me, I won."

"You *won*?" Her voice was filled with relieved disbelief. "I heard they were going to force you to play tonight and what the subsequent punishment was going to be. Knowing Carmine's bunch, I was sure they fixed it so there'd be no way you'd come out unscathed. That's why I didn't want to go to his dinner party and witness it firsthand. But how did you manage to..."

He hastily cut her off, knowing their stateroom phones could be bugged. "Just lucky I guess. Anyway, the reason I called was to ask you for a celebratory drink up in the Crow's Nest. How about it?"

"You bet. Just wait there in your room. I'll be over in ten minutes. Have to throw on something a bit more elegant than these jeans. After all, it is formal night."

"Fine, Doreen. I'm in Cabin 5."

Her thankful voice tingled with excitement. "Be there in a jiff."

Seven put down the phone, took off his dinner jacket, and walked over to the cabin's mini-refrigerator; a built-in *Sanyo* compact, neatly fitted under the dresser. Grabbing a small bottle of cold *Perrier*, the Super Stud began contemplating his impending strategy. After tonight's zany events, he knew he was close to wearing out his welcome with the Gitano gang. In fact, *Don* Carmine might very well have him thrown off at the next port. Or, at the very least, keep everyone, including Doreen, away from him for the remainder of the voyage. Consequently, whatever time left that Seven managed to steal with Doreen, still the weakest and most vulnerable of his four targets, would now be critical. There was still a lot to learn and hopefully he could draw something out of her tonight. Perhaps a few details about Gitano's mysterious submarine or some tidbits about the death of the unfortunate crewman, Rossi. There was also this mysterious Korean plastic surgeon he'd met at dinner.

The Super Stud rubbed his forehead and thought on it further. Above all, he'd have to try and get some definitive proof that these four yacht women were indeed Rhombus. And, if so, find out why they were involved in the murder of Ambassador Dawson. If he could somehow 'turn' Doreen, difficult but not impossible given her feelings for him, maybe she'd reveal something about Dawson's missing documents.

Finishing the Perrier in three quick gulps, Seven sat down with his back to the door and gazed out the cabin's floor-to-ceiling windows. A beautiful full moon was shining down on the placid sea. Still thinking about his next moves, Seven again pondered the swiftly developing events. A moment later, he turned around and was startled to see Doreen standing in the middle of his stateroom. With his back to the door, he hadn't seen or heard her enter. He wondered how she'd gotten into his locked room. She was wearing an elegant, tight-fitting, green dress and looked stunning. Seven smiled up and greeted her.

"Hi. You look wonderful, Doreen. But how'd you get in? I didn't hear you knock and I'm sure my door was locked. Did the steward open it for you?"

Doreen grinned conspiratorially and held up an electronic key card dangling from a long chain. "With this," she confessed. "It's a master passkey. Fits all the passenger cabins. The maids all have them and we four girls bummed a few from them. Makes it easier for us to come and go from each other's rooms, even if no one's home. They're quite handy as we often borrow each other's clothes and makeup."

"Oh, I see," Seven replied, desperately wondering how he could get his hands on one of these magical passkeys. He grinned. "Lucky for you I wasn't showering."

"*Unlucky* you mean." She winked and gave him a grin of her own.

The Super Stud laughed, put his dinner jacket back on, and they were soon making their way up to the Crow's Nest lounge on Deck 9.

Arriving at the now crowded cocktail lounge a few minutes after midnight, Doreen and Seven were welcomed by the pleasant sounds of a young singer/guitarist who was playing *"Yesterday"* over in the corner. Seven requested a table away from the songster, hoping he'd be able to probe his target in relative peace and quiet.

As the headwaiter began escorting them toward a secluded booth in the back of the room, they ran smack into Terry, Anita and Suzanne. They were getting up from their table, preparing to leave. The three of them had just finished drinks with Dr. Huin, the enigmatic Korean VIP.

Huin nodded and grinned when he saw Christopher Seven, still marveling at Seven's escape from the Scegliere game.

"Well, well," Terry greeted. "Looks like sister Doreen was holding out on us. What happened to your *splitting* headache, Dor?"

"Oh, it's much better now," Doreen awkwardly replied. She was obviously embarrassed at getting caught begging out of Gitano's dinner with a lame excuse.

"Yeah," scoffed Anita. "We can see you're feeling better. Quite a miraculous recovery." Anita glared over at Seven. "Well, well, Lover Boy. Not only do you seem to have nine lives, but you don't waste any time with the fair sex, either." She pointed to Doreen. "I guess it's *her* turn now." Anita shook her finger at Seven, admonishingly. "I thought *I* was your date tonight."

"You were," said Seven, winking at the Korean doctor. "But the suave Dr. Huin has successfully whisked you away from me." Everyone laughed except Huin, who merely gave his customary bow.

"We were just on our way to the 12:15 late show in Zephyr's main cabaret lounge," Suzanne informed. "It starts in ten minutes. Some well-known European magician they brought onboard in Monaco. There's also a talented blues singer on the bill. Carmine says it's a long show but a good one. Claims the magician is incredible. You two care to tag along?"

Seven answered for both of them. "No thanks, Suz. Nothing against the act, whoever he is, but I've never been one who enjoys magicians. They're pretty much all the same with their top hats and magic wands. But when and if they have a comic on the bill, let me know. I'd be happy to go to that show with you."

"All right then," said Suz. "We'll see you two lovebirds around." She gave Doreen a stern look. "Just be careful with handsome here if he tries to charm anything out of you, Dor. He's been a bad little boy lately. Almost got a spanking for snooping around where he shouldn't have." And with that, she and the rest of her party exited the lounge and ambled down to the showroom.

Both Seven and Doreen were glad they'd gone, albeit for different reasons. They quickly found their small booth, where the G5 operative ordered two champagnes. After the waiter departed, Doreen asked, "What did Suzanne mean about your *snooping* around?"

"Oh that," scoffed Seven. "I'm really not sure. Apparently, Carmine heard that I was on the top restricted deck and went kind of bonkers about it. *Why* he flipped out, I don't know. I was simply looking for my missing sunglasses. Thought I'd lost them up on Deck 10 when Captain Bacca gave me his 'welcome aboard' safety tour. Can't see what all the fuss was about. I was accompanied by a crewman at all times." Seven shrugged his shoulder. "I still don't understand why Carm went ballistic."

"He's always like that about security," Doreen explained. "But you shouldn't have been up on Deck 10. That's a very firm rule."

"Yeah, I know better now. Believe me, it won't happen again."

Seven suddenly got an inspiration, a means to possibly facilitate his spying. He decided to try it on Doreen. "You know the worst thing about all this? My innocent mistake regarding Deck 10 probably cost us the chance to be with each other for the rest of this voyage."

"What do you mean, Chris?"

"I'm quite sure Carmine won't let me hang around any of you girls after tonight. Mario mentioned that to me as well." Seven gently took her hand in his. "Listen, Doreen, I've been meaning to tell you something. Something that's very important to me." He rubbed her fingers softly. "I don't know how you feel about it, but it seems I've fallen for you. I'm not sure how or when it happened, but I was hoping to spend a lot more time with you during the remainder of this cruise. *Quality* time." He smiled, warmly. "And hopefully for a *long* time after, if you'll let me."

Seven watched her face light up with unmistakable delight.

Perhaps this fish is hooked, he mused, waiting to make sure.

Doreen's expression told the Super Stud agent all he needed to know. Beaming, she kissed his hand, encouraging Seven to go on, which he did. "But now, thanks to my silly blunder on Deck 10, and Mr. Gitano's suspicions about it, I'm certain he'll forbid you and me *ever* getting together. Mario swore that Carmine will probably insist I stay away from you for the rest of the voyage." Seven wiped his brow. "Frankly, after tonight's near-miss with Nalco, I'm edgy about even being *seen* with you. Wouldn't want either one of us to get in trouble!"

She nodded as Seven gloomily added, "So I guess it means that tonight is the end of you and me giving ourselves a chance at something meaningful. According to Mario, Gitano will probably give me his edict first thing tomorrow. And he'll certainly know if I disobey it. Carmine seems to have eyes and ears all over this boat."

Doreen thought on it a moment. Then, as if deciding something, she firmly asserted, "There's always my cabin, Chris. Carmine wouldn't dare invade my privacy there."

Seven reacted with staged excitement. "You *mean* it?"

"Of course I do."

Seven pretended to ponder her suggestion and then nodded. "I guess that's the *only* way, now, Doreen. But we'll have to be extremely discreet about it and stay out of the ship's public areas whenever we're together. If not, Gitano's bound to find out."

The Super Stud seemed to reflect on it further. "I suppose there's no time like the present, Doreen. Especially after my 'near miss' earlier this evening. Tell you what. Why don't you head down to your room, put some champagne on ice and wait for me there. I'll come by in an hour or so. It'll look better if I stay up here awhile. You know, for appearance sake, in case we're being watched. After that, I'll feign going to my room to get some sleep and sneak down to your place. This way, we can finally be alone."

Doreen looked up at him with an endearing expression of desire and contentment, and for a brief moment the G5 operative felt a pang of remorse. He promptly dismissed it as his thoughts quickly returned to using her in any way he could.

"Your plan sounds wonderful, Chris." She smiled warmly. "See? My premonition came true. We *were* meant to be together, albeit on the sly."

"Absolutely, Doreen." He lowered his voice for effect. "But listen. If we're going to keep sneaking in and out of each other's cabins, do you suppose I could borrow one of those passkeys? I can't keep asking the steward to let me in. And if I asked him for a key to your stateroom, Aldo would certainly tell his superiors. Also, I can't pound on your cabin door at all hours of the night either. Not without being noticed. So one of those master passkeys would be the perfect solution."

She frowned at him a moment, clearly apprehensive. Seven kept pressing, however, desperately trying to sway her. "Who knows what special things our time together might lead to?" he pushed. "I just think we owe it to each other to find out."

Still hesitant, Doreen warned, "It *sounds* simple enough, Chris. Me giving you a master key. But I'm not sure. There'd be dire repercussions if Mario or Carmine ever found out. And I mean *dire*."

Yet, as Doreen continued to weigh the pros and cons, Seven could see that she was beginning to weaken. Perhaps thoughts of romantic nights alone with him were starting to sway her.

"Maybe it could work," Doreen finally agreed, though clearly uneasy about it. "And I certainly have a few extra passkeys floating around my cabin. Seems we girls are always misplacing them. But I'm still worried about the whole thing. Especially for you after your Deck 10 fiasco."

Seven scoffed at her hesitance. "Oh, come on, Doreen. My borrowing a passkey for a few days wouldn't be any big breach of security. You four girls are constantly using them anyway. And you said they only open stateroom doors; no other areas. So who am I going to sneak in on? Nalco in the shower? Or Mario's old hag, Tina, curling her hair?"

Doreen chuckled at the images and nimbly handed him the electronic passkey card under the table. "I guess it's all right, since you put it that way. Yet don't breathe a word of this to *anyone*. Not even the other girls."

Seven nodded solemnly. "I promise. Now then, Doreen. Finish the last of your champagne, make a show of saying goodnight to the waiter and telling him how tired you are, and head straight for your cabin. We're probably being watched right now, so I won't be leaving with you. Like I said, I'll probably stick around here for another hour or so. Maybe start up a friendly conversation with the bar staff about soccer. I'll then fake going to my own cabin to retire and come to your stateroom instead." He grinned. "Who knows? Maybe I'll catch *you* by surprise this time."

Doreen giggled excitedly, finished her drink, and then left the Crow's Nest on her own.

After watching her leave, Seven ordered another glass of champagne. He consumed it quickly, got up from the table, and calmly began his trek below to the main passenger deck. Armed with the treasured 'passkey', hopefully the key to the Rhombus kingdom, Seven tried to recall the stateroom numbers of the four yacht women.

~

Twenty minutes later, the Super Stud was cautiously making his way down the passenger deck's extensive hallway, finally remembering the order of the four staterooms. Doreen was in cabin 12, Anita in 14, and Suzanne had mentioned that she was in number 16. As for Terry's cabin number, the G5 operative recalled from that first day onboard that she bunked in stateroom 18. Terry's would be the first one he checked, as she definitely appeared to be the leader of the pack.

Seven glanced down the long, silent hall. Nothing at all was stirring at this hour except the soft whirl of Zephyr's engines. Knowing Doreen was now waiting in her cabin, and that the other three women would hopefully be at the lengthy cabaret show till at least 2 a.m., he glanced at his watch: 12:45 a.m. - Plenty of time to check a few things out.

Alertly making his way down the noiseless passageway, the sweating agent suddenly had an uneasy thought. *What if Terry and the other two women returned prematurely? Perhaps the magician wouldn't be to their liking. Or perhaps one or all of them might get tired and head back to their staterooms.*

The G5 operative wiped his brow, well aware that this passkey gambit was an enormous risk. If some crewman had been callously murdered for merely showing Seven a restricted deck, what would happen if Seven was found openly spying in Terry's cabin? Christopher Seven shuddered, not wanting to think about the consequences. Anyway, this was why he'd come.

After first glancing up at the ceiling to check for any telltale signs of cameras, or an in-house monitoring system, something he'd been thoroughly trained to spot, Seven was confident there were none mounted above the hallway. Carmine Gitano obviously didn't care about the stateroom comings and goings of his hoodlum passengers, preferring instead to scrutinize the restricted open deck areas 24/7.

Cautiously approaching Terry's cabin 18, the Superstud stopped and listened again. All was serene. With a rock-steady hand, he slid the passkey into the door slot and heard the blessed click of the lock opening. He was in!

Guided only by the bright glow of the full moon shining through the cabin's large glass windows and balcony door, Seven dodged a few items of clothing on the floor and made his way over to the small writing desk to his left. Switching on the tiny reading lamp sitting on top of it, he quickly tilted its thin beam away from the door so there'd be no reflection in case anyone passed by Terry's stateroom. Then, gingerly opening the desk's top drawer, he noticed a thick file folder inside it. It contained a number of documents and papers sorted in alphabetical order. He took out the folder and thumbed through it, looking for anything suspicious.

In the middle of the collection, filed under **S** for 'surgeons', was a list of the top plastic surgeons in Europe and Asia, including a lengthy biography of Dr. Huin Kim. Displayed in Kim's bio were several diagrams outlining cosmetic procedures and operations. These included Botox treatments, rhinoplasty and several illustrations on breast-enlargement techniques. Seven narrowed his eyes in puzzlement. *Funny*, he mused. *Neither Terry, nor any of the other shapely yacht women for that matter, needed help in that department. All four of them were very well-stacked. Unless, of course, they'd already received some bolstering.* The agent shrugged his shoulders and kept looking through Terry's files.

The next folder he chose, in the letter **E** slot, contained a short picture file curiously categorized under the label 'escorts'. It contained four photos of good-looking men in their mid-thirties, with brief biographies on each of them. All of their names, both first and last, were blacked out, though, surprisingly, their countries of residence were not. One man lived and worked in London, one hailed from Rome, and another was from Paris. The last man, an American, was from Chicago.

Quickly reading through their short bios, there was really nothing in common between them. Although the first man was a skiing enthusiast and the second fellow a topnotch swimmer. The other two apparently had no athletic prowess, though both were similarly handsome. The only shared connection, if you could even call it that, was that these men either worked in their country's diplomatic sectors, or in their European embassies. All four worked as insignificant, intern-type workers. A penned entry in red ink showed when the yacht women had first met these fellows. Either at embassy parties or diplomatic banquets in Rome or Paris.

Confused, the G5 agent shook his head. *Were these males, like me, merely picked for their looks? 'Trophy catches', to simply use and flaunt as the girls often boasted. Or was there more to this?*

Seven reflected further. *The file disclosed that the four yacht women had met each of these international hunks at parties or banquets. All of those gatherings were either embassy or diplomatic functions. Was there any significance to that? Or were these men simply 'window dressing' as Suzanne liked to phrase it?* Whatever the case, no names were revealed.

He was about to close the 'escort' file when, to his astonishment, he saw that beside each man's photo an illegal narcotic was listed: one drug for each man. The narcotics named were - crystal meth, opium, ecstasy and heroin. There were also large sums of dollars and euros listed by each name. Seven deliberated on what he saw. *Could the yacht women be buying illegal drugs from these guys? Or, conversely, supplying them?*

It was now beginning to get quite warm in the stuffy stateroom. Undeterred, Seven continued his snooping. Under the file letter **N** was a potentially troubling entry. It read; *Terminare Doreen – 9/26 – check with Nalco.* The G5 operative looked at the small calendar date on his watch. That day was less than three weeks away. Seven knew a bit of Italian. Enough to identify the first word as *'Finished'.* But why Doreen? Was she in any danger? Or did this entry merely mean that she was being taken off some singular assignment. Or perhaps Doreen would be dismissed from the group altogether? Then again, with Nalco in on the action, it could mean something much more ominous. If so, should he tell her?

Seven cautioned himself about reading more into these files than was actually there; the plastic surgeons, the possible drug sales, the four male trophy catches, and Doreen's would-be fate. There could be simple, mundane answers to all of these entries. His job was to find and connect any potential dots between a murdered U.S. ambassador and the four women now onboard. Not to try and read into motives.

Doreen's future, some good-looking men on high-priced drugs, or any of the other imagined possibilities admittedly sounded ominous. Yet all of these things could quickly explained as well.

Suddenly, the Super Stud froze! Someone was nearing Terry's cabin. Hearing the approaching footsteps, Seven hurriedly threw the folder back into the drawer, closed it while switching off the small reading lamp, and then dove behind one of the narrow room dividers. Watching breathlessly, he saw the lock on Terry's door slowly being turned.

Crouched in the silent darkness, Christopher Seven nervously envisioned Nalco's huge right hand around his neck!

Chapter 29

'A Fight to the Death'

The cabin door slowly opened. Frozen like a statue, and hiding as best he could behind the thin room divider wall, Seven waited anxiously. He heard a man's voice call out in the thankfully darkened room. "Miss Terry?" There was momentary silence followed by another, "Miss Terry, are you in here?"

The Super Stud recognized both the voice and the inflection. It was the accented tones of room steward, Aldo. The steward called out again, "Miss Terry, are you in the bathroom?" Nothing but silence greeted his query. Fortunately, the lanky crewman didn't bother turning on the cabin's overhead lights. Piloted only by the moonlight shining into the room, Aldo took a cursory glance around the stateroom, shrugged his shoulders, and closed the cabin door behind him. He then made his way back down the hall.

Letting out a sigh of relief, Seven waited till the sound of Aldo's departing footsteps completely diminished. He then switched on the tiny desk lamp again and continued his spying. Not much else was in Terry's file folder except a few receipts from various high-end jewelry stores, and some nebulous notes on the top beaches in Italy. Other than what he'd already seen, there was nothing of further interest. *Best get out of here and live to fight another day,* the G5 agent silently advised himself, still unnerved from yet another close call. Carefully placing everything back exactly as he'd found it, Seven prepared to leave. He was about to turn off the lamp and exit the cabin when, on an impulse, he decided to check out the large dresser's drawers, and also Terry's walk-in closet. Just in case anything of importance was hidden there. Moving over to the small built-in bureau, he noiselessly opened the dresser's draws one by one, gently rummaging through the expensive lingerie and clothing. Unfortunately, nothing was concealed in any of the drawers. He then strolled over to the room's walk-in closet and likewise found nothing of significance inside it. Just some designer dresses and several blouses hanging on the closet's long pole.

Disappointed, Seven took one last glance toward the rear of the closet, zeroing in on the back wall. He suddenly stopped dead in his tracks! Over in the closet's rear corner, concealed behind two large sun umbrellas, was a thin metal item. Carefully removing one of the colorful beach umbrellas, Seven gently picked up the partially hidden metal object behind them. When he did, there was no longer any question as to what it was. Nor any further doubts about Terry and the others being members of Rhombus. For the object Christopher Seven now held in his hand was a branding iron. One with a sinister-looking **R** at the end of it. The *same* letter that had been branded onto Ambassador Dawson's naked body!

Nodding in triumph, the Super Stud again put everything back as he'd found it. He then turned the desk lamp around and switched it off. A few minutes later, he was making the short trek down to Doreen's cabin.

Warily approaching her stateroom door, Seven was just about to take the electronic passkey from his jacket's inside pocket when Aldo's voice startled him from across the hall.

"Good evening, Mr. Seven. May I help you with something?" The wiry steward was standing near a small linen closet, ostensibly looking for some fresh bed sheets. His tone sounded a bit edgy, almost with a trace of suspicion to it.

"Oh, hi Aldo," Seven greeted, affably. "Just came down from the Crow's Nest cocktail lounge. Miss Doreen invited me for a quick nightcap, so here I am."

The steward nodded and observed vigilantly as Seven knocked on her door. "Enjoy the rest of your evening, sir," was all that Aldo said, doing so rather testily. He then grabbed the bedding and walked away.

Seven waited a moment, and then knocked on Doreen's door again. She finally opened it and greeted him, excitedly. Clad only in a short, pink nightshirt, her freshly shampooed hair was parted beguilingly to the side. "Hi again, Chris. But why didn't you use the passkey and surprise me? Didn't it work?"

"I couldn't try it. The steward was standing right outside."

She grinned, teasingly. "That's too bad. I was in the shower."

Doreen winked and sauntered over toward a large champagne bucket. "I put a bottle of *Bollinger* on ice a while ago. Should be nice and chilled by now."

"Sounds great, Doreen."

He watched her skillfully twist the bottle's cork off with a small pop. She looked captivating and very sure of herself, and the sight of her scantily clad body tugged at Seven's senses.

For what seemed like the thousandth time, Christopher Seven again questioned his morals and his beliefs - beliefs forever being tested by his unique profession. He silently reflected on G5's frustrating 'abstinence' theories, rehashing their strict textbook lessons in his mind. *"Seductively tease your target at the beginning stages of the mission, but initially never give in,"* was how one scholarly Yale psychologist had put it. *"If you keep her at bay, while bringing her to the very edge of physical ecstasy, she, like most women, will subconsciously do anything she can to bring you into her world and her heart. In addition to trying to prod physicality on you, she'll likewise try to draw you closer by sharing some of her innermost secrets and concerns. Psychologists call this the 'promulgation response'. Of course, just how far you'll ultimately want to go with her is up to you. Perhaps that will be influenced by how much inside info she's yet to reveal. But rest assured. This methodically tested 'teasing' technique, done in the early stages of any affair, is scientifically sound. It's based on the renowned Kingman essays and it definitely works!"*

Yet, as Seven eyed the voluptuous Doreen, he knew it'd be difficult to follow through with these restrictive classroom ploys. They might be scientifically proven, but right now, *he* was the one being tantalized. Trying to control himself and entice his target to open up her heart and, more importantly, her mouth, the Super Stud walked over and gently kissed her on the lips. When he did, she practically ripped his head off, pulling him closer and kissing him back passionately. Panting heavily, she moaned, "I love you, Chris. I don't know why or how it happened, but I love you with all my heart. I could *never* share you with anyone, not even the other three girls like we've always done in the past. I want you for my *own*!"

She kissed him again. "This has never happened to me before, so it must be love! You're slowly changing my mind about a lot of things. Perhaps, made life worth living again. Just tell me you love me too."

Though startled by her 'life worth living' admission, Christopher Seven knew this was the critical 'turn' moment that he and the G5 psychology experts counted on. He'd been carefully coached to spot it and knew this emotional girl was indeed 'turned'. Her contented sigh and her tears of happiness now revealed what the Super Stud agent needed to know. "Yes, darling," Seven lied, "I love you too. With all my heart. Like you've said, it *must* be love."

Beaming, she put her hands on her shapely hips and teasingly asked, "Then what are we going to do about it?"

Seven grinned back, "Well, for one thing ..." His words were interrupted by a loud banging on the door. It surprised them both. Doreen looked over at Seven with a startled expression. More pounding ensued, followed by Mario's strident voice, "Doreen, open up! It's me, Mario. Mr. Gitano told me to come."

Throwing on the terry cloth bathrobe hanging by her bed, Doreen walked over to the cabin door and angrily opened it. Staring at Mario's menacing face, she greeted him testily, "Look here! I don't like people interrupting my personal time. Carmine knows that. What's this all about?"

Though uninvited to do so, the beefy 'hit man' brazenly strolled into the room. "Well, well," he chirped. "Ain't this cozy. Doreen in her nighties with champagne on ice. Sorry friends, but the party's over." He glared at Christopher Seven. "The boss wants to see you, mister. *Now!*"

Tiring of this bullying punk, and trying to be as spiteful as he could, Seven asked, sarcastically, "Does he, now? Well maybe I don't want to see *him*." The Super Stud chuckled. "Unless good old Carmine's come up with another game for us to play."

Mario bristled at the cutting remark. "Whatever Carm wants is *his* business, punk. He just said to bring you to him, pronto!"

"You better go, Chris," warned Doreen, obviously worried for Seven's sake. "Carmine doesn't like being kept waiting."

"All right. But keep the bubbly cold, Doreen. I'll be back shortly."

Mario frowned and snarled at Seven, "Real sure of yourself, ain't you pal? Oh well, it's your funeral. Let's get going."

The G5 agent did as he was told, dutifully moving toward the elevator, wondering what was in store for him *this* time. Could they have found out he'd been spying in Terry's stateroom? If so, he too might be 'falling' overboard tonight.

Seven and his gangland chaperon rode the elevator in awkward silence, taking it down to Gitano's huge penthouse suite. Mario knocked on the suite's double doors. A gruff "Yeah?" bellowed from inside.

"It's me, boss – Mario. I brought him to you like you ordered."

"OK, enter. The door's unlocked."

Seven was led into a small office located in back of the suite's elegant dining room. The cigar-smoking Gitano was sitting at a large mahogany desk. He pointed to the single chair in front of it.

"Sit," ordered Gitano. He then waved off Mario with a flick of his hand. "Wait outside, Mare. I can handle this pretty boy by myself."

The Mafioso waited for his henchman to leave, and then, looking "Something about you doesn't wash, buddy boy." The mobster sighed. "But I'm tired of trying to figure it out. And tired of you too."

Carmine stared up at the ceiling a moment. "Normally I'd squash a bug like you and forget all about it. But I'm going to cut you a break, fella. Rather than making you 'disappear', a scenario that might have some annoying police complications, I'm simply gonna throw you off my boat once we get to Naples. Kick you off, along with all the other freeloading passengers. I shouldn't have let *any* of you come. You've all become a distraction for me and I got important work to do. So it's goodbye and good riddance to every one of you civvies. Except for the four girls, of course. They're staying."

Seven said nothing, trying to figure out what Gitano was up to. The G5 operative leaned back in his chair and listened closely as Gitano informed, "I probably should have taken care of you tonight once and for all. Have a few of the big boys grab some baseball bats from downstairs and practice their swings on you. But I decided I ain't gonna whack you. Not if you do *exactly* what I tell you."

The mafia kingpin put his elbows on the desk and leaned in closer. "Why am I letting you off the hook, Seven?" Gitano shrugged his shoulders. "I really don't know. Maybe it's your moxie or your guts under pressure. Or maybe it's your boldness. All that stuff appeals to me."

Gitano stood up to stretch his legs. Stubbing out his cigar on the wall behind him, he reached down for the large coffee mug sitting on his desk. He grabbed it and took a swig of the lukewarm brew. Making a sour face as he tasted it, Gitano slammed it back down on his desk, spilling half of it. He then went on with his speech.

"Anyway, as for you. There's a few things I can't figure out. Like who you work for, and how you constantly keep escaping a beating from us." He chuckled and gave Seven a nod of grudging admiration. "Monte Carlo was one thing. But the way you got out of that *Scegliere* fix, unscathed, was a thing of beauty. I thought I finally had you on that one."

The mobster sat back down. "I'm still not sure whether you're working for one of the rival families or not. A guy like you is too clever to be just some yacht-loving gigolo as you claim. I'm betting you have ties to one of the European families. Most likely, Carpi's." Gitano shook his head. "Like I told you, I probably should a just thrown you overboard and been done with it."

Seven shrugged. "I appreciate the reprieve, Carmine. But why *didn't* you?"

"Cause I got bigger fish to fry at the moment. And I don't want no pesky European cops snooping around the Zephyr right now. It's like what Mario said you told him. One death onboard, which we just reported to the Italian Coast Guard by the way, was hard enough to explain. *Two* such mishaps could really cause a long, drawn-out hullabaloo. The Mafia *Don* laughed loudly. "So I guess you lucked out again, mister."

Christopher Seven said nothing as the Mafia chieftain finished up, "Anyway, whichever rival family you might be working for, if any, doesn't really matter to me now. But you better not tell anybody *anything* about my yacht." Gitano used his finger and made a show of pretending to slice Seven's neck with an imaginary knife. "If you do tell them anything, you'll find it's tough to speak without a tongue."

Gitano paused a moment to let his threat sink in. "And believe me, friend, I got *sure* ways of finding out."

Surprisingly, the mobster then took out a thick checkbook from the top drawer of his desk and began writing. "I'm now going to give you some 'going away money', Seven. Payment in advance to keep your trap shut. Like they say in the movies, consider this an offer you *can't* refuse."

Gitano grinned. "Let's call it a 'consolation prize' for your promise to keep silent about *anything* you've seen or heard onboard Zephyr. I figure I owe you that much. Both for your silence and for scaring the pants off of you with my grape game."

Carmine gulped down more of the tepid coffee and pointed his finger ominously at Seven. "This check I'm giving you now squares it with us, friend. Permanently! It means you've been bought off. But it comes with a strict stipulation. One which will start the day after tomorrow. In Italy, we call it a *condizionato*."

Pointing his finger at Seven, the Mafioso began shaking it violently. "After tomorrow, I never want to lay eyes on you again, mister. *Ever!* And I never want you to see, phone, or re-contact *any* of the four women I brought along this trip. *Especially* Doreen." Gitano's widely opened eyes and his crazed expression had the look of a madman. "'Cause if I ever catch you within a hundred miles of *any* of my women, you're a dead man, friend. And your death won't be pretty."

The Super Stud was about to say something, but the mob king held up his right hand for silence and kept railing, "Should you ever cross me on this, mister, it will be the last thing you ever do! *Gridare vendetta,* an old Sicilian ritual, will quickly ensue. In short, it means I'll *personally* cut out your tongue. And that's a promise from me to you."

Gitano leaned forward and handed Seven the check. It was from some Detroit construction company's 'business account', made out to Christopher Seven for $10,000.00.

"That ought to buy you a nice dinner before you fly home," sneered the mobster. He downed the last of his now cold coffee and added, "Tomorrow's stop will be the Isle of Capri. I promised Terry, Suz and Anita that you could come to my afternoon picnic bash there. I always throw one on Capri. Everyone who's anyone comes. It's a big Italian social event. I guess that's why the girls wanted you around. To flaunt you in front of those European blue blooded women they hate so much."

Gitano shrugged his broad shoulders. "Oh well, whatever floats their boat. Anyway, since there's no commercial airport or any train stations on the island itself, so we'll let you and the other civilian passengers stay one more night onboard. That'll give all of you twenty-four hours to get your things together and make travel plans."

"But..."

Seven was immediately cut off. "No *buts*, fella. The day after tomorrow we dock in Naples. And that's where all you civilian spongers are being thrown off. For good!"

Gitano looked away a moment and then informed, "Can't be helped. Something's just come up and I'll need Zephyr for my own business reasons." The capo didn't elaborate, instead giving Seven another warning. "By the way, that's just between *us*. The other passengers will merely be told that some mechanical problems have developed."

The G5 operative wondered what this smokescreen *really* meant and made a mental note to try and find out from Doreen.

"Anyway," Carmine continued, "the day after tomorrow, right after we dock in Naples, you and my other guests will be escorted off. Nice and early. Alternative travel plans shouldn't be a problem. Unlike Capri, Naples has plenty of train and plane connections. Tons of hotels, too, if anyone wants to sightsee. My concierge can make all the departing arrangements, and naturally I'll pay for them." Gitano gave a pompous grin and boasted, "Like they say. Carmine Gitano has deep pockets."

Gitano next advised, "As for you and *your* travel plans, Seven, I strongly suggest you leave Naples as soon as we dock there. Take the first flight out and never look back. Things could have been a lot worse for you. So let's leave it like that."

The mob chief shrugged again. "If you want to stay a few days and see Naples, I really don't give a hoot. Just so long as you keep far away from me, the four girls, and my yacht once we leave you there the day after tomorrow. After that, I don't care what you do so long as I never see you again. Anyway, if I were you, I'd probably find myself some *other* tourist trap to visit. Better for your health that way." The big man forced a smile. "There's an old saying about that city, Seven - 'See Naples and die!'" The mob boss laughed, loudly.

Seven's mind began racing frantically. His main concern now was staying in touch with Doreen. Those thoughts were cut short by Gitano.

"So that's about it pretty boy. By the way, as a final precaution, I'm having you *shadowed* for the rest of your voyage. Both electronically and via one of my crew as a shadow. You'll be watched and listened to 24/7. That means *no* smart phone use, *no* Internet, and *no* computer. For the next day or so, you have *no* contact with the outside world!" Gitano scowled ominously. "This little yacht excursion better be the *last* time I or the girls *ever* lay eyes on you."

The Super Stud sat quietly, not sure what to say or do at this point. He was still determined not to be intimidated by this Mafia bully.

"Now then," growled Gitano, glancing at his expensive watch. "Any final questions or comments?"

Christopher Seven nodded. "Just a few, Carmine. First off, whether you believe me or not, I'm certainly *not* part of any rival gang. Or rival 'families', as you and Mario call them. I was simply invited onboard Zephyr by Terry and her friends, so I came. Who *wouldn't,* when four beautiful women ask you to cruise on a luxury vessel? I knew the girls were using me, so I let myself be used. And I enjoyed every minute of it."

Now it was Seven's turn to point a finger at his gangland host. "I also want you to know that despite everything - the rough stuff included - I appreciated your hospitality. I knew you weren't thrilled to have me along, yet you let me come anyway. That showed me something too. Anyway, your yacht is as magnificent as I thought she'd be. Sorry you and I didn't hit it off. Maybe we could have under different circumstances."

Seven's straightforward, appreciative words, even at this tense moment, seemed to temporarily disarm the gangster. For a brief moment, Gitano let his guard down. "Maybe we could have been 'simpatico' at that, Seven. I could have used a guy like you from time to time. Cool under pressure, shifty and cunning, and great with the dames too. Those traits come in handy in my world. Oh well - c´est la vie."

After musing on it a moment, Gitano's coarse Mafia demeanor quickly returned - in spades. "Yet I meant *every* word I said about your last two days here, Seven. You'll have no communications with anyone, unless it's a medical emergency we can't handle; or personally OK'd by me! For you, everything's 'off limits', staring now!"

"I understand," Seven replied, as a germ of an idea gradually came to him. "Yet you might have a big problem with Doreen about all that. She and I seemed to have really hit it off, and she won't take my leaving her 'for good' very well. *If* you know what I mean. From what I've learned about her, she'll undoubtedly blame *you*."

"So?"

"So, why don't you leave that to me, Carm? I'll smooth things out with Doreen, tell her it's 'goodbye', and make sure you won't have any lingering problems with her."

"Whatta ya driving at, Seven?"

"Well, if it's okay with you, I'd like to have one last day with her tomorrow on Capri. Take her for lunch at a place I read about called *La Fontelina.* This way I can have some personal time with her. Time enough to say my final 'goodbyes' and explain things a bit more eloquently. I'll put all the blame on myself and my job back home. This way, since you won't be involved, she won't be upset with you. As for your afternoon picnic, we can join you there a bit later."

Gitano thought on it a minute, his face initially showing uncertainty. Then, figuring nothing underhanded could really occur in that short a time period, and planning to have Seven 'shadowed' and firmly 'talked to' by a few of his Capri shore side goons anyway, he agreed.

"Like I said, Seven, you're a real smooth operator when it comes to women." The gangster rubbed his chin in thought and then slowly approved. "Okay, I guess that'll be all right. But don't tell her *I* had anything to do with your leaving her or I'll never hear the end of it! Like you said, just make up some story and leave me out of it. Anything to take the blame away from me. That broad can be a royal pain with all of her moods." Gitano's face suddenly showed concern. "And right now, I need *all* four of those women happy and contented." He quickly covered his last revelation. "For *business* reasons."

The Super Stud remained silent, inwardly glad he'd now have one last crack at Doreen. One final opportunity to try and arrange a covert way to continue seeing her after he was booted off the yacht. The exact *opposite* of what this Mafioso was now demanding. Even so, Seven was well aware that disobeying *Don* Carmine Gitano now might cost him his tongue, and almost certainly, his life as well!

"That's it," Gitano announced, again glancing down at his watch. "Meeting's over. I hope, for your sake, that we understand each other on this."

Seven nodded.

"Phone me or Mario if you need to make a business or personal call. I'll look it over before approving it or not.

Seven nodded his head, though knowing full well that he was planning to defy a solemn Cosa Nostra decree. Reflecting on the Mafioso's ominous *'gridare vendetta'* warning, the secret agent suddenly sensed a foreboding feeling of mortal danger.

Walking out of Gitano's plush suite, Christopher Seven now realized that he wouldn't be playing some childish game this time around. This wasn't going to be a petty poker contest or some ancient grape game. No indeed! Somehow, the Super Stud was certain that his next battle of wills against this powerful Mafia *Don* was going to be a fight to the death!

The following morning, a gloriously sunny Friday, Zephyr arrived in the busy Bay of Napoli an hour or so after daybreak. Dropping anchor just outside the Isle of Capri, her crew readied the yacht for passenger tender service to and back from the famous island. While the Zephyr swayed softly in the gentle breeze, four of her crewmen began lowering one of the tenders to test the sea conditions. Still joking among themselves about the 'accidental' death of fellow crewman Emilio Rossi, they knew better than to let any of the passengers overhear their Italian gallows humor. Despite the crew's frivolity, Rossi's death served as another chilling reminder to them. No one *ever* crosses *Don* Gitano and lives to tell about it!

Restlessly stirring in his comfortable cabin bed, Christopher Seven awoke for good shortly after 8:00 a.m., stirred by the noise and vibration of Zephyr's anchor being lowered. The Super Stud had experienced a very uneasy night, tossing and turning while speculating on what strategy to pursue next. Right after last night's tense meeting with Carmine Gitano had ended, Seven compliantly went straight to his cabin, doing so on direct orders from the Mafia *Don* himself. Seven vividly recalled Gitano's parting words to him. "Now that we understand each other, I want you to go back to your stateroom and *stay* there. Forget about Doreen and the other three women tonight."

Seven nodded meekly as Carmine concluded, "I'll give you permission to see Doreen one *last* time like you've asked for. Tomorrow you can escort her on the Isle of Capri. And, if you think it would help your saying goodbye to her *'permanently,'* you two can also have a *last* dinner together tomorrow night onboard the yacht. But after that, it's *over* between you and Doreen...*Capiche?*"

Still worrying about what he'd learned spying in Terry's cabin, and the troublesome *"terminate Doreen"* directive, Christopher Seven had dutifully exited Gitano's suite and phoned Doreen, from his room. Once connected to Doreen, the G5 operative quickly begged off going back to her stateroom, claiming he was "feeling a bit seasick." Good naturedly laughing at his bout with *'mal de mer,'* Doreen told him she looked forward to their lunch tomorrow, and to the rest of their day on Capri. With that, they had bid each other a pleasant good night, with visions of the Isle of Capri on both their minds, albeit for entirely different reasons.

Seven knew that he'd have to work fast and furiously today on Capri, since he, and all the other 'civilian passengers,' were being put off the yacht tomorrow morning. The main thing now was to keep his relationship with Doreen working, *despite* last night's chilling warning from Gitano. Then, under the pretense of 'love,' and perhaps even 'marriage,' arrange to meet up with Doreen after she and the Zephyr returned to Monaco next week. If Seven could reunite with her then, and somehow manipulate this impressionable young woman to be an unwitting inside source, maybe there was hope of discovering something meaningful regarding Terry's branding iron and Gitano's future plans.

After that, Interpol and the CIA could connect the rest of the dots, all the way up to the Rhombus foursome. Maybe even to Carmine Gitano himself. If so, Seven would take great pleasure in bringing down the arrogant Mafioso and his pretty cohorts; regrettably, Doreen included.

After a shower and shave, Seven walked over to the phone and ordered a quick room-service breakfast to be delivered in half an hour: "Fresh-squeezed orange juice, coffee, a lightly toasted bran muffin with butter and jelly on the side, and some fresh fruit."

Seven then changed into a pair of tan Levi's, a yellow pique-knit *Nautica* deck shirt, white cotton crew socks and a new pair of white *New Balance* walking shoes. Exactly thirty minutes later, there was a knock on the door. His breakfast, delivered by room steward Aldo, had promptly arrived.

"Good morning, sir," smiled the steward, seemingly in a much friendlier mood than when he'd seen Seven the night before at Doreen's door. "It's a lovely day. Should I place the tray on the outside balcony?"

"Thanks, Aldo. That'll be fine."

"Very good, sir." The humming steward deftly set the food items on top of the veranda's small glass table, bowed smartly, and took his leave.

Seven walked outside onto his stateroom's balcony, sat down and, after saying grace, consumed the delicious continental breakfast. Eating in reflective silence, he stared out at the glistening water. Now facing the starboard side, the G5 agent saw nothing but endless sea in front of him.

Wondering for a moment what types of predator fish, such as sharks or barracuda, might be lurking below, Seven's thoughts turned to Emilio Rossi, the unfortunate crewman whose corpse Gitano's thugs had callously thrown into the open waters. At least the strangled Rossi had been killed *before* being tossed overboard, and therefore wouldn't have felt the panic of possibly being devoured by some ravenous sea creature.

Guiltily reflecting on Emilio and his two young daughters, innocent girls who would now be fatherless, Christopher Seven pounded his fist on the table. Still feeling responsible for Rossi's death, all the Super Stud could do now was to try and upset Gitano's approaching plans; *whatever* they might be. For Seven's acute 'sixed sense' was telling him that Carmine Gitano was planning something really big!

Seven frowned as he perused this morning's *Yacht and News* information sheet. It mentioned that Gitano and Captain Bacca had given Emilio Rossi a 'traditional naval funeral at sea.' Tossing the crewman's body, draped in an Italian flag, into the open waters, after a few Italian Bible passages were read, Carmine Gitano had misleadingly stated that this sham memorial service was "what Emilio would have wanted."

In truth, Seven knew the *real* reason for this so-called 'sailor's funeral.' It was simply a clever ruse to keep the authorities away from Emilio's corpse and the knowledge that Rossi had first been strangled onboard. Shaking his head in disgust, Seven hoped that by helping to take down Rhombus and Gitano, a small dose of revenge would be gained for Emilio. Sighing softly, Seven glumly finished the rest of his breakfast.

Heading back inside, the G5 agent brushed his teeth again and grabbed his cellphone, mindful that Gitano had 'allowed' him "only *one* onboard call today." Carmine had also hinted that Seven's phone conversation might be recorded, like *all* passenger phone calls made on Zephyr. Seven was thus happy that he and Fieri both knew the federal interdepartmental *'nicety code.'*

Glancing at the four signal bars, which showed that Seven's phone reception was surprisingly strong, he clicked in Vin Fieri's cell number. The doc answered woozily, apparently still half asleep, as Seven began speaking in the rudimentary code they'd rehearsed. Just in case Zephyr's sophisticated electronics could indeed listen in.

"Good morning from the beautiful Isle of Capri, Vin. It's now 8:44 a.m. and the weather outside is hot and sunny."

Knowing that they were most likely talking on an 'open' line, Fieri was likewise guarded. "Morning, Chris. What's up?"

"I'm afraid there's been a change of plans, Vin. My cruise was cut short. All passengers have to leave the yacht first thing tomorrow."

"Sorry to hear that," Doc Fieri replied.

"Courteously, the yacht's owner has been kind enough to pay for everyone's alternative traveling bills," Seven further explained. "Anyway, all passengers are to leave the yacht once we get into Naples tomorrow morning. Some problem with the yacht's fresh water storage."

"Oh well," Fieri replied. "Can't be helped. Anyhow, with the stock market going wild the past few days, it's probably just as well you have to depart."

"Probably," Seven agreed. "Although I'll certainly miss my *four* new friends who got me on this magnificent vessel and cruise. By the way, the gals are staying onboard. So no chance of getting together with them in Monaco."

"As you know, Chris," the doc further explained, "we have some *volatile* new stocks in our portfolio. And this recent plunge seems serious. It will need our immediate attention, *or else.* I don't think it can wait."

"I agree," Seven responded. "Anyway, there's really no choice. Since I can't stay on the Zephyr any longer, I was wondering if you could join me in Naples tomorrow. That way we can still attend to those four attractive blue-chip options we've been talking about and keep a close watch on them. We can also call my New York exchange to see what they suggest. In the meantime, since we'll probably be forced to stick around Naples a few days, maybe we can take in a few of the *sights* I've always wanted to *view.* You know, *before* flying back to New York."

The doc remained silent, so Seven went on, "Naturally, I'd like to leave Naples as soon as we can, Vin. After our portfolio work, of course. It'll probably be difficult to get a flight out of there on the weekend. But come Monday or Tuesday, I want to leave the city like I promised the *boss* if the market turns any worse."

Fieri quickly picked up on *all* of Seven's coded meanings. The *four* attractive *yacht women* and the fact that they'd be *staying* onboard Gitano's vessel. Seven's wish to *continue* spying on them, even though the G5 agent was now 'persona non grata' with mob *boss* Carmine Gitano. And the fact that he'd been 'ordered' to leave Zephyr and stay away.

The doc paused a moment before adding, "As for sightseeing on the weekend, there's a lot worse places to be stuck than Naples. Plenty to see in the area, including Vesuvius and that *Museo Archeologico* I told you about. Anyway, what's better than two old high school chums and future business partners *observing* the treasures of Italy together?"

"Sounds good," Seven declared. His voice then became somber. "Unfortunately, I have some sad news, Vin. One of Zephyr's crewmen had an unfortunate *accident* yesterday. The poor chap is dead. Fell overboard. He seemed like a really nice fellow. I was just talking with him a few hours before it happened. Do you think we should send flowers?"

"Yes," the doc replied, rightly surmising that Seven wanted him to notify CIA and their *inside* moles and see what the scuttlebutt was. "I'll follow up on it."

"Thanks, Vin. By the way, where should I meet you tomorrow?"

"I know a little spot called Riviera 231," Fieri advised. "It's an elegant B&B with only four bedrooms. The manager's a good friend."

Seven knew this was code for someone on CIA's payroll.

"She might even be able to put us up gratis for a night or two," Fieri explained. "Anyway, the cabbies should know the place. Just tell your driver 'Chiaia 231.'"

Seven reached for the small pad and pen on the nearby desk and wrote it all down. "Got it, Vin."

"And listen, Chris. If you get there before I do, which you probably will, mention my name and ask for *Elena*. Hopefully she'll take good care of us. We can grab lunch tomorrow at 231 and use their house computer in case we want to make any stock or funding transfers. If anything more complex is needed, we can search for a full-fledged *business center*."

Christopher Seven knew this meant seeking out CIA's covert headquarters somewhere in the area. He continued jotting down the info, while Vin finished up with some final details.

"Sounds like a plan then, Chris. Well, so long. Sorry your cruise was called to a halt. See you tomorrow."

Feeling better about having an ally joining him soon, Seven was satisfied that even if this phone conversation was recorded and played back for Gitano, nothing of importance was revealed thanks to the code.

The Super Stud sat down on his stateroom bed a moment and began thinking about the fabulous Isle of Capri, now just a short tender ride away. He'd never been to this romantic paradise before, but of course had heard a great deal about it. Italy's breathtaking never-never land that has been charming tourists for almost 2000 years.

Getting up off the bed, Seven contemplated his day ahead with Doreen. Perhaps it would be best to take a taxi tour first and visit a few of the major sights before moving on to the restaurant. Maybe go to *Anacapri's* bluff-top village he'd read so much about. Or see *I Faraglioni* and the fabulous Blue Grotto. It was definitely doable, since Zephyr would be in Capri's scenic harbor all day. And most of the night as well; leaving for Naples in the wee hours.

Quickly remembering his assignment, the Super Stud shook his head and crossly admonished himself to stop acting like a wide-eyed tourist and to act more like an agent. There was serious work to be done here. The mission came first, and that meant convincing Doreen of several things today. His thoughts were interrupted by the metallic voice of Captain Bacca coming through the stateroom's overhead speakers.

"Good morning, ladies and gentlemen. This is your Captain speaking. Welcome to beautiful Capri, the *reginetta di bellezza* of Italy. It's precisely 8:45 a.m. and we've just been cleared by the local authorities. You are now free to embark the tenders for the short ride in to shore. Tender service to and from Capri's Marina Grande will be running continuously, with the last boat back to the ship at 3:30 a.m. We sail for Naples shortly afterward. I ask you to stay seated during the tender ride and to keep your hands and arms inside the tender at all times."

There was a brief silence followed by, "Regrettably, I have some disappointing information to convey this morning. Sadly, our cruise must come to a premature end. As some of you may have already heard, due to an unforeseen problem with our onboard water desalination equipment, passengers will be required to disembark Zephyr tomorrow morning in Naples. Most of our desalination machinery will then be turned off, sometime tomorrow, resulting in a very limited supply of fresh water for the bathrooms and kitchens. Italian passenger regulations dictate that Zephyr can now only take a very limited amount of people back to Monaco, as the fresh water problem can't be fixed until we return there and get the needed parts. In order to comply with this maritime edict, as well as for your safety and comfort, it's been decided to disembark most all passengers tomorrow morning."

There was a further pause and then, "On behalf of Mr. Gitano, I offer you his sincere apology. He also wanted me to assure you that he will personally take care of all your travel costs. Should any of you need airline help or travel advice, those arrangements can be handled by our yacht's concierge. On behalf of the crew and myself, let me likewise apologize for this unforeseen glitch, and say that it's been a pleasure to serve you, albeit for a shorter time than we expected. Perhaps I'll see some of you again on a future Zephyr voyage."

Christopher Seven shook his head, wondering what this contrived fresh water hogwash was all about. What was Gitano *really* up to, and why did he suddenly want all passengers off his yacht? The agent shrugged his shoulders. Perhaps Doreen could shed some light on it.

Just as Seven grabbed his beach bag and prepared to leave, the cabin phone rang. It was Doreen, her voice happy and excited. "Morning, Chris. Hope you're feeling better."

"Much better, thanks. It's been a long time since I've been seasick."

Doreen chuckled and chided, "Some sailor you are. Anyway, I've had my breakfast and I'm ready to go when you are. It'd be good to get an early start. There's so much I want to show you on Capri, so leave things to me. I've hired a car and driver, a young friend of mine named Marco, who runs his own sightseeing company. He speaks English better than we do and knows all the best spots. More importantly, since he's a resident of Capri, he's allowed to have a car. Only locals can have automobiles on the island in season. Visitors can't drive or even rent one. And they're likewise prohibited from bringing them in by the ferries. Marco will be meeting us by the marina around 9:30 a.m. I'll bring along his cell number in case we don't spot him."

The Super Stud was bitterly disappointed by the news. Was it some type of 'shadow' Gitano privately arranged? Or was Doreen telling the truth about her friend? In any case, Seven wanted to be alone with Doreen...not with some Italian chaperon getting in the way. Seven's voice showed obvious displeasure.

"Well, if that's what you want, Doreen. But frankly, I was hoping we'd have some time alone. After all, Capri is said to be a romantic paradise for lovers. And well..." He left the rest unsaid.

Doreen giggled into the phone. "Don't worry, Romeo. Marco knows the score. He'll simply drop us off, where and when we want, and come back later. Capri is a very small island with only a few drivable roads anyway. So having a hired local driver, instead of fighting the crowds, or trying to hail one of those large open-air cabs, is better."

Seven frowned, still disappointed, as Doreen continued explaining, "We probably won't have time to get a swim in today, but bring along your bathing suit just in case. Don't fret, Chris. We'll get in our *private moments*, as you call them, and have that scrumptious lunch you promised me, too."

She paused a moment, and her next words took on an annoyed tone. "Oh, yeah, I almost forgot. Carmine called a few minutes ago. Said he expects us to join him for his silly picnic ritual. I suppose we've got to go." She shook her head, irritably. "And Terry, Suz, and Anita are expecting you there too. Guess you'll have to do your 'window dressing' duties so they can show you off in front of all those hated female bluebloods." Doreen sighed into the phone. "But I adamantly told them that we wouldn't be there until *after* 3:00 p.m. That'll give us most of the day to ourselves. Anyway, I'll see you downstairs by the tenders in five minutes. Bye."

Smiling confidently, Christopher Seven grabbed his wallet and beach gear and walked over to the door. As Seven exited his stateroom, Aldo, his wiry room steward, observed him closely. Hidden behind a small supply closet door, and with a sly grin on his bony face, the shadowy steward glanced at his wristwatch and noted the time. He was soon on his smartphone calling the bridge!

Chapter 31

The Black Car

The tender ride from the anchored yacht to Capri's picturesque harbor was smooth and uneventful. The small craft pulled into a private berth adjacent to the main pier, bumping gently against the rubber pylons that cushioned the auxiliary wharf. Seven and Doreen quickly debarked and made their way over to Capri's bustling *Marina Grande.*

The Super Stud looked around at the sizable throng of tourists making their way inland despite the early hour. By noon, he reflected, this entire area would be filled with throngs of happy visitors coming to the Isle of Capri via the ferries from Naples and Sorrento.

"There's Marco!" Doreen called out. Grinning widely, she pointed toward a thin young man in his early twenties. He had curly black hair, an angular, nice-looking face, and the stubble-growth of a three-day beard. He waved back and made his way over to them.

"Saluti, signorina! Welcome back to Capri."

"Thank you, Marco." Doreen kissed him on both cheeks and introduced Seven as they walked over to Marco's tiny blue Fiat. "This is my good friend, Christopher."

"Glad to meet you, signore Christopher. Welcome."

"Thanks, Marco. Your beautiful island has a famed reputation. Too bad our time here is short. I'll have to return for a longer visit one day."

The Italian grinned. "Si, signore. That's one of Capri's oldest maxims. Those who come here for a first time *always* return."

Seven smiled uneasily, hoping the old adage would prove true. With *Don* Gitano's menacing warnings last night, and Seven's plans to blatantly ignore them, the agent's chances of returning *anywhere* didn't look too promising. He nodded his head dourly.

"You should probably drive us to the funicular station first," suggested Doreen as Marco's car pulled out of the small waterside parking lot. "Chris and I can ride the funicular over to Capri Town, taking in the aerial views, and then meet you later at La Piazzetta."

"Si, Miss Doreen. I'll be waiting there."

Doreen turned around and faced Seven, who had just wedged himself into the Fiat's miniscule back seat. "After that, we can then go by *Villa Lysis.* Wait till you see it, Chris. It was built by the poet Fersen, and it's one of the most beautiful private homes you'll ever lay eyes on. We can also grab a quick look at *Villa Jovis,* Tiberius's mountaintop retreat."

"Sounds good," Seven replied, anxiously wondering when he'd get some time alone with her.

As if reading Seven's mind, Doreen assured him, "But after that it's just you and me on one of Capri's most isolated shorelines. A while back, Marco and I found a seldom-visited spot between the *Arco Naturale* and the *Grotta di Matermania.* And though the area is quite spectacular and ruggedly beautiful, it's one of the few areas on the island that's almost always deserted. No tourists and maybe a few locals. We nicknamed it 'Beach Extraordinaire.' Most folks have never heard about it."

"She's right, signore Christopher," smiled Marco. "I first showed it to Miss Doreen and her friends several years ago. It's still our little secret."

Doreen nodded. "It sure is, Marco. You can drop us off there and come back later to drive us to lunch." She then winked at the young driver. "I forgot to tell you, Marco. My friend Chris here is a wolf in sheep's clothing. Seems all he wants is to be alone with me."

Marco grinned and whistled. "I don't blame him, signorina."

~

The various Capri landmarks, seen from high above via the quaint cable car, were just as astounding as advertised, particularly the ride over the Piazza Umberto, the island's most famous square. The bustling venue below, aptly dubbed 'the little theatre of the world,' was extraordinary. And as they glided above the Isle of Capri, Seven could see why this awe-inspiring atoll was one of the most celebrated spots in the world. Each successive aerial view was more amazing than the next.

Marco's small compact dutifully met them at the inland station, and soon they were motoring on one of the island's very few 'through roads,' driving to a lesser-known section of Capri's magnificent shoreline. Marco dropped them off at Doreen's secluded seashore, her '*Beach Extraordinaire,*' which was located somewhere south of Augusto. The deserted beach was primitive but hauntingly beautiful, especially the distant views surrounding it.

At last alone, Doreen and Seven strolled toward the water for a closer look. They stood speechless for a moment, surveying the far horizon. The panoramic vista in front of them was marvelous! Several phenomenal rock formations could be seen in the distance, a truly awesome sight. Arm in arm, they continued walking, ambling out to the edge of a small overhang where they again gaped at the stunning view.

"One of those rock formations is over 300 feet tall," Doreen finally commented. "Coupled with the turquoise water encircling it, this is one of the island's most dramatic views. I could gaze at it for hours."

Christopher Seven moved closer and kissed her softly. It was simply a kiss of gratitude for allowing him to see such a remarkable sight.

"Thanks for bringing me here, Doreen. I'll never forget this place. And I'll always remember you by it."

She looked over at him with a strange expression, an odd mixture of gloom and contentment. Staring out at the sea, she dolefully whispered, "You're welcome. Unfortunately, this is the last time I'll ever see it."

Confused, Seven merely looked away, not quite sure what she meant by the statement. Did Doreen have bad memories of this secluded rocky waterfront? Or was it simply just another upshot of her erratic moods? Like the one the Super Stud had seen during their drive to Eze?

Seemingly in a brief trance, Doreen gradually came out of it and advised, "I guess we won't have enough time for a swim today, though I'd like to stay near the water's edge. Somewhere we can relax and talk."

Seven's senses heightened. *This might be it!* He and his attractive quarry would finally be alone in a sequestered setting. Or, as G5 euphemistically called it during training - *'a Stud rendezvous site.'* Christopher Seven had used such sites before, all around the world. Out-of-the-way beaches, candlelit backrooms, remote ski gondolas, and even a deserted cave on one successful mission in northern Mexico. These secluded rendezvous locales were ideal locales for Super Stud agents. Isolated spots where operatives could talk with, influence, and, often, even *'turn'* their targets completely.

He and his shapely companion walked back to the rocky shoreline, where a few plastic beach chairs and some shabby wooden picnic tables were located. They sat down at one of them, side by side, and silently watched a moment as the waves gently made their way toward the shore. Doreen suddenly threw her arms around him and kissed him passionately. "I've been waiting since last night to continue," she sighed. "Have you missed me too?"

"Yes, darling." Smiling warmly, he kissed her gently on the neck and face. "You know, Doreen, I've read many stories about the romantic influence of the Isle of Capri. I can see now that they're all true. Especially when experiencing it with a woman like you." Taking her in his arms, Seven kissed her again, this time on the lips with forceful, persuasive passion.

The next forty minutes were pure bliss. They took off their socks and shoes, rolled up their pant legs, and strolled along the shoreline, their bare feet free to enjoy the cool refreshing water. Seven picked up several colorful shells, which they neatly stacked in the sand. For the moment, at least, the G5 operative tried to forget that he was frolicking with a charter member of one of the world's most lethal criminal organizations.

How can it be? Doreen looked so innocent and childlike as she played with the sand and shells. But then, recalling the file photos of Ambassador Dawson's tortured body, and remembering the sinister looking branding iron he'd uncovered in Terry's room, Christopher Seven knew it was time to get down to business.

He walked Doreen back to the chairs and dried her wet ankles and feet with one of the towels he'd brought. Dropping the towel, he massaged her toes sensually, knowing it was exciting her. He then sat down beside her on the adjoining beach chair. "What a wonderful paradise this is, Doreen. Yet tell me, what did you mean by this being the *last* time you'll ever see it?"

She looked away a moment as that now familiar distant gaze of hers returned. Silent awhile, she at last replied, "It's something I can't really discuss, Chris. Something between me and the three other girls. We've made a pact. One that will prevent me from ever coming back here."

Stroking his hair, she looked at him, affectionately. "That's all I can really say about it. Except that, had I known I'd be meeting you, and falling in love, I probably wouldn't have agreed to it."

Seven again tried to speculate on what this was all about. He listened closely as she continued, "You see, Chris, I've made a solemn pledge to myself, and to others, including my late mother. That pledge is sacred to me, and it *must* be honored above everything else."

Doreen noticed the confused expression on Seven's face. Though knowing he'd never understand, she went on explaining anyway. "It's an oath I've honored unquestionably, sworn on my late mother's soul. So I can't go back on it now. Nor am I sure I'd want to."

She again gazed out toward the sea, slowly recalling, "Despite my ups and downs with her, I loved my mother in spite of her foibles. Her unique ambitions and goals eventually became sacrosanct to me. After Dad died, she was all I had, and my whole life slowly, but irrevocably, converted to hers. Years ago, I finally began to appreciate and fully understand Mother's world. Near the end of her life, I promised her that I'd fulfill all of her hopes and dreams for me. Her goals, ambitions, and her resolve to be the best."

Still reliving the past, Doreen resolutely declared, "I'm absolutely *certain* that mother would expect me to see my pledge through - completely and to the end." She nodded halfheartedly, as if trying to convince herself of something she really didn't believe. Tears began welling up in her eyes. "It's all so complicated, Chris. Things you would never, ever comprehend or agree with. Things I can't speak about. For your safety as well as mine. Besides, it's too late to stop now. Arrangements have been made that can't be altered or postponed."

Seven knew instinctively that whatever Doreen's pledge was regarding her late mother's wishes, along with her 'pact' with the other Rhombus women, this *pledge* of hers was the key to it all. The key to something very big. The whole thing had an aura of death and conspiracy surrounding it. Was it some sort of risky Rhombus assignment Doreen was hinting at? One that might end in the loss of her life? Did it involve mob boss Carmine Gitano, or anything found in Ambassador Dawson's missing papers? The Super Stud gently pressed her with an expert's touch.

"Listen Doreen, I meant what I said about being in love with you. And you've told me that you love me too. I don't care about your past or your other three friends. It's *you* I've fallen for. I want to spend the rest of my life with you. Do so without any secrets or troubles hanging over us."

He took her hand, kissed it and continued to hold it gently. With absolutely no remorse about lying to her now, Seven kept on with his approach. "You can't just shut me out, Doreen. Not now with the way we feel about each other. That isn't fair to me *or* to you. So, please tell me what this is all about. Maybe I can help in some way."

Doreen narrowed her eyes, not sure if she should be angry, thankful, or suspicious with his last statement. After all, what did she really know about this incredible-looking man? Someone with whom she'd fallen so madly and swiftly in love. The man of all her fantasies and dreams whom she was foolishly going to give up. Do so for a cause she wasn't even sure she believed in anymore.

What's happening here? Doreen silently asked herself. *Am I foolishly going to throw away the chance to spend my life with someone I love and who loves me? Throw away everything I've privately dreamt about for some outdated mantra my mind doesn't really want to honor anymore? This is my one chance for a decent life. The lifestyle for which Father said I should strive. Maybe it could be possible with Chris, provided he'd be willing to except my past sins and go along with some drastic, lifelong changes. Perhaps agree to live in a distant, remote part of the world if he truly loves me, and never, ever look back.*

She shook her head and continued reflecting. *Oh, who am I kidding? I'm in it too far and too deep now. And part of me still wants to be in on Rhombus's greatest triumph. If only to honor my mother's last command.*

Doreen thought on it further. *And what about that pledge to Mother, the woman who founded and developed Rhombus? The sacred society I still belong to, up to the neck! The organization to which I've given everything. The one I've lived for, robbed for, extorted for, and yes, even helped kill for! I swore to Mother on her deathbed that I'd never betray her or Rhombus - no matter what. Vowed I'd give my life for it if necessary. Just like she gave her life for me when those police bullets, aimed at me, hit her instead. After she bravely and lovingly dove in front of them to save my life. That's when I made my sacred promise to her, right before she died in my arms in our speeding getaway car. Mother gave her life for me.*

Doreen wiped a single tear from her eye, vividly recalling that fateful day when her mom sacrificed her life for her daughter's. *That's when I swore my vow,* Doreen remembered. *The oath that's consumed and enslaved me ever since. How can I go back on it now, no matter how much I love this man? Besides, they'd hunt me down to the ends of the earth - and him, too, if I dared betray them.*

Christopher Seven slid over and gently put his arm around this enigmatic young woman. For a brief moment, *not* as a cold, uncaring agent. But as someone truly concerned for her. Despite all the Gitano and Rhombus baggage she carried, he still wanted to help this confused girl if he could. Find a way to shield her from the dreadful world she'd somehow gotten herself into. *Perhaps there's a way,* Seven mused. *Some type of witness-protection program or plea-bargain deal that Colonel McPhail might be able to arrange - leniency in exchange for cooperation.*

Yet, all of that would initially depend on Seven's talking Doreen into allowing him to keep their relationship going. Do so despite the vindictive Carmine Gitano. That would have to be his first priority now, even though it meant keeping her on a string with romantic promises and falsehoods. Leaning back in the rickety beach chair, he gave it a try.

"Listen, Doreen, as you heard this morning, Carmine is putting me and the rest of the passengers off the ship tomorrow."

"Yes, I know."

"Well, what you *don't* know is that he's also forbidden me to ever see you again after today."

"What?!" she exclaimed, angrily.

"It's true. Gitano gave me the edict last night." Seeing her resentment grow, the Super Stud kept pressing. "Look, I certainly don't mind missing the rest of this cruise. But I can't stand the thought of losing you forever just because of Carmine's jealousy." He nodded at her. "That's what it is, you know. Sheer jealousy."

Doreen nodded as Seven went on, "Even so, I wouldn't want to lose you. Not without giving our relationship a fighting chance. Remember, I want to spend the rest of my life with you."

Seven closed his eyes a moment and then said truthfully, "I also want to help get you out of whatever corner you've painted yourself into. And I think I can. But I've got to hear *all* the details before I try."

"I don't know, Chris. It's rather involved and dramatic. You won't like most of it. Probably won't like me much either."

He kissed her tenderly and assured, "Let *me* be the judge of that. And as for Carmine Gitano and his people, I know the score. I'm certainly aware that he's not a man to disobey or say 'no' to. Yet despite all that, we have to figure out a way to continue to stay together. We *must*, if we want to think about a possible life together. We've got to come up with a viable plan or method to secretly meet again, regardless of Gitano. Like I've said, we owe it to ourselves to at least try. Whatever you decide after that, so be it. All I ask is that we give me a chance. I want to take you away from all this."

Seven nodded, knowing this last promise was at least true. He waited anxiously for Doreen's reaction.

She looked over at him affectionately, though her eyes had genuine fear and uncertainty in them. "It *sounds* fine, but like I told you, Chris, there'd be real danger for you if Carmine's people..."

Seven gently put two of his fingers over her mouth. "No more of that, darling. All I know is I'm not going to lose you. After I hear the details of whatever it is you're facing, I'll try to figure out a way to free you from it. You're going to have to trust me, though. That is, if you think I'm worth it."

Smiling at him lovingly, Doreen continued to contemplate the future. She was about to agree on what he'd said, at least the part about seeing him again once they both returned to Monaco, when Seven's worried voice brought her out of her dreamy meditation.

"Doreen, quick! Look over there, across the street. That long black car that just pulled up. Do you recognize any of the four men sitting in it? They seemed to be staring right at us the past few minutes."

She glanced over at the car, an old-fashioned, converted *Cabriolet* convertible, and let out a frightened gasp. "Yes, I know them. They're from Carmine's Napoli band. One of his European hit squads. Gitano's uncle is one of them. He's the old guy sitting in the front seat."

Still gazing at the long black roadster, now parked on the side of the road, Seven worriedly informed, "They've gotten out of their vehicle and they're still staring straight at us. They sure don't look friendly."

"They're not, Chris. That tall, muscular thug is Roddy Batto, a notorious mob enforcer from Sorrento. He's the big galoot on the left."

Seven nodded. "I see him, and his three pals too. Unfortunately, they're heading this way."

Chapter 32

"We'll slice your friend's ears off!"

As the four gangsters approached the beach, Christopher Seven wondered if another planned beating, or worse, was in store for him. If so, he intended to go down fighting this time, using every tactic he knew, clean *or* underhanded. Including what he'd been recently practicing during his martial arts training. Grabbing a good-sized rock from the stony shoreline, Seven deftly palmed it and then slickly hid his improvised 'brass knuckles' in his closed right hand. Waiting tensely for the four goons to reach Doreen and Seven, the G5 operative had no illusions. These mobsters looked like born killers, cold and vicious. Seven shrugged his shoulders, resignedly, knowing that if Gitano's four hoods were planning to overpower him, there was really nothing he could do to prevent it.

"Hi, Doreen," Roddy Batto greeted in a piercing, shrill voice. He took out a black revolver and spun it theatrically in his right hand, cowboy-style, obviously hoping to impress Seven and Doreen. Seven smirked at the overdramatic gesture as Batto continued, "Long time no see, doll. I think it was Holland last time."

Doreen frowned at him. "Hello, Roddy. Small world. You boys here for a swim?"

Batto grinned at her remark. "Nope, we came here to have a talk with you and Lover Boy here. We've been watching with binoculars from that hill." He pointed to the rise behind them. "There seemed to be a lot of cozy talking going on so we've decided to join you." He again twirled his gun. "Just what have you been telling this handsome punk?" The gangster frowned, menacingly. "And you better spill, sweetheart, or I'll just have to beat it out of your boyfriend here."

"It's none of your business," snapped Seven, his boldness momentarily throwing the Mafia thug off. "I cleared all this with Mr. Gitano last night. As a matter of fact, Carmine's expecting us at his party in a few hours, presumably in one piece. So back off, friend!"

"Shut your mouth," the gangster growled, "or, I'll shut it for you. You only talk when I *tell* you to!" Batto grabbed the butt end of his revolver and pointed it threateningly at Seven's skull. "We was told to have a little *chat* with you people, and that's what we're gonna do."

Seven tried to remain calm, counting on the assumption that Carmine Gitano wouldn't want any serious bloodshed, or any ugly, publicized incidents, at this point. Knowing from similar situations that the best defense was always a good offense, the G5 agent kept replying in kind. "I'll talk whenever I want to, chum. So why don't you take your little toy gun and go play in the sand."

Unimpressed with the bravado, Roddy Batto merely grinned. Noting the mobster's calm self-assurance, the Super Stud knew instantly that he'd misjudged the situation. This confident hood wasn't backing down. He was obviously a seasoned pro. One who had every intention of using some type of punishment or force. Batto stepped forward, revolver in hand. "I think a smack in your mouth with this, along with a few missing teeth, should shut you up for a while." Batto raised his revolver in the air, clearly preparing to strike Seven's head or face.

Christopher Seven had little time to react. Fortunately, parrying an attacker coming at him with a club or weapon was one of the most practiced counters he rehearsed during his martial training. In fact, he'd spent an hour on this very move during his recent sessions in Monaco.

Secure in this practiced technique, Seven raised his right arm just as the mobster charged. Turning quickly aside to avoid the man's thrust, the G5 agent used a *Gato* karate chop with his right arm. Then, slashing down firmly across his attacker's raised gun arm, Seven immediately followed it up with a powerful right elbow into Batto's chin. He followed this solid left-handed punch to the gangster's face with his rock-enclosed fist.

The gun of Seven's startled assailant went flying, as blood spurted down Roddy Batto's cheek. He fell backward to the ground, seething with fury now. Seven watched guardedly as the mobster slowly got up, shaking his head to clear the cobwebs. He glared angrily at Seven, who was now on the balls of his feet in a classic karate stance. The enraged hit-man shook his head again and cautiously readied himself to attack Seven. Batto's big fists were tightly clenched.

Glancing over at the burly hoodlum, Seven saw a perfect opportunity to utilize his proficient leg strength training. This time using his right foot, Seven gave a powerful *Savate* kick directly into Batto's vulnerable, unprotected groin. Screaming in pain, Roddy Batto once more fell to the ground.

"Hold it, you two!" yelled a gruff voice from behind them. Seven and Batto both glanced over to see who was speaking. It was Carmine Gitano's uncle, Salvatore. He was a thin, wiry man with what seemed to be a chiseled smirk plastered on his raw-boned face. He addressed Roddy Batto angrily. "What's wrong with you, Roddy? I distinctly told you - '*no physical stuff*'! Though from the looks of you, you're lucky I stopped it!"

Though livid and still on the ground, Batto dutifully answered the older man. "This guy here was getting too big for his britches, Sal. I was worried for Doreen's sake. My orders were to grill both of them hard. So I figured a little rough stuff might be in order. That's all."

Salvatore Gitano's face showed irritated frustration. "Looks like he grilled *you*. Right into the ground." The oldster impatiently motioned

Batto away. "Scram, Roddy. I'll handle this." Batto reluctantly stomped away, his angry eyes still glued on Seven.

'Uncle Sal' waited a moment and then, smiling cordially, explained, "Don't mind Roddy, mister. He never knows when to back off." The elderly mob boss held up the palms of his hands apologetically. "Sorry about all that. My nephew, Carmine, told us to make sure you two were okay. I can see you are. So, just go back to your shells and your sunning, and we'll go back up the hill. Maybe watch another few minutes." He grinned. "In case we're still *needed*."

Salvatore sat down on one of the beach chairs and moaned exaggeratedly, "Man, it feels good to sit. These old bones ain't so strong no more." He looked over at Seven while advising, "Listen, Mister. Why don't you take some sage advice from an old man?" The gangster tapped his chest to better make his point. "Forget whatever you heard today from this girl. You see, our mutual friend here, the lovely Miss Doreen, has a bad habit of sometimes talking too much. We've all warned her about it. Told her that people who talk too much, especially about *certain* things, sometimes get their tongues cut out. Or their hands and feet sliced off. "Sal sneered, forebodingly. "Capiche, mister?"

The oldster then turned toward Doreen, his tone all business now. "And as for you, Little Miss *Talker.* You better make certain you keep your trap shut. And keep your discussions with your friend here off other people's business. Or he's gonna be your *late* friend."

The wily old mobster knew from the fearful look on Doreen's face that he'd made his point. He smirked over at her. "Like I advised, Dor. You can have a good time today. You know, talk about the weather. Or the beautiful view here. Or the birds and the bees. But *nothing* else! That way, no one gets hurt." Sal kept staring at her. "And we wouldn't want your handsome young companion to get hurt, now would we, Missy?"

Doreen, worried for Seven's sake, nodded nervously.

"Because," Salvatore continued, "if we happen to hear that your friend here was told something he *shouldn't* have been told, well . . . we'd just have to slice his ears off. Along with his tongue and a few other *private* body parts." The gangster again shrugged his shoulders. "And that wouldn't be very pleasant for him, would it, Sweetie?"

Uncle Sal grinned affably, his sinister warning duly delivered. "So, consider yourselves 'talked to' and forewarned, my friends." With that, Salvatore Gitano slowly got up from his chair, rejoined his men, and returned to the long black vehicle parked across the street.

Both of them visibly shaken, Seven and Doreen remained silent for a full three minutes. The angry squeal of tires, as the gangland car finally screeched away, broke the tense stillness.

Christopher Seven turned toward his attractive companion. "Well, that was interesting. Wonder what it was all about?"

"Three guesses," Doreen sullenly replied, now convinced that Seven was doomed if she ever breathed a word to him about Carmine Gitano's upcoming plans. Or Rhombus's role in it. She turned and faced him, fear and apprehension clearly showing on her lovely face. "Listen, Chris, we better leave here before they come back. I'll phone Marco's cell and get him back here pronto."

Seven nodded.

After contacting Marco, Doreen walked over to her small beach bag and grabbed her comb and one of the towels. She wiped her face and sighed, dejectedly. "Looks like I have some real thinking to do. The last thing I'd ever want to do is to get you hurt. Or *worse.* Those near misses with Nalco were nothing compared to what might happen if they somehow found out I told you anything I shouldn't have. Like Uncle Sal said, they'd cut off your ears, tongue, and probably a lot *more* of you, if I ever crossed them now. Sending Sal and his men to 'talk' to us was Carmine's way of giving us one last warning. Yet I can assure you. Those men were deadly serious with their threats."

Tiring of all this gangster lingo, Seven pulled her closer and kissed her full on the lips. Softly stroking her hair, he pleaded genuinely, "Let me take you away from this rotten lifestyle, Doreen. *Whatever* it involves. Just tell me what's really going on and let me help you. I have some good contacts in the States and I honestly think I can. That way, you'll be free from these hoods and their threats."

She gazed back at him blankly with a look of sad resignation rather than encouragement. "Believe me, Chris, part of me would like nothing better. But leaving *my* world, and then trying to run away to *yours*, is something that can never be. You see, I've made my bed with these people. So I guess I'll have to sleep in it now." Doreen gazed out at the sea a moment. "Seems I've messed up my life for good." She sighed again. "And I certainly don't want to mess up *yours.*"

That despondent, faraway expression, which Seven was now accustomed to, once more came over her. She looked at him perplexedly and softly declared, "Your promise to help me, and your marriage proposal, if that's what it was, *sounds* like the perfect scenario. Yet it might come at too steep a price if it fails." She smiled dreamily a moment, imagining it happening. "Not that I haven't thought about all those things, mind you. Marriage, the chance at a normal life, and maybe even a family someday. It's everything my father would have wanted for me."

Doreen's pensive smile quickly turned into an apathetic frown. "Unfortunately, Daddy was a wishful dreamer. Most of his hopes were merely dreams that can never be now. I guess mother and I have seen to that. Mom's forceful life choices for me, as well as a few I've made on my own, have made those decent things impossible. For reasons you'd never understand." Tears welled up in her eyes again, and she buried her head in her hands and moaned, "It's all so difficult."

Gently taking Doreen's hands away from her face and holding them softly in his, Christopher Seven fought off a growing urge to level with her. Inform this bewildered girl that he was a federal agent who could help and protect her. Yet, stoically thinking of the mission first, he once again feigned his 'love' for her. His professional duty to use her was still paramount. A strange wave of culpability came over him as he mouthed the shallow words, "Listen, Doreen, we can conquer all these obstacles. Just trust me and my love for you." He closed his eyes, trying to wipe away the guilt. "But first, we'll have to figure out how I can continue to see you. Some way we can still keep in touch, despite Gitano. After all, I think you owe me *that* much."

Still worried about his safety, she patted her tears dry and shrugged her shoulders halfheartedly as Seven continued, "Your father was right. A girl like you doesn't belong in *any* of this. If you've made some mistakes, we'll just have to try and rectify them. It's plain to see that you're different from Carmine Gitano and your other three friends. Yet, you've got to get away from them *now!* Get away from all they represent. Give life a chance before it's too late."

Seven nodded and consoled her, "I obviously don't know *all* of the details. But I do know one thing...I want to be with you from now on." "Our future together is the only thing that matters to me." Seven frowned inwardly, hoping he wasn't pouring it on too thick.

"I love you, Chris. And I trust you. But I have to be sure that I'm not *condemning* you. I could never live with that."

As she looked at him with a loving, childlike expression, another surge of conscience came over him. Genuinely touched by her emergent faith in him, the Super Stud silently vowed to try and help her escape if he could. Perhaps the Colonel could use his 'witness protection' contacts as well. Nonetheless, he knew his mission came first.

Doreen gently lowered her head onto Seven's lean chest. "The future always sounds so wonderful when you talk about it, Chris. But I still have to weigh the consequences and risks. I'll need a little time."

"Of course, darling. So long as we can keep seeing each other. That's all that matters."

She smiled up at him with unexpected optimism and asked, "Do you *really* think we can get away from all this, Chris?"

"Yes, my love, I do."

~

Twenty minutes later, Marco's Fiat returned. Taking the center road, he drove them through the main hub area and then dropped them off at *La Fontelina,* the charming beach club eatery just below Punta

Tragara. Here they split a plate of homemade *bucatini amatriciana* after first sampling a glass of the house's famous Sangria drink, a delicious concoction of white wine and fresh fruit. It was highly recommended by the gregarious owner, and both the drink and the food were wonderful.

During lunch, the eager agent continued his amorous pleas. He again stressed his desire to whisk Doreen away from her risky mob ties, and from her three hard-nosed girlfriends as well. Though she listened attentively, Doreen was still closed-mouth about her decisions, and maddeningly evasive about the possibility of seeing him again in Monaco.

But then, near the end of the meal, much to the Seven's relief, Doreen finally agreed to covertly meet up with him again once they both returned to the Monaco area. The couple accordingly made tentative plans to get together after she and the *Zephyr* arrived back in Monte Carlo in six days. That was the date Doreen was scheduled to begin a two-week stay at Carmine Gitano's luxurious château in the south of France. The massive seaside estate he owned near Cap Ferrat, appropriately named 'Grandview.'

Whether Doreen was being truthful about seeing him again, or merely mouthing upbeat assurances just to keep their fading time together joyful, was hard to tell. Though the Super Stud had his doubts, all he could do at this point was hope for the best.

At least one thing was evident. Whenever Seven spoke about how a life of normalcy, or the prospect of marriage and family might be, Doreen's eyes lit up with genuine exhilaration. Her candid excitement when discussing these things seemed sincere, and the G5 operative again felt bad about callously misleading her.

"Once Gitano's yacht gets back to Monaco and you're back on land in France, we can stay in touch through this," Seven informed. He then discretely handed her a new smartphone underneath the table, the extra phone he'd brought along on the beach trip for just this purpose. It was an agency spare, one with no owner's record or serial number. And like Seven's cell, it too had a 'secured' line.

"But I already *have* a cellphone," Doreen protested.

"I know. But those electronic experts of Carmine's are quite knowledgeable when it comes to gadgets and monitoring. They probably have a trace on yours already."

"I never thought of that," she admitted.

"Anyway," continued Seven, "sometime late next week, once you're back on terra firma, I'll call you on your new phone. I have the number. We can then meet up someplace away from Gitano's estate and carefully plan our next moves." He purposely didn't give her his own cell number, and thankfully she never asked. "It's better that I call you," Seven advised. "Or that you phone me at my hotel," was all he said to prevent any further communication questions.

The Super Stud waited a few minutes and then tactfully asked her about Carmine Gitano's sudden 'business plans' onboard the yacht. And why they facilitated Seven, and most of the other passengers as well, being forced off the Zephyr prematurely.

Again thinking of Seven's well-being, Doreen was initially hesitant talking about it. Yet she finally divulged, "Oh, these sudden 'business changes' of Carmine's often come up. This one involves some deep-sea water tests he told us he's making out in the Mediterranean this weekend. I really don't know much about it. All Carm said was that one of his European firms is working on some sort of hydroelectric thingamajig. Supposed to make big bucks for him. I guess he's afraid that you, or one of the other civilian passengers, is going to steal his ideas."

Seven shrugged as Doreen further explained, "That's undoubtedly why Carmine's putting most everyone off his yacht. He told Anita and me that these deep-water tests were unexpectedly 'moved up,' and that they had to do them sooner than first planned. He's thus flying in three hydroelectric engineers who'll board the Zephyr tomorrow afternoon. Although that part's very 'hush-hush.' Doubtless it's just another one of Carm's impulsive business decisions. Happens all the time. I wouldn't worry about it. It's certainly nothing that concerns you."

"I see," said Seven, wondering how he could covertly spy on Gitano's alleged 'deep sea tests.' Most likely there was a lot more to it. Though certain that Doreen was holding back a few things, most likely to protect him, the G5 operative decided not to press her any further.

Finishing off their meal with a frothy cappuccino and some tasty handmade biscotti cookies, Seven ducked into the men's room for his tooth brushing ritual. After saying goodbye to the restaurant's affable owner, he and Doreen waited outside for Marco to swing by. They were soon back in his Fiat heading toward the outskirts of Capri Town, over near *Don* Gitano's winery near Moneta.

Arriving at the sprawling vineyard, an immense 20-acre operation, Doreen and Seven said a fond farewell to Marco, knowing they could get back to the tender area via one of Carmine's hired cars. The couple was then ushered out to the picturesque picnic grounds by two armed guards.

The Mafioso's bash was in full swing, complete with an eight-piece band. Sixty or so dancing and drinking guests, an incongruous mixture of gangsters, politicians and Italian VIPs, were eating heartily at elegant picnic tables. Full-service bars were set up to the right of each table, where smartly-dressed bartenders kept the Gitano-labeled wines flowing copiously. Armed sentries were positioned on a small hilltop above the grounds, diligently monitoring the festivities. It reminded Seven of Don Corleone's wedding reception held for his daughter in the first *Godfather* movie.

"Ah, there you are," greeted Gitano, as Seven and Doreen approached his massive table. "Thought you two might have met with an accident." The mob boss roared with laughter and added, "Then again, I heard from the grapevine that you can handle yourself pretty good when it comes to the rough stuff, poker boy." Pointing toward Roddy Batto, who was sitting at the next table with a big gash under his chin, Carmine grinned smugly. "Still claiming you ain't with some other gang, Seven?"

The Super Stud smiled back and replied, "Oh, I've been in my share of scuffs from time to time. But I'm definitely a lover, *not* a gangster."

The mob boss just nodded. "Sure, sure, whatever you say." He gestured toward two empty chairs at the end of the long table. "Anyway, have a seat and relax." Gitano then made a show of introducing all his seated guests, including the other three Rhombus women. "You know the girls of course. And you've already met Mario, Gladys, and Dr. Huin." He gestured toward a seated group of unsmiling, powerfully-built hoods who were also at his table. These other six guys here are from various places. Some of my fellow *business* people." Gitano didn't elaborate. "Now then, have you and Dor had lunch yet?"

"Yes," replied Seven, "back in Tragara. We're stuffed. But I wouldn't mind a glass of your namesake wine, Carmine." Seven grinned sheepishly. "After all, since I correctly identified your green grapes from your red grapes, I think I'm entitled to the finished product."

Gitano gave him a confused look and then, slowly getting Seven's gist, exclaimed, "Oh, yeah, I get it. My little scegliere grape game."

The mob chieftain brusquely snapped his fingers and yelled out to one of the waiters, "Vito. Two glasses of my Chianti for these folks." With that, he sat back down in his seat and resumed the role of amiable host.

What followed was two hours of singing, dancing and smutty jokes, the latter mostly handled by Gladys, Mario's uncouth gun moll. Completely sloshed, she slurred most of the words to her filthy stories, in-between several unsuccessful tries at grabbing and seducing Seven.

Sometime around 6:00 p.m., after Terry, Anita, and Suzanne had brazenly danced with, paraded, and displayed Christopher Seven to the envious female guests, Gitano motioned for Seven and Mario to join him in the small supply shed located behind his table.

Once inside the shed, eerily lit by two small candles, Mario ceremonially stood at attention to Carmine Gitano's right. A hefty revolver bulged noticeably in the hit man's stained sport coat, and he had a strange, forbidding expression on his face. *Don* Gitano waited a moment and then sat down at the room's small desk, his rugged face looking sinister and evil in the glow of the candlelight. Seven stood directly in front, now facing both mobsters. The whole thing reminded him of some weird sect gathering, or some society group's somber initiation ceremony.

Finally breaking the eerie silence, Gitano again reaffirmed his authoritative Cosa Nostra edict. "I'm gonna say this one more time, mister. The *last* time. After today, you *never* come near me, my yacht, or any of the four women again."

Christopher Seven said nothing so Gitano added, "And one more thing, Seven."

"Yes?"

"I meant what I said about my *gridare* vendetta last night. So you better make sure you keep your end of the agreement – *dead* sure! Cause if you don't, I'll personally blow your brains out."

This time the G5 agent nodded his understanding.

"Now swear it, Seven. On your life."

"I swear."

"Good," said the mob boss. "This way there can't be any misunderstanding of the code." The Mafia Don briefly closed his eyes and uncharacteristically crossed himself.

Sweating profusely, Seven wiped his brow. This disturbing gangland setting, along with the ominous pledge, had effectively unnerved him. He looked away a moment, silently reflecting on what had just occurred. Aware that he'd defiantly made plans to meet up with Doreen in less than a week, the Super Stud knew he'd just violated a direct pledge to a Mafia chieftain. His hope now was that he hadn't signed his own death warrant in doing so.

Carmine Gitano, who likewise knew that Seven was shaken by the eerie moment, was rightly proud of himself. The Mafioso Don had efficiently made his point.

As Seven readied himself to rejoin Doreen, Gitano glanced down at the small desk he was sitting at and spotted an ant unhurriedly crawling across it. The Mafioso smiled cruelly, aimed his finger at the desk and slowly crushed the insect with his pudgy right thumb. He then looked up at Christopher Seven, knowing his symbolic message was unmistakable.

Nodding resolutely, the brawny gangster stood up and walked out of the room.

Chapter 33

'Passion from a real woman!'

Back on the yacht some three hours later, Christopher Seven finished up the last of his packing in preparation for tomorrow's forced departure from Zephyr. After first taking out some fresh clothing and toiletries for this evening and tomorrow, he locked both of his suitcases, removed the luggage from the top of his bed, and stood the heavy cases up on the floor. Right after doing so, there was a knock on his cabin door. Half expecting one of Gitano's goons, Seven uneasily opened it.

"Hello, handsome. Mind if I come in?"

The G5 agent was surprised to see the fiery Terry standing in the doorway. She was dressed to kill, in a skin-tight, black outfit. Carrying an opened bottle of *Veuve Clicquot* champagne and two glasses, she brazenly walked in without waiting for his answer.

"Hi, Terry. Nice to see you. But I'm not sure Mr. Gitano would approve of the visit."

"Don't worry about him. I do what I want and Carmine knows it."

Strolling into the cabin, she pushed the door closed with her left foot and turned around to lock it. "Thought we might have a farewell drink together," she cooed. "We never did have time alone this trip."

Seven said nothing, observing her carefully as she kicked off her shoes, walked over to the small glass table next to his bed, and poured two drinks. She handed him one of the flutes. "So, here's to finally being alone."

They clinked glasses and each took a long pull of the ice-cold bubbly. Terry gazed over at him, her expression guarded yet friendly. "You know, Seven, I've been meaning to ask you something."

"Yes?"

"What was *really* up between you and Doreen, before Carm put a stop to it? That's all I kept hearing from Dor this entire voyage. You, as her wonderful lover boy." Terry smirked. "Somehow, the two of you being an item just doesn't fit." Terry paused a moment and then added, "The whole thing with Doreen was hard to swallow, so I'm glad it's over. To tell you the truth, it was somewhat troubling to me."

"*Troubling*, Terry? How so?"

"You see, Seven, we four women have been together a long time and I'm kind of the unofficial 'watchdog' of the group. As such, I know each of my gals pretty good." She eyed him brashly from head to toe. "I also know men. And you're one of the best-looking, smooth-talking males I've ever encountered. So when it comes to choosing a woman, I figure you can have the cream of the crop."

Terry shook her head. "Funny. Our little Miss Doreen, though fine looks-wise, just doesn't fit my concept of someone you'd get serious with. So tell me, friend, what's this all about?"

Seven knew there could be last-minute trouble brewing. Angry at Doreen's naivety, after hearing she'd foolishly been bragging about their growing relationship, the Super Stud decided he'd better answer carefully. "First off, Terry - and with all due respect - I'm not sure it's any of your business. But like you said, Carmine put the kibosh on things, so what's the point anyway?"

Seven took another sip of champagne and continued, "Yet, if you must know, Doreen is a smart and attractive young lady. In my mind, she *is* near the cream of the crop, as you call it. I enjoyed her beauty *and* her brains. Sure, I've had many women in my life. And perhaps some of them were more glamorous than Doreen. But that's just appearance and fashion on the *outside*. That's not what really interests me. You may find this hard to believe, Terry, but I look for brainpower and warmth when I think about a meaningful relationship. Doreen's soft intelligence, plus the heady way she looks at life, really got to me."

"Did you ever propose marriage?"

Seven growled his reply, "That's definitely *my* business and Doreen's. Ours alone." He glared at Terry harshly, trying to take the initiative away from her. "Besides, it's over now, so what's it to you?"

"It's *everything* to me. In addition to our friendship, we four women are also, ah, business partners. We share our work as well as our play. So if one of us was to get hurt or used, it might have severe consequences for the other three. Let's just say it's my obligation to make sure that doesn't happen to *any* of my girls. If I thought it might, I'd just have to take care of whoever was doing the manipulating. Take care of them *my* way!" Terry left her warning at that.

Tiring of all these threats from Carmine Gitano and the others, Seven chuckled his reply, "Oh, stop it, Terry. You sound like Gitano now. Your concern is admirable, but you can relax. I'd never hurt or use Doreen in any way. I have too much respect for her. But it's over now."

She gave him a long, suspicious stare. "Somehow I don't buy all that, handsome. It's a good thing you're getting off this boat tomorrow. And a good thing Carmine forbids you from *ever* coming near any of us again. *Especially* the yappy Miss Doreen. Just remember, friend. When Carmine Gitano forbids something, it better *stay* forbidden. 'Nuff said."

Unpredictably, Terry then strolled over and ran her hands through his hair. "You want to know *why* I don't buy much of your Doreen fairytale. It's because Doreen's not the kind of woman who could ever turn a man like you on." She grinned, seductively. "*I* am!"

Terry suddenly grabbed Seven's neck and forcefully pulled him toward her, kissing him hungrily and then biting his neck. Eyes aflame, she used her tongue and teeth wildly, trying to bite his face as well, all the while laughing with crazed, erotic pleasure. Stunned by her passionate rage and surprising strength, Seven tried in vain to fend her off as she clawed at his body with her long, sharp fingernails, violently ripping the polo shirt he was wearing.

Glancing down at his chest, the Super Stud saw a trickle of blood slowly oozing from his midsection. Noting the strange, sadistic look of desire in Terry's eyes, and amazed by her power, it took all of his strength to force her away from him. "Terry, calm down!" was all he could manage to shout as he finally pushed her away.

Still panting, she laughed at him and hissed, "*That's* what all you men want, Seven! You included. Rough, painful passion from a *real* woman. Not some gloomy banter from a disloyal, moody schoolgirl like Doreen." Terry winked at him. "Just phone my cabin if you want more of me tonight. I'll be ready." And with that, she picked up her shoes, sauntered toward the door, and calmly made her exit.

~

The following morning, a few minutes after 6:00 a.m., the Zephyr raised anchor and made the short trek from Capri's scenic harbor over to her docking birth in Naples. Two hours later, after the yacht had been cleared by the local authorities, Christopher Seven made his way down Zephyr's main gangway. A tough-looking crewman followed him, pushing a baggage cart containing Seven's luggage. Two other sailors watched from the railing, nasty scowls on both their scarred faces. One of them glared directly at Seven and spit into the water. It was obvious that Gitano's lackeys were happy to see Seven go.

Hurried through customs by the yacht's concierge, along with a bunch of other Zephyr passengers who preceded him, the G5 agent made his way over to a waiting taxi cab. Though disappointed about being forced off Carmine Gitano's mega yacht, at least he'd gotten off relatively unscathed. It had been a tense four days. Several times during the short, voyage, the Super Stud wasn't sure if he'd leave the Zephyr in one piece. Or even alive for that matter.

Placing his luggage into the taxi's open trunk, without any help from the overweight Italian cab driver, the Super Stud gave the cabbie his destination from the backseat.

"I'm going to Chiaia 231. The bed and breakfast place."

"Si, Signore, I know it."

A half hour later, they arrived at a small, pleasant inn, directly across from the *Villa Comunale Park*. Seven liked the location immediately, smack in the center of the charming 18th-century Palazzo San Teodoro.

He was promptly met by the B&B's singular bellman who whisked his suitcases over to the front desk. Seven paid the cabbie and followed his luggage inside, where he was welcomed by an attractive, middle-aged woman named Elena.

"Buongiorno, Signore Seven! Vincenzo Fieri mentioned you'd both be coming to us today. I set two rooms aside, one for each of you, up on the second floor. Yours is cleaned and ready should you want to freshen up or grab a nap. There's satellite TV in the room and a small laptop computer there as well, with full Wi-Fi service."

"Thank you, Elena. That nap sounds good to me. I didn't get much sleep last night."

"Molto buono, Signore." She glanced toward the young bellman. "Fredo, please take Mr. Seven's luggage up to room 2 and see that he's comfortable."

"Si, Signorina."

The Super Stud followed Fredo up a small set of stairs and was soon standing inside his comfortable guestroom. Accented in gray and burgundy, the room was decorated in a modern, attractive style with a private bathroom attached to it. Seven thanked and tipped the bellman, drowsily watched him leave, and sat down at the room's small writing desk. He suddenly felt tired and drained, undoubtedly a result of all the tension these past few days.

Rubbing his hand through his hair, the weary operative slowly replayed all of last night's events aboard Zephyr, including Terry's wild, amorous actions in his cabin. That bizarre episode had been followed by a rather subdued 'going away' meal with Doreen. A quiet, candlelit dinner for two in the main dining salon after first getting Carmine Gitano's permission to see Doreen "this one last time."

Over a tasty prime rib dinner, the couple had quietly reaffirmed their covert plans to get together again, once Doreen was back on dry land and comfortably ensconced at Gitano's French chateau near Beaulieu. Though knowing it'd be extremely risky to ignore the Mafioso's warning to 'never see each other again,' both Seven and Doreen had reasons to disobey the gangland edict. She, to find out if her growing love for Christopher Seven was worth giving up everything she'd pledged and lived for. And he, to hopefully uncover what Rhombus and Gitano were up to.

During the meal, the G5 agent had finally decided to give Doreen a subtle word of warning about the possibility of her life being in danger. Though he couldn't divulge his source without admitting he'd been spying in Terry's cabin, Seven nonetheless felt he owed her as much. He now recalled his warning to her. "If I were you, Doreen, I'd change my mind about going to Carmine's French villa when Zephyr returns to Monaco. I'd get out of France ASAP, and go as far away as I could from

Gitano, Nalco, and your three so-called 'friends.' That beach encounter we had with Gitano's uncle makes me think Carmine could definitely be gunning for you. It'd be much safer for you, and for me as well, to meet up somewhere in the States."

From the little he knew about Gitano's plans, and Terry's notes and branding iron, Seven's advice had been sincere. Nonetheless, Doreen glibly dismissed it out of hand. "Nothing's going to happen to me, Chris. It's *you* I'm worried about." Doreen smiled. "Carmine wouldn't dare let anything ominous occur to one of us four gals now." Her face reddened slightly. "He kind of *needs* us at the moment. Terry would *never* allow it either. We four women have had our differences, of course. But Terry always looks out for us. It's sort of a *pact* we have. A unique bond between us. I don't want to get into it now, but believe me - I'll be fine."

"Okay," scolded Seven, "if you say so. But please, for my sake, be on your toes the next few weeks." He left it at that, still anxious for her.

Continuing to reflect on last night's events, Seven now wondered if the impulsive Doreen would even see him again, once she was in the familiar clutches of a powerful Mafia boss and her three persuasive partners. Would Doreen, who had repeatedly shown to be changeable and impulsive, live up to her promise to meet up with Seven again? Or, swayed by her cohorts, would she again change her mind and revert back to her '*Rhombian* roots'?

The frustrated G5 operative rubbed his brow and anxiously asked himself: *Have I successfully convinced Doreen of my love for her? Sufficiently captivated and tempted her, enough so that she'll consider leaving everything for me? In a week or two, I'll know.* Sighing reflectively, Christopher Seven lay down on the comfortable queen-size bed and tried to catch up on some much-needed sleep.

~

Three restful hours passed. Coming out of a dreamless sleep, Seven heard the familiar ring of his travel alarm. He rolled over to his left and checked the time, half past noon. Yawning contentedly, he hopped out of bed and made his way to the bathroom.

Following a revitalizing shower, he went through his standard hygiene routines and put on a fresh change of clothes. Reenergized, he opened the room's small laptop and sent a heavily coded e-mail to headquarters, apprising them of everything that was happening.

Right after turning off the computer, the G5 agent heard the familiar voice of Vin Fieri outside his door. The 'doc' was thanking Elena for the room courtesies. A knock on Seven's door was quickly followed by Fieri's playful greeting, "Okay, playboy, wake up! You've wasted enough time gallivanting around the Mediterranean on your mega-yacht."

Christopher Seven unbolted his door and grinned back at Fieri's smiling face, happy to finally see a friendly one after his nerve-racking days alone on the Zephyr. What was the old saying? *Two is only one more than one. But after you've been on your own awhile, it seems like more.*

Seven reached out and shook the doc's hand. "What took you so long, Vin? Couldn't you get a better flight with your bogus air miles?"

Fieri strolled into the room, locked the door behind him and sardonically replied, "You're lucky I came at all. I met a gorgeous college girl in Monaco yesterday. Rutgers grad like me. The two of us were planning a romantic jaunt to Saint-Tropez today. That is, before you and your gangster friends rudely interrupted things."

The Super Stud laughed as the doc lowered his voice to inform, "But at least I come bearing important news, courtesy of my outfit. It's about your pal, Carmine."

Seven's mood quickly became serious again, hoping that the CIA was on to something. *"What* gives, Vin?"

Fieri again lowered his voice. "My agency received a tip early this morning. Came from an attractive female bartender we have in place at *Grotto's Lounge* on Capri. Seems some of Zephyr's crew were in late last night drinking up a storm. One crewman, who had way too many drinks, was trying to impress the pretty barkeep. Attempting to do so, he carelessly blurted out that his boss, Carmine Gitano, is planning a 'test run' of his new toy tonight, after Zephyr leaves Naples. Seems Gitano's 'toy' is a *private* submarine."

Seven's ears picked up as Fieri went on, "From what our barkeep-informant learned, Gitano is planning his submarine drill for late this evening. Somewhere out on the Mediterranean. Carmine plans to launch the sub from his yacht a few miles off the *Isola di Nisida.* It's going to be a "unique, hush-hush maneuver" was how the flirting seaman put it. There's also going to be some special "gangland fireworks," according to this crewman's boasts." The doc frowned. "Wonder what that's about?"

"I don't know, Vin. Although I did get a quick look at Gitano's mini submarine. It's an Alvis." Seven angrily pounded his right fist into his left palm. "Too bad I was kicked off Carmine's yacht, Vin. I might have been able to get a glimpse of what's taking place. But that's obviously why I, and all the other passengers, sans the four girls, were given the boot. Who knows what these crooks are up to now?" Seven shook his head. "Sure wish I could have been there tonight to see the 'mob fireworks' that barroom drunk talked about, and whatever else they're doing vis-à-vis that mini-sub."

Fieri grinned, widely. "I thought you'd say that, Chris. So, with CIA's help, along with secret Italian 'behind-the-scenes' assistance, I've set up a covert rendezvous with the Zephyr tonight. Out at sea, frogman-style. A clandestine encounter that Carmine and his cronies won't even know is taking place."

The doc sat down on the small desk chair and explained more. "In addition to having a peek at what those mobsters may be rehearsing for, my agency wants me to attach a tiny magnetic beacon onto Gitano's sub. Attach it underwater so that no one will notice it unless they're specifically told about it. Which is *not* the case here so it should work."

Seven nodded as Fieri further explained, "CIA's technical team assured me that once this tiny homing device is fastened tightly to the sub's keel, it will be undetectable to the naked eye. They've also told me just *where* and *how* it should best be attached. And they've assured me that I'll have plenty of time to secure it while the *Alvis* is bobbing in the water getting ready to submerge."

The doc shrugged his shoulders. "That's the one drawback with this particular type of mini-sub, Chris. Once it's initially launched into the water, it takes almost three hours of preparation before it can actually dive. They'll need several lengthy equipment tests and a bunch of time-consuming safety checks tonight."

Fieri got up off the chair, walked over to the room's mini-bar, and grabbed himself a beer. He then sat back down and grinned slyly. "I thought that maybe you'd like to come along with me tonight - *scuba* style. Get yourself a firsthand look at whatever Carmine and those four girlies of his are up to."

Seeing the look of fascinated attraction on his colleague's face, the doc grinned wider and finished his spiel. "The Italians will take us out to sea via a small, fully crewed spy boat from the *Sicurezza Interna.* That's the Italian secret service. They're also supplying us with their newest, classified scuba equipment. State-of-the-art triple air tanks, top quality spear guns, and two long-range undersea scooters. You know, those battery-powered *pull-along* vehicles that can noiselessly whisk us underwater. Quickly and effortlessly. Seems the Italians have come up with a new, top-secret *extended*-range scooter that can go for miles."

Doc Fieri gave Seven a smug nod. "I had a hunch you be interested in coming along with me tonight. So I took the liberty of telling them that there'd be *two* of us making the lengthy underwater trek to Gitano's sub. With any luck, we just might see firsthand what these mobsters are conniving."

"I sure hope so, Doc."

"There is *one* stipulation, however," Fieri cautioned. "Anything we witness tonight must be kept absolutely 'hush-hush.' Strictly between us, our agencies, and the Italian Secret Service. No matter what we see or uncover, we can't involve Italy's Navy, her Coast Guard, or even local law enforcement. Absolutely no exposure or publicity regardless of *what* we uncover. Whatever we encounter, the Italian government cannot and will not act on it. Or even acknowledge they helped us. That edict comes straight from Italy's president, with assurances from the White House."

Seven nodded.

"In any event, Chris, I wouldn't be surprised if your four friends from Rhombus somehow fit into the scheme of things."

"Could be," Seven replied, now thinking of Doreen. "But even though I now know it was Terry who tortured Ambassador Dawson with that branding iron. And Terry, Rhombus's team leader, who undoubtedly planned the whole thing. I really didn't uncover any indications of some foreign governmental plot. And I never witnessed any real violence onboard either. Other than that poor crewman, Rossi, being eliminated for helping me. But that was really Gitano's doing."

The Super Stud thought on it again and admitted, "Of course, there were those things I e-mailed you about. Terry's branding iron and the files about the four embassy trainees and their illegal drugs."

The doc scratched his forehead. "Yeah, that part was a bit strange, Chris. Maybe Gitano and his girlfriends are handling some high-end narcotics, which they're planning to deliver via the sub. Could be that this Terry woman and her 'sisters' are blackmailing those four diplomatic interns, or the countries they work for. Trying to squeeze government secrets out of them, which Rhombus can then sell to the highest bidder."

"I don't think so, Vin. Those good-looking embassy guys were strictly small potatoes from the little I discovered about them. I doubt Terry and her three partners would be part of anything that mundane."

Seven frowned with annoyance and went on, "Unfortunately, their names weren't revealed. Nor were their political offices. So there's really no way for us to check up on any of them. For all I know, they could simply be what Rhombus calls 'window dressing'...four attractive men whom the girls wanted to show off. Similar to what they kept saying about me."

Fieri chuckled as Seven added, "Those four guys seemed like insignificant embassy trainees from what I read about them in Terry's notes. Strictly minor-league."

The doc nodded his head.

"Besides," Seven continued, "That type of petty extortion just doesn't seem to fit the MO of the egotistical, pompous women I met onboard Zephyr. Three of them anyway. Simple blackmail or drug sales would be much too trivial for them. Not fanatical enough. At times, Terry, Anita, and Suzanne seemed crazed with power, driven by some mystical 'esprit de corps.' Furthermore, the initial files I studied indicated that the Rhombus sisterhood would be after far higher objectives."

"Where does this wacky plastic surgeon you e-mailed me about fit into the picture? The Korean. Could *he* be supplying the drugs?"

Seven shook his head. "I don't know, Vin. But all my instincts tell me that Gitano's submarine is being used for something a lot bigger than narcotics sales or petty blackmail. More likely, it's some grandiose plan that Carmine or the Rhombus women have cooked up."

"You're probably right, Chris. But without any proof, or even some basic clues, we can't be sure. The Italian authorities would want detailed proof and full names and addresses before they'd even consider speaking with Gitano. He's got the whole area bribed. Oh, well, at least we'll get a sneak peek at *Don* Carmine's toy sub tonight. And a ringside seat for whatever secret maneuvers and 'fireworks' they're talking about." The doc looked over at Seven. "By the way, how are your scuba skills?"

"Just so-so. But I can handle rudimentary dives fairly well. I took a three-week course with the Navy SEALS a good while back. It was a belated 'thank you' from the SEALS to McPhail after G5 helped them on that *bin Laden* thing. My diving course was pretty basic, though. You know, 'Scuba 101.'" Seven shrugged. "Hope I won't be a burden to you."

"Don't fret, Mr. Seven. I was CIA trained for underwater missions like this one. Most all field agents are. The firm puts us through frequent scuba courses. Besides, those new Italian scooters will do most of the work. All you have to do is hold on to your scooter and follow mine."

Seven grinned. "I *hope* it's that easy. Then again, if my scooter conks out, I'll just grab your leg and you can pull me along that way."

Fieri laughed. "Sounds like a plan, Chris. In any case, we'll be the only ones making the undersea trek to Gitano's sub tonight. The Italians aren't allowed to participate in our jaunt over to the Zephyr, or join us in the actual foray. Strict government orders. They'll simply get us in position for the dive and supply the classified equipment. And like I said, they'll flatly deny anything we claim we discovered. Probably have us deported or shot if we ever mention being on their spy boat."

"Why the paranoia, Vin?"

"They're adamant about not being caught helping other foreign agencies - *especially* American." The doc shrugged. "I'm sure politics has something to do with it. In truth, though, they only agreed to supply the boat and equipment after some strong pressure from Washington."

"I see."

"Whatever their reasons, everyone, including the White House, has made it crystal clear that we're strictly on our own after we hit the water. I guess it'll be the old 'disavowing everything' by the Washington politicos, should you or I be captured or killed while nosing around."

The Super Stud frowned as his CIA sidekick further warned, "So don't expect any rescue bugles or last-minute help from the Italian cavalry if trouble arises, which it probably will. 'Cause I wouldn't be surprised if good old *Don* Carmine has a few undersea scuba guards patrolling the entire sub area."

His statement startled Seven. "Did you say *undersea* guards, Vin?"

"Yep. If my guess is right, there'll probably be some frogmen sentries combing the vicinity, armed and dangerous. So we'll have to be on our toes, or rather, our fins, at all times." He gave a cynical grin. "If the sharks and barracuda don't get us first, the gangsters probably will."

Seven shrugged uneasily, as Vin exclaimed, "And now, my G5 friend, what do you say we go downstairs to the hotel's restaurant and have a heaping plate of *tagliolini con tartufi?* I hear it's the house specialty."

Fieri got up from his chair and tossed his empty beer can into the small garbage container by the desk. "I guess if we're going to be devoured by sharks later tonight, the least we can do is give those hungry man-eaters well-fed bodies!"

Chapter 34

The Big Visitor

The white *Merretti* luxury yacht bobbed gently in the pitch-black Mediterranean Sea. Looking dark and lonely, with most of its interior lights turned off, and as the only vessel around for miles, it was now preparing to drop anchor. Had anyone seen it, the sleek craft would look to be just another high-priced yacht touring the Riviera. Purchased in Antibes, as are many of the luxury crafts in Italy and France, they'd simply think that the ultra-modern vessel was just another high-priced play-toy of the rich and famous. In reality, however, it was one of Italy's top-secret spy boats, equipped with the latest seagoing spyware. Including classified *Scopinni* radar and precision K4 sonar sounders.

The vessel, manned by eight special agents from Italy's secret service, is primarily utilized to ferret out illegal narcotics. Shipments mostly distributed via Sicily's drug cartels. Other Italian naval agencies occasionally used this sophisticated spy craft as well, mainly to track down and monitor Russian submarines venturing into Italy's waters.

This evening, however, neither of those duties was its role. Tonight, thanks to a hush-hush request from Washington DC, it had motored out to the deep Mediterranean to clandestinely rendezvous a few miles south from where Carmine Gitano's Zephyr was similarly anchored. Accordingly, the *Merretti* was now carrying two American agents: CIA's Vin Fieri and Christopher Seven, from some anonymous US agency.

"We've arrived, gentlemen," advised one of the Italian operatives, a slender agent named Pietro, doing so in excellent English. "This is as close as we agreed to go."

Seven and Fieri nodded simultaneously, as the boat's weighty anchor was being lowered. Pietro glanced down at some notes the navigator had just handed him. "It's exactly 10:15 p.m. now, gentlemen. According to our calculations, along with the latest info from the spy plane that's been shadowing Zephyr, Mr. Gitano's yacht left Naples about four hours ago. Sometime around 6:20 p.m. We should now be about three miles from where his Zephyr is presently anchored. We received radio confirmation of that fact from our scout airplane a few minutes ago. And we've likewise spotted Mr. Gitano's vessel via our own radar."

Doc Fieri nodded his head again, as Pietro further informed, "Arrigo, our acting captain, says we're far enough away from the Zephyr to not be spotted by binoculars or the naked eye, though we'll certainly be a small, stationary dot on Zephyr's radar screen."

Pietro saw the concerned look on the faces of Seven and Fieri. "Don't worry, gentlemen. Our presence here shouldn't draw any undue suspicion. First of all, plenty of fishing crafts and luxury vessels frequently travel or party at night. The fisherman come to catch the big fish that only emerge after dark. And the yachts anchor here for a pleasant night under the stars. So on Zephyr's radar we'll simply appear to be one of those."

The relieved American agents again nodded their heads as the Italian added, "And secondly, we're too far from Zephyr to trigger any concerns to Gitano's people. Whatever they're planning or doing, a craft almost three miles away from them wouldn't really be able to observe things closely. And thankfully, our radar shows no other boats are in the area."

Fieri and Seven listened attentively as the Italian agent further expounded, "From what we know about the Alvis mini-sub, it will take them a good four hours to properly prep and launch. And the final report from our spy plane, which was conveyed to us a few minutes ago, said that Zephyr had just dropped anchor. Since they haven't even started any of the sub's safety and equipment tests, you two should have plenty of time to get to her." Pietro glanced at his wristwatch. "I'd say it'll be at least four hours or so before that sub is ready to dive. Certainly not before two in the morning." Pietro's face flashed a trace of pride. "Utilizing our new undersea high-speed scooters, you fellows should easily arrive on time to get a firsthand look at whatever's taking place."

"That's fine, Pietro," Doc Fieri replied. "We'll ride the scooters out to Zephyr's anchorage area, using our underwater GPS devices and following the coordinates your navigator supplies us with. His directions should lead us straight to the Zephyr and safely back here again. Once we arrive near Gitano's yacht, we can dive deeper, and then come up slowly and noiselessly beneath the sub's deep hull. That's where I'll plant CIA's homing device."

Vin grinned, smugly and informed, "By the way, guys, I was briefed all morning on the Alvis sub's hull. CIA experts showed me the best placement for the homer's magnetic attachment. Fortunately it's a very small device. No one would see or detect it unless they knew where to look. One thing's in our favor. All Alvis mini-subs have a very *deep* hull. That's how they were designed, I guess. Their sizable bottom and their deep draft makes them sit deep down in the water. That's a big plus for us as it will better hide us underneath. As will tonight's black water." Fieri shook his head. "We're just lucky there's no moon this evening."

Seven pointed to the round sausage-shaped tube Fieri was now grasping. It was about 4 feet long with three buttons on it. "What's that tube you're holding, Vin?"

"That's called a *'CKI placement extender,'* Chris. The Koreans came up with it during their war. It allows an approaching frogman or assassin to stay well *below* its quarry's hull, and *robotically* place a magnetized item onto the mini-sub's keel. In our case, the tiny CIA tracking device. After firmly placing its magnetized attachment, the red button is pushed, and the extender then deactivates, its package securely attached. Here, let me show you."

The doc pushed the green button on it, and the extender, powered by a small marine battery, zeroed in on the boat's teak railing. He then pushed the *red* button and the extender's metal arm folded back to him.

Fieri smiled "With this extender and the sub's deep draft, we'll be over 16 feet below the surface. Impossible to spot or detect. Especially on this pitch-black night. The bobbing and the engine noise above us will also help, along with the heavy swells and waves forecast for tonight."

Seven shook his head, "What will they think of *next?*"

The doc then held up his small undersea camera, showing it to the others. "I can also take some quick photos my agency wants, via this *Epoque EHD-900 Ai.* This submersible model can even take close-ups."

"After we take care of our two tasks, planting the homer onto the sub's bottom with the extender and taking a few undersea photos, we'll move far away from the Alvis and observe from a safe distance."

"What, exactly, will you fellows be looking for?" Pietro asked.

"We're not really sure, Pietro. Chris and I were just talking about that this afternoon. Best we can figure, this submarine of Gitano's might have something to do with those four yacht women. The ones Chris was assigned to. Maybe they're planning a blackmail scheme regarding government workers from various embassies." The doc shrugged. "Or it could just be a covert drug operation. Something run by the mob, utilizing Gitano's submarine as a way to deliver the goods undetected. But all that is purely speculation. It'll be our job to try and figure out what's *really* happening out there after we get a closer look tonight."

"Oh, well, I'll leave all that to you two," said Pietro. "As you know, we can't play any part in it. Or confirm your findings, no matter *what* you discover. Our only role in this is to get you to the Zephyr and then back to shore again."

The Italian operative glanced at his watch. "It's nearly 10:30, gentlemen. We've been instructed to wait here for you till 3:30 a.m. Not a minute longer. After that, it's arrivederci." He held up his hands apologetically. "Sorry, boys. Strict government orders."

Christopher Seven smiled and assured, "We understand, Pietro. And don't fret about your time limit. According to the esteemed scuba expert standing next to me, he and I will either be back well before three, or we'll be in the jaws of some big shark."

Fieri and Seven laughed at their gallows humor, but the Italian agent did not. He just stared at them somberly and replied, "Hopefully you won't see any sharks tonight. They're pretty rare around here, but they're definitely around. Mainly blue sharks, hammerheads, and, occasionally, some great whites. The last fatal shark encounter we had in these waters took place two years ago. A diver was attacked and eaten not too far from here." Pietro bowed his head at the memory and crossed himself. "Since then, there's been several close calls in these waters involving sharks and barracuda. But that diver was the last actual fatality. Scientists think the number of sharks in the Mediterranean is slowly diminishing, although swimmers and divers are still occasionally harassed by them." Bowing politely, Pietro then walked away.

"Let's take one last look at our equipment, Chris," ordered Fieri, trying to get images of sharks and barracuda out of his head. "We can also recheck the air tanks. Pietro says they're specially made triple tanks, supplying tons of air. And more than enough time. The new *Gamma* racing scooters the Italians are loaning us can pull us the few miles we need to travel in under an hour. Those top-secret scooters may be small and silent, but they're fast as lightening. They're highly-rated speed-wise, and they're completely noiseless, too. The high-end lithium-ion batteries they run on can keep 'em going for hours. Amazing! One of the Italians told me that the prototype scooters we'll be using are indispensable during longer undersea military jaunts."

Seven nodded his head, duly impressed, as Vin added, "Hopefully we won't need them, but we've also been provided with first-rate spear guns, just in case. JBL Gulf Magnum XHD Triple Slings. I can't wait to hold one of those babies. They're supposed to have real stopping power."

Tense, but confident, the two operatives then made their way below to ready themselves for the dive.

~

At exactly 10:45 p.m., Seven and Fieri, now filled with anticipation in place of their earlier apprehension, slipped off the boat into the dark, churning sea. The two bat-like figures felt warm and comfortable in their wetsuits and scuba masks, warmer than if they'd been swimming in bathing trunks during the day.

Watching them from the railing, Pietro and three other men gently lowered a pair of high-tech undersea scooters into the water. The Americans gave the small group above the 'OK' sign and swam over to retrieve them. They found the battery-powered 'pull alongs,' as the Italians had nicknamed them, surprisingly light and compact.

Taking hold of his scooter, Fieri decided they should both try a practice run around and then underneath the Italian spy boat. Observing

Seven as he struggled to control his scooter, the doc removed his scuba mask and shouted, "Don't fight it, Chris! Gently press the scooter's accelerator and then let *it* take *you* along. Nice and easy."

Pushing the small accelerator button on the left of the steering handle, the Super Stud did just that. Quickly getting the hang of it, he followed Fieri out, and they circumvented the Italian spy vessel in a large, leisurely circle. The doc then led him down and they dove beneath the choppy waves with surprising speed and comfort.

Seven found the scooter ride quite enjoyable, akin to touring in an underwater moped. Led by the small GPS device bolted to the right side of his scooter's steering column, Vin gave him the 'thumbs up' sign and they then dove deeper, aiming their scooters due north to begin the undersea trek toward their rendezvous with Zephyr.

Thankfully, the current wasn't very strong, and they zipped through the water effortlessly. Led by each scooter's diminutive headlight, the agents were being propelled at over three miles per hour. At this rate, Fieri figured they'd be at the Zephyr in less than an hour.

In addition to the small headlight mounted on the front of each scooter, equipped with an on/off switch to deactivate the beam when they got nearer their target, both men carried two underwater searchlights strapped to his waist belt. An *Intova Nova Torch 4.7-watt* for brighter coverage, and a multi-function LED pencil torch for any lesser lighting or signaling needs. For now, their scooter's single beam headlight was the only illumination, a soft, tiny beacon to help them ascertain what was up ahead.

Though he tried, the Super Stud couldn't see very much up ahead via his scooter's miniscule headlight. Just the back of Vin's legs and fins and the constant glow of the blinking green GPS directions that flashed on Fieri's hand bar. Seven found this feeling of semi-blindness a bit disconcerting. The sea and the murky blackness surrounding them seemed dark and foreboding, and the G5 agent wondered what was lurking to his sides and directly behind him.

Reflecting on it, Seven envisioned the round, probing eyes of dangerous sea creatures watching their every move…perhaps the eyes of the big dwellers like the barracuda, stingrays, and sharks, or the lesser eyes of the smaller killers, such as deadly sea snakes, the moray eels, and the venomous lionfish. *Would the inner antennae of these undersea creatures detect a new presence this very moment? If so, what were these dangerous creatures contemplating? Did their instincts tell them to ignore the scuba intruders? Or did it signal them that these men and their strange vehicles were good to eat?* Christopher Seven shuddered at the thought. With visions of fearsome predators sizing him up in the darkness, he kept his focus straight ahead, desperately trying to erase thoughts of sinister sea monsters from his mind.

Thirty uneventful minutes went by. They were making excellent progress, better than either had anticipated. Their silent undersea *'pull alongs'* drew them along with remarkable ease and power. The scooters, set on medium speed, probably could have been set to go even faster. But the two agents certainly didn't want their masks being blown off by the faster propulsion if they went *too* fast. Thus far, the small Plexiglas windshield on each scooter's front kept their masks from coming off.

The rest of their specially developed Italian equipment was also functioning perfectly. The indicator meters on the extra-capacity, triple air tanks showed over six hours of reserve; more than sufficient. And the battery levels of their scooters likewise indicated more than enough reserve. Sufficiently armed with high-tech spear guns, both men now took comfort in the excellent Italian gear.

Doc Fieri, by far the more experienced diver, led the way, guided by his aquatic GPS device. Continually checking his wrist-mounted compass, Fieri skillfully followed the coordinated directions: due north, then slightly east; another mile or so to Zephyr.

Staying close behind, the Super Stud made sure to keep up with the doc's swift pace, not wanting to lose him. For even though Seven also had the same underwater compass strapped to his wrist, the thought of finding his way alone in this shadowy, undersea world was daunting.

The going continued to be smooth and without incident, and Fieri made plenty of periodic rest stops. Taking out his *Intova* light, he playfully shined it on any fish gliding by them whenever they paused to rest. Thankfully none of the 'big boys' were about, though Seven warily recalled Vin's erudite admonition: *"If we see a shark or any large barracuda, stay composed and keep riding through the water calmly and naturally. The big fish are rare in these waters, and they shouldn't bother us even if they do show up. So keep your spear gun in its holder unless that's the only remaining option. The last thing we need is some wounded man-eater angrily thrashing around us with a spear in his side. Remember, large predator fish in the Mediterranean typically leave divers alone, unless they sense blood, heavy vibrations, or panic. Awkward movements or blood in the water sometimes sends them into an attacking mode. But if we stay calm, so should they."* Seven shivered again as he replayed the doc's words, once more thinking of the poor Zephyr seaman whom Gitano's thugs had thrown into the sea.

Fifteen minutes after their second rest stop, they paused for a third. Vin pointed upward, and they rode their scooters to the top, floating leisurely on the surface for a few minutes. There was absolutely no sound or movement about. Only darkness and the shimmering, pitch- black water, which was now kicking up via small waves and underwater swells. Shining the small light at his watertight marine watch, Fieri took off his mask to talk.

"We've been traveling nonstop with no interruptions, so we're right on schedule. Should be there in another twenty minutes or so. We'll arrive near Zephyr's anchorage while Gitano's sub is still in the middle of her lengthy pre-dive checks." Fieri wiped some water from his eyes. "We'll be well hidden underwater in this moonless darkness. So unless someone knows we're coming, we should be able to complete our agenda and then safely watch from afar. Then, while the coast is still clear, we'll take the scooters deep and silently come up under the sub. That's where I'll attach the homer and get some underwater photos."

"Won't they hear us, Vin? Seven asked.

"No. The amazing thing about Pietro's scooters is that they have absolutely *no* sound to trace. They're battery powered so they're completely silent."

"Sounds okay," said Seven, "but you know, Vin, maybe all this submarine gossip is much ado about nothing. Conceivably, Carmine just wants to show off his new toy to impress the four girls."

"Maybe," agreed the doc, "but it's definitely worth finding out if anything *else* is on tap. And once I fasten the homing device onto Gitano's sub, CIA's radio teams can easily track its *future* destinations." Fieri pointed downward. "Let's get moving, Chris. They're probably through with the opening pre-checks already."

The two operatives pushed their scooters' accelerator buttons and dove down again, making their way east. This time Fieri took them deeper, and Christopher Seven felt a slight clogging in his ears. The seawater seemed to be colder here, and the current much stronger now. Both scooters had to struggle to the task.

As they got closer to Zephyr, Seven suddenly had the distinct feeling that someone or something was following them. *Could a Gitano sentry be patrolling this area frogman-style just like Vin and Pietro had cautioned?*

Holding the scooter handle with one hand, Seven turned around slowly and shined his small LED flashlight directly behind him. When he did, he saw an enormous smooth-skinned hammerhead shark, accompanied by two smaller 'pilot fish.' This sizeable predator, aptly known as the *'great* hammerhead,' was only ten yards away and it definitely seemed to be following them. Trying to control his momentary panic, Seven tapped Fieri on the back of the leg with his tiny light.

Doc promptly took his hand off the accelerator, bringing his scooter to a stop. Spinning around, he immediately spotted the hammerhead slowly circling toward them. Keeping a wary eye on the big visitor, Vin made a gentle 'OK' sign with his two fingers and waited a moment. The shark stared at them a few seconds and then, with a bored, indifferent glance, it made a quick turn to the left and leisurely swam away. Fieri grinned widely, feigned rubbing some sweat from his forehead, and continued guiding them toward their submarine rendezvous.

Some fifteen minutes later, the doc again brought his scooter to a gradual halt and turned off the craft's small headlight. He raised his right hand to indicate that Seven should do the same. That done, they headed their now-darkened 'pull-alongs' toward the surface and quietly punched through the quicksilver canopy of water above them.

Removing his mask, the doc gave a 'thumbs up' and calmly announced, "We're here, Chris. See those lights up ahead?"

After the continuous darkness of their underwater trek, Seven had to take a few seconds to refocus his eyes. Soon, he too could see the sleek silhouette of Gitano's luxury vessel, now some 500 yards away. Zephyr's amber cabin lights made the yacht look warm and comfortable, and the Super Stud wondered if the yacht's small pubs and cocktail lounges were still open for business.

Positioned in the front of the Zephyr was a single work spotlight, its beam shining down on something in the water. Seven focused in on the large cylinder-shaped object and squinted. *Yes!* It was the Alvis mini-sub swaying in the open sea. Christopher Seven felt his pulse quicken!

Gitano's crew was less than halfway through the submarine's initial pre-dive checks. Fieri tapped Seven on the shoulder and softly informed, "We'll have to whisper, or, better yet, use hand gestures, from now on, Chris. Whenever we're on the surface or as we get nearer the sub. Just in case our friend Carmine has any perimeter swimmers, sound-sensing devises, or scuba men patrolling the area. I doubt they'd be patrolling this far away from Zephyr, but you never know."

Seven nodded as the doc added, "Like I said before, we'll move in slowly and take the scooters deep, well below the submarine's keel. Then, gradually coming up at a snail's pace, and while we're completely hidden by the mounting waves and the sub's sizeable hull, I'll attach the tiny homing device to the Alvis's bottom and silently take some photos. Should only take me 5 or 10 minutes. Once I'm finished, we'll dive back down and get well away from the Zephyr's immediate area. Once we're back here, or even farther away, you and I can safely observe things before the sub actually dives. I brought along a small pair of waterproof binoculars for that task, and there's no way we'd be spotted watching from this far out. Especially, in total darkness. But before that submarine actually begins her last pre-test, the 'ballast' check, we'll have to hightail it out of this area pronto. No telling *which* way that sub will eventually be heading, including over or through us."

Vin passed the small, waterproof *Steiner* binoculars hanging around his neck over to Seven. "Here, take these and see if anything's up onboard the yacht yet. You know Zephyr's cast of characters a lot better than I do. Maybe you'll be able to tell who's staying onboard and who's going for a sub ride."

As their dark black scooters bobbed in the water, Seven grabbed the binoculars and zeroed in on both the Zephyr and the mini-sub. While he observed them, Fieri grabbed the GPS navigation device and carefully reset the return coordinates for the trek back to the Italian spy boat.

"All set," the doc informed. "We're safely dialed in for the journey home - due south, then slightly west. Our equipment's in great shape too. Believe it or not, there's still over four hours of battery power for the scooters and more than enough air left in our scuba tanks. Fortunately we won't be draining either while we watch from here, so I guess everything's a 'go' now." Fieri smirked. "Let's just hope our *hammerhead* friend isn't around for the trip back."

Seven grinned, uneasily.

"Now for the tough part, Chris. Getting below that submarine without being spotted. Oh, well, it's got to be done." Fieri took the binoculars back and zeroed in on the feverish activity now taking place on and around the submarine. "Right now they're starting the engine testing," Vin explained. "I'd say they have at least another half hour before they finish that. They'll then make their flooding and navigation checks. Once those two tests are completed, they'll be ready to dive."

Forty minutes later the doc again handed Seven the binoculars. "Here, take these for a few more minutes, Chris. See if your Rhombus friends are around. After that, though, we'll have to make our move."

While Seven adjusted the binocs, Fieri repeated the drill. "Okay, one last time. We dive deep, get under the sub, and slowly come up under its wide hull. That'll assure we avoid Zephyr's singular work spotlight."

"What about that spotlight, Vin? Won't it be a problem for us?"

Fieri's next words came out confidently. "No worries. That type of singular-direction spotlight is only used for illuminating a very *specific* area...well above the water and away from where we'll be. Plus, they'll be working near the *front* of the sub while we're doing our job near the *back* of her."

Seven nodded as Fieri went on, "That singular-beam spotlight they're using for pre-dive is only good for a smaller, stationary, area. It's no good for lighting up wider areas. Nor is it suitable for spotting anything *under* the water. Its stream of light, though fairly powerful, can't penetrate below the surface. Its beam is far too narrow. There's no way they'd spot us with it unless we swam *above* the surface right into its limited light path. Plus, we've got the sub's wide hull hiding us, along with the waves and the deep water."

Fieri again shook his head. "But absolutely *no* using any of our own lights from here on in, Chris. Except for the thin LED penlights once we're well underneath the sub's wide keel. The penlights are specifically designed *not* to throw any residual light out or around them. They only illuminate one very thin area. So, we'll just have to make do with those."

"Understood, Vin."

"Any accidental noises we make, which should be negligible, will be obscured by the sub's loud testing maneuvers," assured the doc. "And don't worry about our scooters. Remember, they were specially designed to be completely noiseless. Now make it snappy with those binocs, Chris. We've got to get cracking soon."

The Super Stud hurriedly focused in on Gitano's yacht, hoping to see something of interest. Suddenly, his eyes lit up. "*Yes!*" he whispered excitedly. "It's them! Three of the Rhombus girls minus Doreen."

Seven adjusted the binoculars to get a clearer view. Focusing in on the open promenade deck, he saw Terry, Anita, and Suzanne walking out with Carmine Gitano. They were laughing heartily, making their way over to six trembling captives, who were tied at the wrists and legs via thick leather bindings. All of the prisoners were naked, with a pair of gangland 'cement shoes' molded to their feet.

Terry, now grinning cruelly, was carrying a thin metal object. Seven again fine-tuned the binoculars and zoomed in on it. Of course! It was an ominous-looking branding iron, undoubtedly the very iron Seven had uncovered in Terry's closet during his brief spying venture. Even from here, the G5 operative could see that the end of the iron was red hot and smoldering. And judging from the hideous red burn marks on the prisoners' exposed bodies, it was obvious that Terry had been using it liberally on the unfortunate captives.

Seven wiped some saltwater off his brow and whispered to Fieri, "We better stay put a moment. Something's happening on the yacht!"

Chapter 35

'Giustizia di Mafioso'

oncealed in the pitch-black darkness on this moonless night, and completely clad in black rubber wetsuits, secret agents Christopher Seven and Vin Fieri were virtually invisible in the water. The swaying waves, that had suddenly begun churning, also helped keep them undetectable, as the two secret agents blended perfectly with the sea.

Trying to use Vin's nautical binoculars, despite the annoying movement of the waves, Seven kept a constant eye on the Zephyr's outside promenade deck. From what he could make out, there appeared to be several small groups on the outside deck. As for Seven's frogman partner, the doc likewise kept busy, checking and rechecking CIA's small homing device, hoping that he'd prepared the diminutive tracking device correctly. And also hoping that he would attach the magnetized tracking apparatus to the submarine precisely where the CIA experts had told him to.

Floating silently in the pitching water, each man kept one hand on his scooter, even though the scooters were fastened to their wetsuits via a long metal leash.

Thinking about the next part of their mission, Christopher Seven contemplated the situation. Vin's final strategy seemed sound enough. They would initially stop their scooters a mile or so from Carmine's yacht, rest for 15 minutes topside, and then slowly begin the dangerous trek toward Gitano's submarine. This 15-minute pause was a strategic precaution in case any spotlights or sentries were in the area. Yet both men knew that, like them, tonight's murky waters would hide any Gitano frogmen who might be patrolling the target area. Seven shrugged his shoulders, knowing it was a risk they'd just have to take. He watched as Fieri glanced at his GPS 'image finder,' readying himself to lead them to the sub's bottom.

Observing from afar with Vin's binoculars, Seven wished they could *hear* as well as see what was taking place on Carmine's yacht. Had they been able to listen in, however, they would have been sickened by what was taking place.

~

Carmine Gitano and the three Rhombus women, Terry, Anita, and Suzanne, were laughing loudly as they scrutinized the bloodied nude captives standing before them. The bound Capo victims, Joey Taba, Sino Fressi, and 'Little Willie' T., along with their three personal bodyguards, had all been cruelly worked over by Terry's branding iron. There was blood everywhere, and ghastly red marks burned across their bodies. Zeroing in via the watertight binoculars, Seven thought he could see several letter *R*s seared on the captives' brutalized flesh. All six prisoners, seemingly in a stunned terrified daze, were having trouble standing on the concrete blocks now molded to their feet. Every time one of them lost his balance and fell to the deck, the Rhombus women laughed with delight.

Though unable to hear what was happening, Seven correctly assumed that these six prisoners were rival mobsters; mobsters who'd somehow betrayed the mighty *Don* Gitano. The six captives would likely be tossed overboard soon, doomed to the bottom of the sea via their cement shoes. It was obvious that Gitano was planning an extensive and cruel Mafia rubout!

Seven continued to watch as Gitano walked over to the tallest of his prisoners and slapped him hard on the face. Pulling the man's hair back, Gitano gruffly explained, "Terry's artistry with the branding iron tonight was payback on you punks for greedily holding me up for more money. That last minute double-cross of yours really ticked me off. So I decided it was time for some old-fashioned mafia justice - *Giustizia di Mafioso.*"

Gitano let go of the man's hair and further declared, "Seems these onboard 'hits' of mine are becoming a regular feature onboard Zephyr. I knocked off three Carpi bums on my yacht, including old man Carpi, just a week ago. The Carpi gang got theirs like you guys are going to get yours."

Gitano grinned, smugly. "Of course I cleared it with your mob 'families' first. As I always do. And, just like I thought they would, the underbosses of your three families readily agreed to my eliminating you. Right after I assured them that they'd have the European Syndicate's blessings to run your factions themselves. They'll take over after you boys are whacked tonight. In fact, the *new* bosses of each of your mobs were ecstatic about it. You'd be surprised how quickly a hundred million bucks or so, split among your replacement capos, changed their loyalties. They'll take over tomorrow, with my blessings."

Don Gitano then turned toward the three Rhombus women. "You see ladies, I always verify before eliminating Mafia *capos* or their bodyguards. Better for business and better for my health that way."

The three women laughed. Carmine smiled back at them and continued addressing the prisoners. "And now that the various NATO tasks you were each responsible for have been started - and in some cases *completed* - your services are no longer required anyway. Your successors can finish anything that still needs to be carried out."

Gitano glanced over at the drooling Nalco. The broad-shouldered enforcer was standing off to the side eagerly awaiting the 'treat' *Don* Carmine had promised him earlier. Nalco soon received it when his boss walked over to Sino Fressi, the youngest of the three captives, and informed him, "Sorry, Sino, but you drew the short straw. I told Nalco he could have one of you bums tonight. And you're the lucky guy."

Carmine moved a few steps back and pointed toward Fressi. "Okay, Nalc, he's all yours."

Snarling loudly, much like a salivating pit bull, Nalco rushed over to Sino Fressi, grabbed Fressi's neck with his huge right hand, and slowly began squeezing it in a ferocious, vise-like grasp. Sino's face began turning a purplish blue, while his tongue, reacting to the immense pressure, slowly slid out to the right side of his mouth. As Nalco squeezed harder, Fressi fell to his knees, urinating on himself in a helpless reflex reaction. This last pathetic response brought roars of laughter from Rhombus.

Nalco kept it going for a full ten minutes, bringing the gagging gangster to and from the brink of death several times. It was obvious that Nalco had executed this torture before, always doing so with a sadist's touch. The torment finally ended when a sharp crackling noise was heard; the telltale sound that Sino's neck had been broken.

Watching Nalco finish his sinister handiwork, Carmine Gitano and the three Rhombus women gave him loud applause. Two of Gitano's goons promptly picked up Fressi's lifeless body, now drenched in sweat and urine, and threw it into the sea. They quickly made their way over to the other trembling captives. One by one, the five screaming victims were tossed into the sea as well. Each man sank quickly via his concrete shoes.

Smiling with cold satisfaction, Carmine Gitano rubbed his hands together and turned his attention back to the mini-sub. "Well, ladies and gents, fun's over for tonight. It's time to get my submarine ready for launch." He yelled down to the sailors performing their safety checks on the Alvis. "How's it going, guys?"

"Fine, Mr. Gitano," one of them shouted back. "We'll be set to go in another forty-five minutes or so. Have to finish the remaining maneuvers. Takes a while, but we want everything shipshape."

"Hurry it up, if you can," barked Gitano. "It's time we get this submarine show on the road. I don't know why, exactly, but I'm getting an uneasy feeling tonight. It's kinda spooky way out here alone, with no other boats for miles. Can't say why I'm uneasy. Just a feeling I guess. That's why I've got an undersea security guard patrolling this whole area. Big Tony Dappo, one of my best soldiers from Detroit.

Gitano gestured toward the dark ocean surrounding them. Tony's circling underwater somewhere out there now, frogman-style. I told him to patrol as much area as he can, to go as deep and as far as possible."

Gitano grinned. "No problem for Dappo. He swims and dives like a fish. And Tony's tough as nails. And if I know Dappo, he'll circle as far and as wide an area as anyone could. He told me he'd travel a mile or more from here, as far as the eye can see. Dressed in his scuba gear and armed to the teeth." Carmine gave an apologetic shrug of his shoulders to the three Rhombus women. "I know, I'm probably just being overcautious. But, hey, you never know."

The mob boss walked over to the yacht's side railing and called out to his submarine crew again. "Hey, fellas. Is it okay if I take the three girls and Dr. Huin onboard the sub now? While you guys finish up your tests? I'd like to show them around the Alvis before we shove off. Get 'em acquainted with the sub and that fancy air they'll be breathing inside. Or whatever those scientific eggheads call it."

"Sure, Mr. Gitano," answered the head crewman, a bald sailor with a colorful tattoo on his arm. "You can bring your guests down. You won't be in our way."

Carmine yelled down his appreciation. "Thanks, Mack!" Gitano excitedly turned toward the Rhombus trio, who'd just been joined by the Korean plastic surgeon, Huin Kim. Gitano nodded a 'hello' to Kim and proudly declared, "Okay, folks, let's tour the sub, and see for yourselves why I was right. Having this submarine will come in handy for our little billion-dollar venture. It'll also be good practice for the *real* thing. Avoiding the Cannes area's security nets on 'D-Day.'"

The Korean and the three females nodded their agreement. And with that, Gitano, Dr. Huin, and the Rhombus women, minus Doreen, made their way down a set of metal stairs and onto the anchored mini-sub.

~

Under the cover of darkness, a mile or so from Gitano's two vessels, Seven and Fieri bobbed softly in the open sea. Now ready to make their way over to the submarine's broad bottom, only their black hooded heads were currently out of the water. The rest of their wetsuit bodies were completely concealed under the black sea.

Stunned by the brutal gangland killings they'd just witnessed, the two American agents wondered what it was all about. The only thing they'd discerned thus far, besides witnessing six coldblooded mob executions, was the sub's upcoming passenger list. Along with the five crewman manning the submarine, the other passengers for the dive looked to be Gitano himself, three of the Rhombus gals, and lastly, the shadowy Korean plastic surgeon. Seven again worried about Doreen. Where was she? Was she part of any of this? Seven's instincts told him she wasn't. Hopefully she was still alive and safe.

Making a mental note of everything they'd witnessed, Seven and Fieri grabbed their scooters and readied themselves to begin their lengthy one-mile trek over to the submarine's hull. Both knew that this would be the most perilous part of tonight's mission.

"I'll go first," Fieri advised. "We're still okay, time-wise. I make it an hour or so before Carmine's submarine can actually move. And it should only take me ten or fifteen minutes to complete my handiwork. Even so, we better get moving now. Afterward, we can return right here and keep on observing. May not see anything as dramatic as you just did. But at least we'll know which way they're heading. And after I attach the homer to the sub, the CIA can track it fulltime."

Still shaken by the six repulsive murders, particularly Nalco's barbaric handiwork, Seven passed the binoculars back to Fieri and slipped on his mask again. The Super Stud shuddered a moment, knowing if he was caught spying now, Carmine Gitano would have no mercy on him. Especially with Gitano's *Cosa Nostra* pledge to "personally" take care of Seven" if he ever came near again. Thinking about the consequences of being captured, Seven pressed his scooter's noiseless accelerator and tensely followed Doc Fieri down.

Diving extra deep, with still a mile to go, Vin turned around, grinned confidently at Seven, and put his first two fingers together, making his now familiar 'OK' sign. A few seconds after doing so, the bright glare of a large underwater spotlight hit Fieri square in the eyes, momentarily blinding him. It was immediately followed by a whizzing spear, shot from a powerful *Mares* Pneumatic Spear Gun. The barbed mini-harpoon struck Fieri hard, puncturing the left side of his chest. Blood spurt out of his wet suit as he moaned in pain.

Stunned by the surprise attack, Christopher Seven, trailing a few yards behind his badly wounded partner, looked to the right and saw Gitano's frogman sentry swimming his way. Spear gun in hand, the nimble gangster was preparing to strike again!

Sensing that his surprise attack had given him the upper hand, Gitano's hitman quickly let go of his large buoyant diver's spotlight. The oversized light hovered motionlessly and illuminated the entire area.

Now able to see clearly in the bright lighting, Seven noticed that another deadly spear was now loaded in the thug's dual-chamber gun, ready to fire. Knowing there was no time to get to his own spear gun, the G5 agent swam toward the burly attacker, hoping to grab his arm. As Seven did so, a second spear whizzed by him, narrowly missing his head.

Before his assailant could reload, Seven grabbed the man's right arm and kicked him hard in the groin, forcing the weapon out of his hands. They then began grappling hand-to-hand, as the mobster tried desperately to reach for the large marine knife strapped to his side.

While the two combatants wrestled savagely, the wounded and debilitated Fieri looked on. The barbed spear was still firmly in his chest and blood was now flowing faster from his pierced body. Getting weaker by the second, the doc watched helplessly as his G5 sidekick tried to keep the strapping gangster away from his glistening knife.

The two combatants fought savagely, a blur of flailing arms and legs. Then, with one well-disguised powerful kick, Gitano's henchman sent Seven flying across the water! The G5 operative hadn't seen it coming, and the violent blow partially dislodged Seven's mask. It also undid the spear gun strapped to Seven's back, sending it to the bottom. With both his opponents completely unarmed, the mobster's hands were free to act!

Grinning widely through his black scuba mask, the hood reached down and confidently grabbed his large *Tang UK* knife from its sheath. Seven could plainly see the man's cruel smile as his attacker readied himself to apply the killing stabs.

The Super Stud was now in mortal danger! He had no weapon or shield to counter his knife-wielding assailant. Quickly readjusting his mask, Seven raised his two hands in front of his body for what he knew would almost certainly be a futile attempt at parrying the upcoming knife thrusts.

Suddenly there was a great commotion in the water as a foaming whirlpool of bubbles began to engulf them! It was as if a large cement mixer had just been turned on. Momentarily confused, Seven then heard a terrified scream coming from the mobster, muffled somewhat by the hit-man's scuba mask. A thick red substance rapidly began mixing in with the churning water. It was blood - the blood of Seven's attacker!

Seven couldn't figure out what was happening, partially blinded by the foaming maze of bubbles and blood. Trying to clear his head, he finally realized what had occurred. Lured by the blood and the vigorous commotion in the water, a huge hammerhead shark, most likely the one that had been shadowing him and Fieri, had grabbed hold of Gitano's hitman in a swift, ferocious attack from behind. The shark now had the mobster by the torso, its great jaws tearing the screaming man like a rag doll. Chewing and shaking its hideous head violently, the big fish was ripping off parts of the man's body! Fortunately for Seven and Fieri, the ravenous shark had attacked the first victim it came to and not them!

Christopher Seven watched disbelievingly, temporarily frozen as the giant hammerhead tore off the gangster's left hand at the wrist and swallowed it whole. While it did so, bits of shredded flesh and offal slowly made their way toward Seven. Staring incredulously, the sickening scene made the G5 operative retch through his mask.

Quickly regaining his wits, Seven grabbed Fieri by the arm and pulled him away from the shark attack. Retrieving the two hovering scooters, which were finally starting to float upwards, Seven somehow managed to get Vin's arm on the handlebar of one of them and motioned for him to press the accelerator button. The doc, with the spear still in him, nodded his head feebly.

Fortunately, Seven was now using the scooter with the attached GPS device. He turned it on, hurriedly perused the directions, and headed them southwest, trying to get away from the feasting hammerhead as swiftly as possible. He prayed the big shark would be kept occupied by its ongoing attack, while he and Vin got away.

After twenty minutes of rapid scooter movement, with no further signs of the big shark, both agents were now fairly certain that the giant hammerhead hadn't followed them. They surfaced and paused a moment for a much-needed rest. After pulling the spear out of Vin's chest, a task that made both of them cringe, Seven made a makeshift tourniquet for the doc by using pieces of his wet-suit ripped from the arms and legs. It was crude but it seemed to stop most of the bleeding.

An hour later, they were mercifully approaching the Italian spy boat, exhausted and drained. Though Fieri's bleeding had finally stopped, he was getting weaker. Several times during their trek back he'd nearly passed out. Thankfully, he had somehow managed to hang on to his scooter and ride it forward, doing so by sheer willpower.

"Quick, I need some help down here!" Seven yelled up to the two Italian agents standing by the railing as the scooters approached.

"Right away!" one of them yelled back. Reaching down, they gently lifted Fieri up the side of the boat and then helped Seven as well.

Worried for his CIA sidekick, who'd lost a good amount of blood, the Super Stud followed anxiously as they carried Vin down to the hold and applied the best first-aid treatment they could. Using fresh bandages, several injections, and a sedative from their well-stocked pharmaceutical cabinet, the Italian crew did a passable job of patching Vin up.

"I think he'll make it," advised Pietro. "But the immediate worry is infection. I'm not a doctor, but from what I can see, that could be a problem."

After yet another injection, this one for pain, followed by a stiff shot of bourbon, Fieri, though drowsy, seemed to be feeling better. Sitting up on the small cot near the first aid table, he grinned at Seven apologetically. "Sorry I wasn't much help back there, partner. It's kind of tough to lend a hand with a spear sticking in your chest. Anyway, our friend the hammerhead took care of things pretty good."

"I'll say," Seven replied. "That could have been *us* in the shark's jaws instead of Gitano's man. In any case, it's too bad we never got your CIA homing device onto the submarine. Or discovered where he was taking the girls and that Korean quack."

"Or *why* they tortured and killed six men in one fell swoop," the Doc sleepily added. "Oh, well. I guess there's only *one* way we're going to find out what this is all about, Chris, and put an end to whatever *Don* Gitano is planning."

"I know," nodded Seven. "It's up to me to re-contact Doreen and somehow coax every last detail out of her."

Fieri groggily nodded back and closed his eyes. He was soon asleep.

Watching his wounded colleague drift into slumber, the G5 operative began thinking about meeting up with Doreen again. As he did so, he once more recalled Carmine Gitano's dire warning about staying away from her –*"or else*!" After tonight's events, Seven had seen for himself how permanent and cruel the Mafioso's *"or else"* could be.

Right after Pietro phoned ahead for a hospital ambulance to meet them at the pier, the Italian boat's powerful engines started up and began rushing them back to shore. Still down in the hold with the now sleeping Fieri, Seven got up from the small chair he was sitting on and walked away from Vin's bedside a moment. The Super Stud wanted to be alone with his thoughts and his fears.

Seven strolled over to the hold's small porthole and stared out at the dark, churning sea. He sighed resignedly and replayed the horrors of everything he'd witnessed tonight.

Reflecting on all of it, Christopher Seven now wondered if he'd be the next victim to fall prey to Nalco's murderous right hand, Gitano's cement shoes, or Terry's scorching branding iron!

Chapter 36

Tryst or Trap?

Twelve frustrating days passed after the close call with the Hammerhead shark and Gitano's underwater security guard. Christopher Seven, now back at the *Hotel de Paris* in Monaco, hadn't heard a thing from Doreen. It had been nearly two weeks of absolute silence; no calls, no emails, no communication at all. The only information that Seven had ascertained, using a phony name during a brief cell phone conversation with a dock administrator, was that Gitano's yacht had unexpectedly spent several *additional* days out at sea – eight days more than Zephyr's initial manifest. No one knew why the lavish yacht had changed its course and had stayed out at sea. This eerie silence, with virtually all of CIA's and Interpol's sources drying up at the exact *same* time, was quite unusual. Consequently, Seven's keen instincts were now telling him that something really *big* was up.

During these last twelve days of maddening silence, the anxious Super Stud had doggedly phoned the number of the secured smartphone he'd given Doreen on Capri. And though Seven had continually left dire messages, Doreen hadn't responded to *any* of them. Strictly forbidden by G5 headquarters from going anywhere near Gitano's French chateau, unless Doreen called or contacted him, there was nothing Seven could do but keep on waiting.

The Super Stud was now troubled about *two* possibilities, both of them portentous. One: that Doreen had reverted back to her rigid Rhombus loyalties under the constant companionship and pressure from her three Rhombus 'sisters.' Or, two: that she'd incurred the fatal wrath of Carmine Gitano and been eliminated by the Mafioso after Gitano had somehow learned of her plans to meet up with Seven again. As the G5 operative thought on this second scenario, his mind kept going back to the file notes he'd found in Terry's stateroom, specifically the entry that read: '*Terminare* Doreen – 9/26; *re* Nalco.' Today was September 25th! Had Doreen been 'dismissed' or *worse*?

Feeling culpable for not fully informing her during their last night together, as well as genuine fear for Doreen's safety, Seven decided to try and reconnect with Doreen one last time. His tentative plan, admittedly a very risky one, was to first phone New York headquarters and get them to relent. Convince them to let him drive out to Gitano's enormous Antibes estate and somehow slip onto the chateau's spacious grounds during the cover of darkness. Once there, see if he could furtively find or communicate with Doreen again. Perhaps meet up with her while she was taking one of her daily 'solitary walks.' Or maybe spot her sitting alone somewhere around the Mafioso's sprawling six acres of gardens. Then, if he could convince her she was in extreme danger, whisk her away from Gitano and her three Rhombus partners. Once Doreen saw for herself that Seven had risked his life to help her, perhaps she'd come with him.

Earlier that morning, during Seven's ensuing call to New York, this 'suicidal tactic,' as the G5 higher-ups initially called it, was discussed, dissected, and debated at the top levels of headquarters. Seven's chief, Colonel McPhail, was at first vehemently against it. But then, after listening to the other feeble options put forth by his staff, he finally agreed with his Super Stud agent that the only way to find out for sure about Doreen was to indeed sneak over to and into Gitano's huge villa. Then, provided she was still alive, he could hopefully make contact with her by cellphone or face-to-face, doing so despite *Don* Gitano's dire warning and the six sadistic murders Seven had witnessed onboard the Zephyr.

Hank Carson, G5's second-in-command, adamantly disagreed with Seven's plan, as did the three other agency honchos who were also in on the conference call. These four dissenting voters felt Seven's plan was far too dangerous for the classified secrecy of the Super Stud sector.

As Carson firmly explained, to attempt a break-in to Gitano's villa now, especially with the Mafia chieftain very much on the warpath, was utter madness. Like Seven, Hank Carson suspected that the reason Doreen hadn't called the Super Stud back was because she was either dead or was again a devoted and compliant member of Rhombus. Once more, citing the security of the G5 agency as well as Seven's top-secret 'stud' division should Seven be caught and tortured, Carson preferred to let the CIA proceed alone at this juncture and to carry on *without* Seven's help.

As in most G5 stalemates like this one, Colonel McPhail left the final decision up to his agent. Accordingly, after calling back New York and thanking all of the execs for their input, Christopher Seven informed his superiors that he'd like to see it through. He still wanted to try and exploit his self-orchestrated relationship with Doreen, provided she hadn't already been 'hit' or dismissed by Gitano. As for the risks, so be it. He owed it to the girl and to his wounded CIA colleague still in the hospital. Seven further pointed out that he was well-trained for covert break-ins like this one and promised to abort the mission if things became too dicey. With that, the G5 honchos reluctantly agreed to let Seven try.

Thinking on things now, a few hours after his morning phone call with New York, Seven was convinced he'd made the right decision. Via his carefully orchestrated and nurtured 'relationship' with Doreen, the Super Stud knew he was the *sole* conduit through which any significant information could be obtained. And despite the unreturned phone calls, and the very real possibility that Doreen had been re-indoctrinated with Rhombus 'Kool-Aid', the G5 operative still had confidence in his abilities. He'd wait one more day, and then formulate a plan to sneak over to *Don Gitano's* chateau.

Seven's decision had been soundly supported by CIA agent Vin Fieri, who was now at Monaco's Princess Grace Hospital Centre recuperating from the spear damage and the lingering infection in his wounded chest. During Seven's call to the hospital some twenty minutes earlier, Fieri had dejectedly admitted that without the homing device attached to Gitano's submarine, there was little chance of the CIA keeping tabs on either the Mafioso or the Rhombus women now. The Italian government had steadfastly refused to get involved, as did Interpol and the French Coast Guard. All of these bureaus were writing off the six Zephyr murders the American agents 'alleged' they'd viewed from afar as simply 'gangland rub-outs.' Or, more likely, overdramatic 'American hearsay.' As far as the European police agencies were concerned, if Fieri's and Seven's story was true, the more crooks eliminated, the better. Hence, with all of these foreign investigative agencies taking an unconcerned 'hands-off,' as far as Fieri and his CIA bosses were concerned, Christopher Seven, via his tryst with Doreen, was their only hope now.

~

A few hours later, while Seven was finishing a tasty club sandwich out on the veranda of his hotel suite, the decision on whether to try and discover Doreen's fate became a moot point. After wolfing down the last of his room service lunch, Seven's cellphone rang out loudly. Answering it on the first ring, the agent was thrilled and greatly relieved to hear Doreen's voice. "*Thank God!*" he exclaimed with real feeling.

Though noticeably apprehensive about having finally phoned him, Doreen likewise seemed happy to hear his voice again.

"Please don't be angry with me, Chris, and don't ask me why I haven't returned any of your calls. It's been absolute mayhem these past two weeks. Carmine's gone bonkers. He's totally paranoid about everything, and his goons are keeping a short leash on everybody... including us four girls. Apparently, a few weeks ago, one of his most reliable patrol guards went missing while scuba diving near the Zephyr. Ever since then, he's increased security and kept an eye on everyone."

Seven said nothing, though inwardly happy that he, Fieri, and the hammerhead shark had at least put some anxiety into Gitano. He listened closely as Doreen went on, "All I can say is that I've missed you terribly. And I've wanted to call you back several times. Yet, each time I started to, I thought of your safety and vowed never to see you again. Today..." she paused..."is definitely my last chance to ever speak to you."

"But why, Doreen? Seven asked. "I thought we talked all this out. I've *got* to see you, and as soon as possible. There are still important things to sort out. Dangerous things even *without* me. We promised each other we'd calmly discuss things once you got off the Zephyr. You promised me one final heart-to-heart talk."

"I know, but all that's changed now. There's no reason for it any longer, although I can't tell you why. Let's just say terrible things have happened onboard Carmine's yacht. I won't say anything more. It'd be much too dangerous for *you* if I did."

She paused again and then explained, "And secondly...well let's just say you wouldn't be very proud of me. Nor of my past or future once you heard the whole story." She sighed. "Anyway, after thinking on things while I was alone, I've made my decision. And it's final. You're better off without me. That's why I never called you back. For fear you'd try to change my mind."

"But Doreen..."

"No *buts*, Chris. Things aren't the same. We could never meet up without Carmine and his contacts knowing. Not ever. Like I said, he's boosted security, and he never lets me out of his sight for very long." Her face reddened, "He's got a very important *business* deal coming up, which we four women are part of." That's all I can really tell you."

Doreen wouldn't elaborate any further, and Seven wondered how he could coax her to do so. If only he could get that one last chance to try.

"Trust me," she continued. "Carmine's wound tight as a drum now, ready to explode. He's been gunning for *everybody* lately."

Seven silently nodded his head, recalling the six gruesome murders he'd witnessed aboard Zephyr as Doreen nervously went on, "The awful things I saw and heard the last twelve days made me think of you, Chris. What would happen to *you* if we ever violated Carmine's decree. I decided it's better and safer for you if we ended things between us *–forever.* With my uncertain future, short as it may be, our parting is really no loss anyway. "

Christopher Seven was dumfounded, having thought he'd successfully 'turned' his target back on Capri; he thought he had made her want to see him again, no matter *what* the dangers. Her words of rejection totally deflated him. Staring at his iPhone, Seven grudgingly admitted to himself that his wounded pride stung almost as much as his genuine concern for her.

The Super Stud listened halfheartedly as Doreen added, "I want you to go on living, my love. Live life as it *should* be lived. As *I* should have lived it." A small tear welled up in her eye. Seven could hear the gloom in in her voice. "Live life for me, Chris, for you and me can never be. My destiny has already been decreed. It was shaped years ago. Way back when I chose my mother's way instead of my father's."

Still speechless, the G5 agent wasn't sure what this gloomy, brooding about 'life' and 'destiny' was all about. Was she perhaps considering suicide? Or was this simply more of Doreen's recurring histrionics? Most importantly to Seven, was it crucial to Gitano and Rhombus's plans?

"I don't understand," Seven gently replied. "We could have so much to live for. You make it seem like life itself is coming to an end. What's it all about, Doreen?"

She remained silent, so Seven kept pressing.

"I've thought of nothing but *you* these past two weeks, Doreen. Worried myself sick thinking something had happened to you. My love for you hasn't changed." Seven looked away a moment, after reluctantly using the practiced Super Stud half-truths he'd learned at G5. His worry for her safety was genuine, however, and he firmly said so. "I think I can get you through whatever fix you're in, Doreen. But you've got to trust me. Give me and the future a chance before it's too late."

For a precious few moments Doreen desperately wanted to believe him...do so if only in her dreams. Her heart, however, was telling her it was already too late.

Sensing she might be weakening, Seven decided to go for broke. "Listen, I'm back in Monte Carlo now, not too far from Antibes. I can be there with you in less than an hour. It sounds like you're in real trouble or considering something reckless. Just promise me you won't decide on anything until we meet. I may have wonderful news for you – a workable way out."

"No, Chris!" she exclaimed. "No more pipedreams. Not with Carmine and the risk. It's just too..."

"Why don't you give me a chance?" Seven interrupted. "Or at least hear me out today. If you don't like what I'm offering, then we'll say 'goodbye' for good. I promise. No strings. Yet I'm telling you the truth. There *is* a way out."

His last statement had an element of validity in it. He was already thinking about some type of witness-protection deal for her, hoping to explain it when and *if* they got together. Then – provided she showed interest, and provided the CIA and Interpol agreed to it – he would whisk her away today into Interpol's safe hands before Gitano could act on her. There was no time to lose now. Seven was convinced that *Don* Gitano and her Rhombus 'sisters' were planning to do away with her very soon.

The Super Stud, again, heard her sigh into the phone. Was it a sigh of consideration or one of negativity? Either way, Seven kept pushing.

"Listen, Doreen. Is there some rendezvous spot nearby that you could somehow get to? Someplace away from Carmine's villa where we can talk things out?"

Doreen went silent again, her mind spinning. After another tense pause, she finally agreed. "Well, I guess I owe you *that* much, Chris. And there won't be another chance. Let me think a moment."

As the G5 operative nervously held his breath, Doreen replied, "There's a small, deserted children's park, called *Anges*, on the outskirts of Antibes. My father used to take me there. It's right next door to *Fort Carré*, the main landmark of the city. You can't miss it as you drive into town via the Rue Central. The playground is pretty shabby now so no one visits it anymore. We should be alone."

She glanced down at her watch. It read 2PM. "I can meet you there at three o'clock. We can't be very long though. Even though Carmine still allows me to take my walks, and my solo car drives, he gets edgy and suspicious whenever I'm gone *too* long from his villa."

"That rundown playground sounds perfect," said a relieved Seven. But then, after reflecting on her precise meeting spot, and her quick and explicit directions, almost as if they'd been planned ahead of time, the G5 agent was suddenly wary. He wondered if Doreen had reverted back to her sordid past and was now setting him up for a gangland trap.

"We can meet by the kiddy swings," Doreen nervously advised. "They're near the rear exit of the park, ragged and abandoned. You'll see them near some large spruce trees in the back."

"Okay," Seven replied, now uneasy about the whole thing. "I'll see you there at 3."

~

Arriving at the outskirts of Antibes an hour later, Seven parked his rented Mercedes several blocks from the Anges playground. Doing so in case anyone was waiting to ambush him there. Wary of a Mafia trap, he walked to the park's front entrance guardedly. Wearing dark sunglasses, Seven cautiously approached his destination, surveying the surroundings from across the street. He noted the dilapidated swing sets at the rear of the small playground, exactly where Doreen said they'd be. There were also several large leafy trees, clumped together, which made it hard to see into this area. No one was about and there was no traffic or any parked cars nearby. If Gitano's thugs were hidden by the trees, waiting to jump him, this would be an ideal spot for it.

Ten more minutes passed. Still watching from across the road, Seven saw the shapely figure of Doreen approaching the playground from the opposite direction. She was alone and seemed to be quite stressed, looking around constantly. Knowing it was now or never, the Super Stud crossed the street and made his way toward her. "Hello, Doreen," he greeted, about to embrace her.

"Thank goodness you made it," she replied, brusquely pushing his hug away. "But we've got troubles. We have to get out of here. *Now!*"

"What's wrong?" Seven asked, alarmed by her worried expression.

"I just saw Nalco and three of his hoods circling this area. They were driving Carmine's white Hummer. I don't think they spotted me but who knows? One of them might have seen me as I was parking my car." She lowered her head, dejectedly. "When I saw them here, I initially thought someone may have been listening outside my bedroom when I phoned you. That still might be the case. Then I remembered Nalco and his pals like to visit *Scandia's* pizza joint for a late lunch, right here in Antibes." She pounded her right fist into her left palm. "Just our luck."

Knowing there was real danger brewing, but still wary of the whole situation, Seven wondered if Doreen's look of concern was sincere or staged. "What do you suggest we do now, Doreen?"

"Normally, I'd say we just hide out here awhile. But there's another hitch, Chris. I'm due back at the villa by 3:35 for an emergency meeting that Carm *just* called. He said it was imperative that *all* four girls be there. So if I don't get back to the villa in half an hour or less, he's bound to become suspicious. He'd probably send his people out to find me, if he hasn't sent some of them out already. Like Nalco's crew. So we better move quickly."

Seven tried to read Doreen's expression as she ran her hands through her hair, worriedly. Was it genuine fear or superb playacting?

"I don't know what this unexpected, hastily-called conference is all about," Doreen declared, "but Carmine definitely expects me to show. He mentioned the meeting and its importance just as I was leaving to come here to you. I told him I was just going out for my daily car ride and that I'd either drive to town or up to the *Garden Exotica* like I always do. Either way, I promised Carm that I'd be back in time. He said okay, but to be 'quick' about it. My fear now is that Carmine has already sent out his men to shadow me and that they're on patrol now. Hence my seeing Nalco's squad just now."

Fed up with being at the mercy and whims of Doreen's Rhombus and Mafia masters, Seven decided it was time to make her choose. "Why don't you let me take you away from all of this, Doreen? Come with me now, back to Monaco and then to New York. I have a safe way to do it. A way that you'll never have to be afraid of Carmine Gitano or anyone else again. I was planning to tell you all about it here."

Before Doreen had a chance to reply, her face grimaced in near panic. "Chris, get down! It's Nalco's car. That big white vehicle stopped at the corner light over there."

Seven dove under one of the spruce trees while Doreen kept an eye on the street.

"It's okay now," she advised a minute or so later. "They've passed. I don't think anyone saw us but they definitely seemed to be circling the block looking for somebody. Most likely me."

Seven knew they'd probably be spotted any minute now. Trying to control his mounting trepidation, he ordered, "We've got to get away now, Doreen. Although that might prove tricky. For me, anyway. I'm parked several blocks from here, so there's a good chance they'd see me standing here alone once you go. Or spot me walking back to my car. But you might make it safely out of here if you leave now."

"Follow me, Chris. My Jag's right out front."

They rushed to Doreen's car, a roomy Jaguar XJ 4-door sedan, just as Nalco's Hummer began circling the block again. Fortunately it was still up the road a ways. "Quick, get in the trunk, Chris."

"The *trunk?*"

"Don't argue – just do it! Nalco and his boys will be here any moment and they're sure to stop once they see me by my car. You'll be fine in there. Cramped but fine. There's an emergency pull release inside the trunk, so you won't be trapped in there if I have to leave you awhile. Once they've gone, I can drop you off back at your own car. Now hurry and get in the trunk. They'll be here any minute!"

Seven did as he was told, still unsure if he was being set up or not. Though hesitant, he nevertheless scrunched his lean body inside the Jaguar's trunk and waited.

Sure enough, a few minutes later, Nalco's car made another circling search, driving slowly up the playground's narrow street. Finally spotting Doreen, Nalco waved to her, beeped his horn, and pulled up to the playground's potholed driveway. From his cramped hiding place, Seven heard them get out of their car and approach Doreen.

"Hi ya, Miss D," barked Nalco, in his gruff, accented voice. "The boss sent'a us out to find a' you. Said you'd probably be'a around here or at the *Garden Exotica.* Tosca's crew is searching at the *Garden,* so we just started lookin' for you'a here." Nalco glanced around, suspiciously. "Didn't think'a you'd be in some kids' park."

"Sometimes I come here to meditate and be alone," Doreen nervously but firmly informed. "This abandoned playground is quiet and secluded. It brings back fond memories of my father and my childhood."

Nalco merely shrugged his broad shoulders.

"You gotta get back to the boss's villa pronto, Miss D," said one of the other goons, a scar-faced shorter man. "Seems Mr. Gitano needs you earlier than planned. And you know Mr. G. He don't like to be kept waiting."

"Sure, Steno," Doreen replied, her voice straining with tension. "I was about to drive back there now anyway."

"We'll follow'a you," Nalco harshly informed. He smirked, smugly. "And just'a in case we lose'a you again – Steno's gonna ride'a wit you. Make'a sure you get'a home quick and safe."

From his cramped position in Doreen's trunk, Seven heard and felt Steno get into the front passenger seat while the other three men walked back to their Hummer parked directly in front of Doreen's Jag. A few minutes later the G5 agent was bouncing uncomfortably in the trunk as

Doreen's sedan made its way back to the villa. She was closely followed by Nalco in the Hummer.

Christopher Seven, trying his best to settle in for the bumpy twenty-minute ride, was grateful, at least, that he wasn't at all claustrophobic. Still wondering if all this was cleverly orchestrated, the Super Stud wasn't sure how, when, or *if* he'd be able to escape!

Chapter 37

Warped Legacy

Waved through the wrought iron entrance gates by two armed guards, Doreen anxiously maneuvered her Jaguar onto the sprawling driveway of Carmine Gitano's château. With Seven still hiding uncomfortably in the trunk, her car was closely followed in by Nalco's Hummer. Pulling up to the villa's huge 3-car garage, Doreen nervously called out to one of the sentries, "Okay for me to park inside the garage, Pesaro? I don't want my car's leather seats to get too hot out in the sun."

"Si, senora." He pointed toward the windowless 3-door garage door. "Plenty of room inside. Only the chief's two limos are in there. His long black *Cadillac Brougham* limo, and his white *Lincoln MKT limousine.* We got one more empty parking space inside if you want it. "

Doreen nodded affirmably and then turned to her gangland chaperon sitting in the Jag's front passenger seat. 'Thanks for riding with me, Steno."

"No problem, Missy." Steno jumped out and walked over to join Nalco and the other goons in the Hummer. Doreen waited a moment, pushed the electronic garage door opener attached to the visor, and pulled her car through the garage's wide open door.

Watching her closely, as the massive garage door opened and then closed, Nalco's crew finally relaxed. Grinning to himself, Nalco slowly drove away, parking the Hummer over by the swimming pool area. The first part of his mission was now completed. He'd brought Doreen back to the villa and would make sure she stayed there. *Permanently!* The brawny hitman licked his lips, dreamily visualizing the next part of his assignment!

~

At last alone in the empty garage, Doreen turned off the car engine and tried to calm her frayed nerves. Hopping out of the Jag, she quickly moved toward the trunk. "Coast's clear, Chris. Are you all right in there?"

Seven pulled the inside emergency toggle release and held onto the bottom of the trunk as it popped opened. He let it go halfway up and caustically replied, "Now I know what a sardine feels like."

Doreen frowned. "At least you're not a *dead* sardine."

Pushing the trunk open, the Super Stud jumped out and had a quick look around. The château's spacious garage was cavernous, with two other vehicles parked in it now; a pair of well-appointed stretch limousines. One was a long black *Cadillac* limo, and the other a stretched white *Lincoln Town Car.* Doreen's Jaguar, a sizable sedan in its own right, actually looked small lined up next to the two elongated limos. Fortunately there were not any windows on the garage doors, so Seven would have more room to move around unseen.

"What happens *now*, Doreen?" he asked, still worried.

"I'm not sure, but you're probably going to have to stay put in this garage awhile. Maybe even get back in that trunk for short spurts, as cramped as that might be. There are just too many guards keeping watch and combing the grounds at the moment. In fact, Carmine's entertaining some of the *Carpi* gang now. Right here at this château. Some sort of hastily called peace conference. So there's plenty of thugs and heavy artillery around."

"Oh, that's just great," moaned Seven.

Doreen put her hand to her forehead and tried to think. "Like I said, it's best you hide out here in the garage for the time being. There shouldn't be any more cars pulling in here today, as they won't need the limos 'til tomorrow. That gives us the rest of the day and evening to slip you out of here."

She gave him a soft kiss of encouragement. "Listen Chris, I got you into this mess and I'm going to get you out. Hopefully right after Carmine's upcoming meeting ends. Once that's over, I'll make up some excuse about going out for another short solo drive. Tell Carm that my first ride was cut short by his meeting. Then, once we're away from here, I'll get you out of the trunk and back to your own car."

Seven nodded, calmed by her sincere strategy to conceal him.

"And if that plan's not workable," Doreen continued, "we'll just have to wait till nighttime and come up with something else. Luckily, my bedroom, the one called the Blue Room Suite, is right above us. So my comings and goings through this garage won't draw any undo suspicion. I usually enter and exit the main house through this garage since my suite is directly above us. Via that side door over there." She pointed toward a small single door in front of the limos. "I generally walk past the servant's quarters and then up the first flight of stairs. Luckily there's only a skeleton household staff on duty this week. So not many servants should be around. In any case, I can easily get back down here quickly and unobserved after dark."

Seven filed her household directions into in his excellent memory and glanced at his watch: 4:35 p.m. It was going to be a tense, uncomfortable wait. *Oh well,* he mused, *there's really no other option.*

"You should be fine down here", Doreen assured, "as there's no more parking spaces available. Therefore no one should want to come in." She pointed toward her left. "If need be, there's a large supply closet over there to hole up in. Yet I wouldn't stray too far from the car trunk. That's still the best hiding place until I get back. If I get an inkling of anything brewing, or learn they're coming for the limos a bit earlier, we'll obviously have to try plan B. Whatever turns out, I still have your cellphone number. So I can always warn you from inside the house. Just make sure you set your phone's ringing onto its *vibrate* mode. Not on any ring modes. She smiled warmly. "Don't worry, I'll think of something, Chris. Even if it means sneaking you upstairs and hiding you in my room for the night."

Seven nodded again, though he knew that any attempt to hide *inside* Gitano's villa would probably be suicidal.

Doreen suddenly shook her head angrily, as if recalling something troubling. "Unfortunately, I just remembered, Chris. You're definitely going to have to get back in that trunk in the next half-hour or so anyway. And *stay* in there for a while."

"Why's that?"

"Because Carmine's sentries always make a 5 p.m. security stroll through the house and the garage. Purely routine. But they'll probably check that supply closet. Good thing I remembered."

"I'll say, Doreen."

She hugged him, reassuringly. "Don't fret, darling. Everything's going to be fine. With any luck, no one will come back in here after that routine security check. So once my meeting's over, and I let Carmine know that I'd like to go out again, we can hopefully slip away in the Jag. She beamed, excitedly. "By the way, I can't wait to hear about your idea for getting me free of this mess. That's all I've thought about since you mentioned it this morning. Who knows? Maybe you really *can* get me out of this lifestyle into a new one - one with a future."

"I know I can," Seven assured her.

"Oh well, we'll just have to see about that, Chris. But at least I can *dream* about it." On her way out of the garage, she blew him another kiss. "I'll come back for you as soon as I can, my love." Turning toward the garage's small side door, she then quietly made her exit, slowly marching up the stairs and into the house via the servant's wing.

Christopher Seven watched her leave and then walked over to the musty supply closet. It was filled with tools, large tiers and spare auto parts. Once inside, he hid behind some large boxes in the closet's far corner, switched his cellphone from the audible ring mode to the silent vibration-only selection, and waited edgily.

An uneventful fifteen minutes went by. Noting it was getting closer to the villa's 5 p.m. security check, the anxious G5 agent made his way back to Doreen's Jaguar. He hopped into the trunk again and slowly pulled it closed. No matter how uncomfortable, Seven instinctively new that continuing to hide in the trunk of Doreen's Jag was still his best shot at staying undetected. He then took out his small penlight and shined it on the trunk's emergency exit toggle. Reassured that he could get in and out of the trunk again, he turned off his tiny flashlight and tried to make himself as comfortable as the constricted conditions allowed.

Twenty minutes later, while he was silently struggling to stretch out his cramped legs, Seven suddenly heard voices; the sounds of several men, not just two. They were entering through the same side door Doreen had used. By the sound of all the footsteps, this obviously wasn't the two-man security team. It seemed to be a gathering of people. As one of them called the impromptu meeting to order, Seven recognized the gruff baritone voice. It belonged to Carmine Gitano!

The Super Stud stiffened his body and tried to remain calm. He reminded himself that covertly eavesdropping on encounters like this was often the most vital part of his job; the mainstay of any secret agent's role. How many times had he overheard something significant while hiding in a back room, a closet or even kneeling by someone's keyhole? Hoping his car trunk hideout would likewise garner valuable information, Seven braced himself and listened closely as *Don* Carmine began his speech.

"Okay, boys, we only got ten minutes or so in here. Anita and Suzanne are giving the Carpi crew a tour of the grounds. Flirting openly with them and plying 'em with booze while they do.

I told the girls to keep those Carpi bums over at the far section of the villa for as long as they can. Away from the garage. That gives us one last chance to go over tomorrow's car bomb details. This will have to be our *final* run-through, however. We can't risk any more meetings in here while young Carpi and his four bodyguards are visiting."

Seven heard the shuffling of feet as the men gathered around their chief. "My own security team will be making their standard 'inside the villa' checks in ten minutes or so," Gitano continued. "After that, Carpi's people will have pretty much a limited free reign here at the château. For appearance sake, I want them to feel safe and welcome. So this will be our last conference regarding tomorrow night's NATO events as well."

The big man wiped some sweat off his brow and then rested his brawny arms on top of the trunk of Doreen's Jaguar. Crunched directly below, in his confined cocoon hiding place, Christopher Seven could almost *feel* the mobster's arms on top of him. The G5 operative prayed he wouldn't give himself away with a cough or a sneeze.

"As you know," Gitano informed, "only *three* of the Rhombus women will actually be attending the NATO dinner tomorrow, armed with their explosives. You guys know how we're gonna pull that off with security so tight." Gitano smiled widely. "All I can say is that this Korean doctor, Dr. Huin, is a genius!"

"What about that Rhombus chick, Doreen?" asked one of the men.

"She's waiting upstairs for some imaginary meeting I told her about. But suffice to say she's out now."

"What do you mean, *out*, boss?" a high-pitched voice asked.

"I mean out. Out for the count. *Kaput, finite, dead.* I'm getting rid of her later tonight. Nalco's gonna make the hit."

There were several satisfied grunts. "We're better off without that screwy broad," another one of the mobsters chimed in.

"I know," agreed Gitano. "Doreen's been nothing but trouble lately. Too much emotional baggage." He pointed his finger at his men, sternly. "But don't confuse Doreen with the other Rhombus women. Those other three are tops in my book. Remember, guys. Terry, Suzanne, and Anita are giving their lives for this venture of ours. They, along with everyone else at tomorrow night's NATO gala, are gonna be blown to smithereens. And the only thing Rhombus wants out of it is my assurance that the world will know *they* did it. I gave them my word on that and I meant it."

There was a respectful silence in the room. *Don* Gitano waited a moment and then broke it. "According to our experts, it'll be a colossal explosion. No one at the NATO festivities will know what hit 'em. And nobody will survive it. The Rhombus threesome will die, but so will the president of the United States, France and Italy's two leaders, and Britain's prime minister. It will be the biggest mob 'hit' in the history of organized crime, and it's gonna net us one *billion* smackeroos!"

Murmurs of satisfaction could be heard as Gitano further explained, "True, there won't be *four* explosions going off, like we originally planned. But three is more than enough according to the Korean. In any case, we just couldn't count on Doreen. She's become weak and unreliable. And this job is too important and too profitable to have some basket case messing things up last-minute." Gitano beamed confidently. "But don't worry, fellas. Doc Huin's scientific eggheads assured me that the three massive explosions, going off simultaneously, will take down the catering hall and most of the neighborhood as well. It'll be more destructive than a small nuclear blast!"

"Getting back to tonight, Don Gitano. What will happen to Doreen's body *after* Nalco makes the 'hit ' on her?" a fourth voice asked. "We certainly don't want no police inquiries or shocked witnesses, boss."

"It's all taken care of, Benny," Carmine coldly informed. "Nalco will throw her body into the Bizet River later tonight." Carmine Gitano reflected a moment. "Too bad. I kind of had a *thing* for that chick. Even with all her emotional garbage. But she's gotta go. Terry kept telling me that Doreen couldn't be trusted no more. Said she went soft on them." The big man frowned. "Even so, the other three girls had originally agreed that if Doreen came around, fine. They'd still allow her to take part in the NATO job like the others. If not, we'd whack her shortly beforehand." The mob boss casually glanced at his watch. "Doreen never did come around, so Nalc's gonna take care of her a few hours from now."

Christopher Seven, listening intently from his cramped hiding place in the Jaguar's trunk, got an instant chill up his spine. His growing worries about Doreen's fate had been well-founded. She'd already been condemned by the merciless Gitano. Sweating profusely, Seven remained motionless as the Mafioso outlined the rest of his plans.

The thug with the high-pitched voice then asked, "Didn't Doreen get suspicious when you told her she wouldn't be attending the Cannes gala dinner tomorrow night?"

"We *didn't* tell her," barked Gitano. "Doreen still thinks she's going. And she still believes she's going to die along with her Rhombus sisters this evening. As a tribute to her mother, whatever *that* means."

Carmine moved in closer to his men and assured, "Don't worry. Doreen ain't the least bit suspicious."

"Now, as for why we're meeting in the garage here", barked Gitano. "Away from Carpi's tribe. Here's the deal. You see those two limousines parked here now? One is my personal limo - the black Cadillac. And the other one is our *house* limousine - the white Lincoln Town Car. The one we use to pick up mob bigwigs; like the Carpi's. The white Lincoln is the vehicle that will be used to drive young Carpi and his body guards back to Monaco tomorrow. Or so they *think*." Carmine pounded his chest angrily. "I found out a few days ago, through my paid moles in Carpi's gang, that Frankie Carpi is planning to have me *whacked* sometime in the next three weeks. He's also planning to take over my territory and the NATO job profits once I'm dead." Gitano sneered. "The lousy bum! After all I did to try and make peace with him. Oh well. He'll get his, tomorrow, just like his old man did."

The mob king walked his lackeys over to the white Lincoln Town Car and motioned toward a thin gangster name Cano. "Cano here has put a timed VBIED car bomb under the white Lincoln. Did so the middle of last night. That car bomb is set to go off tomorrow afternoon at precisely one in the afternoon. Just when young Carpi and his pals are halfway back to Monte Carlo."

Gitano grinned satisfactorily and addressed Cano Ralfi by his nickname. "Cane. Slide under the white Town Car limo one last time and take a final looksee. Make sure the bomb is attached tightly and that it's well hidden."

Cano promptly got down on the floor and obediently slid under the white limo. "The bomb's fine, boss," he assured. "Tight and secure, and completely concealed by the dark grease that Nicky and I slathered over it. It's armed and ready to go off tomorrow afternoon at *exactly* 1:00 p.m. Just like you ordered."

"Excellent," growled Gitano. "By then, I'll be on my way with the three Rhombus girls in my private black Cadillac limo, taking them to their date with immortality.

The Mafia Don tapped the hood of his black Caddy parked alongside the white limousine. "Ironic, ain't it? I get to take the Rhombus women to the biggest, most profitable mob hit ever; while young Carpi, who prides himself on his Mafia legacy, gets blown up into little pieces."

In an air of false sympathy, Gitano then stated, "Too bad that my own man, Enzi, will be driving them in the white limo, and will also have to die. But if I didn't have one of my most beloved guys driving the white Lincoln, Carpi's boys might have smelled a rat. Oh well, that's the way the billion dollar cookie crumbles."

Carmine shrugged his shoulders and ordered Cano back out from under the Town Car. "Okay, Cane, crawl back out. And that's the *last* time I want you or anyone else examining that bomb any longer. There's no need to fine-tune it anymore. We've done it three times this week already and it's in perfect shape. So no sense taking a chance of being spotted rechecking it again. Not with young Carpi and his bodyguards roaming around the place. I don't want *anything* calling attention to this garage or that white limo at this point." Gitano grinned. "Besides. When Cano Ralfi says a bomb is armed and ready to go, it's ready. Cane's the best there is."

There were satisfied grins from the group as *Don* Gitano proudly exclaimed, "So, while Carpi and his boys are being blown to kingdom come, I'll be in the black Cadillac here riding with the three Rhombus women to *Saint Paul de Vence.* That's a little town outside of Cannes. We have a suite booked for them at the *Cantemerle Hotel.* That's where the gals will change into their formal duds, and where Doc Huin will make certain that everything's ready to go for the NATO fireworks. That's also where their three embassy dates will be picking the girls up to escort them to the gala."

Gitano was silent a moment, genuinely moved. "I'm really gonna miss those three women. They've got real guts. That's why I wanted to personally drive with them over to Vence tomorrow. Out of respect."

The mobster beamed proudly. "Like I said, I've sworn that the whole world will know it was them. Rhombus. The organization that pulled off the NATO hit."

Gitano raised both his palms up. "That's all they've asked for, so that's what they'll get. I promised them. And I also made a pledge to them to use some of my fees to make sure that the four *new* women they've handpicked for the *next* version of Rhombus glide smoothly into place." While his men watched, transfixed, an uncharacteristic tear welled up in their chief's eye.

"What about the payoff, boss?" asked the high-pitched hood. "Your fees. I understand that right after the 'fireworks' tomorrow you'll be meeting up with your clients' couriers. Rienzo told me you're planning to meet them somewhere near St. Tropez. Ain't that a bit risky, boss?"

Gitano frowned. "Risky? Why?"

"Well, that's only a half-hour or so from where the NATO job in Cannes is going to take place." Gitano's man shrugged, apologetically. "I don't mean to tell you your business, Mr. Gitano, but Tropez is darn close to Cannes. And from what we expect tomorrow, every cop and government agency, including the US Secret Service, the FBI and the Sûreté of France will be scouring the entire area right after the dust clears. It'll probably be the biggest manhunt in history. There's no way you, a known gangster like us, would escape *that* wide a dragnet."

Carmine Gitano sneered as he answered. "All those government and police scum, including the French Coast Guard, will be looking for suspects above the sea - not *under* it." The Mafioso grinned. "As soon as we get final word on the NATO explosion, and the subsequent carnage, I, along with the North Korean and Iranian paymasters, will escape in my submarine swiftly and secretly. After I drop the girls off in Vence, my Caddy limo will drive me to meet our clients at a deserted beach locale on the south shore of Henri Provence."

Carmine cleared his throat and added, "Immediately after the blasts and resulting destruction have been confirmed, a speed boat will whisk us out to the sub, where we'll secretly board her. Far away from any public sighting areas. That whole south shore area is permanently deserted."

Gitano shrugged unconcernedly as he envisioned it all. "There might be a few crazy rumors of something strange in the water, but no one will know who and what it was *really* all about. Not unless a naval destroyer armed with depth charges happens to be stationed directly off the extensive Côte d'Azur coast. And last time I looked, there weren't many destroyers patrolling the chic Riviera resorts and nude beaches."

The gangsters all laughed loudly as Carmine further explained, "My submarine will meet up with Zephyr late that evening. And from there my yacht will speed me away to parts unknown."

Don Gitano excitedly rubbed his hands together and smiled widely. "Now, as for the billion-dollar fee. I've already received some of it. And confidential Swiss bank arrangements have been put into motion for the balance. Several checks, to be made out to various anonymous holding companies. It's just awaiting our clients' fiduciary e-mail 'okay' and code word. That will be done electronically once we're back onboard the Zephyr."

The Mafioso gloated confidently. "Don't worry, fellas. There won't be any problems with the money. In fact, our two customers, Iran and North Korea, have already discussed some other ventures with me." Gitano pounded his barreled chest arrogantly. "So, when all is said and done tomorrow, I'm gonna pull off the *biggest* coup in the annals of organized crime."

Seven could hear Gitano's men applauding their chief. The mob king pompously acknowledged their applause. "Thank you, boys. And don't forget – sizable bonuses are in store for you guys, too. Good money, and well-earned satisfaction for your parts in various things." He gestured toward them. "You boys should be real proud. After all, it ain't every day that a small pack of 'wise guys' knock off all the world leaders in one shot!"

As more exuberance and applause ensued, Carmine Gitano ended his impromptu garage meeting. "Well guys, it's almost time for Nalco's hit on Doreen, so I gotta go." He looked over at his motley crew. "Try to get some rest, if you can, fellas. Tomorrow's gonna be a busy day." And with that, *Don* Gitano and his team exited the garage, going out the same side door from which they'd entered.

Still scrunched in the Jaguar's trunk, Seven was stunned by what he'd just overheard. He twisted his body in a startled reflex reaction. So, *that* was the score! What Doreen had meant about Gitano's 'important business deal', the one she thought she'd soon be dying for. It was also how the Rhombus women fit into the picture and why they'd needed Ambassador Dawson's NATO papers. These fanatical females, minus the doomed Doreen, were planning to blow up several leaders of the free world in a crazed suicide mission. Doing it simply to bolster their warped legacy.

Yet how were they possibly going to get away with it when the tightest security on the planet would be in place at tomorrow night's NATO gala?

As Christopher Seven continued asking himself that question, over and over and over again, he was somehow certain that Carmine Gitano, along with the women of Rhombus, had a plausible way to actually pull it off!

Chapter 38

'What on Earth do you mean?'

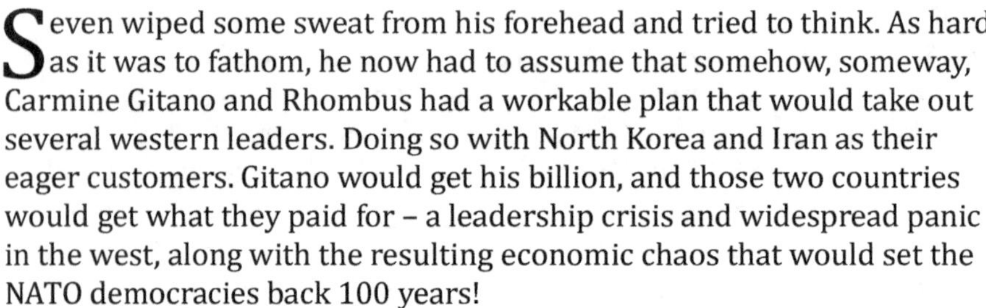

Seven wiped some sweat from his forehead and tried to think. As hard as it was to fathom, he now had to assume that somehow, someway, Carmine Gitano and Rhombus had a workable plan that would take out several western leaders. Doing so with North Korea and Iran as their eager customers. Gitano would get his billion, and those two countries would get what they paid for – a leadership crisis and widespread panic in the west, along with the resulting economic chaos that would set the NATO democracies back 100 years!

The Super Stud quickly flipped over his cellphone and looked for a signal. As he feared, there was none. Doreen had been wrong about their smart phones continuing to work here, erroneously assuming that her cell, and any others here in the villa, would remain functioning like her phone did earlier that morning. Knowing Gitano's propensity for seclusion when the stakes were this high, the Mafioso had undoubtedly put out the word to begin blocking all inside and outside communication. The mob chieftain had undoubtedly given orders to jam any transmissions or cellphone reception.

The G5 agent sighed, aware that the odds of his escaping from Carmine's château fortress were slim. Consequently, it might be best to try to do something here and now, something to hinder the frightening plans he'd just overheard. Yet, what could he do or attempt at this point? Other than perhaps getting hold of a stray weapon and trying to kill Carmine Gitano or the Rhombus threesome, in a suicide charge. Seven frowned glumly, knowing that wasn't realistic. No...short of escaping to warn Interpol, hopefully with the condemned Doreen by his side, there was really nothing the G5 operative could think of doing.

But then, Seven remembered Gitano's boasting about the car bomb. The VBIED timed explosive was attached under the white Lincoln Town Car right here in the garage! Seven had been schooled in similar bomb weaponry, working with a variety of limpet mines and timed explosives during a munitions course at the FBI Academy in Quantico.

Thinking on it, a germ of an idea slowly came to him. If he could somehow switch the white car's attached bomb and plant it under the other vehicle, Gitano's personal black Cadillac limo, conceivably Carmine and the Rhombus women might be eliminated instead of the visiting rival mobsters. Yet, wouldn't Gitano's goon check the Lincoln Town Car again... to make sure the explosive was still armed and ready before it left with the Carpi gang tomorrow? Probably not. Gitano himself had decreed that rechecking the car bomb was no longer an option. Not with the intended victims milling about the villa. Besides, Carmine's explosives expert had just checked on the white Town Car's bomb for a third and final time.

No, Seven assured himself. *With any luck, they wouldn't be checking under the white limo anymore.* Pondering the situation, Seven decided it just might work. In any case, switching the bomb from one limo to the other was all he could conjure up at this juncture.

The Super Stud pulled the inside safety release and jumped out of the Jaguar's trunk. Pausing to stretch his aching bones, he glanced around the dimly lit garage. It was now barely illuminated by a single amber nightlight, making it difficult to see anything at all. At least the garage had no windows, so no one on the outside could look in on him. Seven quickly made his way back inside the supply closet, walking over to a large set of shelves lined with auto parts and accessories. Grabbing a small tool kit and a few larger utensils from the top shelf, he hurriedly approached Gitano's two limousines and nimbly slid under the white Lincoln.

Taking the small but powerful penlight that was attached to his pocket keychain, Seven shined it directly onto the limo's undercarriage, franticly searching for the VBIED bomb. Even knowing what he was looking for, it still took him a few minutes to actually locate the explosive. Gitano's man had done an excellent job of camouflaging it. The bomb was expertly hidden beneath the vehicle, totally covered with thick black grease. The X14 bomb, compact, yet extremely powerful, was tightly attached to the middle of the car via two powerful magnets. It was additionally fastened to the Lincoln by six large screwed-in bolts. Gitano's lackey had done a good job.

Hoping that one of the five wrenches in the tool kit would work, the G5 agent carefully began trying each of them. Momentarily panicking when none of the first four wrenches fit the bolts, he finally relaxed when the last wrench, the largest one, ultimately worked. After unscrewing the six bolts, it still took all of Seven's strength, plus the aid of a small crowbar, to pry the powerfully magnetized bomb from under the white car. He grabbed the explosive firmly in his arms, slid out from beneath the white Lincoln Town Car and then slithered under Gitano's black Caddy.

Just as Christopher Seven situated himself underneath the black Cadillac limo, he heard the garage's small side door open again. Someone was entering the area! The Super Stud had momentarily forgotten about the afternoon security check that Doreen had warned him about. Seven froze, praying he wouldn't be noticed underneath the Caddy by the two guards now inside the blackened garage. Would the darkness of the garage help hide him? Or would they turn on the central overhead light?

One of them, the lead man, turned on his flashlight and had a quick look around, thankfully focusing mainly on the back area walls and ceiling. Satisfied that all was satisfactory, and knowing that Gitano's conference guards had undoubtedly checked out the garage less than an hour ago, he called out to his sidekick standing by the door. "The garage checks out fine, Bill. Figured it'd be safe with the boss just meeting in here. I still wanted to quickly check, though."

"I understand," agreed Bill. "But it beats me why Mario didn't want the guard dogs patrolling today and evening. Guess it was the Carpi group being here and all. Yet, I still say we should have used them."

"You're right, Bill."

Bill chuckled. "Those Dobermans would have loved it too. An unexpected snack of Carpi flesh and blood." The two sentries laughed loudly, switched off the flashlight, and made their exit.

Remaining motionless under the Cadillac, Christopher Seven heaved a huge sigh, thankful he hadn't been spotted. Even so, he knew he had to work fast now. Finish his task and then get out of this garage if he wanted to escape.

With the car bomb firmly in hand, Seven slid closer to the Caddy's undercarriage. Once there, he placed the explosive down on the floor and examined it methodically. Thankfully, both the explosive and its timing mechanism, a simple *Pravix* clock dial, were devices he'd studied at the FBI school. The red digital time and date setting, surprisingly uncomplicated, showed that the bomb was programmed to go off at exactly 1:00 p.m. tomorrow afternoon, just like Gitano had mentioned during his meeting. Seven toyed with resetting the time of the explosion for a bit later in the afternoon, in case there were any delays. But quickly decided he'd better not fool with it. His only worry now was still whether Gitano's goons would give the bottom of the other limo, the white Lincoln, another last-minute look-see. Reflecting on it once more, he again took solace in the fact that Carmine had adamantly ordered "no more bomb rechecks" for fear his Carpi rivals might be tipped off.

Skillfully attaching the car explosive under Gitano's private Cadillac limousine with the wrench, Seven made sure that the six thick connection bolts, along with the explosive's powerful magnets, were firmly in place. Content that the bomb's tight connection was indeed rock-solid, he next took out the rag he'd brought from the closet. This he used to redistribute some of the abundant black grease that was still on the explosive, thoroughly coating the bomb to hide it in its new home. The car bomb was now properly attached and totally hidden by the dark grease.

Nodding with satisfaction, the G5 operative grabbed the tool box, the rag, and the crowbar, and slithered out from under the black limo.

After walking the tools back to the supply area, Seven placed them exactly where he'd found them. Then, aware that escape was highly unlikely, he wiped his hands clean and ditched the black-stained rag under some trash in one of the large garbage bins. Fortunately none of the grease had gotten onto his clothing; something that might have alerted anyone apprehending him.

All tasks completed, the sweating operative rested a moment and reflected on what would happen should he be captured. As long as Gitano and his apes didn't know that Christopher Seven had eavesdropped on their impromptu garage meeting, they'd have no reason to suspect his switching the car bomb from one limo to the other. But now what? There were only *two* options...*one*: try to escape by running away outside after dark and attempt to climb over the wrought iron gate, a task that would be nearly impossible with all the security men, mobsters, and perhaps even hungry Dobermans roaming the grounds. Or...*two*: somehow sneak into the main dwelling. Even though escape from *inside* the château likewise seemed hopeless, Seven chose this second option.

Wiping some sweat from his eyes, the G5 agent was well aware that there was also Doreen to think about. He glanced down at his watch: She was scheduled to die in less than four hours! Nalco, aka *Il Strangolatore*, the vicious Mafia executioner, would soon be trudging up the chateau's lavish staircase to the main bedroom floor in order to surprise and strangle another unfortunate victim – in this case, the unsuspecting Doreen. Seven nervously looked at his watch again. If he didn't act quickly, she'd soon be dead.

Of course, he could callously forget about her and try to escape on his own. It might be easier that way; easier than trying to drag some emotional female along. After all, he'd finally obtained the information that headquarters had sent him to uncover. And as a government agent, it was now his duty to try to get away and warn NATO, and to do so as quickly as possible without regard for *any* individual's safety, including his own. Besides, Doreen was still a member of a criminal organization, one that had killed and tortured many times. As such, perhaps she deserved what she got.

Yet, deep down, Christopher Seven realized he couldn't walk out on her. Doreen had twice saved him from harm's way, and he owed her the same chance. If he deserted her now, the Super Stud knew he'd never be able to live with himself. Come what may, he'd at least have to try and warn Doreen. After that, it was up to her.

There was also another factor to consider now...getting away from this garage and his car bomb switch. That was the most important objective of all. If he was eventually going to be caught, it would be crucial that he be apprehended *away* from the garage so as not to draw any suspicions about his sabotage of the limousine or his overhearing *Don Carmine's* plans. For that reason alone, Doreen's bedroom was a better place to be apprehended than here.

Maybe I can find her, the G5 agent speculated. *If so, she might be aware of somewhere to hide inside this huge mansion. Or know a seldom-*

used exit that I haven't counted on. Then, come nightfall, we can escape together. It's worth a try, and I owe her the chance of rescue, anyway. As he reflected on all of this, the sound of dogs barking grew louder and nearer. It was time to go!

Seven turned on his pocket-sized flashlight and cautiously made his way toward the side door at the far end of the garage. Desperately trying to recall Doreen's sketchy directions, he silently evoked them again: *That side door leads inside the house through the servant's quarters. Hardly anyone's around now as Carmine only has a small, skeleton staff working here this week. My bedroom is right above the garage, just up the first staircase.*

Slowly opening the garage's side door to enter the house, the Super Stud cringed at the creaking noise it made. He waited a moment, relieved to hear nothing stir inside the massive dwelling. He gently closed the door, bringing about another annoying creak, this one much softer.

Carefully creeping inside the villa, Seven began making his way down a dark, narrow passageway, guided by a few tiny nightlights plugged in along the wall. He quickly arrived at a small kitchen area, one probably used by the servants to prepare their own meals. Halting a moment, he shined his penlight to the right and spotted a circular stairway at the end of a short corridor. Hopefully these were the stairs Doreen had mentioned. Readying himself to move toward them, he stepped out of the kitchen into the small vestibule. Suddenly he heard a loud noise behind him, the distinct sound of somebody working in the kitchen! Startled, he stopped dead in his tracks, half-expecting to be discovered at any moment.

Freezing against the wall, Seven waited a few seconds, his ears desperately trying to determine where this noise was coming from. *Yes, there it was again, a dull, clunking, hollow sound. Perhaps someone was filling a plastic cup or a pitcher. Were they working by the kitchen sink?* Still motionless, the G5 agent tried to fight off his mounting panic.

His heart racing, Seven slowly took a few steps back and peered back into the kitchen. When he did, his taut muscles immediately relaxed as he spotted the source of the harmless noise. The kitchen's fancy Sub-Zero refrigerator had an automatic icemaker. The rumbling clunk he'd heard was the sound of fresh ice cubes falling into their inside container. The relieved operative smiled grimly at his overreaction. Running his hands through his hair to release some of the tension, he swiftly made his way over to the stairs.

Now for the tough part, Seven reflected. *Any sound while I'm walking up these stairs, and one of the servants, guards, or houseguests is bound to come running from their room, screaming that there's an intruder about.*

Fortunately, as he tiptoed up the stairs, no such alarm ensued and no one was about. Arriving at the second floor without incident, and aided by the remaining sunshine streaming through the half-opened drapes, Seven promptly spotted his main objective; a closed bedroom door with the 'Blue Room' nameplate on it.

Standing just outside Doreen's suite, the G5 operative wasn't sure how to proceed next. If he just barged in and surprised her, she might let out a reflex scream. Yet, if he knocked on the door, his knock might be heard by someone resting nearby; perhaps one of her Rhombus 'sisters.' Mulling over both choices, Seven finally tapped softly on the outside of the door, pondering for just a nightmarish moment that one of Gitano's goons would answer and ambush him with a gun or a stiletto. Surprisingly, nothing at all happened. There was absolutely no response to his tapping. *Now what?* Seven decided to give the door a louder second knock.

This time he was successful. The door slowly opened, and there, smiling, and clad only in a revealing pink nightshirt, was Doreen. She looked lovely, not at all concerned about the deadly fate awaiting her. Grinning incongruously, she put a finger up to her lips to signify silence, relocked the door, and motioned him in.

Following her directions, Seven was instantly met with a passionate kiss, followed by Doreen's whispering, "Welcome, my love. I was worried for you. I tried to call your cellphone but couldn't get any signal. I don't understand. That phone you gave me was working fine this morning."

"I know," Seven replied, in a similarly quiet voice. "Carmine's apparently blocked all cell reception from this point on. Probably the house phones, too."

Doreen picked up the room phone by her bed and listened. "Yep, dead as a doornail." She smiled. "Oh, well, no need for phones any more. Everything's all right now that you're here."

The Super Stud shook his head, warily. "I wouldn't say that, Doreen. There's definite danger about. Especially for *you.*"

Seven hesitated a moment, now faced with the dilemma of not revealing how he'd heard the news of her pending execution. Doreen, after all, was still an enemy agent, and the Super Stud was firmly resolved not to tell her anything about the car bomb switch. Or even mention all that he'd learned via his eavesdropping on Gitano's garage conference.

Instead, he deceptively informed, "While I was hiding in the Jag's trunk, those two patrolling guards came into the garage for their quick security check. The inspection you warned me about. I overheard one of the guards emphatically say that Gitano had given Nalco firm instructions to eliminate you. Nalco's been ordered to do so any time now. That's why I came up for you as fast as I could, despite the danger. We've got to scram, immediately. Get you out of here for good, like we talked about. Of course, I'll have to know all the details later on if I'm going to be of any help to you."

Seven's face reddened slightly, yet he felt no remorse about continuing to use her. She was still one of his assigned targets and, as such, had to be exploited to the fullest. He shrugged his shoulders in staged confusion and declared, "I hope *you* know what the heck's going on around here, Doreen, 'cause I certainly *don't.* Although, it seems something big is happening with all these hoods around."

Knowing they'd first have to get away if there was any chance of preventing the NATO carnage, Seven promptly asked, "I was also hoping you might know of an emergency exit or secret passageway in this old barn. Some undiscovered nook for us to hide in before we try escaping later on. Lots of these old French mansions have them. Unexplored cubbyholes or attics that even the owners aren't familiar with."

Doreen threw her arms around him, seemingly more pleased with his coming back for her than worried about the danger. "No one's ever loved me that much, Chris. To risk his life for me."

"Listen, Doreen, it's not that I..."

She put her fingers over his lips and admonished, "Hush, my darling. Now that I know how much you love me, I want to give up *everything* for you." Doreen shook her head. "And to think, before I met you, my priorities were such that I was perfectly willing to blow myself up with a suicide bomb. I know it seems crazy or reckless but it's true." An expression of relief came over her pretty face. "I'll tell you all about it later."

Seven gave her another bewildered look of faked shock and confusion. "What in the *world* are you talking about, Doreen? *Suicide* bombings?"

"Not now, Chris. I'll explain it once we get out of here. But don't worry about Nalco or Carmine. Like I've told you before, Terry would *never* let that happen. It's the most sacred pledge between us four girls. A lifetime oath we've taken to protect each other no matter *what*! Trust me, none of us would *ever* break it!"

Doreen's eyes began blazing with an odd hue, as if she'd just been put into a strange trance. Staring at the far wall, she stridently informed, "That part of our sisterhood will *always* be sacrosanct. Especially to Terry. She'll get us out of this mess. You'll see!"

Grimacing angrily, Seven walked over and shook her shoulders, desperately trying to bring her to her senses. "How can you be so naïve, so *stupid*, Doreen?" He frowned at her incredulously and forcefully scolded, "*None* of them can be trusted! *Least* of all, Terry. She's undoubtedly in on the plot to kill you, along with your other so-called sisters. I don't care *what* type of bond you think you have with them. Those three are in on the execution plans."

He again grabbed her shoulders and shook her, much harder this time. "You've got to believe me, Doreen. We have to get out of here – *now!*"

Finally coming out of her dreamy stupor, Doreen's face reddened with perplexed embarrassment. Then, as if her eyes and mind had at last been opened, she contritely informed, "I'm afraid it's too late for that, Chris."

"*Too late*? What on Earth do you mean?"

Before she could answer, Seven heard the sound of footsteps approaching, followed by the jingle of a metal key being put into the old-fashioned style keyhole of Doreen's bedroom door.

Christopher Seven nervously looked over and saw the room's previously locked doorknob begin to turn. Someone was about to enter!

Chapter 39

'Two Things'

T he bedroom door opened widely. Standing there with a smirk on her face was Terry, the iniquitous Rhombus leader. She was holding a small revolver in her right hand and greeted Seven icily. "Hello, friend. Fancy meeting you here." Pushing the door closed with her left arm, she strolled to the center of the bedroom. Still exasperated with Doreen, who had obviously orchestrated this, the stunned Christopher Seven didn't reply.

Situated between Seven and Terry, and showing little, if any concern, Doreen turned to face Seven. "Don't be upset, Chris. A short while ago, Terry and I had a heart-to-heart talk in her room. I explained that you and I were in love with each other and that we were hoping to escape from here later tonight. Like I assured you, Terry reaffirmed that our Rhombus pledge of protection is still binding between us. It stands supreme above everything else. We four are sworn to defend each other to the very end. No matter *what.* Knowing our hallowed mantra on this, I've asked Terry to help us get away. She agreed – one pledged sister to another."

"You *what?*" exclaimed the still seething Super Stud. "You don't actually think you can trust her? Or those other 'sisters' of yours?"

"Of course I can trust them," Doreen confidently countered. "There's an unquestioned vow of protection between us. Our most solemn oath. Terry would never let Nalco, or Carmine, or *anyone* harm me. Nor would Anita or Suzanne." She smiled at her leader. "Would they, Terr?"

Terry stared up at the ceiling a moment, and then, indifferently, snapped, "Let's forget all that *oath* stuff for the moment, Doreen. I want to talk to Handsome here. I need to find out what he knows and what he doesn't know. And whether he's with the cops or working for some rival mob family."

Walking over to the opposite end of the bedroom, Terry cocked her revolver. She kept it pointed at Seven and Doreen while adding, "Yet, surely you must know, Doreen. If you gave away any Rhombus secrets, you've technically forfeited your rights to vowed protection. We'll decide later on what will become of you. In the meantime, sit down on the bed with him and tell me everything you two have been discussing. And I mean *everything.*"

Doreen was quick and explicit with her answer. "I've never told him anything about our upcoming plans," she assured Terry. "Like I told you this morning, I thought it'd be safer for him that way. We only spoke of getting away, and living together without all the bedlam and danger here."

That's correct" echoed Seven. "Whatever plans or secrets you're worried about mean nothing to me. I don't want to know or hear anything about them. I came here only to get Doreen. We only spoke of our future."

"Okay, mister," demanded Terry, her voice confident and businesslike. "Then who *are* you working for? And exactly *when* did you get to this villa? Doreen was a bit vague with some of the details."

The G5 operative smiled amiably, trying to quell some of the tension in the room, while contemplating how he could jump Terry and get hold of her gun. "I'm not working for anyone. I've been all through this with you before, Terry. I'm not connected to any rival mobs and I'm certainly *not* a cop. "He chuckled at the accusation. "Look, it's quite simple. Doreen and I have fallen in love, and we've decided to run off together. With Carmine's crazed jealousy, and his paranoia about my seeing Doreen, what else could I do…other than sneaking in here to take her away?"

Christopher Seven turned his head away from Terry's view a moment and signaled Doreen with two winks of his left eye. She promptly picked up on his blinking signal *not* to correct anything he was about to say.

"Well," Seven continued, "knowing I wanted to sneak Doreen away with me, once escape seemed feasible, I slipped into Gitano's villa last

night. It wasn't easy with all these rival gangsters being here. Or with Carmine's Dobermans running around the area. Because of all that activity, I had to hide up here for a while. Doreen had thankfully told me her room number and location, as our smartphones couldn't get a signal." The agent shrugged his shoulders. "Tonight was going to be our getaway, as there wasn't supposed to be many servants milling around. Only a skeletal staff. So we planned to leave here sometime after two in the morning."

"Is all that true, Doreen?" demanded Terry. "Your life and his may depend on it."

"Yes, it's the truth, Terry. Like he said, Chris has been in my room and hasn't left it. And we've had no phones since then. In any case, our exit hour was later tonight."

"Why didn't you tell me he was here, Doreen?" Terry asked.

"Because I wanted time with him *alone.* Time to discuss everything, including if I should go or stay here and be loyal to the Rhombus mission. Believe it or not, it wasn't an easy choice either way."

"Oh, sure," sneered Terry. She gestured toward Seven and nodded her head.

Terry waved her revolver at Seven menacingly. "You know what I think, pretty boy? I think you've been gunning for us right from the start. Carmine included. You're either doing it for the Italian police or for one of the other mob families. Most likely Carpi's. Yet, whichever it is doesn't matter now. You're a dead man, friend. Doreen should have kept quiet about your plans when she came to see me before. Although I know firsthand that she has trouble keeping her big mouth shut. That's why she'll have to go, too, Rhombus or no Rhombus."

For the first time since Terry had entered the bedroom, Doreen began to worry she'd been duped and betrayed by her former three partners. Doreen's face reddened with shame and disgust as she finally comprehended what a fool she'd been. Despite Terry's sisterly promises and assurances of just a short while ago, her Rhombus leader was acting quite differently now. All those guarantees about preventing anyone from ever harming a fellow sister had obviously been bogus, along with Terry's steadfast assurances to help them get away tonight. It was all a pack of lies!

Doreen lowered her head dejectedly, as the situation became clearer. Rhombus, the secret society for which she'd thrown her life away to honor and defend, was a complete sham. She looked over at Seven with a stunned, defeated expression.

Seven looked down at the floor, trying to avoid Doreen's worried eyes. He then looked back at Terry who continued her tirade. "When Doreen came to me with her tearful plea for help, she said she might have to tell you a few details about us. Some hogwash about it being an 'obligation of love' to inform you about her past sins. That traitorous action sealed the deal, Seven. You'll both have to die now."

"But, Terry," Doreen implored, "you gave me your solemn word as a Rhombus sister that you'd..."

Terry rushed over to the bed and smacked Doreen hard across the face. "Shut up, you filthy turncoat! It's too late for promises and vows. You don't deserve them anyway. You've violated everything we stand for by bringing this man here. Or intending to tell him our secrets." Terry hissed with hatred. "You're not worthy of mercy or protection. Your life means nothing to me anymore. Or to Rhombus. You've become a dangerous millstone around our necks. Your mother would have been ashamed of you!"

She slapped Doreen again and again, this time much harder. Seven winced at the blows as Terry screeched, "We suspected you'd betray us someday, and you almost did."

Still holding the gun in readiness, Terry stepped back a few steps and shrieked, "You should *never* have been part of Rhombus! If it hadn't been for your mother, you'd never have been in. I should have eliminated you long ago. I would have if we weren't all scheduled for this upcoming final mission. It figures you'd back out of that, too. Oh, well. It's better you *won't* be coming with us tomorrow. Better you die here tonight instead. You don't deserve the honor of being part of Rhombus's most notable triumph anyhow."

Seven, noting the tears of disbelief in Doreen's eyes and the crazed expression on Terry's face, knew the situation was dire. Yet how could he wrestle the revolver away without him or Doreen being shot? As he thought on it, the now unlocked bedroom door suddenly banged open again. In marched Anita, Suzanne, and Dr. Huin, the Korean plastic surgeon.

Terry briefly glanced at the three of them, still keeping her focus and gun on Doreen and Seven. "Just in time, folks," Terry greeted. "Told you I'd have a little show for you today. I'm about to put several bullets into Handsome here. Starting with two shots right between his legs."

Anita and Suzanne giggled excitedly as Terry raised her gun. Knowing there were only seconds left, Seven decided to try one last gambit. "Before you start shooting," he countered, "I think all of you ought to know what I can offer you. Perhaps you'd like to hear about it. I think you'll agree it's a lot better than all this mob garbage."

The three Rhombus women showed expressions of amused curiosity rather than actual consideration. "Well," smirked Suzanne as she winked at Terry. "Let's hear it, Handsome."

Hoping for a miracle, Christopher Seven began his pitch. "I'm aware who Carmine Gitano is and that all of you may have done some illicit work for him. So, as I was going to inform Doreen later tonight, I have some excellent contacts with the U.S. Justice Department via a close relative who works there. More specifically, my contact runs the department's *witness-protection* program. I'm sure they'd give each of you a full pardon, without many strings attached. This in exchange for inside information on the mob. Past and present details about your underworld connections, for instance. I enquired about doing this for Doreen, without going into specifics or names, of course. And the initial vibes I got back were quite positive. I'm sure they'd work with all four of you. And with you too, Doctor."

Seven looked them straight in the eyes and asked, "So, how about it, ladies? The chance for a new life and a new future like other women your age. That's a lot better than risking your lives for some Mafia gambit."

Instead of any interest, Seven's offer was met with uproarious laughter. "Us like *other* women?" hooted Terry. "I guess you don't get it, friend. We're not *like* other women. Or other men, for that matter. We're the best there is!"

Terry turned toward Seven and declared, "I guess your sweetie pie, Doreen, didn't tell you, Handsome. Anita, Suz, and I are going to die tomorrow night. In a suicide *gambit* as you called it. And when we die tomorrow night, so will every major NATO leader. Our legacy will surpass all of the other assassins. All the misunderstood giants of our genre. Oswald, bin Laden, Timothy McVeigh, Atta. They'll only be insignificant footnotes compared to us!"

Anita and Suz triumphantly raised their clenched fists in agreement. It was obvious that they also saw tomorrow's explosive finale as a path to immortality, much like Mideast fanatics. More troubling to Seven, however, was the fact that all of them seemed certain that their NATO strategy was workable. Yet how could it be done with the security experts of half the free world inspecting everyone at the door *before* the gala began? Doing so with a plethora of new high-tech screening machines. And with fortification vehicles surrounding the entire banquet hall.

The Super Stud hastily searched his memory for anything he could remember about NATO's international security procedures. Especially whenever one of their functions was being attended by a sitting U.S. president. NATO security squadrons, along with the U.S. Secret Service, would definitely be using the latest WG IS7858 x-ray scanners at every entrance and exit. And probably some new defense wrinkles added as well.

Seven scratched his forehead and continued reflecting on NATO's security. There would undoubtedly be the maximum inspections of everyone arriving, of course, along with rigid pre-event background checks on some of the guests. Especially if anyone had something 'iffy' on their record. Though knowing the Rhombus machine, they'd probably be completely clean with no record at all. Even G5 and the CIA had no names or pertinent background on them.

Seven silently shook his head. *Could Rhombus have found a chink in NATO's armor via Ambassador Dawson's missing papers?* The Super Stud decided to try and bait Terry into talking more about it. And then, somehow try to escape and help prevent it. After all, that was the sworn duty of every secret agent, no matter how dire the situation.

"Okay, girls," laughed Seven, with all the scorn he could muster. "Play your little game of cowboys and Indians tomorrow night. Your juvenile scheme will *never* work. Every two-bit assassin on the planet has fantasized about taking out some VIP world leader. At least I'll go to my grave knowing your insane amateur theatrics will be an embarrassing flop. You three fools actually killing the president? It's laughable."

Seven's strategy worked immediately. Goaded into rebuffing him, Terry brazenly responded, "You just don't understand, do you buster? We're good, *really* good. So before I take care of your manhood, and then your life, it will amuse me to explain just *how* good we really are. This way you'll die knowing that we *will* succeed."

Anita angrily shook her head. "No, Terry!" she barked. "Just kill him and be done with it. Why give this loser any details?"

"'Cause I *want* to," insisted Terry. "If I don't, this arrogant fool will die thinking he's right. I want him to know that Rhombus *never* fails!"

With her pistol still trained on Seven and Doreen, Terry began her boastful spiel. "We know they'll be plenty of security procedures in place at tomorrow night's NATO gala. We're familiar with most of them thanks to a certain deceased ambassador's briefcase. Then, more recently, we learned of some additional security measures that will be in place at tomorrow's NATO dinner."

"I don't believe it," scoffed Seven with contrived skepticism. "*What* details? *What* ambassador? "

Terry simply ignored him and added, "We're now aware of the VIP seating arrangements. And the fact that the five world leaders will be sitting in a separate, cordoned-off area. Using the ambassador's personal notes, we likewise learned that there'll be a special Plexiglas wall, five inches thick, surrounding the world leader's section. In essence, there'll be two separate rooms. One for the guests to dine in and gawk, and the other through which the NATO leaders can be viewed. Sitting safely protected behind a mammoth, Plexiglas shield. The guests will be able to see the bigwig politicos, and hear their short speeches, without being allowed to touch or mingle with them. Those precautions will help make the event planners feel safe."

Terry glanced over at her two cohorts, who likewise seemed to be warming up to putting the cocky Christopher Seven in his place. She smiled at them and further explained, "All five world leaders, including the president, will be wearing specially developed bulletproof vests under their tux jackets, vests impervious to any hand-held guns, or even rifles, for that matter. But that won't be any problem for us."

Seven's face showed uncertainty so the egotistical Rhombus leader continued her boasts, "In case you're wondering how *we* four gals got the invite, our escorts for tomorrow's NATO gala are well-connected diplomatic interns whom Carmine's sources set us up with a while back. They helped us with all the diplomatic arrangements, bringing us along as their 'dates.' Willingly doing so, thanks to a severe drug habit the mob hooked them on."

Seven remained silent as Terry added, "Consequently, it wasn't very difficult getting an invitation to the dinner, provided all of our paperwork checked out okay." Terry laughed, loudly. "Now here's the *best* part of all this. Believe it or not, we four girls passed with flying colors. But that was really no surprise. Because of vigilant secrecy over the years, our *real* names and fingerprints have no notoriety or record. We're clean as a whistle under our *actual* names. Just simple farm girls from the Midwest Bible belt." She beamed, proudly. "In fact, this is the first time we've ever used our *real* names and authentic passports for a Rhombus mission. Yet, giving our names and passports was fine with us." She chuckled. "'Cause after tomorrow we'll never need them again."

Anita and Suzanne also giggled as Terry admitted, "Obviously, NATO was very thorough with security, and their standards were quite impressive. Yet there's one thing that they can't or won't check tomorrow night." Terry grinned and winked at Dr. Kim. "Or should I say *two*."

"And what could that possibly be?" asked Seven, sarcastically, still trying to prod everything out of her that he could. "Just what two things are we talking about?"

Grinning from ear to ear, Terry calmly replied, "Our breasts."

Chapter 40

Hethal

At first, Christopher Seven thought he hadn't heard correctly. Confused, he quickly asked, "Did you say your *breasts*?"

"That's right," confirmed Terry with an amused look on her face. "The shapely new breasts Dr. Huin fitted onto Suzanne, Anita, and me. Thanks to the doc's handiwork, we'll soon have more explosive power in our bosoms than what 500 suicide bombers would be able to carry. And we'll be a thousand times more lethal! Terry gestured toward the Korean plastic surgeon. "But why don't you take it from here, Doctor?"

Huin Kim bowed and began explaining, doing so in excellent English. Until now, Seven had only heard him speak in a few broken sentences.

"Yes, Mr. Seven," said Huin, "Terry is correct on all accounts. A new and very powerful chemical explosive, camouflaged and buried by silicon and human skin, will do the trick tomorrow night. I won't bore you with all the scientific details, Mr. Seven, other than to say that there's a substantial amount of highly concentrated PETN – that's Pentaerythritol tetranitrate – in Anita's, Terry's, and Suzanne's redesigned left bosoms. I've also added an innovative, top-secret ingredient as well. One that makes the PETN and other compounds undetectable in a human's body. It's a ground-breaking mixture. One that I and several of my North Korean colleagues came up with. But unlike the sporadic PETN successes various terrorists have had over the years, no humans, dogs, or machines will be able to detect my PETN presently in Rhombus's left breasts."

Huin bowed proudly, waiting for some type of acknowledgment from Seven. Disappointed when none came, he shrugged his shoulders and went on, "Their *other* breast will soon be filled with a *second* innovative and highly classified additive – *Hethal.* That's my own discovery. One I fostered some ten months ago in Pyongyang."

Dr. Kim again waited for reaction, and this time the Super Stud gave him a grudging nod. The Korean bowed back and then added, "My 'find' was a new and awesome substance, honed later by our North Korean chemical specialists to be even *more* effective."

The doctor smiled sinisterly and added, "Hethal increases the power of most chemical explosives a thousand fold. It's also undetectable on all present X-ray and body-scan apparatuses. Yet it's the unique *combination* of the two substances, Hethal mixed with PETN, which we found produces incredible, cataclysmic power. No one knows why, exactly. But we did discover that when PETN and Hethal are merged together, even in small amounts, the result is earth-shattering. A destructive explosion ensues, in some cases rivaling a nuclear blast!"

The doctor bowed once more, causing Seven to frown at Kim's continual theatrics. Ignoring the frown, the Korean gleefully continued, "To facilitate the eventual joining of these compounds, we'll use two separate sacs made up from each girl's own skin. By using the actual skin of the carrier, these pouches will be imperceptible to any body scanners. Nor will they be seen on the latest X-ray apparatuses, even the newest devices like the 355 X-ray prototypes, the ones the late Ambassador's notes said NATO will be using tomorrow. We've practiced and worked with all of them, and they've revealed nothing.

Seven felt he better say something to keep this Korean quack talking. "Are you *sure* they'll be undetectable, doc?"

"Absolutely. We've done several tests with all those new scan machines that NATO now uses and nothing showed up. Case closed! My surgery will *not* be detected. Not unless each woman attending the dinner is subjected to a long and thorough strip-search. And I doubt that will occur at a festive banquet, with all the ladies dressed in their finest."

Kim again resumed his bragging, "I said two *separate* pouches are needed to hold the chemicals, Mr. Seven. That's because PETN and Hethal are devastatingly volatile when mixed together. And as I've explained, when combined together, their destructive energy is colossal!"

Christopher Seven, now sweating profusely, was beginning to understand why Terry and her cohorts were so confident. Spellbound, the G5 agent listened closely as Kim explained more.

"The basic idea of surgically hiding explosives inside a human body has been attempted before. It was last tried in a few unproductive terrorist attacks in Pakistan and Syria. The results were disappointing. Al-Qaeda and ISIS specialists are working diligently to perfect it. But thus far nothing has been powerful enough to do any serious carnage. Nor has the Taliban, or any other terror organization, been able to conceal explosives very well in human body cavities."

The Korean raised his arms in triumph, blissfully trumpeting his achievement. "But not so with *my* designs. And *my* newfound chemical! The colossal power of my merged compounds will be more deadly and awesome than any terror bomb that's ever been used! Like Terry rightly said – a *thousand* times more powerful. Plus, I've developed a truly non-detectable way to link the two elements."

Terry held up her hand, halting Kim's dissertation. "Sorry, doc, but I noticed Doreen trying to edge away from Lover Boy toward the end of the bed." Terry waved her pistol menacingly and ordered, "You better stay put, sweetie. Or Handsome here is going to die a few minutes earlier than planned." Doreen meekly nodded and slid back, as Dr. Kim resumed.

"Let's see, where was I, Mr. Seven? Oh, yes. How we'll join the two compounds, PETN and Hethal. That's always been the snag. And why Mr. Gitano and his associates began searching for someone who might have the answer. Through his international and Mafia links, Carmine eventually found me, Dr. Huin Kim, renowned plastic surgeon of North Korea. I assured him that I would find a way to do it. For a huge fee, of course." The Korean chuckled, merrily.

Beaming with pride, the wily plastic surgeon leaned back against the wall and admitted, "Believe it or not, Mr. Seven, once I hit on my unique sac design, the solution to joining any two chemicals was fairly straightforward. The three Rhombus women, via my recent breast surgery, now have slightly larger bosoms, equipped with an expandable transparent sac located between their breasts. There's also a minuscule diaphanous surgical string in the middle of their new silicon bosoms. It's well hidden by a piece of their own flesh, which I likewise grafted onto them. This way, nothing unusual will show up on any body scanners. From what we've learned from our 'sources,' those machines can only pick up *non-human* oddities."

Seven opened his eyes wider, showing feigned interest and hoping to buy some more time.

"In any event," Dr. Kim informed, "this strip of thin flesh on their breasts can be pulled away by one strong tug. Easily done in any bathroom stall or locked powder room. Pulling away the concealing flesh covering will reveal my 'see-through' human surgical string, as well as the expandable empty sac. A brief feeling of pain, but necessary."

The Korean grinned, exposing several missing teeth. "Anyway," he added, "when the string is firmly yanked, this will allow the contents of their two augmented breasts to flow together into *one* internal compartment which is the middle surgical sac I've created. It's somewhat similar to a Lap-Ban pocket, similar to saline solution being seeped into a lap-ban ring. More importantly, it's undetectable by any human, dog, or machine."

The Super Stud reluctantly nodded his head as the wild-eyed surgeon assured, "Like I mentioned, all of these steps can be done quickly, easily, and simultaneously, shortly after the world leaders arrive and take their seats behind the Plexiglas wall and begin their speeches. Once the girls are inside, they'll pull off their flesh strips, releasing the two chemicals into one common sac. The two compounds will finally be united and that will be that. Some five minutes later – *bam!* Death will come instantly to the Rhombus girls and to everyone else there. Including the heads of the west's most important nations.

Dr. Kim giggled with glee as the stunned Seven merely kept listening to him. "Everything and everyone in the building, and probably several surrounding buildings as well, will be blown to kingdom come. Including the five leaders of the free world."

The Korean made a throw-away gesture with his left hand and grinned. "Poof! Just like that. Nothing will be left standing and no one will be alive. Our professionals said that one recent experimental blast in Sinuiju measured more strength than a small nuclear device being detonated. That may be a slight exaggeration, but it will certainly obliterate the entire banquet hall and all of its occupants."

Anita and Suzanne giggled delightedly as Dr. Kim concluded. "The beauty of my surgery is in the minuteness and concealment of everything. No present security scanning machine can pick it up, and even a methodical strip-search wouldn't necessarily reveal anything. Unless the searcher knew *exactly* what to look for. Or unless there was going to be a very lengthy and painstaking body exam, using magnifying glasses, on every blue-blood attendee."

Dr. Kim gloated with confidence. "And, thanks to the protocol information provided by the dead ambassador's attaché papers, we know that *won't* be the case tomorrow evening. No one expects these lovely females to go through a lengthy and humiliating process of completely disrobing. Not on the most gala night of their lives. As Terry stated, NATO will depend on their pre-screening, and on the high-tech bulletproof vests the world leaders will wear under their formal shirts. And most of all, they'll rely on the thick Plexiglas wall separating the attendees from the five world leaders."

With escape always on his mind, Christopher Seven made mental notes of everything he was hearing as Dr. Kim ended his talk.

"Perhaps one of the event's security screeners might notice that my three women have had some sort of breast enlargement operation. But that type of body enhancement is quite prevalent nowadays. Kim chuckled again. "And as for guard dogs sniffing out something. Both chemicals I've used have been treated by a new process Iran developed called *sinusoptis.* It renders most compounds, including ours, free of any chemical or explosive scents. Not one dog in our countless tests could detect anything."

Dr. Huin Kim again raised his arms in exultation. "There you have it, Christopher Seven. I assure you. It won't fail. My handiwork and my chemicals are odorless, colorless, imperceptible, and undetectable. The resulting chemical fusion I've designed will bring about three catastrophic explosions – explosions that will shake the entire world!"

So, Seven mused. *These lunatics and their Mafia benefactor really do have a workable scheme.*

His thoughts were cut short by Terry, "The doc is spot-on, Handsome. We *are* going to shake the world. From tomorrow on, the glorious name of *Rhombus* will live forever!"

The Korean plastic surgeon bowed respectfully toward Suzanne, Terry, and Anita and finally finished up. "Naturally, for safety's sake, I won't add the second compound, the Hethal, until sometime late tomorrow afternoon. I'll do that at the Vence hotel just before the three girls head over to the NATO gala. We certainly don't want any inadvertent or premature fireworks going off. For example – if one of the Rhombus women had *both* compounds inside their new breasts now, and then somehow accidentally pulled the connecting string, say in their sleep – it would literally blow this villa, and a few neighboring buildings, into smithereens. And I doubt Carmine would like that very much."

Huin giggled, visualizing the scenario. "Just one such explosion is powerful enough to take out this whole mansion, Mr. Seven. Imagine what *three* will do at the NATO dinner. When all three bosom explosions go off *simultaneously*, it will produce a truly earth-shattering blast!"

Terry glared directly at Seven and pumped her fist, triumphantly. "So, take *that* to your grave, pal! The knowledge that our plot will work perfectly." She paused a moment, waiting for Seven's admission. When none came she added, "And as for our being *lunatics*, as you've called us, the same thing was said about Da Vinci, Michelangelo, Attila, and Napoleon. Artists in their respective fields like we were in ours!"

Tired of talking now, Terry pointed her gun between Seven's legs and declared, "And now, Lover Boy, our little chat has come to an end. Just like your life. It's time for you to start screaming in agony once I shoot off your manhood."

Panting with a sadistic sneer, she excitedly exclaimed, "And then, after we enjoy watching you howl on the floor a few minutes – it'll be time for you to die!"

Chapter 41

'Something I Cherish More'

Watching helplessly as the chuckling Terry aimed her revolver, Christopher Seven wasn't sure if she was pointing her pistol at his crotch or merely preparing to shoot him in the heart to end things quickly. In either case, the G5 agent knew there was no time to lose. His only chance now was to drop to the floor, roll over and plow into her, hopefully knocking her gun away. Maybe he could then somehow get his hands on it in the resulting chaos. The Super Stud knew his plan didn't have much of a chance, yet it was the only maneuver left to him.

But then, just as Terry cocked the revolver and put her finger on the trigger, Doreen, who was sitting beside Seven on the bed, unexpectedly jumped in front of the gun barrel's line of fire. Doreen's intention was clear and heroic – to act as a human shield. The move by Doreen and the firing of Terry's gun transpired simultaneously as two quick shots rang out. The bullets intended for Seven hit Doreen instead, catching her near the arm and shoulder. Blood spurted out as she fell to the floor. After that, everything seemed to stop, and a brief, surreal silence ensued. It was immediately followed by mass confusion.

For some reason, maybe their deep-rooted loyalty to a Rhombus 'sister' after all these years, Suzanne and Anita instinctively rushed over to Doreen. Seven likewise bent down, cradled her in his arms and held her close. She looked up at him with a tender smile and explained, "I knew I was going to die anyway, Chris. I just didn't want *you* to be shot. Not like that and not in front of me. You see, I truly love you." She gave him another thin smile through clenched teeth. "A few weeks ago, I was perfectly willing to die for something I thought I prized more than anything or anyone. Then I met you and all that changed."

"Try not to talk," said Seven, his conscience tugging at him.

"I need to," insisted Doreen, "before it's too late." She coughed softly and cringed in obvious pain. "When I heard Terry's threats toward you just now, I figured I'd much rather die for something I *really* cherish. *You,* my love." She let out another painful cough. "I wanted to give up my life for yours just as my mother did for me. I also thought that seeing me shot would be enough revenge for Terry. Maybe it still will be and she'll let you escape now." Doreen looked over at Terry, pleadingly. "Do it now, Terry – for me. As a last request from a dying Rhombus sister."

"You're not going to die," Seven consoled. "We'll get you a doctor as soon as we can. The bullets seemed to have missed your vital areas. With a bit of medical help, you'll be good as new." He picked her up and gently laid her on the bed. Trying to control his anger and revulsion, Seven addressed Anita and Suzanne harshly. "If your so-called *sisterhood* means anything to you, get a doctor here right away."

The perplexed Rhombus duo looked over at Terry for direction. She was still holding her revolver tightly, likewise uncertain as to what to do next. Suddenly there was the sound of running footsteps coming toward the bedroom. A few moments later, Carmine Gitano, along with Nalco and three other hoods, rushed into the room, their guns drawn. Two of Gitano's men rushed over to Seven, grabbing him tightly from behind. Swiftly and expertly they rendered the Super Stud a helpless prisoner.

"We heard shots," Gitano exclaimed. "What's going on?" He glared over at Seven. "And what in the world is *he* doing here?"

Terry pointed her pistol toward the bed. "You ought to ask Doreen. That is, if she can still talk. Seven's been holed up in here with her the last two days. Apparently, he hasn't left this room. The two of them were planning to sneak out tonight. Luckily I found out about it last minute. Those shots you heard were meant for Seven, but Doreen purposely got in the way. Seems she wanted to save Lover Boy from a nasty end. By the way, she's been telling him all about our plans."

Gitano's face turned red with rage. Trying to control himself, he addressed the three standing Rhombus women. "You girls know what this means. Doreen's betrayed us for some two-bit loser. She could have loused up the whole NATO thing if Terry hadn't caught her." The mafia boss grimaced, angrily. "I'll take care of Seven later, like I vowed. But little miss traitor here, our friend Doreen, needs some *immediate* attention." He frowned at them. "I know Anita and Suzanne still had reservations about actually killing Doreen whenever we've discussed it – all that Rhombus loyalty stuff. But there shouldn't be *any* qualms about it now. She's a confirmed turncoat. Both to your sisterhood and to me. So Doreen's gotta die. Here and *now!*"

Anita, Terry, and Suzanne glanced at each other and then slowly nodded their heads in uneasy agreement.

"The motion's carried," bullied Gitano, pushing his agenda forward, as always. "It'll now be settled *Cosa Nostra* style."

Glowering at Seven with an expression of absolute hatred, the mob boss coldly decreed, "And I think Mr. Seven here should witness it firsthand. See for himself what happens to people who cross me." The Mafioso raised his eyebrows expectantly at the three silent Rhombus women. "Okay for Nalco to proceed, ladies?"

Terry shrugged her OK, as did Anita. Suzanne, however, hesitated, declaring, "I know I shouldn't be, but I'm still grappling with our lifelong loyalty oath." Suz waited a moment and then gave her approval as well.

"I suppose it's like you said, Carm. Doreen violated our most essential statute. As such, she no longer deserves the protection of the Rhombus sisterhood." There was another short pause followed by Suzanne's, "So, yes, you can go ahead with the 'hit.'"

That was all Gitano needed to hear. He nodded to Nalco who now had a look of madness and anticipation on his ugly face. Nalco growled loudly and rushed over to Doreen's bleeding body lying on the bed. He seized her by the hair and jerked her up forcefully, drawing a shriek of pain from the wounded girl. Eyes ablaze, Nalco grabbed Doreen's neck with his powerful right paw, a hand that Seven knew could easily crush billiard balls. Giggling repulsively, Nalco slowly began squeezing the life out of her.

Watching from the other side of the room, Christopher Seven went berserk! Now handcuffed tightly, he tried to kick and flail at his burly captors, doing anything he could to escape and help Doreen. When that failed, he screamed at the mob goons holding him to kill him instead, yelling the same thing to Nalco and the Rhombus women. It was all to no avail.

Gitano's three burly thugs, still holding Seven in a vicelike grip, callously turned Seven's head and forced him to witness the execution.

The G5 agent watched helplessly as Nalco slowly tightened his stranglehold. Doreen's lovely face began turning a purplish hue. Gagging uncontrollably, she desperately tried to breathe in between her muffled cries. Slowly but surely, Nalco increased his deadly grip, forcing Doreen's tongue to bulge out the side of her mouth. The apelike henchman groaned loudly, sensually reveling in his merciless handiwork. Much like a wolf toying with a baby rabbit. Visibly aroused, Nalco moaned with contentment. He was truly a 'death addict' getting his *fix* from yet another killing!

Seven momentarily closed his eyes to the horror and mumbled a quick prayer. When he reopened them, it was mercifully over. Doreen's terrified, lifeless eyes were staring blankly up at the ceiling. And her tongue was protruding out. Doreen, so lovely and soft a moment ago in Seven's arms, was now a lifeless white corpse. Disappointed that his amusement had ended so quickly, Nalco calmly wiped some sweat from his brow, picked up Doreen's flaccid body from the floor, and threw it back on the bed.

Gitano grinned at Seven. "Enjoy the show, pal? You'll be next."

Christopher Seven clenched his teeth and said nothing, still sickened by what he'd just witnessed. Knowing Doreen had bravely saved him from death just a few minutes earlier, Seven now felt responsible for not being able to do the same for her. Filled with loathing toward Carmine Gitano and everyone else in the suddenly silent room, Seven's only solace was in knowing that a powerful explosive was now sitting under Gitano's black Cadillac limousine. A fiery car bomb set to go off at 1:00 p.m. tomorrow afternoon. Hopefully it would blow this disgusting mobster and his Rhombus allies sky-high as they drove toward their sordid date with infamy. Seven knew his vindictive wish wasn't very Christian-like, but revenge was now trumping everything else.

Still seething with revulsion, and longing for vengeance, the Super Stud thought about the car bomb again. Would it go off as scheduled? Demolish Gitano and Rhombus and prevent the NATO calamity? Or had Carmine's lackeys already discovered the swap and placed the explosive back under the white limo?

Seven knew he would never know for sure now, as he would undoubtedly be the next to die. Gitano and the Rhombus women wouldn't wait much longer to eliminate him. The only question at this juncture was what type of excruciating death they had in store for him. A horrifying drowning via the mob's cement shoes, a slow strangulation at the hands of Nalco, or scalded to death by Terry's searing branding iron?

While Seven glumly thought on it, a heavyset goon named Eddie rushed into the bedroom. He had a worried, nervous expression on his plump face. Gitano greeted the worrywart testily, "*Now* what, Eddie?"

"Sorry to interrupt, boss, but young Carpi says he wants to see you and the gals downstairs – pronto. Says it's important. Something about his 'cut,' and more questions about tomorrow's plans."

Carmine shook his head. "It's always *something* with that Carpi guy. So I guess 'pretty boy' will have to wait a while. The girls and I have too much on our plates now to deal with Seven properly." Gitano looked at his watch. "We've already wasted too much time with this Doreen thing." Gitano smiled, cruelly. "But tomorrow's another day."

Don Gitano looked over at Terry. "By the way, Terr, is there any chance Seven could have overheard anything important while he's been holed up in here?"

Hesitant to mention the extent of her and Dr. Kim's boasting about the NATO gala details, for fear Carmine would go bonkers, Terry played it down.

"He certainly couldn't have heard anything while he was up here hiding with Doreen," Terry assured. "And Doreen swore to me that her lover boy hadn't moved from this bedroom. Nor could Seven have texted any warnings via his cell phone. All phone signals were blocked, with no calls or texts accessible in or out. Your private staff made sure of that."

Gitano grunted satisfactorily as Terry added, "Besides, there's nothing Seven could have overheard while hiding up here anyway. All your meetings were done on the ground floors. Or in the heavily guarded conference room. So, you're in the clear. Seven couldn't have overheard anything while in Doreen's bedroom. And he never left here. So, as long

as your boys keep a close watch on Seven *before* you whack him, there's
no possibility of any leaks."

Content with Terry's reassurances, the mob chief nodded his head.
"Excellent." He then turned toward Nalco and the other three hoods. "For
now, take Seven down to the basement. Lock him in the holding cell and
keep two men guarding him at all times. Make sure you chain him up tight.
I'll deal with him later – for good!"

Gitano's lackeys promptly grabbed their prisoner in preparation for
taking him downstairs to the villa's basement.

Slowly rubbing his chin in contemplation, Carmine suddenly called
out, "Hey, wait a minute, I just got a brainwave! Instead of dirtying my
own hands on Seven, I think I'll ask young Carpi to take care of him
during Carpi's limo ride back to Monte Carlo. He and his boys can make
the 'hit' somewhere on the rural outskirts of Monaco. Someplace where
no one will hear Seven's screams. And believe me, he'll be screaming if
Carpi himself performs the hit.

"What do you mean, Carm?" asked Anita.

Gitano grinned his reply. "Well, they say Frankie Carpi gets his
jollies slicing up victims with that big hunting knife he always carries.
I've seen that stiletto of his. It's over a foot long and sharp as can be. Like a
butcher's tool. And young Frankie really knows how to flay people's skin
off with that thing. Some of his own people call him 'The Skinner' behind
his back. Slicing up screaming victims is said to be his one true fetish."
Gitano shrugged his broad shoulders. "I'm not into that flaying stuff
myself. But, as they say, to each his own fantasies. In any event, Seven
here will be a gift from me to Frankie. A trussed up pigeon for young
Carpi to skin."

Gitano winked at Nalco, secure in the knowledge that neither
Frankie Carpi nor Christopher Seven would even get close to Monaco
tomorrow afternoon. They'd all be killed before they were halfway home.
Blown to bits in a grisly explosion via Carmine's car bomb arrangements.
A powerful bomb obliterating the white limo and its passengers at 1:00
p.m. sharp! – Or so Gitano *thought*.

The Mafioso giggled excitedly. He could scarcely hide his little car
bomb secret. He winked over at his henchmen, who were all privy to the
explosive hit on Carpi. "Yes, fellas," Carmine wryly exclaimed, "it should
be a *real* interesting car ride for Mr. Seven tomorrow in that white Lincoln
Town Car. As planned, both limos will be leaving the villa at the exact
same time – 12:30 on the dot. One limousine going east with us, and the
other going west with Carpi and Seven. Bon voyage everyone!"

As the mobsters laughed knowingly, little did they suspect that
Seven was also in on *Don* Gitano's little secret. And that he had done
something about it down in the garage.

Inwardly optimistic as well, the Super Stud followed his captors out the door and down to the villa's basement.

~

Two hours later, while lying on a filthy army cot in the small prison cell located down in the chateau's basement, Christopher Seven tried to rest and gather his thoughts. Locked securely inside the musty chamber, and chained to the wall by way of a long, thick shackle, the secret agent struggled to remain calm. He was quietly optimistic that Gitano's furtive plan to blow him up in the white car's explosion would backfire, hopeful that his switch of the car bomb would destroy the black limo, *NOT* the white one as Gitano had planned.

Yes, Seven pondered, *there might be a real chance for a reprieve now.* If, during their ride to Monaco, Seven could somehow convince Carpi and his bodyguards that Carmine Gitano had deceived them by planting a car bomb under their white limo, one that Seven himself had switched and prevented, maybe they'd consider turning him loose as a token of their appreciation, perhaps doing so to spite Gitano, or simply as a reward for saving their lives. Who knows, with the crazy code of honor these gangsters followed! *Yes*, mused Seven, *riding with the Carpi crew in the white limo tomorrow is an unexpected break, a mistake by the usually shrewd Gitano.*

Seven closed his eyes a moment. He still couldn't get his mind off the brutal murder of Doreen. It had been a ghastly execution, one that would haunt him forever. The only good news was that Gitano and the Rhombus women hadn't killed him already, preferring instead to let him die the following day with the Carpi gang. Luckily for Seven, it was Gitano's *black* limo that was now scheduled to explode, *NOT* the white Lincoln limo which would be carrying Carpi's squad and Seven himself.

Seven again mulled over his strategy. During the start of tomorrow's drive to Monaco with the Carpi crew, Seven would wait until both limousines were on the road at the same time. Both leaving the villa at exactly 12:30 p.m. The Super Stud would then calmly inform Mr. Carpi about the car bomb switch. News that could easily be verified *after* 1:00 p.m. by Carpi's inside contacts. Once young Carpi confirmed Gitano's devious double cross, and learned that it was Seven's handiwork that had eliminated *Don* Gitano instead, Frankie Carpi just might release him, doing so simply to foil Carmine's last wishes.

Why not? Seven asked himself. *There's no reason for young Carpi to suspect I'm a federal agent.*

The G5 agent nodded his head gratefully. Even though his being freed by Carpi was far from a sure thing, at least he'd be in the white Lincoln limo tomorrow rather than in Carmine's doomed Caddy.

Seven's thoughts were interrupted by the sound of approaching footsteps. It was Carmine Gitano and his bodyguards making their way toward the jail cell.

"Hello, dead man," Gitano greeted sarcastically.

Seven looked over with his own indifferent smirk. "Well, if it isn't Don Vito Gitano. What's up, Godfather? Come to put a horsehead in my army cot?"

Gitano's neck turned red with anger. Fighting to control his temper, he loudly exclaimed, "You better keep your trap shut, fella, or I'll have my boys cut your tongue out!"

Christopher Seven smiled, happy he'd gotten the big man's goat. He listened closely as Gitano informed, "It just so happens I've been thinking about my Mafia pledge to you, Seven. You remember. That *Costa Nostra* vengeance oath I made back onboard the Zephyr." Carmine shrugged. "With all that's been going on, lately, I'd almost forgotten that I swore to kill you *myself* if you ever came near me or the four girls again."

Seven's ears perked up. He wondered if he was going to be murdered right then and there.

"I've thus changed my mind about young Carpi making the hit on you," Gitano declared. "I've decided to kill you *myself*, just like I vowed. Do it in front of the Rhombus women so they can see how a worthless coward like you dies."

The Mafioso's tone was confident and forceful. "So, forget Carpi, Seven. You're coming with me tomorrow. Appropriately in my *black* Cadillac limo, which we've occasionally used as a hearse. You're gonna get yours when we take the gals over to Vence."

The big man sneered while clenching his fist. "Tomorrow afternoon I'm going to *personally* 'whack' you. And I'm gonna do it in the most excruciating manner I can dream up!"

U nable to hide his shock and disappointment, Cristopher Seven winced, as if hit by a hard punch in the stomach. His heart, filled with hope and optimism just a few minutes earlier, quickly sank. *So much for escaping in the white Lincoln with the Carpi gang,* Seven bitterly contemplated. *I'm going to die tomorrow after all. Be burned to a crisp with this thug Gitano in an explosive inferno. Ironically, one that I arranged myself.* Unable to conceal this crushing letdown, and his mounting anxiety, the G5 operative sighed openly.

Observing the prisoner's troubled reaction, a grinning Carmine Gitano gloated happily. "You heard right, punk. Tomorrow afternoon, during my final ride with the Rhombus trio, we're going to make a little detour first. A slight deviation up to a secluded forest area I've used before. That's where you're going to get it, friend. From me to you, just like I vowed. I'll make the 'hit' on the way over to Vence tomorrow, right before we drop the women off to Dr. Kim at the hotel. This way, the girls can likewise enjoy watching you die."

Walking closer to Seven's cot, the mob boss informed, "I'm going to kill you myself, just like I pledged. But before I do, I'm gonna make sure Nalco has some fun with you first. Just like he did with your traitorous girlfriend. Only you're going to get Nalco's *full* treatment tomorrow, Seven. A brutal pounding with his fists and his steel-tipped boots. Followed by several near-deaths each time he chokes the breath out of you. Then, after he's done reducing you to a quivering lump of broken bones, I'll finish you off with the tommy gun. Maybe get a little target practice in first. Start with your fingers, kneecaps, and elbows and work my way down before you're toast."

Gitano's stocky arm reached out and pulled Seven's head up by the back of the neck. "Like I said. The Rhombus women will see for themselves how a worthless punk like you croaks. I'm betting you sob like a baby while Nalco dishes it out." He let Seven's head go and barked out a laugh.

Still stunned by this sudden change of plans, the Super Stud silently pondered his situation. *Yes,* he thought. *I'll die tomorrow. But so will you, big man. Along with your three attractive accomplices. We're all going to die together in a blazing inferno, before that NATO gala even begins.*

Seven looked away from his captors a moment, once again thinking about the ironic prospect of having arranged his own death. He closed his eyes and mouthed a silent prayer, as Carmine and his brawny bodyguards made their way out of the locked cell, and made their way up to the main floor of the villa.

~

The next few hours crawled by slowly for Seven, still firmly chained to the wall in the château's basement jail. Early the next morning, after a cold and restless night of sporadic sleep, he awoke for good sometime around 5:30 a.m. He had a slight headache, caused by stress and lack of sleep. Tossing and turning in the chilly darkness, the despondent agent had relived the nightmarish murder of Doreen several times. Still laying on the grimy army cot, he stared at the ceiling and waited in tense silence.

Two hours later, a pockmarked goon brought Seven what looked to be breakfast, pushing a stale roll and a tiny carton of lukewarm apple juice through the bars. It was obvious they wanted to keep the prisoner fully cognizant till the torture began.

Somehow this callous scenario, along with the guard's taunting face, suddenly brought back much of Seven's anger and fighting spirit. Though the situation seemed hopeless, the G5 operative began urging himself to remain positive. He'd been in tight spots before, and like all seasoned undercover agents, Christopher Seven was trained to always focus on escape despite the odds. He thus took the mediocre food, hoping to get some sustenance and to keep up his strength for later.

After washing his hands in the cell's primitive sink, located adjacent to a filthy, antiquated toilet, Seven wolfed down what probably would be his last meal ever. Then, for some ingrained reason, he took out the small travel tooth care kit from his pants pocket and brushed his teeth, doing so as a final tribute to his practiced Super Stud routines. This familiar 'Stud' ritual also helped bolster his spirits.

Lying back down on the cot, the G5 agent tried to visualize what would happen later that afternoon now that Gitano's plans for him had changed. Seven's thoughts now returned to the car bomb he'd switched yesterday, the VBIED explosive that he hoped was still under Gitano's black Cadillac limo. Even though it would mean a violent death for himself, the Super Stud was still bent on payback for the horrible killing of Doreen. Seven now saw it as a small token of revenge for her murder, while also praying that it would prevent Rhombus from carrying out their NATO dirty work.

Another quiet four hours went by, followed by the chimes of the chateau's large courtyard clock promptly striking noon. Through the thick bars on the cell's open window, Seven suddenly heard distant voices coming from outside. One was the familiar voice of Carmine Gitano, who was walking his gangland house guests over to the waiting white limo. Little Frankie Carpi, along with his two strapping bodyguards, were getting ready to leave Gitano's château for their four-hour ride up the high corniche to Frankie's lavish mountaintop retreat some fifteen miles west of Monaco. Another 20 minutes went by, mainly a series of handshakes and small talk.

The Super Stud walked over to the window to get a better look and listen. He watched closely as Carmine said a cheery goodbye to the rival mobsters who were now getting into the white Lincoln Town Car. As they did, Seven's heart momently sank. Where was the *black* limo? Did Gitano's experts find the bomb underneath it? But then, thankfully, the black Caddy limo pulled up next to the white Lincoln limousine ready to drive Gitano's party, including Seven.

"Take care, Frankie boy," boomed Gitano, smiling at his mafia rival. "I'm glad we talked out our differences. And glad you finally understand about your old man. It was purely business, nothing personal. According to the Cosa Nostra council, it had to be done."

"I now understand your reasons," Carpi replied, in a gruff, monotone voice. "But this violence between us must stop if we're ever going to do business with each other again."

Carmine Gitano nodded affirmatively as Little Frankie slid into the limo's rear seat, looked out the Town Car's open door and sternly warned his host, "And speaking of violence, Carm, my father's cut of the NATO fee better be in my Swiss account by early next week – or *else*! After all, it was my old man's contacts that got you those Rhombus diplomatic escorts. We also supplied the drugs that got 'em hooked."

"Don't worry, Frankie," assured Carmine, "your money's coming."

"It *better* be. If not, there'll be more trouble between us. *Big* trouble." Frankie Carpi stared straight at Gitano to emphasize his point. Carpi's two armed bodyguards, sitting on both sides of him in the Lincoln's spacious back seat, likewise glared at Gitano.

Carmine merely smiled, ignoring their menacing stares.

"Well, so long, Carm," Carpi bellowed, after a brief silence. "See you in church."

"Take care, Frankie. And make sure you send my favorite driver, Enzi, back to me in *one* piece. Everyone knows Enzi's like a son to me. Been with me as a driver for over twenty years now."

"Enzi will be fine. We all know that he's one of your pets. But *you* won't be so fine if my money don't come."

Carmine lowered his head and gently shut the Lincoln's rear door. With a hidden pang of guilt, Gitano then gestured to Enzi, one of his most loyal and beloved workers. With that, the long white limo slowly pulled away.

Gitano waited until the limousine carrying Carpi and his men was well out of sight. He then let out a string of harsh obscenities and growled, "Good riddance, punk! And happy landings when the Lincoln blows sky high in an hour or so!" Then, again thinking of his much-loved Enzi, he crossed himself and made his way back into the house.

Ten minutes later, Nalco and two other thugs arrived at Seven's cell. They were all well-armed. "Ten minutes past noon, fella. Time to get moving," ordered the tallest of the mobsters, a towering square-faced goon aptly nicknamed 'Tall Boy' Donnie. Donnie looked at Seven and sneered. "You're about to take your *final* ride, Bub."

The lanky gangster grinned and unhooked the long chain from Seven's legs. Then, with a smug, triumphant look in his eyes, Donnie shockingly informed, "And by the way, Bub. I guess you *thought* you were pretty clever yesterday. But we were cleverer and foiled your two-bit plans."

Tall Boy then began laughing loudly, leaving Seven to wonder if the teasing was merely about Seven's aborted plan to escape with Doreen. Or, more disastrously, if it meant they'd uncovered the car bomb switch. Judging by this thug's self-assured grin, it certainly sounded like the latter. If that was the case, Christopher Seven had run out of miracles. He sighed resignedly and followed his captors out to Gitano's black Caddy.

The limo's engine was idling quietly, with only the driver, a short, pudgy man, sitting inside the vehicle. Seven was roughly pushed into the middle seat and immediately handcuffed to a large metal bolt in front of it. Nalco and Donnie then slid in on both sides of him, wedging the Super Stud in like a sardine.

A few minutes later, Carmine Gitano and the three Rhombus women appeared. The Mafia chieftain and his pretty accomplices were noticeably tense and jittery. Carmine climbed into the front with the driver, while Terry, Anita, and Suzanne, now ashen-faced and mute, silently slid into the limo's rear third row. The mob boss gave a cursory glance behind to make sure his passengers and prisoner were firmly in place. Satisfied, Gitano tapped the driver. "Okay, Peno. Let's move."

The black stretch limo slowly rolled out toward its destination with a veil of heavy tension shrouding it. Everyone, including Seven, was now on edge. The G5 agent awkwardly glanced down at his wristwatch. It showed thirteen minutes passed noon. He frowned at the unlucky number and leaned back in his seat.

The Caddy first drove along a busy highway for twenty minutes or so. Then, just like Gitano had promised, it veered off the highway onto a narrow, rustic side road. After climbing up this disserted rural corridor, the black limousine quickly made its way into an immense evergreen forest somewhere on the outskirts of *Chemin Lasine.*

Seven glumly looked out the window, assuming that this desolate woodland was where Carmine and Nalco were planning to make the 'hit' on him. The only question now was whether the car bomb was still wedged under Gitano's vehicle. Or if Seven's switch had indeed been discovered. Though it meant certain death for him, Christopher Seven prayed the explosive was still there, armed and ready to go off in thirty minutes...at precisely 1:00 p.m. The Super Stud again gazed at his watch: 12:33. In half an hour he'd know for sure...that is, if he hadn't been choked or shot by then.

Another ten minutes went by, feeling more like hours to Seven. *Twenty more to go,* the agent quietly contemplated. Though desperately hoping his handiwork in the garage hadn't been exposed, Christopher Seven couldn't get the confident boast of Tall Boy Donnie out of his mind. What had Donnie meant by "foiling Seven's plans"? Had they found him out? Or was the timed explosive still firmly entrenched beneath them?

A few more tension-filled minutes crawled by. It was almost time. Seven nervously gave another quick glance at his wristwatch, but this time his actions brought a suspicious snarl from Nalco.

"Hey, mister! Why do you keep 'a looking at your watch? Is'a some ting gonna happen *besides* your 'a death? Maybe you got a few mob friends who wanna jump us along da way?" With that, Nalco angrily ripped Seven's watch off and threw it onto the floor. "Now, you don't look 'a no more!"

Seven said nothing, praying he hadn't tipped off his captors. Ironically, it was Carmine Gitano's gruff voice that eased the tension.

"Relax, Nalc. This guy's just worried about when he's going get it. That's natural." Carmine chuckled and turned back around.

Without his watch, the Super Stud could only approximate the time now. As best he could figure, there were five or six minutes left to go, although he might be off by a minute or two. He again leaned back in his seat and tried to mentally count out sixty-second intervals.

After what seemed like three minutes later, Carmine Gitano glanced at his own watch and informed, "It's going on one o'clock, although my watch might be a few minutes fast. It usually is. In any case, our deceitful pal, Frankie Carpi, should be getting his any minute now – *Ka-boom!*" Nalco and Tall Boy Donnie laughed loudly while Gitano added, "Like I said before – good riddance to that lying bum."

Don Gitano waited another minute or two and then tapped the driver's shoulder. "We're here, Peno. Stop the car by that clearing up ahead."

As the limo came to a halt, Seven tried to fight back his mounting panic. Something was wrong! The explosion should have occurred by now. Was Gitano's watch indeed a few minutes fast? Or had all of Seven's efforts been for nothing?

"All right, Nalc," barked the boss. "Time for this punk to meet his maker." Gitano glared at Seven. "I've been waiting a long time for this moment, friend." He grinned and pointed toward a tree lined clearing some fifteen yards from the road.

Christopher Seven said nothing, now anxious to get out and away from the car in case it was going to blow. Thwarting Rhombus was the main thing now. If the Caddy did explode, he'd take his chances with Nalco and Gitano. That is, *if* the bomb was still attached to Carmine's black limo.

Seven's thoughts were cut short by Nalco's gruff orders. "I'm 'a gonna uncuff 'a you now, mister. But my 'a revolver will be 'a pointed at your kneecaps when I do." He took out a small handgun from inside his pants pocket and waved it menacingly. "So, no'a funny business or you punishment will be even worse 'a."

Nalco unlocked Seven's handcuffs and motioned him out of the car and onto the side of the road. Carmine Gitano was already standing there holding a small *Minimi* machine gun in his right hand. The Mafioso again grinned and chillingly informed, "No one will hear your screams up here, friend. And no one should find your body for months."

Gitano shrugged his shoulders. "Too bad we don't have more time. If we had, Terry would have fixed you up good. She's an expert with her branding iron, and I'm sure she'd have loved to play around with it on you. Like she did that ambassador." The mob chief pointed at Nalco. "But don't worry, pretty boy. Big Nalc will make sure your final moments are plenty painful. And right after he's done working his excruciating magic on you, I'm going to slowly finish you off with the 'tommy,' just like I vowed."

Seven, who by now had given up on the car bomb, could clearly hear the sadistic panting of Nalco. It reminded him of Doreen's dreadful ordeal. Gitano heard Nalco's anxious breathing as well and promptly tried to calm his apelike assassin, much like a doting father reassuring a young son waiting for a toy. "Almost time, big boy. You've been real patient."

The obviously aroused Nalco, now gasping even louder, just kept staring at Seven. Now wide-eyed, he was rapidly nodding his head up and down, as if in some sort of blissful fantasy. His dreamy thoughts were interrupted by Carmine Gitano.

"By the way, Nalc, after I've polished Seven off with the machine gun, I want you and Tall Boy to drag his body into the woods and cover it up as best you can."

Nalco gave an impatient grunt of acknowledgment as his chief added, "We've left a getaway car for you and Donnie about a quarter mile down the road. That way." He pointed to his right. "It's a blue Mercedes with Monaco plates. The doors are unlocked and the keys are in the ashtray. I'll catch up with you guys next week, back at our usual rendezvous spot."

The Mafia boss again looked over at Seven. "Okay, mister, the time has come. It'll be interesting to see how you die. This is when you learn the *true* mettle of a man. I ought to know, 'cause I've personally killed lots of 'em." The Mafioso sneered. "And I'm betting that when the chips are down you're gonna go out pleading and screaming."

Carmine then leaned over, stuck his head inside the Cadillac limo, and then addressed the three Rhombus women. "I'll be back shortly, ladies. Any last words for Pretty Boy here before we take him on his death walk?"

Terry, sitting in the back seat, gazed over at Seven with a spiteful scowl and chided, "So long, handsome. It's been fun *using* you. By the way, your offer of a pardon never swayed us. Like I said, we could never be *ordinary* women. That's why we look forward to dying for the Rhombus legacy. Then, after we're gone, a *new* Rhombus foursome will carry on. In fact, they're already in place. And, thanks to Carmine's generous help, they're very well-funded as well. You see, Seven, Rhombus *never* dies. It will live forever. So take *that* to your grave!"

Anita and Suzanne cheered loudly at their leader's proclamation. Terry smiled at them and then gave Seven a final taunt, "Sorry I couldn't burn our trademark *R* onto you with the iron, handsome. But like Carm told you – *bigger* things await us."

Christopher Seven looked at her and slowly replied, "You and your psychotic 'sisters' will soon get what's coming to you, Terry. And that's a final promise from *me*."

The three women stared at him with perplexed expressions. Did their looks show a trace of fear? The G5 operative couldn't tell for sure but took comfort in their uncertainty. He quickly turned away and tried to gather up his courage and his wits.

Seven's only thought now was getting as far from the limo as he could in the unlikely event it went up in flames. *Yet would it?* It had to be past one o'clock by now, or very close to it. Was the bomb's timing clock a bit slow? Or had Seven's efforts with the car bomb been thwarted? *If only he still had his watch!*

"Start moving, pal," ordered Gitano, toting a small machine gun, and walking a few feet behind Seven and Nalco, The mob boss looked back toward the limo a moment and called to his limo driver. "I'll be back in 15 minutes or so, Peno. Donnie will stay with you and the girls in the limo 'til Nalco and I are finished with this bum. "

"Okay, chief."

Gitano was holding the *Minimi* light machine gun in his right hand, pointing it straight at his captive's back. Seven was very familiar with this particular gun, the superb automatic weapon developed by Belgium's *FN Herstal.* The Super Stud had once spent an entire afternoon firing one just like it, doing so at the US Coast Guard's Small Arms Center near Boston.

Seven knew the gun was lethal and deadly accurate. Hastily glancing at it again, the G5 operative was surprised to see that Gitano didn't have the machine gun strapped to his shoulder, holding it loosely in his hands instead. *Perhaps there was a chance to rush the mobster and wrestle it from him,* Seven mused.

"All right, fella," Carmine barked. "By those trees over there. Now!" Seven, sweating profusely, did as he was told, walking with his two captors toward the outer edge of the forest. The Cadillac's engine was still running, and the long stretch limo was idling softly on the side of the road. Seven gazed back at it, knowing there was only one slim chance at this point.

Nalco, now stripped to the waste, was growling loudly. The sight of Nalco's muscular arms and chest quickly brought Seven back to the present.

Nalco grinned excitedly and informed, "I'm 'a gonna start out slow by kicking you in the groin with my steel-tipped boots. Just'a to soften you'a up. I will be without mercy. The louder you'a scream the harder I'll kick. Then'a, my choking will begin; over and over and over again. Your face will turn'a blue, just like'a your girl's. You'll lose'a your breath and come close to death *many* times, begging me to'a finish you off. But I won't let'a you die. Carmine will see to that. And though your actual death won't come from me, I'm still gonna..."

Nalco never finished the sentence. His words were interrupted by an enormous, deafening explosion that shook the entire area! It was followed by a gigantic ball of fire where the limo was parked. The powerful blast knocked the three standing men off their feet. Nalco and his chief were completely taken by surprise! But Seven, who'd been half-expecting it, was not nearly as staggered.

The Super Stud, now on his knees from the fall, glanced to his left where Gitano's tommy gun had conveniently landed. It was lying on the ground, maybe four or five feet away. His captors, likewise, on their knees, were still dazed, and Seven knew this was his chance. As the stunned gangsters gradually began to regain their wits, Christopher Seven deftly rolled to his left, grabbed the machine gun, and readied himself.

Nalco and Gitano, quickly recovering, began reaching into their pants pockets, obviously fumbling for handguns. Seven had no choice. It was kill or be killed. He pointed the *Minimi* gun at the kneeling gangsters and fired away!

The thunderous roar of continuous machine gun bullets was louder than Seven had remembered it on the Coast Guard's rifle range. The noise echoed through the dense forest as the nonstop flurry of shots did its grim job, instantly killing both mobsters who'd somehow managed to get their revolvers out just before they died.

Finally stopping his shooting, Seven looked over at the carnage he'd just wreaked. It had been an extremely brutal execution. Both victims' bloodied bodies had been hurled into midair by the powerful salvo. Their corpses had landed grotesquely to Seven's right, spread-eagled and covered with dirt and pine needles.

Still kneeling, the G5 agent wiped some sweat from his forehead and listened for any signs of life. There was nothing – just a surreal, trance-like silence. A thick cloud of haze slowly began permeating the area. And the smoke from the car bomb, and that of the machine gun bullets, began to mix and saturate the cool air.

Shaking from nerves, Seven slowly got up from his knees and walked over to the bullet-riddled bodies. He looked down at them, again thinking of Doreen, the enigmatic girl who'd been cruelly murdered by these same two mobsters. Reflecting on it a moment, the agent admitted to himself that he felt little remorse about killing these two vicious hoods.

He turned away and glanced over at the limousine, or rather what was left of it. Gitano's car was now a charred, smoking heap of shattered glass and metal. *Nothing could have lived through that,* Seven surmised. Fortunately, the Rhombus women hadn't yet been armed with the *second* half of the Korean's deadly chemical mixture. Had they been, Seven too would have been blown away, along with a few acres of pine trees!

The Super Stud shook his head at the irony of the three women who'd just died inside the exploding limo. Perfectly willing to blow up themselves, and numerous untold innocents, they had died the way they'd planned. Only doing so a few hours earlier than intended.

Despite the bloodshed and death surrounding him, Christopher Seven knew he'd better get out of the area quickly. Get away before Gitano's hoods start checking up on their soon to be tardy boss. Or before some passerby or police car arrived on the scene. Conceivably, someone might have heard the noise of the explosion already and reported it. If so, it was definitely time to leave.

Yet how could he disappear from this isolated forest, out in the middle of nowhere? Seven then remembered Gitano saying that he'd left a getaway car down the road for Nalco and Donnie. Dropping the machine gun, the G5 agent began running toward the parked car.

Ten minutes later, Seven found the blue Mercedes exactly where Carmine said it would be. The keys were in the ashtray, as planned. Jumping into the front seat, Seven turned the car around and raced toward Monte Carlo.

~

Three hours later, he ditched the Mercedes in an empty cobblestone alleyway several blocks from his hotel. Still feeling the numbing effects of being so near to the violent car explosion, and drained by all of the other traumatic events, the Super Stud stumbled toward the Hotel de Paris, not knowing or caring what he'd do next. Arriving at his room, he walked into the bathroom, splashed some cold water on his face and collapsed on the bed.

304

Chapter 43

'Some Machine!'

Seven must have dozed off, fainted, or simply collapsed from sheer exhaustion...because the next thing he was aware of was frantic pounding on his suite's door. Still groggy, he glanced at his bedside alarm clock, astonished that it was now going on 8:30 p.m. He'd been out for nearly five hours!

"Chris! Chris! Open up! It's me, Vin!" The doc's tone had a desperate urgency to it.

Seven was surprised to hear Fieri's voice, thinking his CIA sidekick was still recuperating in a Monaco hospital. Still half asleep, the Super Stud rubbed his eyes and got up from the bed. After viewing Fieri's worried face in the door's peephole, he promptly let him in.

"Thank God!" Doc Fieri exclaimed with genuine feeling.

"It's all right, Vin, I'm fine. And Gitano and those Rhombus women won't be giving us any more trouble. Not unless they can do something from the grave."

"What's happened?"

Seven sat back down on the edge of his bed and began relaying the entire story, leaving nothing out. He methodically gave Vin all the details, including the specifics of the switched car bomb and Rhombus's plans to blow up the NATO gala via Dr. Kim's formidable chemicals.

When he finished, Fieri, who was jotting down a few facts on a small notepad, let out a low whistle and responded, "Well, I knew there were a lot of dead people popping up the last few hours. Thanks to CIA's texting me some frantic French police faxes. But no one seemed to know where *you* fit in. We initially thought you might have been one of the unidentified corpses."

The Doc rubbed his forehead, obviously thankful that Seven was alive and safe. "Well, I guess you've busted up Rhombus for a while, Chris. And put a permanent crimp on the Gitano mob family."

"I guess I did. But there's bound to be some real fallout once everything hits. Both political- and Mafia-related."

"It's already started," informed Fieri. "About six hours ago, a Vence police wagon responded to a phone call from a local lumberjack. The jack claimed he'd heard a big explosion near the *Lasine* forest area. When the policemen arrived on the scene, they found two bullet-riddled corpses in the woods. Both had been peppered with machine-gun bullets. The gendarmes also discovered the charred remains of several other bodies in the smoking wreck of Carmine Gitano's limousine. Almost all of them were unrecognizable."

Seven listened closely as Fieri explained, "The car was identified via one of its license plates, which had somehow survived the explosion. As you can imagine, the minute the local police called in their report, chaos and confusion ensued."

Seeing the anxious look on Seven's face, Fieri held up his hand. "Relax, Chris. Things are quickly quieting down now. Although when the CIA first heard about all the dead people, in all likelihood some of them Americans, they envisioned a full-blown diplomatic crisis with France. Remember. The French and Italian secret services were well aware that you and I were on Gitano's tail."

Seven nodded as Vin resumed, "Surprisingly, neither the French nor the Italian authorities seem all that upset any more. Probably because they soon learned that the two machine-gunned bodies belonged to two notorious mobsters. They also knew the CIA's been after *Don* Gitano and his motley crew."

"We're lucky the French authorities reacted that way, Vin."

"I'll say. But there were still a bunch of loose ends the French cops wanted connected. My CIA chief phoned me at the hospital around 4 p.m. Got me out of my sickbay bed and told me to get cracking and find you – dead or alive. He went over the few sketchy details he had at the time and asked if I knew what was up. I told him the truth. That I hadn't heard from you since you decided to re-contact that Rhombus girl, Doreen, a few days ago. I promised to phone him right away if you turned up."

The doc walked over to the suite's mini-fridge and grabbed himself a can of beer. He popped open the top and began rehashing a few of his afternoon's anxious moments. "I called your hotel and asked to be connected to your room. There was no answer. Same with your private cell." Fieri raised his eyebrows.

"Sorry about that, Vin. Gitano's apes confiscated my cellphone, which didn't work at the villa anyway. As for your call to my hotel room, I must have slept right through it. I was totally out of it. The aftereffects of that explosion put me in what felt like a mini-coma."

Fieri smiled his understanding and then went on, "The first thing I fretted about was that you were one of the unfortunate car bomb victims. Or one of the two unidentified machine-gunned corpses. At the very least, I feared that top-secret agency of yours was going to be completely blown by an embarrassing police investigation, with you smack-dab in the center of it. Provided you weren't dead, that is. I quickly hopped in my rental car and took a ride out to Gitano's Antibes estate. Spent an hour driving around the place, and kept a close watch on things with my binoculars. I got real worried when I didn't see any sign of you. Or those four Rhombus women."

Fieri took another gulp of his beer. "In any case, Chris, I figured if you'd somehow survived and escaped – and those were *big* ifs – everybody from the Mafia to the National Gendarmerie and the French Secret Service would be gunning for you. And probably for me, too. So I promptly contacted CIA's 'disinformation specialists' and told them to be prepared to start spreading some false rumors around. They quickly went into action with their skilled expertise and their inside mob connections, and immediately calmed things down. Figuring correctly that you had something to do with Gitano's car blowing up, CIA's propaganda experts quickly put out a much different spin on things. Substituting your role in the chaos with that of a rival mob. We wanted to take you out of the loop and put the various mob families back in."

"And?" asked Seven.

"It worked. The past few hours, CIA's European front men, along with their contacts in the press and media, have convinced most everyone who's interested – mobsters *and* police – that the whole deal was simply another episode of gangland violence. Merely one mob family making war on another. That's also what our rumor-spreading moles at the French newspapers and television stations will propagate, starting with tonight's TV and news headlines."

Fieri gave Seven his familiar two-fingered, rounded 'OK' sign. "Believe it or not, everyone seems okay with things now. Especially since rumors were *already* ripe that Frankie Carpi was going to 'hit' Carmine Gitano any day now. Or vice versa."

The doc tossed his empty beer can into a nearby wastepaper basket. "And so, my G5 buddy, it seems we're both in the clear vis-à-vis any police investigations. And apparently, we're clean from the bad guys' side of things too. They'll undoubtedly think it was simply Gitano versus Carpi." Vin chuckled loudly. "Looks like neither one of us is going to wind up with a horsehead in our beds."

Seven laughed back as Fieri declared, "Thankfully, there doesn't appear to be too much to worry about, at the moment. Other than mounds of paperwork for me, and getting you out of Europe pronto. Which the French DPSD and Monaco police have *insisted* on, by the way. Things could always change, of course, but I wouldn't sweat it. I think everything's going to be fine and so does my agency. The mob's well-deserved reputation for interfamily violence and gunplay will see to that. Everyone's looking in the mafia's direction now, and forgetting about anyone else. Including you."

"Thank God," Seven exclaimed, now thinking of his boss, Colonel McPhail, and the colonel's penchant for secrecy.

"We were darn lucky, Chris. For a while there, I thought you and your hush-hush department were going to be openly exposed. A full-blown cover story in the *Paris Match Magazine,* complete with some juicy photos." The doc grinned. "No worries on that score now. In addition to the inevitable finger-pointing between the various French and Italian underworld families, CIA will keep the gang warfare rumors ripe. My outfit's influential European contacts, along with their uncanny talent for manipulating false leads, should do wonders. We've got a solid team here in Europe. They'll keep a tight lid on things here, while quietly whisking you off the continent sometime tomorrow."

Christopher Seven lowered his head, appreciatively, thankful for CIA's powerful influence. Leaning back on the bed's headboard, he listened attentively as the doc assured, "So, relax good buddy. I'll call our Paris people to let them know you're fine. Then I'll phone Washington. They'll undoubtedly get a hold of your G5 agency ASAP. Your chief will probably have some more ideas on all this as well."

"You can count on that," laughed Seven. He smiled at the thought of a flustered Colonel McPhail trying to put out a bunch of annoying diplomatic fires. "I never did call New York. I was so dazed after what happened in the woods that I came right up here and conked out."

"Perfectly understandable, Chris. You've been through the wringer. And like you said, that car explosion may have jarred your brain a tad. You just chill a while. I'll handle everything from here." The doc pointed toward the bathroom. "Why don't you take a long, hot shower and have a drink from the mini-bar while I make my cellphone calls? Once I'm through with all the inter-departmental schmoozing, I'll treat you to the best dinner in Monte Carlo. On *me* this time."

Seven dutifully headed for the bath as Fieri grabbed his cell.

~

Forty-five minutes later, after a shower, shave, and change of clothes, Christopher Seven sat outside on the mini-suite's balcony nursing a glass of white wine. Gazing out at the calm Mediterranean Sea, and the harbor's plethora of luxury yachts, he reflected on the entire Rhombus affair. It had been a long, tough assignment.

Trying hard not to let it do so, Seven's mind kept coming back to the bloodshed he'd orchestrated just a few hours earlier in the forest. The Super Stud was keenly aware that he had indirectly or directly taken the lives of seven human beings. Doing so in a violent, brutal manner. *Seven* deaths – his namesake. Would that always be a grim reminder of what he'd done here in the south of France?

Though the carnage had been done purely in self-defense, it still weighed heavily on him. It probably always would, no matter how sinister the people who'd died were. Or no matter how diabolical their plans.

Seven bowed his head a moment and said a quiet prayer, asking for forgiveness and peace. Feeling better after praying, as always, he got up and walked back into the suite, where Vin was saying a few parting words to his CIA bosses. Finishing the call, Fieri flipped down his smartphone. There was a trace of pride on his angular face, more so for his agency than himself.

"Everything's hunky-dory, now, Chris. And believe it or not, that NATO dinner is still going to take place, albeit it a few hours later than planned. Screening and security measures have been tripled, and the five world leaders will now make *separate* and much briefer appearances. The President may not even show at all, although he wants to. Secret Service is still kicking it around."

Looking up toward the ceiling, Fieri somberly informed, "My chief, who just now talked to some of our terror experts, said it was a near thing. Seems Carmine's plan would have definitely worked. A few years back, in the Arabian Peninsula, *al Qaeda* almost succeeded in assassinating a Saudi prince with a bomb believed to be concealed inside a suicide bomber's body cavity. The assassin got very close to his target despite tight security measures. Thankfully, in that attempt, the terrorist's bulk absorbed much of the shock. So the prince, who's friendly toward the United States, was only wounded. But Rhombus's calamitous explosives were in a *much* different league. Infinitely more powerful."

Seven shook his head as Fieri explained more. "Apparently the immense power of those Rhombus compounds would have totally leveled the NATO gala's building. Easily killing everyone inside. I cited everything you told me about the Hethal, PETN, and the transparent body sacs to my boss. He confirmed that it would have been nearly impossible to detect those chemicals due to the unique and natural way it was concealed. Just like that Korean doctor boasted. Without a detailed and very specific strip-search of every woman attending the dinner, nothing could have prevented it. Knowing that now, I'm sure Homeland Security will quickly begin researching ways to combat Dr. Kim's ingenious design."

"Maybe," replied Seven. "Although it seems we're always one step behind the bad guys."

"Seems that way," Fieri concurred. "Anyway, thanks to a strong team effort by the Italian and French Coast Guards, they've located and impounded the Zephyr. They'll probably find that mini-sub next. It's too small to stay under water very long. Once they do, they'll be able to squeeze more of the plot details out of Gitano's crew."

"What about that Korean plastic surgeon, Vin?"

"There's a wide APB out on him, so he won't get very far. Evidently he had some sort of secret laboratory on the Riviera coast where he worked on the Rhombus women. One of the mob stoolies the French police just grilled told us that Gitano often ferried the girls over there via his submarine. Who knows? Maybe the Korean is hiding there now."

Vin glanced down at his handwritten notes. "As for the various Mafia clans, details are now pouring in fast and furious over at CIA's Paris headquarters. Initial snippets from our informants confirm that almost all of the crime families think it was simply gang warfare between the Gitano and Carpi factions. Same deal with the tommy-gunned corpses. With the growing bad blood between Carmine and Frankie it was bound to happen. Those two bodies in the forest, Nalco's and Carmine's, are now being blamed on a squad of Corsican hit men whom the Carpi family frequently uses. Corsicans, who specialize in vengeance machine-gun killings."

"Sounds plausible," agreed Seven, though still worried that his classified Super Stud section might be exposed to the wrong people. "But is the CIA *certain* that my role in this won't come out?"

"Absolutely. My agency is *positive* no one would or could connect some good-looking loner from New York to any of it. Nor would the mob bigwigs ever suspect that CIA would have a hand in this. That just wouldn't make sense to them. Those gangsters know that the CIA seldom, if ever, interferes with European organized crime. Or its warfare. They rightly think we're too busy with the Russians, China, and ISIS."

Fieri shook his head resolutely. "No way would you, or we, *ever* be suspected of knocking off mobsters. The underworld view of all that's happened will simply be the age-old Mafia 'eye for an eye' vendettas. And just to make sure everyone continues seeing it that way, the CIA will keep *that* version going."

"But what about the machine gun itself, Vin? The actual weapon. Remember, I peppered Gitano and Nalco with bullets. My prints, along with Gitano's, are undoubtedly all over that gun. Won't the police or mob insiders be asking questions about *that*?"

The doc grinned his reply. "Already taken care of. Calling in a diplomatic favor, from our President to theirs, CIA got the machine gun back less than three hours after the shootings. This via the French Secret Service. They ordered the local cops to hold off taking prints from the weapon. So the CIA got the weapon *before* any fingerprints were gleaned."

"How'd you manage *that*?" asked Seven.

"Our friends from the French DCRI, Chris. Thanks to them, it's been '*officially*' confirmed that "no prints were ever taken from the gun. That's a polite way of saying that the French government has given us their word on it. And you know the French. Their word of honor means everything to them. They'd rather shoot their firstborn than betray a vow from Mother France. So you're safe, my friend. Completely out of the loop."

"Wow! You guys have some machine here in Europe, Vin. I can't tell you how thankful and impressed I am." The Super Stud chuckled. "And how relieved my chief will be."

"No problem. You and he have nothing further to fret about. Like I said, my CIA is darn good at nurturing rumors. It'll be easy for them to spin this Gitano/Carpi thing, thanks to the mob's infamous reputation for violence. Especially since car bombs and machine guns are the Cosa Nostra's cup of tea. Heck, it wouldn't be a real European summer if some syndicate didn't try blasting another one to smithereens."

Seven laughed as the doc added, "And now that France's Secret Service and its top government leaders are covertly involved, the local police will be ordered *not* to press it any further." Fieri grinned, widely. "You remember the movie, *Casablanca?* When that French police captain, 'Louie,' tells his men to "round up the usual suspects," after plainly seeing Rick shoot the Nazi?"

Seven smiled again, as Vin reassured, "So don't give it a second thought, Chris. This type of professional courtesy between NATO countries happens all the time. The Frenchies may gripe about it, but they usually come around and play ball. Just as we do for them. Like two years ago, when that French undercover agent was rightly suspected of taking files out of the Russian Embassy in Washington. We squashed the whole thing exactly like the Frogs asked us to do."

Seven nodded his head, remembering the case well.

"Besides," Vin added. "Everything that's happened today makes perfect gangland sense. Gitano's people hit Frankie Carpi's father, so Carpi's people hit back. Blew up Carmine's car and machine-gunned him and his hairy-knuckled lieutenant. No big deal. It's a common occurrence in the world of organized crime. Too bad some pretty yacht guests of Gitano's were blown up too, but that's life in the big city. Probably just a few of Carmine's sleazy gun molls anyway."

Christopher Seven saw the logic of what Vin had just stated. Feeling a bit better now, Seven listened to the doc's assurances.

"Just leave it to us, Chris. We'll keep the *real* names out of the headlines and insert the ones we want into it. Nobody but our respective agencies will ever know the whole story."

"If you say so, Vin."

"Yes, I say so, Chris. I also say that you should be very proud of yourself, my G5 buddy. You cracked the case, got Carmine Gitano out of the way, and put an end to Rhombus's catastrophic NATO plans. I don't know about you, but I'm kind of pleased the way things worked out. Proud to have worked with you and proud I had a small part in it."

"You and the CIA had a *big* part in it, Doc. Without you guys, my cover, along with the confidentiality of my department, would now be completely blown. And I'd still be trying to figure out a way to get out of Europe without a mob bullet in my back. Or a long jail sentence in some French prison. You and your agency did *everything* for me behind the scenes. I couldn't have done any of this without you guys. I'll always be grateful, Vin."

Christopher Seven stared admiringly at the lanky CIA operative who was now beaming with pride. McPhail and Admiral Collingwood had been right after all. Thank goodness they'd insisted that 'Doc' Vin Fieri come along on this mission. Seven would have been lost without him, the shadowy undercover agent who initially alarmed him back at JFK Airport. The 'doc' had quickly turned into a trusted ally and a true friend.

A lump came to Seven's throat as Fieri summed things up. "Well, Chris, the hard part's over. Now let's go have a charbroiled cote du boeuf up at the hotel's roof restaurant and make some plans to get you back home."

And with that, the two secret agents made their way to *Le Grill,* the Hotel de Paris' elegant rooftop eatery.

The following morning, a cloudy Thursday, Christopher Seven was finishing up the last of his packing for his flight back to New York that night. Thanks to Vin Fieri and the CIA, no one from Monaco's police force had called on him. Thankfully, neither had any thugs from the Mafia.

Everything was peaceful and quiet now, the first time in days that the G5 agent could actually relax. Headquarters had booked him on the overnight red-eye flight from Nice to New York, which was scheduled to leave that evening at 8:30 p.m. The grinning Super Stud was certain that his G5 travel department buddy, Dave Kelb, must have taken sadistic pleasure in giving him a nighttime departure instead of Seven's preferred morning flights. Thinking of Kelb again, Seven was surprised to find that he was actually looking forward to more of Dave's all-night poker parties. Smiling at the prospect, he dutifully completed his packing.

Finished at last, he shut and locked his suitcases and began contemplating the full day he'd planned for himself, his last one in Europe. At least having a late night flight would give him one more afternoon here on the Riviera. In lieu of tennis, the casino, or a grueling martial arts session, Seven opted, instead, for a return visit to Eze, and another meal at *Château de la Chèvre d'Or*. He knew that visiting the scenic restaurant would be bittersweet without Doreen, yet he still wanted to experience it one last time. The drive to that area would also give him the opportunity to make good on the promise he'd made to himself earlier that morning. In a reflective, quiet moment, the Super Stud had decided to stop at Doreen's father's old villa up near the *Peillon* Mountains...this, in order to pay his private respects to Doreen's memory.

Thankful he hadn't returned his Hertz rented *BMW* convertible yet, which he could now conveniently return when he got to the airport later that night, Seven phoned for the bellman. Then, with a surprising pang of melancholy, he checked out of the *Hotel de Paris* for good a few minutes past 11:00 a.m. Receiving a warm farewell from the hotel's fine staff, Seven waved them a final 'adieu' and hopped into his waiting car brought up by the valet attendant.

After putting down the convertible's top, the Super Stud headed out of town toward the middle *cornice.* Motoring up the picturesque access road, he reflected that he'd sorely miss driving these scenic mountain roads once back in the States. Popping in the *British Invasion* CD he'd brought from home, he softly sang along with Peter & Gordon's classic

"World Without Love." The words to the song were movingly ironic after the last few days.

When he arrived at the elegant *La Chèvre d'Or* restaurant, the G5 operative felt a touch of sadness as he pulled up near the canopied entrance. As expected, thoughts of Doreen and their meal here brought on a mixed bag of memories. Seven shrugged his shoulders and walked in the ornate front doors.

Shown to a corner window table by the genial maître d', the restaurant's amazing panoramic view once again enthralled him. Knowing he'd narrowly escaped a painful death some 24 hours earlier, Seven opted to go 'all out' for his final meal in Europe. He shook his head, knowing the exquisite food here would be a far cry from what he thought would be his final meal *anywhere*; that stale breakfast roll in Carmine Gitano's basement prison.

The G5 operative began his lunch with a small portion of pasta from the menu's appetizer selection, choosing a heavenly pasta *primavera*. Homemade egg *tagliatelle* hand-tossed in a delicious sauce made with just a 'touch' of cream, adorned with plenty of crispy vegetables. It was outstanding! Following the appetizer, his main course was a moist roast chicken from *Bresse,* covered in a pool of natural juices. The tasty *poulet* was flavored with a perfect blend of lemon, vinegar, and tarragon. Then, though knowing he shouldn't have, he ended his lunch with one of the best soufflés he'd ever consumed; a tall and airy raspberry soufflé topped with fresh Chantilly whipped cream.

Ready to explode, the sated operative thanked his waiter, paid the staggering bill, and made his way to the restaurant's men's room where he dutifully brushed his teeth. As he strolled toward the front door, Seven noticed a gorgeous blonde sitting alone at one of the front tables. Nursing an apple martini, her dazzling beauty and well-endowed figure were truly extraordinary, leading him to believe that she had to be an actress, or a top European fashion model. The blonde eyed him unabashedly with a gorgeous smile, one which the Super Stud quickly returned.

Seven suddenly wished he had more time left on the Riviera. Time enough to see if he could have persuaded this voluptuous beauty to join him. She was, without a doubt, one of the most striking women he'd ever laid eyes on, and Seven dreamily fantasized about what the evening might have been like with her. Perhaps the two of them could enjoy a candlelit dinner somewhere in Monaco. Or dine at *Le Moulin de Mougins* up the road a ways. The gourmet restaurant he'd heard so much about. Maybe she would have enjoyed a fun-filled night at Monte Carlo's stylish casino, followed by a quiet moonlight drink near the harbor.

The agent sighed. The sight of a female *this* attractive and shapely always stirred his senses. But then, he quickly reminded himself that the malevolent Rhombus women he'd just battled had likewise lured men with their charismatic beauty. And that a *new* Rhombus squad had recently been formed and was perhaps already operating this very moment. Silently speculating if the stunning blonde sitting alone here was capable of hiding chemical explosives on her well-stacked body, Christopher Seven swiftly walked out the front door, purposely ignoring the blonde as he passed by her table.

~

A half hour later, Seven's *BMW* pulled into the wide, circular driveway of the abandoned *Le Bleu* estate; Doreen's dilapidated childhood home. The gravel and dirt driveway, potted with several holes and rocks, felt just like he remembered it. Looking up toward the old rundown villa, the G5 agent was unexpectedly overcome by a wave of nostalgia and sadness. It was brought on by his vivid memories of the murdered Doreen and the brief, yet poignant, time the two of them had shared here.

Seven hopped out of the car and slowly made his way down a small hill toward the villa's namesake lake. That was the spot where he and Doreen had talked and first caressed. He pictured her lovely face and the tender mannerisms of this devoted, yet puzzling, young woman. One who had twice saved his life. She was truly an enigma – on one hand a charming beauty, soft and childlike – and, on the other, a charter member of the reprehensible Rhombus quartet.

Arriving at the waterside, the Super Stud recalled Doreen's revealing openness here. When she had confessed that she'd been forced into a life she abhorred by an uncaring mother. A mother, as Seven later learned, who had been the fanatical founder of Rhombus itself. *Rhombus* – the merciless female crime consortium that had almost pulled off an unimaginable coup!

Yet, as the G5 agent contemplated all this, he also remembered how Doreen's glowing face had lit up when she spoke of her kind and caring father. Her dad had probably been the only good thing in her young life. Seven lowered his head and moved closer to the tranquil lake.

Walking along the narrow shoreline, Seven smiled gently while evoking Doreen's childhood mermaid story. How her doting father had continually reassured his young daughter that she would always return to this very spot if ever she was hurt or lost. Safely brought back by the legendary '*flower mermaid*' of the Riviera.

Sighing tenderly, Seven recalled the enchanting legend. The charming, innocent fairytale that moved him so when he first heard it, just as it did now. He sighed once more. Sadly, the flower mermaid would never bring Doreen back to this shore again. Carmine Gitano, the apelike Nalco, and her three Rhombus sisters had seen to that.

Just then, a young robin began chirping loudly from a nearby pine tree, interrupting Seven's thoughts. Its high-pitched cry instantly brought the mother bird back to the nest. Doreen loved birds, just as she'd loved flowers, especially roses. Remembering her affection for them, Seven walked over to the beautifully blossomed roses on his right and picked the largest one from the vine.

Thinking of Doreen, he bowed his head and said a short prayer. Then he strolled back to the edge of the water and threw the flower as far as he could out into the lake. It began floating away from him, rapidly making its way to the deeper end toward the other side of the lake. Seven sat down by the shoreline and watched the rose swiftly drift away.

His thoughts again turned to Rhombus, perhaps the most menacing organization he'd ever faced. Terry, its unbending leader, had brashly told him that this quartet of sadistic females would soon reinvent itself with four new members. Boldly resuming its repugnant tradition of murder and mayhem. What was it that Terry had boasted? *"Rhombus never dies. It will go on forever!"*

Seven frowned at the thought. Perhaps, as he'd just reflected in the restaurant, four *new* Rhombus women had already been united. Maybe they were planning a revenge strike right now in memory of their late sisters. The G5 agent shivered slightly, wondering if Rhombus would indeed recreate itself. And, if so, if he'd ever meet up with them again.

Once more thinking of Doreen, the enigmatic fourth member of the group, Seven was still confused. Would she have been happy to learn that he'd foiled Rhombus' calamitous NATO plans? Or would her lifelong membership in her mother's deadly society have made her inwardly angry with him for ruining their most earth-shattering mission? The Super Stud just wasn't sure, uncertain about Doreen's actual mindset. True, she had saved his life by risking her own. Yet, she'd also been strangely proud of Rhombus' iniquitous goals. Their sacred sisterhood bonds and, at times, their infamous reputation. Perhaps this dichotomy of good and evil stemmed from her divergent parents; the father, kind and virtuous, and the mother, evil and overbearing. *Whatever Doreen's actual views were*, Seven reflected, *I'm glad I took care of the people who murdered her.*

The melancholy agent glanced down at his watch. It was time to go. He looked out across the lake again, hoping he could see the floating rose one last time. To him, the rose had now become the flowering symbol of Doreen. The girl who had given her life for his, and who'd thus become so meaningful to him despite her obvious flaws.

Sadly, the flower had disappeared. In all likelihood, it had now descended to the bottom of the lake. Or perhaps it had been blown away by the growing wind. Oh, well. At least the memory of this lovely yet puzzling young woman, unlike the disappearing rose, would never leave him.

About to depart, the Super Stud looked down at the lapping water in front of him, and when he did he couldn't believe his eyes! He smiled widely. *There it was – the rose!*

Just like the young Doreen of her father's mermaid tale, the flower had somehow returned safely to this very shore. For a brief but poignant moment, the spirit of the girl had returned. Seven smiled again. *Had the mythical mermaid of the Riviera brought it back?*

As a small tear welled up in his eye, Christopher Seven picked up the rose, kissed it softly and placed it back near the bush.